W9-BEU-623

The Writers' Club

Bernadette Carson

Copyright © 2004 by Bernadette Carson

*All rights reserved. No part of this book shall be repro-
duced or transmitted in any form or by any means,
electronic, mechanical, magnetic, photographic including
photocopying, recording or by any information storage and
retrieval system, without prior written permission of the
publisher. No patent liability is assumed with respect to
the use of the information contained herein. Although
every precaution has been taken in the preparation of this
book, the publisher and author assume no responsibility for
errors or omissions. Neither is any liability assumed for
damages resulting from the use of the information
contained herein.*

*This is a work of fiction. Names, characters, places, and
incidents either are the product of the author's imagination
or are used fictitiously. Any resemblance to actual events
or locales or persons, living or dead, is entirely coincidental.*

ISBN 0-7414-4954-4

Cover art by Pat Amatulle.

Published by:

INFI(∞)ITY
PUBLISHING.COM

1094 New DeHaven Street, Suite 100
West Conshohocken, PA 19428-2713
Info@buybooksontheweb.com
www.buybooksontheweb.com
Toll-free (877) BUY BOOK
Local Phone (610) 941-9999
Fax (610) 941-9959

Printed in the United States of America

Printed on Recycled Paper

Published September 2008

Acknowledgments

As you can imagine, writing a novel is a concerted effort. The author must rely on assistance from others to authenticate scenes and dialogue unfamiliar to her. In this, my second published novel, I wish to acknowledge with sincere appreciation the following individuals who eagerly answered my questions or read entire chapters where necessary.

Det. Lt. John McAndrew, Orangetown Police Department;

Joy Arzaga, regional theater actor/director;

Blanche Rothstein, community theater actor/director;

Dianne Carbo and Evelyn Sconzo, two nurses in my family who are always there for me;

Bob Trudell and Sharon Aperto, Nyack Library reference librarians;

All my writer friends, too numerous to list, who have become like second family to me;

My husband, Bill, who comes to my rescue when the computer and I are engaged in battle and for his invaluable editing assistance and pride in my work;

To my children, without whose love and support my books would not be possible: Michael and his wife, Ellen, Frank; Bernadette and her husband, Danny, Paul and his wife, Lauren;

To my grandchildren, Andrea, Lauren, Michael, Vincent, Brian and Jaclyn, whose presence in my life brightens my days like the brilliance of a morning sun.

Web Site: BernadetteCarson.com

E-mail: Bernadette057@optonline.net

Characters

Mallory Triana	Wannabe writer who had to put her dreams aside to care for her parents.
Brad Winslow	Longtime boyfriend Mal loves but can't commit to.
Quentin Kingsley	Ambitious actor/writer whose "accident" thrusts him into a web of deceit.
Liz Triana	Mal's mom, struggling to survive cancer.
Russ Triana	Mal's father, confined to a wheelchair.
Georgia Pappas	Creative writing teacher whose shocking discovery impacts her life and her family.
Jordan Hammer	Theatrical producer whose wife was killed in "accident."
Anne Bishop	Wife and mother whose husband was killed in "accident."
Jill Eaton	Brad's co-worker who is determined to win him away from Mal.
Deidre Grange	Quentin's co-star and lover.
Bertie Bookman	Active member of theater where Quentin performs. Her flirtations with him has devastating results.
Alan Bookman	Bertie's "look the other way" husband.
Harry Pappas	Georgia's husband who put a wall of silence between them.

Writers/Students:	Evelyn Shapiro, Walter Paget, Amanda Valentine, Carolyn Graham, Marybeth Fontaine, Philomena Lombardi, Martin Roth
Friends:	Lois (Mal's); Doug, Steve, Lou (Brad's); Althea James, Jennifer Morrison (Georgia's)
Children:	Dorothy, Alex, Elaine (Georgia's); Keith and Adam (Anne's)

Chapter One

By the time Quentin Kingsley turned the bend and saw the parked car, it was too late. He watched, horrified, as his car sent a man's body high into the night air and down the steep jagged cliff. Instinctively, he turned off his headlights.

Gloria Hammer, his 120-pound albatross, went berserk. She threw the door open and went out screaming. "You killed him! You stupid son-of-a-bitch, you killed that guy!" Standing on the protruding roots of a nearby tree, she frantically pulled at her hair, then pounded away at the tree trunk. Her cries became incoherent. Hysterical, her body twisted and circled as though wracked with pain. Except for the moonlight flashing through the leafy branches, darkness blanketed the scene.

Quentin panicked. He had to shut her up. Fear and shock dictated his actions. Petrified that a passing motorist might stop to investigate, or use his cell phone to call for help, Quentin's right hand went over her mouth while his left hand yanked her back towards the car. But Gloria struggled to be free. She pounded his chest screaming muffled profanities through the grip of his fingers, but when her teeth caught his fingertip, she bit down hard. A jolt of pain shot through Quentin's finger. He reacted with a spontaneous slap to her face intended to shut her up, which it did. But Gloria stumbled back a few steps too many. And then she was gone. Only the fading, agonizing sounds of her final screams echoed in the distance. And then they too were gone. Stunned into disbelief, Quentin's entire body numbed. He staggered backwards. This couldn't be happening. It was bizarre. Two lives thrown to certain death, moments apart.

He found himself back behind the wheel of his car. He couldn't help thinking that if he hadn't agreed to see her tonight, this horror would never have happened. He hadn't really wanted to, but when Gloria started pushing, it was easier to give in.

He shook his head as though the last few minutes had been a nightmare he could chase away. But reality set in, plunging his thoughts into action. First, he had to get as far away from the accident scene as possible. *I'm no killer*, he reasoned with his conscience. There was no malicious intent. He had never meant to kill either one. They were accidents, horrible, tragic accidents. But the courts would surely disagree. The police would undoubtedly detect the three vodka martinis he downed before he left to pick up Gloria.

His foot pressed down on the accelerator just as the sky opened up and poured down its rage.

Quentin concentrated on keeping his speedometer within the legal limit. The last thing he needed was to be pulled over for a speeding ticket. To think that only minutes ago, his biggest problem was how to break off his relationship with Gloria. As an actor with a budding career, getting involved with the producer's wife was as stupid as you can get. Lust was the ruination of many a man. But now, that affair was a miniscule problem compared to the events of these last moments.

*   *   *

He had a rough time that night. First, he spent more than an hour in his garage carefully inspecting his car. No visible damage. Fortunately, a heavy downpour followed him all the way home, saving him the trouble of hand-washing his car. Hopefully, that eliminated any tire tracks at the scene.

2

Later, in bed, every sound made him jump. Images of police banging down his door invaded his sleep. By morning, after he'd been through it over and over again, he was finally satisfied that he couldn't be connected to the crime.

He opened his door and reached for the newspaper. He didn't expect to find anything in it yet, but the article glared up at him. How the hell did they find them so fast? They identified the other victim as thirty-nine-year-old Wayne Bishop, husband and father of two. Quentin let a little remorse slip in, but he soon found himself feeling anger towards the guy. The jerk should have stayed in his car and waited for help. His own impatience had cost him his life, and consequently, Gloria's too. Now I have to live with the guilt and fear of being caught, he thought. All because of his stupidity.

He read the part about Gloria. The reporter made her sound like a saint, a pillar of the community. But Quentin knew better. If he could have known how possessive she would be, their affair would never have started. Yet, sexually she far surpassed all the women he had ever known. A fleeting feeling of relief swept through him. He tried not to acknowledge it, but there it was. All he ever wanted from Gloria was her body, and only until the fire burned out. And he never doubted that it would. But Gloria wouldn't settle for sex alone. She wanted his *life.* Maybe if she hadn't been nagging him with her demands, he could have kept his eyes on the road. Maybe he could have swerved in time to avoid hitting this young father. Yes, she too had caused his death, and her own, Quentin concluded. He allowed himself to relax a little, convinced that if the police hadn't come for him after all these hours, he was home free.

He gulped down a glass of orange juice, put on his sweats and sneakers, and went out for his morning run. As usual.

The run helped sort out his thoughts. He focused on his day's mundane schedule and remembered that it was

3

supposed to end at the library with registration for a creative writing class. After last night's hell, his enthusiasm had fizzled out faster than air out of a balloon, but he had already mentioned it to several people. There was no way he'd cancel now. Quentin resolved not to deviate from normalcy. After all, what killer would have the head for such trivialities?

Chapter Two

She felt like a goldfish in a shark tank. What the heck am I doing here? she wondered. Mallory Triana sat on the metal folding chair in the library's conference room, a chill rippling through her chest and back. She didn't know if it was caused by the air conditioning or the anticipation of what she had gotten herself into.

People started to fill the room. Nods of the head and weak, polite smiles were exchanged. She sat erect, forced her shoulders back and clasped her hands in her lap. With a will of their own, her fingers tapped out a silent tune. She hoped her deodorant was as powerful as promised because tonight it would be put to the ultimate test. For the middle of September it was unseasonably hot. The temperature had soared to ninety degrees. But the cold empty room had cooled her the moment she walked in. Mal knew the perspiration creeping into her armpits had nothing to do with the heat wave.

Sixteen people took seats around the table and every face looked stone cold. Until the teacher smiled. A warmth emanated from that simple gesture that allowed Mal's jumpy fingers to relax somewhat.

"Well, it's good to see such a great turnout," she said, scanning their faces. "My name is Georgia Pappas—just 'Georgia' to all of you. As I told you when you responded to my flyer on the library bulletin board, I decided to use my home to conduct a twelve-week creative writing course. After tonight's meeting, those of you who are interested, please stay to sign up. You'll all have an opportunity to ask questions about the course near the end of the meeting."

She paused to pull papers out of her briefcase and came up smiling. "I've been teaching creative writing and poetry for more years than I care to count. I don't want to bore you with the details of my background, so I'm going to distribute handouts listing my credentials."

Mal stole a cursory glance around the table for signs of defrost on those icy faces. A few slight cracks, she noted. Well, at least the teacher seems nice. Fine features set in a round face framed with short, dark hair and eyes. Creamy skin and a wide smile boasting perfectly even, white teeth peeled years off her age. A quick look at her bio revealed the woman had to be in her mid-forties. She looked ten years younger, but, more importantly, a lot of heart poured out of those lips and eyes.

Mal prided herself on only two things; writing and perception. A person's first words and facial expressions were usually indicative of the personality within. Her initial impressions were almost always on target. She drew a breath and placed her hands on the table, fingers laced together.

"Why don't we begin by introducing ourselves," Georgia said. "Feel free to tell a little about your writing background, publications, if any. Or maybe just your interest in writing. Why you're interested in joining the class. If you're uncomfortable, no problem. Just your name and town or village will do for now."

The introductions began at Georgia's left. Mal was seated eighth in position, grateful for the time to plan her words. Writing prose was comfortable for her; verbal expression before an unknown audience was hell. Her heart started to pound. She sneaked a Lifesaver in her mouth to activate the salivary glands that seemed to stop working.

Bracing herself for the impending humiliation, Mal fixed her gaze on the first speaker, Evelyn Shapiro, hoping

6

the woman wouldn't rattle off an impressionable list of degrees and writing credits. *Why do you always try to walk with giants?* she asked herself. Here she was, in the 21st century, a twenty-five-year-old woman, with only secretarial skills and a high school diploma, in this sea of educated faces, this world of educated people. If she were a turtle or a snail, she could crawl back into her shell at moments like these and slither out when it's safe. But Mal had a passion to write, to learn the craft. Her thirst for knowledge was insatiable. Keeping her eye on the prize, she chased her fears away and gave her attention to speaker number one.

Evelyn Shapiro was what might be referred to as "a full-figured woman," somewhere in her sixties, Mal guessed. Her face was pleasant, her voice soft, but friendly and confident. Gray hair, teased and sprayed so that not a single strand dared move, locked her into the 1960s.

"I'm a retired teacher," she said, "trying to fulfill an old dream I never had time for."

A medley of uh-huhs and me-toos echoed Evelyn's sentiments.

"I wrote a few children's stories a few years back, but never got published. I did try a few times though." She shrugged and gave them an indifferent what-are-you-gonna-do-look. But no one was fooled. Most returned empathetic nods.

The thaw had begun.

By the time Mal's turn came, she had shed her inhibitions. Her adrenaline flowed. Yes, from what she had heard so far, her suspicions were correct. She was probably the only one in the room without at least one degree. But she took an immediate liking to the entire group. Maybe it was their common goal; that perpetual quest for publication.

Mal made an impulsive decision to address her problem head on. If she didn't, she'd be awake nights thinking of how she'd handle it at the next meeting. She cleared her throat, drew a breath and tried to look relaxed. "My name is Mal Triana. I've lived here in the county all my life. For the last six years, I've been employed as a legal secretary by the law firm of Marcus & Goodman."

One man started asking questions about the firm, but Georgia steered them back on track. "I don't mean to be rude, but we have to stay on course. We have only two hours, and if we start going far afield, we won't accomplish anything. Mal, will you continue, please?"

"Well, I've loved writing since I was a little kid. I used to write stories and poetry, and loved the composition assignments in school. My English and grammar are good and I read constantly. I'm addicted to books."

Mal paused for an awkward few seconds, but that little voice in her head prodded her. *Here's your chance. Jump in and get it over with.* "But I never had the opportunity to go to college. Family problems, but that's a long story. Hopefully, some day. . ." Her voice faded away with her thoughts. She shook her head and finished off. "For a wannabe writer, I know that's a big disadvantage. I'll just have to try harder. Anyway, I'm excited about this class. I hope it works out because I need some guidance. The craft books are great, but a live teacher you can question is better. Not to mention other students to share the highs and lows."

Supportive comments flowed. Mal felt as if she had lost a thousand pounds. The relief put a wide smile on her face. She turned to the next speaker, eager to hear what he had to say. Yes, she thought, this class is going to be the answer to my prayers.

Chapter Three

The week couldn't pass fast enough. Mal anticipated that Mondays would become the highlight of her week. She seldom had time for friends, except for Brad Winslow, who had been a constant in her life since high school. Brad was like hot chocolate and toasted marshmallows on a bitter cold winter night. At times when their relationship would be more aptly described as a fire out of control, Mal usually put the brakes on. Yes, he was much more than a friend, but she had closed her heart to disallow anything more. Both her parents needed her. For now, love and marriage would have to remain in the romance novels.

She had been honest with Brad about her feelings, and he understood—so he said—but sometimes she wondered how long he could be patient.

*　　*　　*

When Monday finally rolled around, Mal drove her car off at 6:30 that evening, headed for Georgia's house and her first creative writing class. She couldn't keep the smile off her face as she drove. Cher was belting out a song on the radio. Mal turned up the volume and sang along.

She walked into what Georgia called her den, but except for the low ceilings, it looked more like the lobby of a luxury hotel. Two sofas and a matching loveseat, with plushy cushions you could sink into, all in earth tones and arranged before a now dormant fireplace. A dark pine dining room set with twelve matching chairs, resembling Ethan Allen style and quality, awaited the hopeful writers. If that magnificent set was banished to the den, what could she possibly have upstairs?

Adjacent to the sliding glass doors leading to her patio, a buffet table was already set up with a barrel-shaped coffee urn, china cups and exquisite serving platters with miniature pastries on lace doilies. A fully equipped exercise room was visible to the left. Judging by Georgia's tight, trim figure, she put it to good use. No, Mal decided, Georgia Pappas was definitely not doing this for the money.

"At the beginning of each class," Georgia began, "I'll be distributing these sheets which contain excerpts from various books on the craft of writing. These will all become precious tools to help shape your writing into professional manuscripts ready for presentation to a publisher. You won't always heed what you read, but *read, read, read.* Everything you can get your hands on, with particular emphasis on the type of books you want to write. Then *write, write, write.* In this class, it'll be two R's and a W. Reading, research and writing. But the research we'll get to later. There's research you must do to make your novel factually correct, and there's market research. We'll get around to all of it."

At the halfway point, Georgia called a break for re-freshments, after which each person would have fifteen minutes to write about what they hoped to accomplish in the class. A tall young man dressed all in denim offered to pour her a cup of coffee. His straight dark hair looked clean, but was too long to be stylish. Mal accepted the coffee graciously, but when he reached to get her a piece of Danish, she stopped him. There was something about hand-to-mouth contact with a complete stranger that turned her off.

"No, thanks," she said politely, "I had a full meal tonight. I can do without the extra calories." The guy was either starting a beard or hadn't gotten around to shaving for a few days. Tom Cruise or Brad Pitt can get away with it, she thought, but on you it's plain sloppy.

10

He extended a hand. She took it for the handshake and watched him munch on the slice of chocolate cake he had selected. "I'm Quentin Kingsley," he said through chocolate-coated lips. Her mouth watered at the rich, creamy icing in his plate, but after she refused his offer, she couldn't very well reach for a piece herself.

Quentin's eyes swept the room. "I hear Georgia had an overwhelming response for this class. She said she had more calls after the library meeting last week. I hope she doesn't squeeze in any more students. The larger the class, the more we'll have to fight for her attention. And I'm loaded with questions."

"No, that problem's been solved. I guess you weren't here yet, but Georgia told us earlier she's going to conduct two classes. Several people are interested exclusively in poetry. Here, most of us are interested in writing that Great American Novel." She drew quotation marks in the air with her two fingers. "Some wanted help with nonfiction articles. Not parallel roads, in my opinion."

Their eyes met as he fingered his stubbly beard.

"By the way, forgive my appearance. I don't always look this bad, but I'm an actor. I have the lead in Jordan Hammer's new musical, *Crush*. We'll be opening at the Emily Forrester Theater in November. It's set in the 1970's, ergo the long hair and beard." He paused to laugh. "Actually, it'll get worse. I just started to let it grow."

Mal's brows shot up. "Wow! An actor! I'm impressed. Sounds exciting. And you have time for acting and writing?"

"Actually, it's my day job that gets in the way."

"What is your day job?"

"I'm an accountant. But I found out I don't like crunching numbers as much as I used to."

Mal laughed. "Can't say that I blame you. Math was my worst subject. But I admire you for handling it all."

"It's not that bad, really. I set my own hours and keep my clients down to a minimum. During tax season, my retired friends help. I make time for what means most to me. I love the theater, but writing still holds first place here." He tapped his heart. "Maybe someday, I'll finish my play. That was my objective with this class, but plays and novels are totally different. Georgia wasn't too hopeful about getting a class together for wannabe playwrights, though, so I decided to try a novel first. At least I'll be writing. I can always work my way up." He shrugged and smiled. "What the heck. I can dream big, can't I?"

"Why not? I do. We *all* do," she said pleasantly.

There was a brief, awkward silence. Mal wanted to jump right into a conversation about writing, but the words got tangled somewhere in her head. "Beautiful home Georgia has, isn't it?" she said instead.

Quentin gave it a second glance. "Well, figures. Her husband is a successful stockbroker with a prestigious firm. And she's been teaching all her life. Now she has these classes too."

Mal looked up at him. That killer smile was a bit un-nerving. She tried to imagine what he looked like without the beard. As she removed her blazer, she caught his eyes make a quick assessment of what the jacket had concealed. Mal was unsure whether she felt flattered or annoyed.

"Thanks for the coffee," she said. "If you'll excuse me, I'd like to mingle and get to know everyone."

"No problem," he said with a mock salute.

She turned to join a group of three women and fell into their conversation with ease. As long as the topic was writing, Mal was riding high.

Chapter Four

Both her parents were asleep when Mal got home. A wave of guilt washed over her as she peeked in at them. How dare I drown myself in self-pity? What about them? So young, all their dreams snatched away. At least I have youth, good health and Brad.

Brad was her rock. When her dad had that horrific car accident seven years ago that would confine him to a wheelchair for the rest of his life, Brad was there for anything they needed. He couldn't do enough for them.

Later, when the storm of denial had passed, and her father had begun to accept his fate, Brad bought him a second-hand computer. Together, he and Mal had taught him how to enter this new cyberspace world until he was able to explore it on his own. Through that little screen, her father had come to life. No more sitting in that chair, staring into space. His spirits soared now every time he made a new and fascinating discovery. The clicking sound of that keyboard was as soothing to Mal as classical music was to her mom.

Things were looking up again in the Triana household those days until the second bomb fell. Liz's routine mammography had revealed what every woman fears. Breast cancer. A radical mastectomy was performed followed by six months of chemotherapy. At forty-eight years old, Liz Triana was being chased by death.

Mal checked her e-mails as she did every night before going to bed. Only one from Brad. Call me when you get home, it said. Want to hear how your class went.

13

After she had undressed, put on her nightshirt and washed up, she crawled into her bed, propped the pillows behind her and dialed Brad's number. She loved talking to him, but tonight she looked forward to their conversation even more. She knew he would share her enthusiasm, and be happy for her.

"Hi. Did I wake you?"

"No. I was waiting for your call. How did it go?"

"Oh, Brad. I was in seventh heaven. Already I feel like I learned so much. I'm all fired up. When I hang up with you, I'm going to start that first chapter. The story's been dancing around in my head for a long time, as you well know. Now, with the help of the teacher and the other writers, maybe I can shape it into something."

"You will. I'm sure of it. Just don't stay up all night writing. It's not time to quit your day job yet."

Mal laughed. "I wish I could. I need more time to write. We have to bring in a few pages every week to be critiqued, so I can't procrastinate even if I wanted to, which I don't."

Brad's tone faded. "Does this mean you won't have time for me?"

She waved him off as if he were there to see. "Oh, stop it. Of course not. What would I do without my best friend?"

When she heard no response, she said, "Brad, are you there?"

"I'm here."

"What happened? I thought I disconnected you. That happens sometimes when the receiver is on my shoulder."

"No. It was just that 'best friend' thing. Is that all I'll ever be to you, Mal?"

Her spirits deflated. She wasn't ready for this. "Oh, Brad, don't push me into another serious talk. You know my obligation here to my parents. I feel like my life is not my own. I can't put that burden on you too. It wouldn't be fair."

"That should be my decision, or ours, not yours alone. Is that all that's stopping you?"

Mal drew a breath, then exhaled slowly. "I'm not sure, Brad. It's certainly a major contributing factor. Can't we just coast along for a while?"

"Mal, we've been 'coasting' for almost seven years now."

"Oh, c'mon, Brad. That's not fair. Seven years ago, and for a long time after, we were only high school friends."

"Speak for yourself, girl. Why do you think I chose a local college?"

"I thought you preferred St. Thomas?" Mal asked, clearly surprised by his revelation.

"Sure I preferred it. So I could be closer and see you more often."

"I never knew. Not then, Brad."

"But you know now?"

"Yes, of course." A hush fell over their conversation while she battled with her thoughts. "Brad, I don't want to lose you, but I can't hold back your life. I'm not sure what I feel anymore. What I do know is I can't abandon my parents."

"I'm not asking you to."

"I can't commit to anything now, Brad. Every time I look at my mother . . ." Her voice trailed off, then the tears.

"Okay, I'm sorry, Mal. Let's forget it for now. Try to get a good night's sleep. Maybe it is selfish of me to want more now."

She was restless after she hung up. Brad had every right to expect more. She loved him for the special person he was. She had learned to lean on him with every problem or challenge she and her parents faced. If, for some reason, she couldn't see him for a few days, she missed him terribly, needed to be with him. The warmth of his conversations, the laughter he always managed to pull from her, the comfort he offered when she was down, the hugs, the kisses, those fingers through her hair.

She loved it all, enough to consider breaking off with him entirely. For his sake. But, selfishly, the thought of life without Brad made her shiver. Yet, how could she ignore the facts? How could she make any plans for the future with her mom growing weaker every day from the ravages of cancer and its chemotherapy treatment? Her dad was loving and supportive to her mom, but, unquestionably, his physical limitations put the onus on Mal. She couldn't and wouldn't expect anyone to take on her responsibilities. And the situation could easily worsen if the cancer has its way.

The images of what might lie ahead were chilling. Mal fought unsuccessfully to erase them from her mind. She knew there was only one cure-all to dissolve her disturbing thoughts. She reached for the remedy in her night table drawer.

The moment her pen touched the paper in her thick, unused spiral notebook, all fears melted away. Once she got through writing and rewriting that all-important opening "hook" line, it was clear sailing. Immersed in her imaginary world, the words poured out like salt from a shaker. She would bring to life all those faceless, fictitious characters that had been swimming around in her head for months now. They would become her second family.

The digital clock glared 2:30 when Mal reluctantly closed her notebook and slipped it under her pillow. In only four hours the alarm would ring. She forced her eyes closed while her mind raced with new possible characters and subplots for her romantic/suspense novel, *Hold Back the Love*. Careful now, she told herself, don't turn it into an autobiography.

Chapter Five

Russ Triana was already on his computer when Mal yawned her way into the kitchen. She put the coffee on first, then stuck her head in the small bedroom off the kitchen which had become the family office.

"What are you doing up so early, Dad?" she asked.

He shrugged. "Couldn't sleep, obviously. I tried to wait up for you last night. I wanted to hear about your class, but I fell asleep early, right after Mom. How'd it go?"

"Great. The teacher's a sweetheart, and I already started to warm up to some of the other students." Quentin Kingsley's image flashed before her. She blinked it away. "Let me jump in the shower first, Dad. I'll tell you all about it over coffee."

Ten minutes later, Mal, clad in a white terrycloth robe and a white towel wrapped around her head, poured two glasses of orange juice and two mugs of steaming coffee. She watched and cringed silently as her father wheeled his way to the kitchen table. *Almost seven years, and I still can't get used to it.* She could well imagine how he felt. He had been a passionate golfer, good at the game. How he had looked forward to those Saturday morning tee-offs. Now, if only he could take a few steps or stand on his own two feet, they'd be ecstatic.

"So tell me," Russ said, stirring two teaspoons of sugar into his black coffee.

A broad smile crossed Mal's face. She was not usually loquacious in the morning, but her dad had encouraged her favorite subject. Her enthusiasm bubbled over.

"Oh, Dad, it was wonderful. We barely scratched the surface, but already I'm learning. The teacher recommended some good books on the craft of writing. I can't wait to buy them. We started working with one of them last night. You wouldn't believe all the things you have to know. It's mind-boggling!"

Russ smiled at his daughter, his eyes clear reflections of love and pride. "You'll master it all. I have no doubt about that. It'll be challenging and you'll love it."

"I felt a little out of place at first," she said, wrinkling her nose in a frown. "All the other students are college educated, well-read . . . I'm completely out of their league."

Her father's expression made a sudden change; his eyes downcast. Mal silently admonished herself for touching on his sore spot; her college plans cut short because of his accident. She could never convince him that the accident wasn't the sole reason. Probably because it was true.

She forced a smile and tried to steer away from the sensitive subject. "But as soon as these people started to speak, I was instantly at ease. Dad, they're just a nice, down-to-earth bunch who love to write. It's more like a club than a class. That love of writing sort of bonds us. Everyone thought they already knew how difficult it is to get published. But Dad, you have no idea. Some of the things we read in class were real eye-openers. Your chances of getting that first book accepted for publication can be equated with winning the lottery."

Mal popped an English Muffin in the toaster. "Should I throw one in for you, Dad?"

"No. I'll have breakfast with Mom."

If she has an appetite for breakfast, Mal thought. For Liz, a whole slice of dry toast would be considered a banquet. Both Mal and her father fell silent. They shared the same fears, but made it a practice to wear their optimistic masks at all times.

Her dad broke the somber mood. "Back to your writing, Mal. Here's your wise old father's two cents worth of advice. Don't start with a defeatist attitude. You definitely have a talent for writing; you always have. And you love it. That's the underlying winning formula. Just keep at it and believe in yourself. When you're finished and totally satisfied with what you've written, that's when you can start worrying about how to market it."

Mal spread raspberry jam on her warm muffin and bit into it, licking the oozed jam off her lips. "You sound like Georgia, my teacher."

"Good. Then I like her already." He toyed with his coffee spoon while he ruminated, then said, "Mal, how about if I get involved with your writing? Can I help you in some way?"

Mal tried to shield her reaction. She'd never want to hurt her dad's feelings, but this novel had to be hers alone. It would be a part of her mind, her heart, her emotions. "Like how?" she asked. She tried to keep her tone casual, but her father caught her tightened expression.

Russ shook his hand in front of her face. "No, no. I can see what you're thinking," he said with a laugh. "Your writing is your baby. I'm not looking to infringe on that. I'm no writer, you are. But how about if I do your typing? Since you like to write your work out first, wouldn't it save a lot of your time if I typed it up and printed out your chapters while you're at the office?" He threw his shoulders back and gave her a complacent grin. "I'm pretty good now since I bought that touch-typing program. I'm up to fifty words per minute."

19

She darted a look from the corner of her eye. "Promise not to change a word unless you check with me first?"

His hand went to his heart. "Scout's honor," he said.

"Okay, Dad. You've got yourself a job."

"Fantastic! How much will I get paid?" he teased.

"Let's put it this way. When I get paid, you'll get paid. For now, you have to settle for one hug and one kiss for each chapter."

Their cheerful mood instantly faded at the sound of Liz Triana's vomiting. For those brief minutes, Mal had been able to block out that black cloud of cancer that loomed over their family.

Chapter Six

Mal swallowed hard as she went to clear the table after dinner. She dumped the tiny portions of chicken and mashed potatoes from her mother's plate into the garbage. She had known from the start that it would all end up there.

This pretense of normalcy was getting more unbearable with each passing day. Sometimes she wanted to hug her mother, cry on her shoulder, shake her and beg her not to die; to be strong, to fight like hell. As though a strong will could possibly be an effective weapon to beat the devastating disease. Every time she looked at her mother's frail, thin body, her spirits would sink down to reality again.

Those once dancing, happy eyes were vacant now. They carried that glazed, unmistakable look of cancer under drooping, weary lids. Long gone was the thick mane of shiny chocolate-brown hair. Rather than wear that wig she hated, her mom chose a brown cloth turban to become a permanent part of her. But it fooled no one. They all knew what was underneath.

Mal bit back the agony. With nervous energy, she attacked the kitchen until it was spotless and shining. The phone rang just as she was about to help her mother with her nightly shower.

"Mal? Is this Mal?" the voice asked.

"Yes. Who's calling, please?" she answered, annoyed by the interruption.

"Quentin. Quentin Kingsley, from your writing class."

Recognition relaxed her, but she remained nonplussed. She couldn't imagine why he'd call her at home, but greeted him politely. "Oh, yes. I thought your voice was familiar. I don't mean to be rude, but I'm a little busy now, Quentin. What can I do for you?"

"I'm sorry. You were listed in the phone book so I thought I'd call instead of waiting until next week's class. The reason I'm calling is this: a few of us lingered after you left last night. We got into a conversation outside Georgia's house. Anyway, to make it short, we'd like a little more than a once-a-week class. Would you be interested in meeting at the Melville library on Saturdays?"

"To do what?"

"We haven't fine-tuned that yet. Maybe to read aloud some of the craft books, take notes, share our thoughts and problems, come up with pertinent questions for our sessions with Georgia. Whatever. It's just great to get together with people who share your interest."

Mal paused. "You mean just a few students and no teacher?"

"Yeah. We'll see how it goes. If we don't feel we're gaining anything from it, we'll quit. But I think it's worth a try. You interested?"

Mal found it hard to resist any invitation related to writing. But, timewise, she had to be realistic. "For how long?" she asked.

"For only two hours, from 10:00 till noon. My schedule's kind of tight too. I've already checked with the library about availability. They have a small room we can use, and we can start a week from this Saturday."

"Let me sleep on it, Quentin. It sounds good, but there are kinks I have to work out to clear the time. Can I get back to you?"

"Sure. Anytime." He gave her his number and she promised to call him the following day.

Great. Now he has my number and I have his. And we both love to write.

She dismissed the apprehensive, uneasy feeling and led her mom to the shower.

Chapter Seven

Saturdays were brutal. A regular Cinderella story, before the Ball. Mal's mundane routine seldom varied. First, she would tend to her mother's personal needs, help her wash and dress, then try to get a little food in her stomach. Liz's diet consisted of mostly farina and Ensure these days. Next, she'd give their modest ranch-style house a-lick-and-a-promise cleaning, doing laundry in between. The dreaded weekly grocery shopping would come next. By the time she got home, she was exhausted, but never complained. Her dad looked forward to his hot, home-cooked dinners and Mal had no intention of denying him that simple pleasure.

Lately, if she and Brad went to a Saturday night movie, unless it was exceptionally interesting or exciting, she'd doze off on his shoulder. Or her mind would wander off to the sad situation at home. Poor Brad, why he kept coming back for more, she'd never know. But she was glad he did.

Now, to find time for a Saturday morning writing session would be pushing it. Her lips twisted thoughtfully. Well, maybe she could transfer the supermarket chore to a weeknight. The thought put a frown on her face. Not after a day in her hectic office. If someone were to film an average day in the law offices of Marcus & Goodman, all those employees racing to meet schedules would make it look like a silent movie.

But Brad always offers to come shopping with me to help with the packages, she thought. Maybe I'll accept that offer.

*   *   *

"No sweat," he told her when she broached the subject that night. They were enjoying a half pepperoni-half mushroom pizza at Anthony's Pizza Palace, one of their favorite hangouts.

"Sure you don't mind? You don't have to come with me every week," she said, "but I admit it *is* a drag unloading those bags from the car and carrying them all in by myself."

Brad's eyebrows rose to form perfect crescents. Mal never tired of looking at those incredible, sand-colored lashes that made her think of a wheat field. They complemented his mesmerizing eyes, which were the lightest shade of blue she had ever seen.

"If I minded," he said, "I wouldn't have offered in the first place. Of course, if I have to work late, or something else comes up, you're on your own. Otherwise, we'll make Fridays grocery shopping nights. Okay?"

She placed her hand over his on the red and white checkered tablecloth and gave it a squeeze. A lump was forming in her throat. She took a sip of her Diet Coke. "Brad, in case I don't tell you often enough, I want you to know how much I appreciate all you do for me and my parents. A simple 'thank you' just doesn't cut it."

Brad's other hand covered hers. A sly smile tugged at the corners of his lips. "I was thinking of that line you said they keep pounding into you writers: 'Show, don't tell.' Fits perfectly here."

Mal yanked her hand out from his and laughed. "Touché!" She leaned over and smacked a kiss on his lips. "Thank you, Brad," she said with a sugary, teasing tone.

"That's not what I had in mind, Mal."

Her gaze sobered. "I know, Brad. Half of me wants the same thing. The other half has that famous Scarlett O'Hara

25

attitude. Always wants to worry about it tomorrow. That half has too much on her plate today."

Brad brushed away a strand of her chestnut hair that threatened to fall over her almond-shaped brown eyes. His voice deepened. "I know, Mal. You're a wonderful daughter to your parents. I'm sure Somebody Upstairs is watching over you and smiling. That's why I want to help you find all the time you need for your writing. I can see how your eyes light up whenever you talk about it. It's like a surge of electricity shoots through you. And Mal, when you feel good, I feel good. Simple as that."

"Oh, Brad, you're one in a million. I don't know how to tell you—or show you—as you so aptly put it, how much you mean to me."

Those magnetic eyes narrowed mischievously. "I might be able to help you out there," he said.

She threw her napkin at him and laughed again. Heartily this time.

Chapter Eight

Mallory walked the half-mile to the library energized by the crisp, cold air, her spirits better. Liz had managed to hold down a few tablespoons of farina this morning and she seemed a little stronger, more animated than usual. Lately, she seldom got into an actual conversation; nothing more than a few necessary words. But her mother's slight improvement this morning brightened Mal's day.

Quentin spotted her coming up the street and waved to her. When he smiled, gleaming white teeth illuminated his bearded face. He stood on the top concrete step watching her walk towards him. With a quick wave and a polite smile, Mal returned his friendly greeting, but kept her gaze down on the sidewalk.

"Did you just get here?" she asked when she reached him.

"A few minutes," he said, opening the heavy glass door for her. "But I was here yesterday to get a jump on things. All the computers were tied up, so I asked one of the librarians to help me out. She found four books she thought would be useful for our class."

"This class? Our teacherless class?" she asked, trying to make light of it.

Quentin's look turned defensive. "We don't need a teacher for this one," he said, then tapped the pile of books in his hand. "Everything we need we'll find in these."

"Fine with me," Mal said pleasantly. "It certainly can't hurt." But she wondered how effective the class could be without a qualified leader. Maybe they could do themselves more harm than good. Like groping in the dark. Suppose we misinterpret something and apply it to our writing erroneously? We could screw ourselves up big time, she thought. We'd have to unlearn, relearn and rewrite unnecessarily.

* * *

A total of six people showed up for the Saturday Writers Study Group, the name they unanimously chose. Besides Mal and Quentin, there was Walter Paget, a forty-year-old construction worker who had started writing as a hobby. It was an escape from the cacophony of noises at night when his three young boys went from brotherly messing around to all-out fighting in front of a blasting television. Writing was no longer a hobby. Wally's goal now, he said, was to someday have his novels share a library shelf with James Patterson.

The remaining three were women, one of whom was Evelyn Shapiro. Mal was pleased to see her there. She had taken a liking to the older woman the moment she had introduced herself that first night here at the library. There was a softness to her smile that suggested sincerity and a big heart. Mal thought she saw reflections of sadness in the woman's eyes, as though a great deal of sorrow or some kind of deep-seated hurt was buried behind them. Still, Evelyn smiled and greeted everyone warmly. *We all wear our masks,* Mal thought.

Amanda Valentine was another story. Maybe it was her pretentious appearance, the designer clothes, the full makeup and all that jewelry that turned Mal off. Amanda's whole image was that of a self-indulgent, materialistic person, but Mal promised herself she'd give the woman a chance. For some people, all that stuff is their security blanket.

Carolyn Graham was another woman of means. For one thing, she drove a recent model Jaguar. Mal guessed that Carolyn was between forty-five to fifty, well-dressed, well-read and well-spoken. Her husband was a successful defense attorney whose face was often in the newspapers or on television. Carolyn was a classy lady who took her wealth for granted. Her one endearing charm was a naiveté that bordered on adorable. Extremely friendly, she beamed with delight every time she spoke and talked to everyone as though they were all lifelong friends. But Carolyn had one problem everyone but she was aware of. She couldn't write. When Carolyn had read her piece, Mal had silently cringed for her, and had discreetly searched the other faces at the table. Their expressions were transparent. But who knows? They were all gathered together to sharpen their skills and learn the craft of writing. Who's to say Carolyn couldn't excel and shoot past them all with the first publication? Miracles happen.

Quentin stood up and called for everyone's attention. Apparently, he'd be running this show. "Okay, people, I hope no one minds, but I took the liberty of browsing through a few books earlier and made a selection for today's class. I thought it might be a good idea to begin with point of view first. Is that okay with everyone?"

Everyone nodded, except for Carolyn, who, in her cheery voice, asked, "How are we going to do this? Don't we all need a book too?"

Quentin, who had appointed himself leader, answered her question. "Yes. I intend to read through all these books this week. I'll then decide which one would be most beneficial to us. Then we can order the copies from Barnes & Noble. For today, I'll make photocopies of this POV section and we can work from there. Don't worry about the charges for the copies. I'll handle it."

Big sport, Mal thought, as he headed for the copying machine. A split second later, her thoughts reversed. After all, this class was his idea. He's putting it together, he should be in charge. *And he does have that killer smile.*

Chapter Nine

Brad spent Saturday morning helping his friend Doug move out. Four of them had shared the five-room apartment almost eight years, since their freshman year in college. It had worked out surprisingly well, and the location couldn't be beat. The convenience of a ten-minute walk to campus had convinced them to take it. The rent had been more than they had planned, but they all had jobs, plus some help from their parents.

One of the guys, Steve Owens, was the neat freak of the bunch. Steve had always kept everyone in check, made sure each one did his share. He would prepare a schedule of assigned duties every week, on a rotating basis, and post it on the refrigerator. Brad, Doug and Lou had laughed and teased him about it at first, but agreed to give it a try.

Brad smiled as he carried a carton out to Doug's van. He reminisced about those early days of college. Now the schedule was still on the refrigerator, but Doug's name had been deleted. A sentimental sadness filled him. The Fearless Four were slowly breaking up. Doug was off to Morristown to be closer to his new job, Steve would be getting married in a few months, and Lou was getting serious with a girl he had been dating. He had already mentioned the possibility of moving in with her.

After only one month of bouncing around on interviews, Brad had been lucky to land a decent job with Paragon Consultants, a successful business in real estate and construction. But the rent was a lot higher now, and for more rooms than he'd need. It was time to make new plans. But those plans would not include Mal, at least not in the immediate future. He blinked away the horrible thought of what would set her free. Her mom still had a fighting chance to beat her cancer, and Brad sincerely hoped she would make it. Her dad's disability was also a strong concern to Mal, but at least his condition wasn't life-threatening. The emotional trauma Russ had experienced over the years had been far worse to deal with than the physical impact. But he seemed to be coming around now.

The sound of Lou's and Steve's heavy footsteps on the stairs broke Brad's reverie. "Hey, Doug, take a break," Brad called out. His almost ex-roommate was in his bedroom, busy packing his computer equipment. "The guys are back with the food."

The aroma of that fresh, mellow Dunkin' Donuts coffee brought them all to the kitchen table. The four young men attacked the bag of donuts and bagels and sipped the steaming coffee.

Brad couldn't shake the blues and all his friends noticed. "What the hell's bugging you today, Brad? You look down, like you lost your best friend," Lou said.

Brad's quick laugh had a bitter edge. "Bad choice of words, Lou. That's pretty much what it's all about. We're pushing eight years together. Now that Fat Ass is going," he said, using the nickname they had tagged on their slightly overweight friend, "that great part of our lives is coming to an end."

Lou nodded, empathizing. "And soon Mr. Clean will be leaving us," he said, his gaze shifting to Steve. "Now he'll have a wife to drive crazy. You gonna follow her around with your spray bottle too?" he teased.

"Yeah, yeah, go ahead and laugh," Steve said. "But once I'm gone, you guys are gonna miss me. I can just imagine what a pigsty this place will become."

"Not for long, I'm afraid," Brad said. His serious tone caught the attention of his friends.

"What's that supposed to mean?" Doug asked. "You getting married too?"

Brad's lips twisted. His gaze fell downward, fixed on his half-eaten bagel. "I wish," he said.

"Don't let it drag you down," Steve said with a quick squeeze to Brad's shoulder. "Mal's boxed in a bad situation. Did you ever think maybe she loves you too much to dump her troubles on you on a permanent basis?"

"Sometimes I wonder," Brad answered, with a sour twist of his mouth. "After all this time, she should know me better. I've told her a million times that I don't mind helping out and spending time with her parents. They're great people." He wrinkled his nose in thought. "Maybe it's more than that. Who knows? Mal puts a wall up between us. We're very close, no question about that, but we rarely get time alone. *Really* alone. But it doesn't seem to bother her as much as it does me."

Steve raised a brow in disbelief. He hesitated before he spoke. "Are you saying what I think you're saying? Don't tell me you guys are just great *friends.*"

Brad laughed. "No, it's not that bad . . ." His thoughts were suspended in air for a moment. "Just practically never," he said with a shrug of his shoulders.

Lou jumped in. "He means few and far between, right, Brad?"

Brad nodded with an embarrassed grin. "You could put it that way," he answered his friend.

"Geez, how the hell do you do it?" Doug asked, truly surprised.

"I don't know. I keep hoping things will get better, I guess. I'll tell you guys one thing. Cold showers don't work."

All three of them looked at Brad, shaking their heads. Their expressions were identical. A mix between bewildered admiration and sympathy.

Chapter Ten

Opening night for *Crush* was only three weeks away. The cast and crew were at their Manhattan studio, where they would rehearse for the next two weeks. After that, the exodus would begin to the Emily Forrester Theater upstate for "tech week," their third and final week of rehearsals. A concerted effort would then be made to polish it all to perfection.

At first, the mood was awkward and somber. Everyone was uncomfortable being in Jordan Hammer's company after the news of his wife's shocking death. Maxwell Carter, the director, decided to meet the problem head on. He made a brief announcement extending condolences to Jordan on behalf of the entire company, which was followed by a moment of silence. Short, tasteful, respectful. Then back to business.

Oblivious to all the hustle and bustle around him, Quentin's eyes were glued to Deirdre Grange. That flaming red hair flew seductively as she went through her dance routine. This one had him spellbound from that first moment he saw her when she auditioned for the part of the fiery Melina. It was no surprise that she had been selected. She hadn't even needed her connections. Her performance had snuffed out the dreams of the myriad hopefuls who had tried for the sought-after part that could launch a career.

When she completed her number, his applause might have been a bit too enthusiastic, but he doubted that anyone noticed. Most eyes were on Deirdre, and those that were not were absorbed in their work. Something stirred inside Quentin unlike anything he had ever known. His reactions when he watched her were more than sexual. Her total presence obsessed him. Her striking good looks were unique. Sometimes she looked as wholesome as his grandmother's apple pie, and sometimes all he could visualize was that gorgeous body stretched out in front of a roaring fire, her arms outstretched invitingly.

Their eyes locked for a fleeting moment when she flashed that electrifying smile at her small captive audience. Applause will thunder in that theater for her, Quentin thought. Heat rose in his cheeks. And elsewhere. Deirdre Grange had unknowingly—or perhaps knowingly—snaked herself into his bloodstream. He had to know her better, to touch her, to have her.

Quentin was well aware of his reputation as a womanizer, and he had every intention of maintaining that image. Especially now while the accident was still under investigation. There would be no change in his routine or demeanor. No shadows of doubt to be cast on his innocence or integrity should homicide be suspected.

Bearing that in mind, much later, when they had wrapped for the day, Quentin locked his dressing room door and tapped out her cell number, hoping she hadn't left yet. At the sound of her whispered "hello," Quentin sucked in a deep breath, as though he could drink her in.

"Deirdre, it's Quentin. I can't believe how you light up that stage. We all needed that escape today. Everyone is still shook up about Gloria." He paused before returning to his friendly, casual tone. "Anyway, I just thought I'd grab a minute to tell you so."

"Quentin, that's so nice! Coming from you, that's a compliment I'll treasure. Nothing like being accepted by your peers. And I'm kind of in awe of you too."

Quentin visualized those full, red sensual lips framing her perfect white teeth. He imagined his tongue exploring the depth of that dimple in her right cheek and the crevices of those tiny ears hiding behind her thick mane of hair.

His voice was raspy when he spoke again. "I was wondering if you were free for dinner tonight. There's a new French restaurant on Forty-eighth Street near Lexington that I'd like to try. *A Touch of Paris,* it's called, and I'd love to have you join me." He lowered his tone intentionally. "I've been in a down mood watching Jordan. Your good company could work wonders."

Her long pause made Quentin brace himself for rejection. He didn't really know much about her. Maybe she already has a man in her life.

"It hit me like a ton of bricks too, Quentin. That poor woman. I didn't get to know her very well, but still . . ." She left the sentence hanging, then said, "Well, I'd love to accept your invitation, but I need some time. Can I have an hour?"

"You can have all the time you need."

"Good. I can meet you there at seven."

*   *   *

When Quentin left for the restaurant, he filled his mind with pleasant thoughts and grinned. He couldn't believe his luck lately. First, getting a lead part in a Jordan Hammer musical, then, it was just a matter of time—a short time, probably—when he'd enjoy a sizzling affair with Deirdre Grange, a woman who could take his mind off Gloria Hammer, Wayne Bishop and that one night in hell.

Strangely, his thoughts drifted to his writing classes. He had been immediately attracted to that Mal Triana. Something fresh and unique about her. A certain innocence that set her apart from the others. Well, he couldn't think about her now. He focused on his dinner date with Deirdre.

Everything would be moving along perfectly, if only he weren't constantly haunted by those two terrified faces falling to their deaths.

Chapter Eleven

Once she got into it, she couldn't stop writing. Mal's fingers raced over her steno pad before the words and phrases escaped her. Occasionally, she'd stop to jot down a thought for a new scene, a new character or a possible plot twist, but the words flowed like music coming towards her from a distance. Like a marching band drumming out patriotic tunes to swell the heart. She became lost in her writing, closing her mind to the heartaches and unpleasantries of her everyday life.

After spending all those hours on *Hold Back the Love,* Mal chose to abandon it for a while. It had begun to show shades of her own life, her own feelings. Knowing her dad would read every word, she had become dispirited. If she had to whitewash the story, there would be no story.

Instead, Mal chose to attempt a Civil War saga. Quite a challenge for a novice writer, but she had always been moved by stories of the Old South and the devastation caused by a war that pitted brother against brother. She had read probably a dozen such stories after reading *Gone With the Wind,* but most of them paled by comparison to Margaret Mitchell's immortal classic. Still, most were well-written and well-researched. *Who am I to think I can follow in the footsteps of those masters?* Well, maybe I can't follow in their footsteps, she decided, but I can emulate and, hopefully, my own voice will shine through. Like Quentin said, why not dream big?

She used *On This Rich Earth* as her working title, and worked long into the night. From the very first page, Mal knew she had found her niche. This was the era in which she belonged. She left several blanks on her pages. Extensive research would be required to accurately describe life as Americans knew it then, nearly a century and a half ago. She made a mental note to work on a glossary of necessary descriptive words.

Reluctantly, she turned off her lamp at 2:05 a.m. Two active files in her office required motion papers to be prepared and mailed out to the court and opposing counsel before five o'clock the next day. There would be no margin for error or allowances for drowsiness or bloodshot eyes.

Mal forced her eyes shut, but her mind wouldn't turn off. Scenes for *On This Rich Earth* played in her mind. She fell asleep hoping she'd remember them in the morning.

*   *   *

The next day she spent her lunch hour at the library. She left with a documentary tape and two thick nonfiction books depicting life in America before, during and after the Civil War. How and when she'd find time to digest it all, she couldn't imagine, but flipping through the pages had already started her adrenaline pumping.

Her story was becoming an obsession, Mal realized when she caught herself attaching the wrong exhibit to her motion papers. Concentration on anything else had been a struggle all day. The up side was her thoughts rarely drifted to her mother's cancer, or her dad's immobile legs.

Mal knew she had lost it when Lois, the receptionist, brought back the court's cover letter that Mal had given her to photocopy. "Mal, where the hell is your head today? First you almost screwed up the exhibits and now this."

Nonplussed, Mal reexamined the letter and gasped. "Boy, Lois, do I owe you for catching this! They would have shown no mercy for this bungle," she said, referring to the law partners who paid her salary. Quickly, she brought the letter up on her computer screen to correct her error. Opposing counsel, Robert E. Lowry, was to receive a copy. Mal had typed "Robert E. Lee." If it weren't such a stupid, serious mistake, she could have enjoyed a good laugh at its absurdity.

"No problem. You don't owe me anything," Lois said with a shrug of her shoulders. "But maybe a pizza for lunch tomorrow might be nice."

"You're on," Mal answered. Silently, she promised herself to stay attuned to her job responsibilities and keep her writing at home where it belonged.

Instead, her mind wandered to how fast she could get through dinner and her mom's shower in order to watch the Civil War tape. Then she'd still need some time to write.

And then there was Brad. They were supposed to go out for a while. Oh, well, she thought, he'd probably enjoy watching the tape anyway.

Chapter Twelve

At nine o'clock Liz excused herself and went to bed. Mal jumped right up to slip the Civil War tape into the video cassette player. Not only did Brad watch the tape with her that night, but so did her dad. Russ hadn't intended to. Whenever Brad was there, in order to give them privacy, Russ always found some pressing reason to get back to his computer. But he was hooked the moment the tape started to roll.

"I really should get back to the computer. I have a few new Web sites to check out," he said after the first few minutes. "I can always watch it tomorrow or whenever."

Mal put her hand over her father's to stop him from wheeling away. "No, Dad, stay. Don't tie this TV up. You know Mom prefers to watch her talk shows and soaps out here. Why should she be cooped up in your bedroom?"

Russ heaved a sigh and nodded. That simple nod of his head and the rise and fall of his Adam's apple revealed to Mal her father's thoughts and feelings.

When Russ's gaze met Brad's, Brad recognized that he was waiting for his invitation as well. Brad straightened himself on the sofa and gave Russ the encouragement he needed. "Mal's right, Russ. It's always better to have a little company. And as long as Mal needs to soak up some facts for her novel, three heads are better than one."

But by the second hour, both male heads nodded off while Mal sat up with rapt attention, jotting down pertinent information she might use in her story.

Her father looked so uncomfortable with his head slumped over his shoulder, that she stopped the tape to wake him. "Dad, why don't you go to bed? You can't keep your eyes open."

Brad stood up and stretched. "Can I get you anything, Russ? Do anything?"

Russ patted his hand. "No, no. After all these years, I have it down to a science."

Mal grimaced silently at the bitter edge in her father's voice.

With Russ out of the room, Brad put his arm around Mal. She welcomed his comfort and snuggled her head on his shoulder. He brushed her face with two gentle kisses, one on her lips, one on her forehead.

She smiled up at him and caressed his face as an invitation for more.

While the Union and Confederate armies blazed in battle on a 25-inch screen, Brad pulled her closer, kissed her with a passion beyond sexual desire. More like a desperation to hold on to someone who was slowly slipping away.

"I don't know how long I can keep this up, Mal."

Tears welled in her eyes. She kissed his neck, savoring its warmth and the lingering masculine smell of his skin. "I don't know what to tell you, Brad. I wish I had some answers you want to hear. All I know is I don't want to lose you." She let the tears flow while Brad raked his fingers through her hair. The light from the television acted as a magnet in the darkened room. His eyes stared at it, unseeing.

*　　　*　　　*

To lighten their mood the next night, after a quick supper of cold salads, they went to see a comedy movie, then stopped at Starbuck's afterwards for coffee and a muffin. They found themselves talking and laughing nonstop.

"Gee, it did feel good to get out, I must admit," Mal said. They walked up the flagstone path to her front door.

"We *can* do it more often, Mal. Your dad can look after your mother. He does it all day." Brad slipped his arms inside her jacket and rubbed her back. His fingers tingled at the feel of her soft skin.

"I know, Brad, but that's the point. It isn't fair to him. He needs the help and companionship too. How can I go out to enjoy myself every night and close the door on those two sad souls? *They're my parents.* Now I'm out on Monday nights and Saturday mornings for my writing. I'd hate to give that up. That's my salvation."

"No one is asking you to. I just wish I were your salvation."

She squeezed the tip of his nose and flashed a wide smile. "Oh, Brad. We had such fun tonight. Let's leave on that note. Now give me a big hug and say goodnight. We both have to get up early for work tomorrow."

He gave her the big hug but he couldn't match her wide smile as he walked away to his car.

Chapter Thirteen

Georgia was her usual congenial self at the next class. In awe of her knowledge on the subject of writing, everyone listened attentively to her every word.

Mal had completed the first chapter of her novel after making countless revisions. She couldn't help but wonder whether her first draft was better. One of the first things Georgia had told the class was to write with passion and edit with reason. Maybe her editing had knocked out all the passion. She'd soon find out because it was almost her turn to read.

Her mouth went dry and her tongue felt like it was coated with sawdust. She helped herself to one of the butterscotch candies from Georgia's Lenox candy dish and read Carolyn Graham's pages as Carolyn read her copy aloud. Her voice was strong and proud; her face beamed with confidence. But the poor woman needed so much help with her writing. Seated to Carolyn's left, Mal would be first to comment, followed by the others, leaving Georgia to make the final analysis. To critique her work honestly, Mal would have comments about every paragraph, but didn't have the heart to come down that hard. She decided to mention, as gently as possible, only the most glaring errors. Not that she considered herself a paragon by any means, but some things were basic. *Compliment, correct, compliment,* she reminded herself.

"Carolyn, this sounds like the beginning of a great plot, but I have two comments to make. I think you could use a little dialogue to bring this scene to life. We're all familiar with those haunting words, 'show, don't tell.' And secondly, where is this scene? We have no idea. Give us a brief description of where this takes place so we can visualize the characters in that setting."

The smile never left Carolyn's face. Nothing would shoot her down. "Oh, you're right. I never thought of that." She turned to Georgia. "Sorry, you did talk to us about that last week, Georgia. I guess it didn't sink in yet."

Georgia waved off Carolyn's apology. "No problem, Carolyn. No one here is expected to memorize everything I say. It'll all come in time." She turned to the next speaker, Marybeth Fontaine, a 30-year-old stay-at-home mom whose goal was to become the next Nora Roberts. After hearing her first reading, Mal considered that a strong possibility if someone gave her that first break. Marybeth's critique of Carolyn's work covered some points Mal had chosen to ignore. And so it went around the table until it reached Georgia.

"Carolyn, first let me say that I admire your ability to accept criticism. Some students I've had will fight you tooth and nail. But that's what this class is all about; revision, polishing your story into a marketable product that will catch an editor's eye. Most of the remarks made on your work were valid; others I disagree with. Let's go over those now . . ."

Mal watched Carolyn as they listened to Georgia's critique. On a scale of one to ten, Carolyn's enthusiasm was an eleven. She certainly had the right attitude. Everything was a learning experience to her and nothing could break her spirit. Between Carolyn and Evelyn Shapiro, she couldn't figure out which one she liked more.

"Okay, Mal, you're next," Georgia announced. "Then we'll take our break. Ready?"

"I guess so," Mal said. She hated to get started. When she had completed that first chapter of *On This Rich Earth,* she was pleased with it. Not at first, but after a few rounds of revisions, she felt she would not be embarrassed to read it in class. Now she had her doubts. *Here goes. Sink or swim.*

"Emma watched through the brush till the wagon was no longer visible on the graveled road. She hurt everywhere. One eye was swollen shut, her jaw ached and throbbed; her teeth had bitten through her lip. Her groin, hips and legs felt as though they had been hammered into the ground. The bodice of her new dress was ripped to shreds from when they had savagely feasted on her breasts. With nothing to hold on to for support, she turned on her knees to crawl. The ground was sticky and damp with a dark substance. She crawled away to a nearby magnolia tree where she grabbed a branch and pulled herself up. Alone and desperate, she cried and screamed. How could she go back home looking like this? Pa would tan her hide and ask questions later. Luellen would help her. If only she could get to her first.

As she took her first shaky steps, she felt a hot trickle run down her legs. Blood. Blood and the filthy seeds of those bastards. The realization of what they had done exploded within her. Her head jerked back and lurched forward. She vomited violently. When nothing was left in her stomach, she slowly dragged herself to the brook and immersed her body in the icy water. But nothing would wash away the disgrace, and nothing would ever replace what the Gallagher brothers had stolen from her. Fueled by fury, she vowed never to rest until she could watch them hanging from a tree."

When Mal finally finished reading her five pages, no one said a word. She sunk a little in her seat and waited, hands clasped in her lap.

Quentin broke the silence. "Geez, Mal, I'm a man and I could almost feel what Emma was feeling."

The rest of the class chimed in with more words of praise. A few offered constructive criticism, some of which she agreed with, but most comments were favorable. Georgia put the icing on the cake when she simply said, "Mal, I think you have something great going here. I'd like to hold on to these pages till next week to take a closer look. Is that okay with you?"

Mal beamed. "Are you kidding?"

Quentin never gave her a chance to get into conversation with anyone else. "Young lady, let me buy you a cup of coffee," he said, leading her to Georgia's buffet table. "You are one hell of a writer."

Mal took the coffee and this time helped herself to an éclair too. This was a night to celebrate.

Quentin raised his cup. "To us," he said.

"To us," Mal repeated, following his lead. She caught the double-entendre in his words, but pretended not to notice. Maybe it was intended for their writing success, but instinct told her there was something more behind his words.

Chapter Fourteen

Jordan Hammer and Quentin sat in the rehearsal studio watching a conflict brew between the choreographer and the musical director while twelve dancers stood idle waiting for direction. With opening night only two weeks away, tension was high. Everyone was focused on the success of the play and his or her individual performance or responsibility. Even all the gossip about the scandalous death of the producer's wife had died down.

"Once we open, it'll be smeared all over the morning papers again," Jordan told Quentin. "Those damn newspapers and rag sheets eat up this stuff. They don't give a damn how many lives they ruin, as long as they sell their friggin' papers."

"Hang in there, Jordan. It'll die down soon enough. It was just an accident they've been trying to sensationalize. How long can they write about an affair? What's newsworthy about that in this day and age? Sure, your name is known around the theater, but let's face it, Jordan, you're no Bill Clinton."

Quentin felt a smile tug at the corners of his mouth. He had a hell of a time controlling it, but this was where the actor in him had to jump to the rescue. The deaths of Gloria Hammer and Wayne Bishop had been ruled accidental, Jordan had told him. Soon after the police spotted the abandoned car, the bodies were discovered. In no time crime scene investigators, police and the medical examiner's personnel were at the scene. When their investigations were completed, all had concluded that the couple had been involved in an extramarital affair, although no evidence of recent sexual activity had been found on either victim. It was assumed that tragedy had obviously struck before they had the opportunity to indulge. Apparently, Wayne Bishop's car had broken down before they reached their destination. The experts had theorized that panic caused by fear of discovery had probably provoked an argument between the two lovers, a struggle ensued, and both fell to their deaths.

For Quentin, the story was tailor-made. The press had already played up the affair. Gloria Hammer, although new to the theater, was going places. She had both talent and stage presence. But without the help of her producer husband, she probably would have joined the ranks of gifted performers who never got a break.

Jordan Hammer had been testing the waters with his beautiful and talented wife. Out-of-town audience reaction had been more than favorable. One more year and she would have been ready for Broadway.

Quentin wrapped a brotherly arm around Jordan's shoulder. "This is pretty shitty, Jordan. I can imagine. It's bad enough to lose your wife, but to find out at the same time that she'd been seeing another man . . ." He paused, shook his head as though the thought was inconceivable. "That's enough to blow you out of the water. Look, I'm here if you want to talk. If not, I understand. But these are the times when you need your friends. However you want it, Jordan. You tell me."

Jordan raked his fingers through his thick graying hair. "I'm not in the mood to go home yet. Why don't we go across the street to Benny's? I could use a good stiff drink."

"You got it, buddy. But I'm buying."

There were several stools available up front at the bar, but they chose a back booth where they could speak privately.

"Thanks for keeping me company, Quentin," Jordan said after the waiter brought their drinks. "Since Gloria's death, the days have been sheer hell and the nights ten times worse. I keep thinking it's like one horrific nightmare . . . that I'll wake up eventually, Gloria will be with me, alive and well, and I can have my normal life back." He twirled the stirrer in his glass and watched the ice circle around in his scotch. "But that's not gonna happen."

Quentin was baffled at Jordan's blatant depression. Knowing the real Gloria, not just her fabulous packaging, he couldn't understand the guy's grief. Had she behaved so differently with her husband that he never got to know the bitch within? He has everything going for him, good looks, talent, charisma, a name that was gaining recognition in the New York theater district, and money. Buckets of money, he suspected. He'd have dozens of Glorias waiting in line to soothe his grieving soul.

"Jordan, like I said, you're suffering a double tragedy here. The loss of your wife and the shock of her involvement with another man. But why not turn that around? They told you there was no evidence of sexual activity on either of them, correct?"

"Right."

"Then isn't it possible it was something entirely different that brought them together? Maybe this Wayne Bishop was someone from her past. For all we know, he could have tried to blackmail her for some buried secret. Anything's possible. I'm sure you're aware, Jordan, your wealth would make her a target."

Jordan's eyebrows rose and his lips twisted, revealing his thoughts before the words were spoken. "That's ludicrous, Quentin. A little too imaginative."

"Yes, I agree it's a stretch, but anything is possible. Not necessarily about Gloria herself, but maybe she wanted to protect a family member, a father, a brother. Who knows?"

Jordan waved it off. "Forget it, Quentin. I know what you're trying to do, but you're way off. Gloria's family are all financially sound in their own right, all responsible people who have the smarts never to box themselves into such a predicament."

Quentin shrugged. "Maybe. You're probably right. You know them. I don't. But you can't assume to know everything that goes on in their private lives. Sometimes people create an image to cover a dark side of their past." *Like me,* he thought.

Jordan responded with a condescending laugh. "Quentin, my guess is you're secretly a lover of mystery novels. Your imagination is bizarre."

Quentin conceded with a nod of his head. "Yeah, maybe so, but I can't seem to swallow this other man's story. I know the pieces fit, but I was always under the impression you and Gloria had a pretty good marriage going. I don't mean to pry, but . . ."

"We did, but we had our storms to ride, like most couples, I suppose. But once Gloria got involved in her own career, things changed. We were never as close as we were in the beginning. I sure as shit loved her . . ." He signaled the waiter for their fourth round of drinks. Quentin had switched to club soda after his first two shots of vodka. He didn't dare have a conversation with Jordan without being in total control.

"Let's change the subject before I start telling you my life story," Jordan said, his words slightly slurred. "I don't want to say anything I'll regret in the morning."

"Let's take off after this last round, Jordan. I think you're ready to hit the sack."

"I'll be okay. Guess I should have eaten something before drinking." Tears glazed his eyes. "That's the worst part, you know."

"What?"

"Hitting the sack. Reaching out for her and coming up empty. That sucks."

Quentin paid the check, hailed a cab and took Jordan back to his two-story, four-bedroom apartment on 65th Street. He was sobbing like a baby by the time they got off the elevator.

"Sorry if I talked too much tonight, Quentin. Didn't mean to dump my troubles on you. Whatever I said, it's just between us, right?"

"Of course. Hey, I'm your friend. You can trust me. Now get a good night's sleep and make sure you eat a good breakfast in the morning. You need your strength to get through this. Don't hesitate to call if you need me, regardless of the time."

"You're a good friend, Quentin. Thanks again, for everything."

When the door closed, Quentin allowed the smile to break through on his face. "That was one of my best performances," he murmured complacently.

Chapter Fifteen

The next day Quentin called Mal at the office. "I remembered hearing you say you worked for the Marcus law firm, so I looked up the number. Is it okay that I called you at work? Do they get uptight about personal calls?"

This guy is a little too pushy, Mal thought, but kept her voice even and polite. "Well, it's not that they don't allow it, but they do frown on abuse of the privilege. This place is a madhouse, anyway, Quentin. I really can't take the time for lingering social conversations." *There now, that should set him straight.* She had enjoyed talking to him at the class the night before, but Mal abhorred people who were too forward. Calling her at the office had put him in that category.

"Why *did* you call me here, Quentin? Is it about Saturday's class? Do we have to cancel?"

"No. On the contrary. I'm looking to extend it, sort of. I thought maybe we could go out for something afterwards. I love hearing your thoughts on writing, and I enjoy your company. You're a nice person. Plain and simple."

"Well, thanks for the compliment. I enjoyed our conversation too, but I don't think I'll have time for a leisurely lunch. My Saturdays are extremely busy," she said.

"So are mine. I have to get to the theater, but we can just do coffee and something fast. There's a diner right down the street. We can be out in a half-hour."

"Okay," she relented, "but I'll hold you to that half-hour." When she hung up the phone, she clung to the receiver a few moments, her brows furrowed. If he hadn't caught her by surprise, she would have refused him. What had compelled her to accept? Pondering the thought had given her an uneasy feeling. She dismissed it by focusing on the mountain of work on her desk.

*   *   *

The Saturday class had certain advantages. First and foremost, they read and discussed chapters from various how-to books on writing. There was so much to learn that setting this time aside disciplined them to study their craft. They also took ten minutes for spontaneous writing. They would choose a common line and everyone would write from there. If was fun to hear the variations and it also helped develop new story ideas.

Wally Paget gave Quentin a pat on the back when the class broke up at noon. "I'm glad you thought of this, Quentin. It forces us to study. If I had to find time for this at home, it would never work out."

"Listen guys, I skipped breakfast and I'm starving," Evelyn Shapiro said. "Would any of you like to join me for a bite to eat? I'm going to the diner down the street."

Mal and Quentin locked eyes. Both smiled as though they were harboring a secret. Which they were.

"Fine with me, Evelyn," Mal said. "But I can't stay too long."

Five minutes later, everyone left for the diner, with the exception of Amanda Valentine, who begged off claiming to have other pressing plans.

*   *   *

The five of them sat in the crescent-shaped corner booth where they chatted amiably about their present projects. They threw questions and answers at each other across the

53

table. The open exchange of thoughts was another opportunity to hone their skills.

After forty minutes, Mal was the first to rise. She left a few singles to cover her coffee and muffin and said, "I hate to break this up, but I really have to leave. It's been fun. I'll see you all at Georgia's on Monday."

Evelyn signaled the waitress for a refill on her coffee. "We should do this every Saturday after the library," she said. "It was good to have open, undisciplined conversation where we can throw out anything that comes in our heads."

Wally and Carolyn were quick to agree, while Quentin and Mal were conspicuously silent. Mal jumped in to break the awkward moment. "Look guys, you know I love all this writing stuff, but I can't make any promises. I'll join you whenever I can, but I have a full-time job and two sick parents who depend on me."

She had wanted to leave it at that, but their faces all went serious, waiting for more. Seeing their concern and sympathy, she explained, "My dad's not really sick, but he had an accident years ago that left him confined to a wheelchair. My mom, unfortunately, is in worse shape. She has cancer. And I don't think I have to explain to any of you what those chemo treatments do to a person . . ." She hadn't felt the tears coming, but there they were, filling her eyes. Embarrassed, she swallowed the lump in her throat, tightened her lips, waved to all of them, and left.

The moment she stepped on the sidewalk outside, she let those few tears fall. Then she inhaled, filling her lungs with fresh air. She refused to yield to them. That would only make her feel worse. As she walked to her car, she brought her thoughts back to the class. And Quentin. She was relieved when Evelyn suggested that the group gather at the diner on a regular basis after their Saturday classes. That obliterated the chances of going alone with Quentin.

Mal struggled with her feelings as she drove out of the parking lot and into the busy traffic. There's a part of him I definitely don't like, she thought. It's more than his forwardness, but I can't put my finger on it. So why did I feel this pang of disappointment when Evelyn unknowingly threw a monkey wrench into our impromptu date?

Chapter Sixteen

Brad sat at his desk listening to the mesmerizing sound of raindrops tapping the windows like tiny bullets. In the street below, passing cars and trucks made gushy sounds on the rain-slicked streets. He was glad he had decided to order lunch in for a change. With almost everyone out of the office, it was a welcome respite from the usual bedlam.

At first he thought he could never accept the Atlanta job offer. But now he was having second thoughts. Especially after he had called Mal to tell her about it. The only reason he did was because the offer alone made him feel damn proud. For a 25-year-old guy to be considered for such a challenging and responsible position—not to mention the $25,000 boost in pay—was quite an accomplishment.

But Mal's response was not what he had hoped. Foolishly, he had imagined that she'd sound frightened by the news, hoping that he would refuse it. But that wasn't what he had gleaned from their brief phone conversation. She had said nothing for a moment or two, then sounded genuinely happy for him and asked if he was going to accept the offer. Maybe it's because I called her at work, he thought. She has no privacy there. That was stupid.

He got through the rest of his workday telling himself that was the reason for her reaction. Tonight, when the subject comes up again, he'd try to read her face. This was one time he wanted to see sadness in those magnetic eyes of hers.

Unexpectedly, he got stuck working late and couldn't get to Mal's until almost nine that night. If it weren't for the fact that Russ needed help on a computer problem, he wouldn't have gone at all. But he didn't have the heart to disappoint the guy. Besides, he wanted the chance to broach the subject of Altanta with Mal face-to-face.

*   *   *

When they were finally alone, it was past ten o'clock. Brian Williams' newscast had initially grabbed Mal's attention, but after the first ten minutes, Brad was glad to see her reach for the remote. They needed to talk.

"Do you mind if I turn this off?" she asked. "It seems that every night the news is one long horror story. Ever since 9/11, I haven't been able to watch the news before going to bed. The nightmares are terrifying."

Brad's brows furrowed with concern. He reached for her hands and laced his fingers with hers. "You never told me that, Mal. If it's that bad, maybe you should get some help."

She gave him a smirk. "Like I have time to add therapy sessions to my daily schedule?"

"Well, it wouldn't have to be daily . . ."

"Forget it, Brad. It's not a consideration. I don't like to talk about it. Besides, we have more important things to discuss. Like your new job opportunity. Let me put on some relaxing music and we'll talk."

While she fingered through her CDs, she remained silent, then chose Kenny G and rejoined him on the sofa. Her smile was somewhat strained, unnatural, for which Brad was grateful. "You don't seem too upset about it," he said.

She looked him square in the face. "Of course, I'm upset, Brad, but I'm happy for you too—proud of you. I wouldn't dream of trying to talk you out of an opportunity like that. How selfish do you think I am?"

He tucked the persistent strand of hair that always fell over her eye behind her ear and stared at her for a moment. "Not selfish enough," he answered, pulling her closer. He kissed her gently at first, then with more urgency, as though trying to ignite in her the same stirrings that burned inside him. Instead, with their faces cheek-to-cheek, he saw her one eye pop open.

"What's that supposed to mean?"

"What's *what* supposed to mean?" he asked back. For the moment, he was more interested in nibbling at her neck than getting into analytical conversation.

She pulled away. "Not selfish enough."

Seeing her folded arms across her chest sent a clear message to Brad that their lovemaking would be put on hold until she had an answer. Exasperated, he drew a breath and blew it out slowly. "It means you deserve a life of your own, Mal."

"I have a life, thank you."

"Not the kind of life a woman your age should be enjoying."

"I'm playing with the cards that were dealt me the best way I can, Brad. And I *do* take time for myself. I spend time with you, and now I have my writing. If it weren't for my parents' troubles, I'd be perfectly happy."

"And as far as we're concerned, you'd be content with the status quo indefinitely, right?"

Her voice softened. "It's not that I don't want more, Brad. You know I love you and I'd be lost without you. You're my closest friend in the whole world. I've told you a hundred times."

His bitter words spilled out laced with sarcasm. "That's it in a nutshell, Mal. I don't want to be 'your closest friend in the whole world'; I want to be your husband, your lover."

Her eyes glazed with tears. She blinked them back. "For now you want too much, Brad."

The mellow sound of Kenny G's music switched from romantic to mournful as Brad grabbed his jacket and reached for the door. He realized they had never gotten around to discussing the job in Atlanta. But then again, even without the exchange of words, maybe they had.

Chapter Seventeen

Too stunned to move, Mal remained on the sofa with her legs curled under her. Brad had abruptly walked out without looking back. She tried to rub the chill out of her arms, but it wasn't working. Silent tears filled her eyes. She and Brad had been through this before, but tonight was different. A sense of finality hovered over her. Brad had pushed for that commitment she couldn't give him.

Would he have turned down the job offer if she had committed? She'd never know for certain because their discussion never got that far. One thing she *did* know for certain was in those last moments of their conversation, Brad had made his decision. She was about to lose him, and there wasn't a damn thing she could do about it.

She let out an involuntary sigh, grabbed a tissue and blew her nose.

"Mal, are you all right?"

Her mother's voice was behind her. Mal shot up from the sofa and tried her best to hide her emotions. "Mom, what are you doing up? Is something wrong?"

"Nothing's wrong with me. I'm fine. It's you I'm worried about. Want to talk?"

She's fine, she says. That's probably the most overused white lie, Mal thought. A brief blanket statement that hides a multitude of troubles.

Mal shrugged, but said nothing for fear her words would drown in sobs.

"I couldn't help but hear you and Brad. I didn't hear what was said, but the tone came through loud and clear. You argued about something, didn't you?"

Mal sucked in a breath to offer her mother a modified explanation, but Liz put a hand over her daughter's mouth. "You don't have to tell me anything if you don't want to. I just figured while you still have a mother, you might want to make use of her." She said it with a smile as though the fact that she might die was no big deal.

"Mom, I hate when you start with that fatalistic talk! Not everyone with cancer dies, you know."

Liz pursed her lips. "No, but many do. Anyway, forget that for now. I asked you if you want to talk. If not, I'll go back to bed. We'll both go to bed."

"Well, the good part is Brad's been offered a promotion with a big raise," Mal blurted out.

Liz waited for the catch. "And?"

"The bad part is it's in Atlanta. And I think he's going to take it."

"And he wants you to go with him." It was more of a statement than a question.

"He never said that," was the only response she could give. How could she tell her mother that he'd stay if she'd commit to him and she certainly would if it weren't for her parents' hardships.

"He doesn't have to. Some things you take for granted. Do you *want* to go? To marry Brad? To spend your life with him?"

Mal snapped back. "No, of course I don't want to go. My home is here. What would I do in Atlanta?"

"Okay, but you only answered part of my question. What about the other part? The Brad part."

Mal cupped her face in her hands and answered without meeting her mother's gaze. "I don't know what I want, Mom. I just don't know for sure."

"Do you love him, Mal?"

"I love him, but I don't like to feel pressured."

Liz paused a few moments, then said. "My dear daughter, if he makes you feel pressured, you don't love him. Not enough to marry him, anyway. Are you sure it's not something else?"

"No, I'm not sure of anything, Mom. But the thought of never seeing Brad again . . ."

Mal couldn't finish, but she didn't need to. Liz held her daughter and patted her back while she shed a few tears of her own.

Chapter Eighteen

By their third dinner date, Quentin and Deirdre were fast friends. With their love for the theater in common, they were never at a loss for words. Their spirits were high. Next week *Crush* would open here in Brockford, New York.

This time he took her to a Mexican restaurant overlooking the Hudson River where the food was spicy and loaded with cheese, but outrageously delicious. With friendly greetings and happy music, the owners and their staff made certain their customers enjoyed generous doses of food and ambiance.

Quentin and Deirdre had a romantic, dimly lit corner table where they sat on high-back wicker chairs. Their conversation was pleasantly interrupted by three guitarists decked out in typical Mexican attire—at least typical to what tourists would expect to see on a Mexican vacation. They wore sombreros trimmed with little black balls that swayed with the rhythm of their music, sequined, colorful vests with cummerbunds to match. The couple smiled politely as the men sang to them. When Quentin slipped the lead singer a ten-dollar bill, they all nodded graciously and moved on to the next table.

"So, where were we?" Quentin asked. Pretending to be unaware of his own actions, he took her hand and gently rubbed a finger along each of hers. Deirdre looked at him guardedly, but never removed her hand from his. The moment passed and they picked up their conversation where they had left off. Quentin confessed to her that although he hoped to someday be lucky enough to find himself on the Broadway stage, his secret dream had always been to be a successful writer.

"You're kidding!" Taken by surprise, Deirdre's reaction came off louder than she had intended. Embarrassed, she lowered her head, rounded her shoulders and met Quentin's gaze with an apologetic grin. "Sorry," she murmured.

"Don't be," he said. "That seems to be the general reaction whenever I mention it." He thought of Mal. She too had been surprised. Surprised and impressed.

"No, I think that's great, Quentin. I just took it for granted that most people, once they have a taste of that stage and the heat of the theater lights flooding them, they're hooked. Not to mention applause. That's the grand prize."

He stared at her in silence for a few moments, basking in that Mother Goose and apple pie smile of hers. Without moving his eyes, he scanned the rest of her sensuous body. What he couldn't see, he imagined. Mother Goose and apple pie had no business there. He scooped up some salsa onto his tortilla chip, put the whole thing in his mouth, washed it down with sangria. He liked to watch Deirdre's unconscious habit of running her tongue along her bottom lip as she sipped the fruity wine.

"You're absolutely right," he said finally. "And I'm no exception. I fall right in with 'the smell of the greasepaint, roar of the crowd' bunch. But who says I can't be an actor and a writer at the same time?"

Deirdre's hand went up like a stop sign. "Fine. Nobody says you can't. But they're both special crafts that require a lot of sacrifice and dedication. I doubt that I'd have the stamina for both. If you do, I say go for it. Half the battle is won if your goals are set and your desire to achieve is strong enough."

Quentin offered no response. His eyes were fixed on Deirdre and his mind was clouded with pleasurable thoughts.

"Quentin, why do I get the feeling you're not listening to me?"

He threw his head back, laughing, then reduced it to his sexiest smile. "Sorry. It's just that you're so incredibly beautiful, I find it hard to concentrate. My mind is elsewhere."

Deirdre cleared her throat and clutched her wineglass with both hands. Her voice grew deeper, throaty. "And where *is* your mind, Quentin?"

"I think you know the answer to that, and I hope your mind is in the same place."

Deirdre met his gaze and whispered, "It is."

The waiter wheeled his cart over with their sizzling entrees, making small talk as he served them. With diminished appetites, they merely picked at the succulent dishes they had earlier planned to attack. The air was thick between them. If anyone looked, it would be plain to see there was more sizzling at their table than steak and onions.

Quentin turned his attention away from his plate and reached over to stroke her bare arm. "No coffee, no dessert tonight. That okay with you?"

She flashed him a smile loaded with innuendoes. "Certainly," she said.

Chapter Nineteen

Hours before the opening night performance, Jordan Hammer decided to disappear, to slip out quietly before the final bows. Before the accident—if it was an accident—he had looked forward to this night. Something told him this one was going to launch him over the top. Every time he saw or felt something exceptional, he'd get a ripple up his back, and that feeling had been strong with *Crush*. He had dreamed this play's success could be comparable to *Chicago* or *Cabaret*. How the thought had excited him then! Tonight, once he had seen the audience reaction, he knew his instincts had been right. But now, since Gloria's death, and the way she died, how the hell could he hang around to celebrate?

He thought he'd scream if one more person threw one of the usual cliché lines at him: "Life goes on, Jordan"; "You have to think of yourself now, Jordan"; "You have to move on, Jordan." All that crap they feed him, but Jordan knew well what unsaid words were prevalent in their minds.

He wasn't sure how the press would handle his absence. He assumed they'd play up the grief angle and rehash the accident, soap opera style.

To block the wind off his neck, Jordan flipped up the collar of his coat. He started walking away from the theater and down towards the river. Empty benches faced the blackened water, which was angered by the whipping wind. Jordan tried to imagine happier times with Gloria, those summer days when they would sit on one of those benches looking out at the boats on the river, watching the shimmering golden stripe of sunlight on the water. They'd sit there sharing their dreams and ambitions. There was a time when Gloria's dreams were his dreams, when what excited him excited her. Then, before he realized it was happening, they began to drift apart. He never stopped loving her for a minute, but never took the time to tell her, to show her. His love for the theater, for his work, took precedence over all else. Gloria followed his lead; wrapped herself in her own theatrical career, set her goals and went after them. Like the proverbial two ships that pass in the night, their marriage stayed afloat because neither took the time to notice it sinking.

Common sense told him a dark, lonely park was no place to hang out your troubles. He might as well put a sign on his back: Mug Me. But cold air has a way of clearing your head; unscrambling your thoughts. You can line up your problems in the order of their importance and decide which ones to deal with first. Good plan when it works.

He pulled a cigarette from the pack in his pocket, lit it and watched the wind blow the smoke away. He had been doing so well beating the addiction until the accident. That same haunting scene flashed before him again, as it did every day, every hour of the day. The night when the police came to the door. One look at those faces and he knew he had lost her. He thought nothing could be worse than hearing that Gloria was dead until he heard about this Wayne Bishop. Who the hell was he really? How the hell did she become involved with him? A part of him wanted to know and a part of him didn't. The part of him that did turned around and headed home. He felt better and quickened his pace, confident he had made the right decision. Soon, very soon, he'd pay a visit to Mrs. Wayne Bishop. Maybe she needs to know too.

Chapter Twenty

Quentin was proud of his performance. Being offered the lead in a musical had surprised him. There were several others whose singing and dancing were superior to his—as much as he hated to admit it—but the director had favored him and Quentin wasn't about to give him an argument.

Hands joined across the stage, he and the rest of the cast took their bows and basked in the thunderous applause. Many in the audience were on their feet cheering. True, opening night performances were full of family and close friends, but so what? It still felt marvelous. Absolutely marvelous. Deirdre was on his left. She squeezed his hand and sneaked him an I-told-you-so smile.

Jordan had gladly paid for the opening night party held in Alfredo's northern Italian restaurant, but didn't attend. Quentin and Deirdre, on the other hand, enjoyed every moment and drank in all the accolades. Tonight he found Deirdre particularly desirable, probably because they couldn't be alone together. Long before they became lovers, Deirdre had made plans to celebrate opening night with her family. Their celebration would take place tomorrow night. After their matinee performance, she'd have dinner with her parents and sister before they headed back to Pennsylvania. From there she'd go directly to the Marriott Hotel in the city where he would be waiting. He had ordered two dozen roses and champagne.

A familiar voice calling his name interrupted his thoughts.

"Quentin Kingsley! Let me congratulate you. You were *fabulous.*" The open arms coming towards him belonged to Roberta Bookman, an active member and benefactor of the Emily Forrester Theater.

"Hi, Bertie," Quentin said. He gave her a hug, then lowered his head to accept her kiss. "It was great, wasn't it? Everyone was in top form tonight."

"Yes, everyone in the show is talented and entertaining," she said, then with a hand on his shoulder, she whispered, "but you, my dear man, are mesmerizing. You have that something special that clicks with the audience. Charisma, stage presence, whatever you want to call it, you've got it, baby."

Quentin bowed his head in thanks. "Well, aren't you sweet for saying that. Now if only we could get the Big Guns in New York to agree with you."

"I think they would if we could get them up here to see the play."

"I hear Jordan is working on that. He wants to see us on Broadway as much as we do."

"Hey, can't blame him. It's his play." The smile disappeared from her face. "Poor guy. I hope things work out for him." She shielded her lips with her hand then lowered her voice to a whisper. "At least he never found out that the guy she died with wasn't the only one."

Quentin, who was only half-listening, did a double take. "Bertie, that's an awful thing to say. The woman is dead and can't defend herself. I don't think it's fair to make such wild accusations."

She threw him a slanted look. "Come off it, Quentin. You can drop the noble act with me. I won't tell your little secret. I like the guy. Why break his heart? Truthfully though, I was a bit curious about how *you* felt when she was found with Wayne Bishop."

Quentin's empty stomach was doing somersaults.

He welcomed Bertie's rambling because he was too shocked to come up with the appropriate response. He had no idea if what she said was based on supposition or an eyewitness accounting. A look of shocked confusion was all he offered.

"But it's none of my business," she went on. "Forget what I said, Quentin. Go. Enjoy your big night. Deirdre is throwing me daggers through her smiling face for monopolizing you. Time for me to mingle. Cheers, baby."

Deirdre was waiting to introduce him to her family. With a champagne glass in her hand, she waved him over to join them, but Quentin was no longer in a celebratory mood. Not wanting Bertie to see him unnerved, he started towards her anyway. Other well-wishers blocked his path and showered him with words of praise. Ordinarily, he would have been eating it all up, but suddenly he had no patience for congeniality.

That bitch had ruined his night. Top priority in his mind was to find out what she knew and how to shut her up.

Chapter Twenty-one

All the alcohol he had consumed at the party dulled his brain enough to cloud his fears. He slept through till morning, but awoke to her image. To Quentin, Roberta Bookman was a time bomb about to explode. She monopolized all his thoughts while he trimmed his beard, showered and dressed for his celebration date with Deirdre at the Marriott.

Certainly, it was too late to reverse courses now, but he hated himself for not reporting the accidents that killed Gloria and Wayne Bishop. Still, if he had to do it all over again, he probably would have made the same decision. The repercussions would have ruined him. Although both deaths were truly accidental, chances are no one would have believed him. And then, of course, there was that little detail that couldn't be overlooked; the three martinis. An ambitious prosecutor looking to climb the political ladder, and a jury looking for justice for the victims' loved ones, would probably have sent him away for life.

Even if he were able to escape the worst, Jordan Hammer, his friend, producer, and husband of his deceased lover, would have crushed Quentin's theatrical ambitions for good.

He knew Bertie had the hots for him. She wasn't exactly repulsive, but she had at least ten years on him and was fighting the battle of the bulge. Her layered outfits helped somewhat, but the swell of her stomach and her thickening waistline were out to destroy her femininity and whatever sex appeal she had left. Her husband, Alan, was fifteen years older than she; short, bald and heavy enough to make Bertie look good, but Alan was friendly, good-natured and gifted with a comical flair. Everyone enjoyed his company except his wife. Apparently, those attributes were not enough for Bertie.

Befriend your enemies. Yes, those were words of wisdom he would live by in the wake of that fateful fall night. But he had to move slowly and cautiously with Bertie. She was no dummy and would recognize his motivations in a flash. For tonight, he resolved to sweep Bertie from his head and replace her with thoughts only of Deirdre. Sensual thoughts.

Before slipping into his black leather three-quarter coat, he checked himself once more in the living room mirror. He raked his fingers through his thick black hair and fussed with the turtleneck collar of his burgundy sweater. He pursed his lips and studied his long hair and beard, which were both meticulously trimmed. They were starting to grow on him, literally and figuratively. Deirdre had fallen into the habit of twisting her fingers in his beard, or absentmindedly curling the hair at the nape of his neck whenever she was in a talkative mood. Almost always, after they made love, she wanted to talk and he wanted to doze off. They compromised. He listened to her with his eyes half-closed.

He felt the stirring in his loins just thinking about those fingers of hers. If they weren't in his hair, they were busy elsewhere.

As he drove, the Bertie Bookman problem sobered his mood. He had to develop a plan; subtle, but effective. If necessary, should his affair with Gloria be exposed, Quentin was prepared to play the role of the penitent sinner. He'd admit to the affair, but would claim he felt as shocked and betrayed as Jordan was when he learned she had died with another lover. Except for the fact that his career would be immediately extinguished, that would work. At least he'd protect himself from a life behind bars.

His fingers tapped the steering wheel as he waited at a red light. Then, satisfied with his line of defense should he need a Plan B, he put on an optimistic grin and took off to weave his way through the thickening traffic.

His mind filled with fresh thoughts. The chapter he would read at Georgia's tomorrow night, and, more importantly, how the hell he was going to squeeze Mal into his social life. Mal Triana was an itch that needed scratching, but he had to prioritize. Bertie had to be dealt with first. But Mal had recently split up with her boyfriend, which meant she would welcome his sympathetic shoulder and be ripe for picking.

No. Not yet, Quentin decided. Mal would have to be put on hold for now.

Chapter Twenty-two

He awoke that Monday morning in the luxury suite that had cost him megabucks. Deirdre purred beside him in a deep, contented sleep. The lacy Victoria's Secret nightgown she had bought for the special occasion lay strewn on the plush champagne-colored carpeting at the foot of the bed. Under different circumstances, he would have nibbled at her neck to pick up where they had left off last night.

A throbbing headache dragged him out of bed. He picked up the phone and ordered a continental breakfast for two. That done, he downed two Extra-Strength Tylenol, stepped into the glass-enclosed shower and let the steamy, needle-like spray penetrate his pores. He helped himself to one of the thick, white terrycloth robes that hung on oversized antique brass hooks.

By the time room service knocked on the door, Quentin was completely dressed, minus shoes. Deirdre looked like she might be good for a few more hours and he toyed with the idea of leaving her there. He could write her a note, leave money for a cab and take off. The thought was tempting, but ludicrous.

Instead, he woke her up with a kiss and a smile, like Snow White's prince. "C'mon, sleeping beauty, I hate to cut our festivities short, but I have a tight schedule today." He busied himself with the breakfast tray to avoid her gaze.

Deirdre slipped her nightgown back on and joined him at the table. He poured her coffee, which she accepted politely, as if the night before had never happened.

"I see you're dressed and ready to run. Did something happen to prompt this sudden rush?" she asked, her voice dripping with sarcasm. "It's only nine o'clock, Quentin."

Her obvious annoyance only cemented Quentin's decision to check out early. His life was his own, and he answered to no one. Sure, she was gorgeous, good company; particularly since they shared a common interest. And not to be overlooked, a dynamite sexual partner. But although Deirdre was his "pleasure in progress," he knew she could easily be replaced.

Still, he masked his feelings and forced a smile. "I realize I never got around to mentioning an early checkout, but I do have things to handle today, Deirdre. It can't be helped."

She pouted seductively, stood behind him and wrapped her arms around his waist. "Can't you spare another hour? What do you have to do that's so important? It's not as if you have to rush through your day for a performance tonight. It's Monday, we're off." She threw him a sarcastic smirk. "Oh, I know you have your writing class tonight—God forbid you should miss that—but that's not until seven o'clock. What's the hurry?"

Quentin steeled himself to hold back the rising fury. He had neither the time nor the patience for an argumentative discussion. Or worse. He unclasped her hands and turned around to face her. "Deirdre, I have things to take care of before my writing class. I don't think I have to provide you with details. And, by the way, I didn't appreciate your sarcastic remark about my writing class." His tone of voice welcomed no further discussion.

Deirdre stared at him for a few seconds, baffled by his behavior, a complete reversal of the man she slept with the night before. "Okay, forget it," she said, one hand raised. "Do you think you can spare me a half hour to shower and dress?"

"Of course."

She started for the bathroom, then turned around. "Just one thing, Quentin . . . what the hell happened to last night?"

He shrugged. "I was drunk last night. I'm sober now."

Deirdre took a deep breath and closed her eyes, as though that could erase the hurt. Then calmly, she said, "Look, Quentin, something's obviously upset you terribly. I don't know and I don't care what it is, but I think you should leave now. I'll find my own way home."

"I'll leave you money for a cab."

Her temper rose. "I can pay for my own damn cab, thank you. Just go, Quentin."

He picked up his coat, stopped at the door, and very softly said, "Don't choke me, Deirdre. Just don't choke me."

Chapter Twenty-three

Carolyn introduced the subject at the coffee break during class. "So, Quentin, how's the play going? You never talk about it. I hear you're great."

He faked a modest smile. "The feedback has been good for all of us, yes."

Amanda Valentine had been chatting with Philomena Lombardi, an introverted woman in her fifties who had made the move from Italy to this country only seven years before. Philomena said little in class and spoke with a thick accent, but her novel about an Italian family trying to survive during World War II was poignant and powerfully written. Amanda had been picking Philomena's brain for information she needed for her own novel until she heard the other conversation switch to Quentin's play. She left Philomena abruptly and shifted to that group. Her hand went up for Quentin's attention, sending six chunky gold bracelets on a collision course up her arm.

"Yes, Quentin, I've been meaning to ask you about your play too," Amanda said. Her eyes were fixed on Quentin only, oblivious to everyone else. "You never say two words about it. I saw the ad in the paper and would love to see it."

Quentin knew a come-on when he saw one and he had seen Amanda's several times before, but had been turned off by her not-so-subtle advances. He liked to do the chasing himself. It was much more fun and much more rewarding when he succeeded, which was more often than not.

Quentin tilted his head and raised his brows. "Well, we all try to respect that unwritten rule we have here about not drifting off to any subjects unrelated to writing. And it's a good rule. We're only here two hours a week, and we have to make every minute count."

Amanda gave him a conceding smile. "I can't argue with that, but I'd still like to see it."

Several others expressed the same interest.

"Fine. Glad to have your support, but you'll have to call the box office to check on ticket availability."

Martin Roth, a local realtor who joined the class to sharpen his mystery writing skills, chimed in with a suggestion. "Why don't we all get tickets for the same night? Maybe we can meet for an early dinner, then see the show. It'll give us a chance to socialize before Quentin entertains us with his talents."

Quentin feigned modesty again. "Well, even if I disappoint you, I'm certain that you'll be more than pleased with some of the other performers. Deirdre Grange and Jack Borden are a dynamite dance team, for openers, and there are a few others who are worthy of honorable mention."

"I'm sure that includes you as well, Quentin," Wally Paget said, then focused his attention on Martin Roth. "Martin, are you suggesting that we do that dinner/theater thing for the class only, or are husbands, wives or partners included? I, personally, would prefer to take my wife. If that's not okay, we'll get our own tickets."

Georgia clapped her hands. "Excuse me, class," she said. "Can we take our seats now and get back to work? Not that I'm against what you're trying to plan, but Quentin is right. We can't get into that now. You can make those arrangements after class. I'd be happy to join you if I can, but we're usually loaded with social and business engagements, so I can't make any commitments." Then, to Quentin, "But I will see your play, Quentin, I promise."

When the class was over, Quentin walked Mal to her car, making small talk. He stalled her until everyone else was out of earshot. "I was flattered that everyone wanted to watch me perform, but disappointed in a way."

"Why?"

"Because I've been wanting to invite you alone. Then maybe go out for something afterwards." The moment the words spilled out of his mouth, Quentin was annoyed with himself. He knew better than to speak without thinking first. Since the night of Gloria Hammer's and Wayne Bishop's deaths, he had trained himself to be particularly cautious every time he spoke. This was the second time in one day he had put his foot in his mouth. First, this morning, when the tension of his encounter with Bertie had frayed his nerves, he had snapped biting words at Deirdre without cause, and now again, he had spoken too soon.

As far as Mal was concerned, although he fully intended to get around to her eventually, he had no intentions of inviting her to the theater. After showering Deirdre with remorseful apologies this morning and begging like a puppy before she reluctantly forgave him, he wasn't about to jeopardize their relationship. Not yet. Besides he suspected the slower he moved with Mal, the more receptive she'd be when he was ready. Yes, Quentin decided, slow cooking always tenderizes the meat.

Mal had one ear on the other lingering conversation. "It sounds like plans are under way to get tickets for the class. I'd hate to exclude myself from that get-together. I'm sure everyone else will probably go."

"Yeah, sure. I guess you're right," Quentin said, with a silent sigh of relief.

Chapter Twenty-four

Brad battled with his thoughts and made the wrong decision anyway. Mal had told him several times all about Georgia's gorgeous home, on a gorgeous street, in a gorgeous neighborhood, and exactly where it was. Her writing classes ran from seven to nine o'clock on Monday nights, but there was usually a ten-to-fifteen-minute period of lingering conversation at the door, Mal had said.

He arrived there about ten minutes before nine and parked across the street, waiting for her to come out. One more try, he promised himself. Maybe the weeks of separation had a positive effect. Maybe she had missed him as much as he had missed her. If so, she'd come flying into his arms as soon as he called her name. "Stop dreaming, kid," he mumbled, "It ain't gonna happen." But he waited anyway, just in case.

At 9:20 that door finally opened. Happy, animated people started pouring out. If Mal had been suffering these past weeks from a broken heart, there certainly were no visual traces evident tonight. She was laughing and talking nonstop. He was about to call her name, but remained with his mouth open. A tall, lanky-looking guy with long hair and beard who looked like Abe Lincoln was leading her to his car. Her car was parked right in front of his. He couldn't hear the whole conversation, but what he did hear was enough. "Why should you bother to take your car? I'll drive you back here later to pick it up."

Where the hell was she going with him? Who the hell was he? Then he remembered. The long hair and beard clicked. He's the actor Mal had mentioned. Brad hadn't paid too much attention then, but the creep sure grabbed his attention now.

After they pulled away, still talking and laughing, Brad started his car. See, jackass? he said to himself. Forget it. She has her writing to make her happy and now this . . . She sure isn't pining away for you, boy. It's over.

*   *   *

When he opened the door to his apartment, he found the television on, the volume up too high, and Larry King's face on the screen thanking his guests and saying goodnight to his audience. Steve was spread out on the sofa, snoring away. Brad shook him awake. "C'mon, Steve. Either sit up and watch television or go to bed. I can't sit in this room and listen to you snore."

Steve was upright in a flash, as though surprised that he had fallen asleep. He yawned and rubbed his eyes. "Boy! You're in a hell of a mood, aren't you?"

"I'm not in a hell of a mood. It's just that you fall asleep on this sofa so often, no one else can sit here. You're getting to be a couch potato. Once you're married, I doubt that Karen is gonna like that."

Steve stood up now and pointed a warning finger at Brad. "What Karen likes and doesn't like is none of your damn business. Why the hell do you have a bug up your ass tonight?"

Instant remorse hit Brad. He hated himself for the way he had lashed out at his friend. "Sorry, Steve. You're right. I do have a bug up my ass, but I don't want to talk about it now, okay? Where's Lou? Is he home yet?"

Lou had been in his room on the phone with his girl. He cut the conversation short when he heard the heated discussion. "What the hell's going on in here?"

"Nothing. I'm in a shitty mood, and I don't feel like talking, except to say one thing to you, Lou. You don't have to look for another roommate to share the expenses after Steve gets married. I changed my mind about the Atlanta job. Initially, I said yes to that for all the wrong reasons. But they had given me another week to think it through before I made a final decision. And I decided I'm staying right here in New York where I belong."

Lou extended his right hand. "Hey, good for you, buddy. That's great news for us."

Steve shook Brad's hand too, but said nothing at first. Then he hugged his friend and said, "Whenever you want to talk, we're here to listen, pal. You have a big fire to put out. I can tell."

Brad felt a lump in his throat the size of an apple. "Thanks," he said, then went to the kitchen, popped open a beer and wiped the moisture from his eyes.

Chapter Twenty-five

Georgia was grateful that she didn't have high blood pressure because the bastard she was married to would have given her a stroke years ago with his polite poison. How she had gotten through twenty-six years of marriage with Harry Pappas was still beyond her comprehension. The months and years just roll into each other, and before you know it, you're forty-seven years old fighting wrinkles and cellulite.

But Georgia couldn't dispute the fact that there were certain immeasurable rewards. The first were her children, Dorothy, Alex and Elaine, although there wasn't an angel in the bunch. Their teenage years had put plenty of gray hairs in her head, if gray hair can be blamed on stress. But now, with all three in college, they were all finally maturing into young adulthood.

Harry's warm relationship with his children was also a plus, and his sharp business acumen provided Georgia and her family with a more than comfortable lifestyle.

She had called in sick today, but it was actually a planned R & R day. Her students would have their own rest and relaxation day by driving the sub crazy. For the record, Georgia taught English to high school seniors, but half the time was spent being a disciplinarian. Two-thirds of the class were bright, attentive and enthusiastic students who would have no trouble finding their way in this world, but the others . . . She didn't want to think about those thorns in her side right now. She had to leave for the city to meet friends for lunch at Antoine's on 52nd Street.

*   *   *

Jennifer Morrison and Althea James were her closest friends in college and the three had stuck to their promise never to lose touch. Barring illness or emergencies, they met in the city every other month, each time at a different restaurant. All three were married and in their late forties now, but liked to roll back the years when they were together. They exchanged stories, some pleasant, some not so pleasant, but they always found reason to laugh. Maybe their good moods were launched by the cocktails they had first, but whatever it was, it worked for all three of them.

"No, I could never fault him for being an unaffectionate or inattentive father," Georgia was saying, "It's just me he hates."

"Oh, stop it," Jennifer said, with a half-smile. "I don't believe he hates you. From what you tell us, he isn't *that* bad."

"Okay, so maybe hate is too strong a word. How about ignore? He certainly ignores me. As much as I hate to admit it, I'm convinced he has someone on the side. In his business, he has plenty of opportunity to take off unexpectedly for days at a time. And he does."

Althea took the floor. "Now, wait a minute, Georgia. Just because a guy has a job that requires travel, that doesn't mean he's cheating on his wife. My Max travels two or three times a month, and I don't get those vibes."

"Does he ignore you?"

Althea's brows furrowed in thought. "What do you mean 'ignore'?"

"I mean it in the full sense of the word."

Jennifer leaned forward on the table and spoke in a whisper. "Georgia, are you telling us you have no sex life?"

"Zilch. It's been years now. Fifteen to be exact." Georgia grinned and shrugged her shoulders, as though it were funny and unimportant, but nobody laughed.

84

"Geez, Georgia. You never told us," Althea said.

"It never came up, if you'll forgive the pun." Again nobody laughed. "Besides, it's not something a woman wants to admit, not even to her best friends."

Perplexed, Jennifer sat with her arms crossed over her chest, looking at Georgia as though examining her for flaws she hadn't noticed before. "I don't get it. You're still a good-looking woman——no, not good-looking, beautiful. You have a figure like a thirty-year-old, you're intelligent, have a big heart and a great personality. What the hell more does he want?"

Georgia bit her bottom lip and kept her eyes focused on the teaspoon she was playing with. "Beats me."

"Well, haven't you confronted him?" Jennifer continued. "It's not normal, you know."

"I haven't confronted him verbally, but a few times when we were in bed—you know." She squared her shoulders and looked Jennifer straight in the eye. "Then I just didn't give a damn anymore. I'm not about to beg him to love me. It's either there or it isn't. Now I hardly ever think about it. We're polite to each other, pretend nothing is wrong, especially in front of the children, but when we're alone in the house, he does his thing and I do mine."

"And you accept that kind of existence?" Althea asked. "Georgia, I can't believe you can have such an indifferent attitude. Let it out. Tell us what you're really feeling."

Georgia's elbow was on the table and two fingers went to her cheek. She wrinkled her brows and slipped into a pensive moment. "Actually," she said, "I hate the bastard and wish he were dead."

The line rendered her friends speechless.

Chapter Twenty-six

Two weeks after that scene at the hotel, Deirdre was still pissed. Although they still had a few late dinners together, she was finding one excuse after another to keep Quentin out of her bed. Whether she was trying to torture him and teach him a lesson, or simply keeping her guard up, he wasn't sure, but his patience was running thin. How many times did she expect him to apologize?

Quentin shook his head thinking what a jackass he had been that morning. That sort of erratic behavior was exactly what he had to watch out for and avoid. Bertie had put him in such a sour mood the night before that he had lashed out at Deirdre. Still, as much as he missed her sexually, he was confident he could win her over eventually, if he wanted to.

Just as well, he thought. He could work this temporary rift to his advantage. Without being too obvious, he would ease his way into a relationship with Bertie. For over ten years, Bertie had been an active member and strong financial supporter of the theater. She availed her services wherever she was needed and was present at the beginning or end of nearly every performance. Still, Quentin hadn't been able to find the chance to talk to her alone. Somehow, he had to make the connection. Since opening night, when she had teased him with that devastating remark she casually threw at him, he hadn't had one decent night's sleep.

Bertie, on the other hand, being the extroverted, liberal-minded person she is, probably never gave it a second thought. It's not as if she'd go and tell Jordan, and certainly it never dawned on her to connect him to Gloria's death. But her loose tongue posed a serious threat to Quentin. How could he know she hadn't told anyone else what she knew or suspected, and, if so, whether that person would connect the dots?

For now, the only solution he could come up with would be to charm her into an affair, which required little effort, he thought confidently. If he had something to hold over her head, she'd think twice about divulging his affair with Gloria.

He grimaced at the thought of a sexual relationship with Bertie. To go from Deirdre to Bertie would be such a sharp contrast he hoped he'd be able to perform. He'd have to concentrate on memories of sex with Deirdre and expectations of sex with Mal.

Mal was beginning to look better and better to him now since his relationship with Deirdre had cooled, and more particularly since he had resolved to make Bertie his priority. Yet, since passion has a way of quashing reason, he felt compelled to approach Mal again.

Quentin put the copies of his chapter to be read at tonight's class in his folder and took off for Georgia's house. With the theater dark on Mondays, this was his only full night off and he couldn't think of a better way to spend the time. His writing class was a surefire way to tune out the Bertie problem for a few hours.

*   *   *

At the coffee break, he joined right in the conversation among Mal, Evelyn and Philomena. He gave them all equal attention at first, then found his opening. First, he boosted the egos of the other two women by pouring on words of praise. Both were proficient writers, albeit in different genres, so his words were sincere despite their underlying purpose. His intent was to steer the conversation to Mal and keep it alive there. When Wally Paget joined them, Evelyn and Philomena got into a separate conversation with him, which fit perfectly into Quentin's plan.

Finally, he turned to her. "And you, Mal . . ." He paused, shook his head in awe and disbelief. "I'm amazed at your story. Maybe I find yours particularly compelling because I'm a Civil War buff myself, but your knowledge of the chronology and the way you present it through your characters is superb. Obviously, you've done your homework. I imagine the research is time-consuming. I'd be happy to help you out a little."

Mal laughed as though his offer was absurd. "Quentin, how can you even consider making such an offer? Even if you do control your hours, you do have a day job plus your work in the theater. That plus your writing is a heavy load already."

"If I couldn't handle it, I wouldn't offer."

She waved him off. "Thanks anyway, Quentin, but I wouldn't dream of accepting your help. My father would be devastated." She went on to explain how her dad got involved in her story. "Sometimes I think working on my novel excites him more than it does me. You should see his face when he finds the information we need on the Internet. It's wonderful to see him so enthused and excited. Since his accident, that computer is the best thing that's happened to him."

His eyes met hers and lingered a brief moment, as though probing, searching her thoughts. "It must be rough on you at home, I imagine, from the little you've told us."

Mal forced a smile. "Not really."

Quentin spotted Georgia headed back to the table. He had to move fast. "Listen, how about pizza after class? Just the two of us. We can pick each other's brain."

Mal's nose wrinkled in indecision, which Quentin considered better than a flat refusal. He was about to coax her into it when Georgia called the class back to the table. He flashed her his most innocent schoolboy smile as they walked back into the den. "Think about it," he said. "Half-hour or so."

"Okay. I did want to ask you a few questions about the play you're starring in and your writing."

Satisfied with his coffee-break accomplishment, Quentin took his place at the table for the second half of the class. Before he could give Georgia his full attention, he had to figure out how to break away with Mal before any others invited themselves along.

Quentin loved this class. Not once had Bertie Bookman entered his mind. Tonight he would work on Priority No. 2, Mal Triana. Maybe just until he got Deirdre back completely or got rid of the Bertie problem, whichever came first.

Chapter Twenty-seven

Mal enjoyed her forty-minute bus ride to work. She liked looking out the window and being alone with her thoughts. Sometimes she'd read, write, invent plot twists and create new characters for her novel. Lately though, all she could think of was Brad. After three weeks passed without a call from him, Mal tried to con herself into thinking it was all for the best.

At first her feelings were similar to those of tornado survivors. That devil in the sky rips through a town, flattening it into total devastation. As though it never existed. How do you pick up the pieces and go on when part of your life is suddenly whipped away?

But Brad loved her. He had for years, and that's why this breakup was necessary. His love was unconditional; hers was not. Mal never doubted that if she had said she'd marry him with the stipulation that they live right there in her parents' home, like one big, happy family, he'd agree in a flash. Sure, he got along with her parents, and had sincere affection for them. But could he take it on a daily basis? Never. He'd eventually want his own privacy, his own home and his wife, all to himself. The depression in the Triana household would kill him. So it's better that he left now, before it could reach that point, she told herself. He told her she deserves a life of her own. Well, so does he.

Mal drew a breath, determined to sweep him from her mind. For now, at least. When she felt her eyes glazing over again, she pulled a book from the attaché case she carried with her every day. Not that she wanted to impress anyone with the professional touch, but her current chapter and related paraphernalia accompanied her everywhere. Just in case she got a brainstorm.

She opened the book on Civil War history that she had found in the library. The text and illustrations offered plenty of useful information for her novel, but today she didn't have the concentration for research. Although her eyes scanned the words, her comprehension was nil. Her thoughts wandered. When Brad's face wasn't flashing in her mind, the image of her dad in his wheelchair or her mom sick in the bathroom did. At least the chemo was over for now. Thankfully, the Cancer Society had provided volunteer drivers to transport Liz to and from her treatments every week. Next week she was scheduled for a CAT scan of her chest, abdomen/pelvis and bones to see if the cancer had metastasized. God, she hoped not.

*   *   *

Second only to her writing, work was Mal's therapy. Her job was always insanely busy leaving little chance to get lost in her musings. She tucked her troubles away in some dark corner of her mind and threw herself into her work. She was fine until one of the young lawyers stopped at her desk with an affirmation that needed revisions.

"Mal, before we go over these changes I scribbled," Chuck began, "I haven't had much time to talk to you lately. How are things going at home with your parents?"

She gave him a good-as-can-be-expected shrug and opened her mouth to speak, but Chuck cut in.

"Good thing you have Brad to help you get through this, Mal. That guy's been a godsend to you. I know how rough a caretaker's job can be when you're handling it alone."

Oh, shit, she mumbled to herself. *Not here.* Chuck had hit a nerve. There was no stopping those tears. She had stored them up too long and they wanted out. She grabbed her bag and raced to the ladies' room, leaving Chuck standing there, sorry he had brought up the sensitive subject.

She lucked out. The bathroom was empty. Mal wasn't sure herself whether she had cried for Brad, her parents or herself. Probably a combination of all. She made a fast repair job on her makeup and felt better. As long as no one said a word to her, she'd be fine. Why can't people understand that when someone is in an emotional state, the worst thing they can say to that person is "Are you okay?" or words to that effect. It's as if they pressed a button marked "Release Tears."

Which is exactly what Lois did when she opened the bathroom door a moment later.

Chapter Twenty-eight

Mal sat up in bed promising herself she wouldn't write for more than an hour tonight. *On This Rich Earth,* her Civil War story, had developed into more of a challenge than she had anticipated. Rather than slow down the pace of her writing, she'd highlight any areas that needed to be authenticated by research; a task her dad took on eagerly. He had become invaluable in that respect.

Russ was asleep when Mal got home at 10:30, but he had left her a printout on the kitchen table covering certain Civil War battles. Perfect. She smiled as she glanced through it, happy to have the pertinent details she needed to fill in some blanks, and happy for her father. She knew what a charge it gave him when his research efforts were successful.

But tonight the words wouldn't come. Her thoughts were flooded with images of Brad and her mother. She wondered if he was already in Atlanta, if he missed her, or if he had erased her from his mind. When she wasn't thinking of Brad, she thought of her mother's upcoming CAT scan. If the results weren't good, how would she and her dad handle it? More importantly, how would her mother handle it?

She fell asleep with a troubled mind and woke up at 5:20 in a sweat, her heart palpitating. Memories of a terrifying nightmare surfaced. Her mother was drowning in the ocean, drifting far out to sea. Mal tried to swim towards her, but the waves kept pushing her back to shore where her father sat helplessly in his chair, tears streaming down his face. Brad stood there with him, his feet buried in the sand, his arms folded. She called out to him to help, but he stood there in silence, watching her desperation.

Instead of trying to sleep for another hour and risk another nightmare, she turned off the alarm and got out of bed to begin her morning routine. She heard the sound of water pouring in the kitchen. Her father was already awake, making coffee. She kept her voice down to a whisper and went to him.

"Dad, what the heck are you doing up so early?"

Russ's lips tightened. He didn't turn to meet his daughter's gaze, but continued busying himself with the coffee. "I've been up for hours. Couldn't sleep," he said with a shrug.

"Me too. Probably for the same reason. Were you thinking about Mom's CAT scan tomorrow?"

He nodded and kept his eyes fixed on the coffee slowly dripping into the glass pot. "It's like the day of reckoning, Mal. I want to know, and yet I don't. I'm afraid for her, for you, for myself. I'll go crazy if . . ." His voice broke up.

Mal bent over, hugged her father, and kissed his cheek. "Me too, Dad. I wish I could cheer you up, but I feel exactly the same. I'm taking off tomorrow. We'll all go together."

"No, Mal. Save the day for when you really need it. I'll be with her, and it's not as if we'll get immediate results."

Mal put her finger over her lips to silence him. "Forget it, Dad. I already told them I won't be in. It's not a problem."

Russ reached for his daughter's arm as she stepped away. "Mal, have you heard from Brad at all? I miss him myself. I haven't brought up the subject because I can imagine how you must be hurting."

Mal heaved a sigh. "No, Dad. I haven't heard from him, and yes, I miss him too, but I don't want to talk about him or think about him. I have too much on my plate right now. My first concern is Mom." *And you're my second,* she thought.

"Okay, I understand. Go take your shower. When we have our breakfast, we'll talk about something pleasant. I have an idea for a plot twist on your book that you might like."

"Good, because I have a hell of a time getting out of some situations I box myself into. Creating conflict is easy, but finding solutions is tough. And by the way, Dad, thanks for that printout you left last night. I read through it. That's exactly what I needed."

Russ smiled. "See what a great team we are? When you get published, you can give thanks to your old dad on your acknowledgment page."

Mal laughed. "Yeah, sure. When I get published. Don't hold your breath."

Chapter Twenty-nine

After talking to Jennifer and Althea at lunch two weeks ago, Georgia felt as though she had burst through the confinement of a straitjacket. So often when she spoke to these dear friends on the phone, she had wanted to dump her marital problems on them, but never got around to it. Either she wasn't in the mood to bare her soul or the opportunity for a long conversation hadn't presented itself.

She had driven home from the restaurant that day with a new sense of freedom. Getting those words out, telling them quite matter-of-factly that she hated him and wished him dead had been more than satisfying. Shades of guilt had run through her for the "wish him dead" part, though. Their children loved him and that was reason enough for him to stay alive.

But last night had changed everything. She called Althea late that afternoon, as she promised she would when she had the privacy to talk.

"Oh, Georgia, you just caught me," she said. "I had an early shoot in the city and I just got in." Althea was a widely respected free-lance photographer. "I was about to soak in a nice hot bath and rest my weary bones."

"Guess I didn't pick a good time to talk then. Go relax in your tub. It's not important."

"Yes, it *is* important, Georgia. My tub will still be there when we're through talking. I told you to call me for my sake as well as yours. You really upset us that day. Jennifer and I had no idea you had such an empty marriage. Maybe instead of turning a blind eye, you should sit him down and force him to tell you where you stand. The underlying problem might be workable. Even another woman. He won't be the first decent husband who strayed. Sometimes it's just a passing thing. One of those 'I love my wife, but oh, you kid' situations. Heaven knows what's been going on in his mind. Maybe he thinks you're the one who's been ignoring him."

Georgia was shaking her head as she let Althea go on with her analyses. She drew a breath and interrupted her. "No, Althea. I wish it were that easy. I'm afraid it's much worse than that."

"What are you talking about, Georgia? I don't like the tone of your voice."

"I overheard something last night that has me very suspicious. Actually, not suspicious, convinced."

"Convinced of what? Georgia, get to the point. You're scaring me."

Georgia's voice cracked. For some crazy reason, the words she had to spit out were worse than saying she wished him dead.

"Okay, here goes. Late last night I came downstairs intending to get the novel I had left in the kitchen. I had been having a bout with insomnia and wanted to read for a while. I had heard the phone ring ten or fifteen minutes before, but assumed it was for him. No one calls me that late. Well, I never made it to the kitchen because I stopped short when I heard his voice. He was still on the telephone, whispering, laughing a little. Unquestionably, he was talking to his lover. I couldn't pick up the conversation, but I did hear him say, 'I miss you too.'"

A gasp from Althea. "Oh, no," was all she said.

"I know he never heard me come down," Georgia continued. "He was too engrossed in his romantic conversation and I was barefoot. I went back upstairs and curled up like a snail in my bed, pretending to be asleep. Later, much later, when I heard that steady snore and knew he was dead to the world, I went downstairs again. I wanted to check the last incoming call. When the number came up, I recognized it instantly." Georgia paused, hating to get that last part out.

Concern for her friend came through when Althea spoke. "Georgia, are you all right? Who was it? Was it someone you know?"

"It was one of the partners in Harry's firm. He was just made a partner sometime last year. I've met him several times. His name is Jeffrey Townsend. Harry even had the nerve to bring him here and let me serve him dinner! Can you imagine? Those bastards. I don't know which one I want to kill more."

Althea was at a loss. After a few seconds of silence, she found her voice. "Georgia, are you sure you heard right? I can't believe what you're saying."

"Believe it. It all makes sense now. It's funny, I kind of suspected this guy was gay. There was something about him . . . but it was none of my business and it wasn't important, so I put it out of my mind. Stupid, wasn't I? I never dreamed that *he* was the one. Sometimes we can't see the forest for the trees."

"Geez, Georgia. I'm in shock. I want to help you, but I don't know what to say."

"That's okay, Althea. I just had to tell someone. It was reaching a boiling point inside my gut."

"Listen, Georgia. I think we need to get together again, not in a restaurant this time. We'll do it here, in my house, where we can have privacy. How about if I call Jennifer and set it up?"

"Fine," Georgia mumbled, but her emotions were about to let loose and she couldn't continue.

"I'll get back to you. Promise. Hang in there."

Georgia only nodded into the phone, then hung up.

Later, she had no choice but to pull herself off the living room chair because she needed to use the bathroom. She caught a glimpse of her face in the mirror. Her eyes were red and puffy from crying. She had to get herself together and try to patch up the damage. Like it or not, she had to function; to distract herself with daily normalcies, like driving over to CVS for another bottle of Advil. Judging by the throbbing headache she had last night, she suspected she'd need a healthy supply.

She washed her face clean and wondered what happened to that beautiful woman Jennifer had described. "You look like hell," she said to the image in the mirror. What's worse, she thought to herself, is that I don't give a shit.

Chapter Thirty

Three frightened faces waited for Dr. Elena Vargas to speak, all afraid to hear what she would tell them, but hopeful that the news would be good.

The doctor leaned forward on her desk and clasped her hands. When she smiled at them, the three faces relaxed somewhat and braced themselves.

"Yes, Liz, you responded well to the treatment. Your blood work is good. Once a month, we'll check it, but for now it looks good."

Liz let out a long sigh of relief. Russ couldn't reach her face from his chair, but he grabbed her hand and kissed it. "Thank God, thank God," he murmured, swallowing the sob that had rushed to his throat.

Mal squeezed her mother's other hand and kept her eyes focused on the young oncologist. Her tall frame was lean and firm from what she could see under her white coat. Her face was devoid of makeup, her clothing as casual as you can get, jeans and sneakers. Warm brown hair was pulled back and piled on her head, fastened haphazardly with a large plastic clip.

The "for now" tagged on the end of the doctor's words made Mal sense a "but" coming. She encouraged her to continue. "So what does this mean to us, Doctor?"

"It means that your mom can take a break from the treatment, but after three months we'll do another CAT scan and take a look."

Relief flooded Liz's face. "Thank you, Doctor. You can't imagine—"

Dr. Vargas interrupted. "Yes, I can imagine, Liz. Although I never experienced the disease personally, I see and listen to my patients every day. And I lived through it in my own family."

"I'm sorry," Liz said. "I didn't mean to imply that you were insensitive."

The doctor flashed a warmer smile to put her at ease. "No problem. I understand. Now, I want you to go home and do the best you can to enjoy yourself. You'll be getting your strength back after a while and you should take advantage. Plan pleasant things to do, a vacation, maybe. Whatever. Go enjoy your life a little. I know you've been through the mill. Now you can celebrate. I'll see you again in three months. Of course, if you notice any changes in the way you feel, don't hesitate to call me."

Three months. Three glorious months without watching her mother suffer through those treatments. Maybe she can put a little weight back on. Maybe they can spend a Saturday out shopping together and stopping somewhere special for a nice, relaxing lunch like they used to before cancer knocked on their door.

She wished she could tell Brad. He would have been so happy for Liz, for all of them. Maybe he'll call. He knew when she was scheduled to go for the CAT scan and see the doctor. He couldn't have hardened that much. And if he did, he wasn't the super Mr. Wonderful she had always thought him to be.

Chapter Thirty-one

Jill Eaton's jaw tightened and her teeth clenched at the mere mention of that name: Mal Triana, her nemesis. She had never laid eyes on her except for that haunting, framed photo on his desk. Two smiling faces embraced in a hug, standing in front of a Christmas tree, both wearing red sweaters and Brad in a Santa hat. How very merry. Jill wanted to vomit every time she saw it.

But today it was conspicuously absent. With all the work-related debris on his desk, someone else might not have noticed, but for Jill it was as though bells had rung. Was the photo's disappearance an all-clear signal? Had he finally wised up and given up on that bitch? She'd been using him and taking advantage of him for years. He knew it too, Jill was certain. He just didn't want to face it. If he did, he'd have to deal with it and let her go.

Well, maybe now he had.

She waited for the right moment to make her move. Through the corner of her eye, she watched him. Her intent was to worm her way into his lunch hour, whether he was eating in or out. She hoped he had no plans to join the guys at Romero's across the street. It had become a regular lunchtime hangout for some of the office staff.

Jill put her idea into action. She posed her question in the form of a general announcement to the three coworkers within earshot, one of whom was Brad. "Does anybody want to order in? I can't decide whether to go out or not . . ."

Two of them cut her off with a thanks-but-no-thanks, just as she had known they would. She had overheard them earlier making plans to lunch together. That left Brad.

"How about you, Brad? Eating in or out?"

He stretched his arms out and rolled his chair away from his desk. He laced his fingers behind his head. His look was indecisive. "I'm not sure what the heck I want to do."

"I'm not in the mood to eat in myself. The day seems too long if I don't get out. But I couldn't leave at twelve when the girls left. I had to finish my report so I could eat lunch with a clear head." She met his gaze with a feigned look of impromptu thought. "Brad, they have a new chef at that seafood place on 55th Street. I heard the food is great. Want to try it with me? I hate to sit alone. My treat."

Brad wheeled back to his desk, closed out the document on his computer screen, and stood up. "Sounds good to me. I could use the walk and the fresh air too. But I'm buying."

Jill felt her heart thumping. She hadn't expected it to be this easy. Needing a few minutes to organize her thoughts and carefully plan her conversation, she excused herself to the ladies' room and arranged to meet him at the elevators in five minutes. She couldn't wait to find out if Mal Triana was past tense. And, if so, she had no qualms about getting him on the rebound. She had been lusting for Brad Winslow for too long.

*   *   *

They started with white wine at the bar while they waited for their table. Shop talk kept their conversation light and impersonal. When Brad's name was called, they lifted their glasses and followed the hostess to a table in the back room, which Jill thought was a little overdone in seafaring style. But the mood was captured and the place was mobbed. She ignored all the hanging fishnets and plaques of various sea creatures plastered to the walls. The lights and colorful fish in a gigantic tank along the back wall added a warm glow to the dark, wood-paneled room.

She felt the blush in her cheeks caused by the wine and the nearness of Brad Winslow. *Easy girl, you've got him nibbling at your bait. Don't let him slip away.* Food was the last thing on her mind, but she chose salmon from the list of specials while Brad decided on the sole florentine. That done, she steered the conversation back to the usual office buzz. When the waiter brought their food, Jill welcomed the interruption. She only had a lunch hour to get to first base and needed to switch gears.

After a few silent minutes as they ate, Jill took the plunge. She had decided not to mention the missing photo. Someone who had no particular interest in him might have been oblivious to its presence or absence. She moved in what she deemed to be the more natural direction. "Brad, I know it's none of my business, so you can just ask me to shut up if you like, but I haven't heard you say a word about Mal lately. Are things okay with you?" And then, before he could answer, she added with a wave of her hand, "Oh, forget it. I don't want to stick my nose where it doesn't belong. It's just that you seem a little quieter than usual lately. I got the distinct impression something's bothering you."

"No, it's okay. I don't mind your asking. It's just that I don't like getting into that stuff at the office. Mal and I broke up weeks ago. We had problems that we couldn't iron out. It's better this way. I think we both needed a fresh start."

"Well, I don't want to see you hurting, Brad. But maybe a fresh start *is* what you need. Sometimes when the problems are overwhelming, it's like beating a dead horse."

Brad nodded and went back to his food. "Maybe so. But if you don't mind, I'd rather change the subject, okay?"

He's all yours. Reel him in.

Chapter Thirty-two

Russ had already typed eight double-spaced pages of Mal's work from the night before. Seated at the living room window, he enjoyed the morning sun and watched the usual signs of everyday life unfolding. His eyes were fixed on the postal worker as she briskly walked up the driveways of his neighbors and stuffed their mailboxes with what was probably mostly junk mail.

Bored after five minutes of watching the mundane chore, he wheeled back to the computer room to retrieve the day's typed pages. He beamed as he reread them, while marking a few spots with his yellow highlighter. There were always questions pertaining to grammar, punctuation or plot development that he would discuss with Mal at night. But he smiled down at the pages, in awe of his daughter's writing ability. *On This Rich Earth* was developing into a compelling, poignant story with strong characters, powerful plot twists and cliff-hanging chapter endings. Sure, his view was prejudiced, but he still knew a good story when he read one.

"Have more pages for me to read?"

Russ was startled, albeit pleasantly, by the sound of his wife's voice. She bent to kiss him good morning and he gazed up at her with brightened eyes. "Yes, I think you're gonna love this chapter, Liz. I think I see the buds of another Margaret Mitchell in our darling daughter."

Liz raised her eyes to the sky, as though only a heavenly act could create such a miracle. "We wish," she said with a smile.

"No, don't give me that look like it's impossible. Mal really has talent." He slapped the printed manuscript pages. "This story is as good as dozens I've read, and better than many."

Liz's hand went up. "Hey, I'm not disagreeing with you. I'm just as proud of Mal as you are. It's just that I think she's setting herself up for heartaches. Writers need a tough skin. I don't want to see the disappointment in her face when those rejection letters start pouring in."

"She can handle it. Mal is tougher than you think. She's enthusiastic and confident about her work, and it'll be up to us to keep her spirits strong through the low periods." He wheeled himself closer to her chair. His voice lowered. "Speaking of lifted spirits, Liz, do you know what it does to me to see you looking stronger and happy again? It broke my heart not to be able to help you when you were feeling so sick."

She patted her husband's hand and shrugged. "You did help. You were there. There wasn't much you or anyone else could do, anyway. That damn chemo is no stroll in the park. I still don't feel that great, but just knowing I have a three-month break makes me feel reborn."

The sound of the phone stopped Russ from saying anything further. "That has to be Mal. You notice how she's been calling me every morning to ask my opinion on her latest chapter? I love that." Then, into the phone, "Mal?" His face grew serious. "It's Brad," he mouthed to his wife. Then, "Good to hear from you, Brad . . .Yes, she did go, and we got great news." Russ filled Brad in with the details of their conversation with Dr. Vargas. " . . .Yes, sure you can say hello." He handed the phone to Liz. Russ watched her and listened for the subject to change to Mal, but the only reference was Liz's polite "Yes, she's fine."

"What's the story with him?" he asked when she hung up. "Did he say anything about Mal?"

Nonplussed, Liz shook her head. "Not really. Only to ask how she is. Then in the same breath, he rolled away from the subject. He wished us all luck—sounded very formal— not the same Brad we all loved."

"Maybe we should have asked him to stop by and say hello. He might have opened up to us a little."

Liz gave him a sideways glance. "I doubt it, Russ. He said he was calling from Atlanta. I can't believe he made that move. Between his family and Mal, I thought for sure he'd turn the offer down."

"I think it was *because of* Mal that he accepted it."

Together, they decided not to mention the call at all to Mal. The hurt was still raw. Better to let sleeping dogs lie, Russ had told his wife, but he wondered if those dogs were actually sleeping.

Chapter Thirty-three

It had taken Jordan Hammer three weeks to work up the courage, but today he impulsively flipped through the telephone directory and there it was—Anne and Wayne Bishop, 331 Jackson Avenue. He entered the address into the computer, using the theater as his point of origin. The printout said it would be a twenty-eight minute ride to his destination. He knew the area vaguely. All the streets are named after presidents.

He thought about calling first, but was afraid she'd hang up before he had a chance to speak. But maybe not. In all probability, Anne Bishop was being tormented with the same unanswered questions.

His courage began to slip away as he drove into the quiet, tree-lined neighborhood. Bags of autumn leaves were lined up at the curbsides of the high-ranch houses waiting for morning pickup. Two teenage boys were shooting baskets in the driveway next door to the Bishop house. With the car still running, he parked in the street. What the hell am I doing here? Jordan asked himself. He was about to pull away and head home when a light blue SUV swerved in front of him and pulled into the driveway. The streetlights and the van's headlights afforded visibility and instant recognition. Her look was hesitant and cautious at first, but stiffened to anger when she realized who he was. Jordan put his car in park, shook his head, and, with a long, rueful look, apologized for being there.

Before he had a chance to pull out and take off, Anne Bishop was out of her SUV and boldly approaching his car. Jordan lowered his window halfway to mumble his apologies, but she never gave him the chance.

"You're her husband, aren't you? I know that face from the newspapers. Hers too. Your bitch of a wife. What are you doing here?" she yelled at him. "What *the hell* are you doing here? Did you stop by to torture me a little more?"

Impulsively, Jordan got out of the car, hoping to allay her fears with a stream of apologies.

She shot up towards the side entrance of her house, leaving the SUV at the foot of her driveway. Floodlights splashed across the lawn and drive.

"Please, Mrs. Bishop, I realized the moment I saw you that this was a dumb mistake. I just had this wild idea that maybe you and I could put our thoughts together . . ." Jordan shrugged and threw his hands out in a gesture of hopelessness. "It was a bad idea and I'm sorry," he said, his eyes cast downward. He bit down hard on his dry lips, feeling like a fool and an ass because he couldn't stop the tears that were filling his eyelids.

Anne Bishop's voice remained angry, laced with the bitter taste of her husband's indiscretion with the wife of this broken down man who stood before her. "What did you expect to gain by coming here? Did you think we could talk our way into finding them innocent?"

Jordan's emotions wouldn't yet allow him to speak. He responded with another shrug, then lifted his face to meet her gaze. "Something like that," he said finally. His tears embarrassed him, but he made no attempt to hide them. Standing on the concrete steps outside her kitchen door, she loomed over him. The anger drained from her face. Her eyes bore down on him for one long, hard moment. Then, as though a dam had burst, she buried her face in her hands and sobbed uncontrollably.

Jordan fought the compelling feeling to comfort her, to put his arms around her. Theirs was a common pain that went far beyond the parameters of grief caused by the unexpected death of a loved one. Those flames of betrayal would never burn out.

She struggled to pull herself together, inhaling deeply to suck those sobs back in. "Mr. Hammer, I'm not sure this is a good idea either, but I'm going to let you in for a while. But I only have a half-hour or so before I have to leave again. My boys are at basketball practice and I have to pick them up."

"That's absolutely fine, Mrs. Bishop," Jordan said with as much humility as he could muster. "I'd appreciate any time you could offer. So much of this nightmare doesn't make sense, and I thought . . . I don't know what I thought."

"Come in, Mr. Hammer," she said with a sigh. "I doubt that we'll find any answers. Facts are facts, as they say, but maybe talking it out will do us each some good."

"I hope so, for both our sakes," Jordan said, and stepped into the kitchen of Anne Bishop's home.

Jordan was having second thoughts about this visit. Not that she was rude or uncooperative, but he felt intrusive. Before they had a chance to begin the conversation he had hoped for, the phone rang. Her mother, she mouthed. Jordan sat at her kitchen table smiling politely as the young widow rolled her eyes and tapped her foot. She shot him an apologetic look and kept nodding her head as her mother's words apparently went in one ear and out the other.

When she finally ran out of steam and Anne got the chance to offer one complete sentence to the phone conversation, she begged off with the excuse that she absolutely had to leave to pick the boys up from practice.

"I'm sorry," she said when she hung up. "My mother is a wonderful woman who means well, but she completely overlooks the fact that I'm all grown up now and like to make my own decisions, right or wrong. And ever since Wayne is gone, she's much worse; more protective than ever."

"Sounds like a typical mother," Jordan said with a smile, "The kind a lot of people wish they had."

"Oh, don't misunderstand. I'm not complaining. I love her to pieces, but she never stops mothering."

Without asking, she made two mugs of hot chocolate, threw a few miniature marshmallows on top of each, and sat at the table to give Jordan her attention. He was silently amused as he sipped the soothing warm drink, thinking that he probably hadn't had hot chocolate since he was a kid.

"But you're not here to talk about my mother, Mr. Hammer. What exactly brought you here?"

He never got the chance to get into it. The phone rang again. This time it was another mother asking if Anne could possibly do her the favor of picking up her son from practice and taking him home with her. The woman was obviously detained somewhere, and judging by Anne's response, was apologizing profoundly for imposing.

By the time that second call concluded, Jordan gulped down the last of his hot chocolate and got up to leave. Embarrassed, he mumbled an apology for showing up unexpectedly and invading her time.

"I'm sorry, Mr. Hammer. In my house, this is par for the course. Maybe we could meet one day for coffee while my boys are in school. We won't have the interruption of my constantly ringing phone. I'll even turn off my cell phone."

Recalling her initial hostility and anger, Jordan was touched by her sincerity. He returned a warm smile and said, "That sounds like a good idea. What day is good for you?"

Chapter Thirty-four

Torrential rain and wind had forced Mal and Lois to do lunch at the ground floor deli in their office building. They both ordered the soup of the day, beef barley, and one turkey club sandwich to share.

"Why don't you call him, Mal?"

Mal's eyes rolled upward. She couldn't remember how the conversation got centered on Brad again. She thought she had made it clear that she'd rather not discuss Brad, but Lois had a way of sucking out Mal's innermost feelings. Not that she resented the intrusion; she knew Lois meant well, but talking or thinking about Brad always put her in a down mood these days. She worked hard to drive him out of her mind.

"What would be the purpose of calling him, Lois? He's hundreds of miles away in Atlanta. He made his choices and I can't say that I blame him. Let him get on with his life and I'll get on with mine." She pulled one of the pink cellophane-wrapped toothpicks out of a sandwich wedge and bit into it, hoping to dismiss the subject. But Lois wasn't ready to let go.

"Mal, do your parents have any idea what caused the breakup?"

Mal's sandwich went back to her plate. "Lois, my parents have nothing to do with any of this. Brad made it clear to me that he was perfectly willing to move in and take care of us all."

"So? What's wrong with that?"

Mal shot her a look that needed no explanatory words, but she offered them anyway. "Lois, I can't do that to him or anyone. My burdens are mine alone. Not that I consider my parents burdens. I love them both and never resent for one minute anything I do for them. But for anyone else who isn't bound by that strong family love, it would never work. There's no sense kidding ourselves."

"How do you know that?"

"I know it. Trust me. Lois, I don't mean to sound sharp, but you're on the outside looking in. You can't imagine all the everyday pleasures Brad would be denied if he hooked up permanently with me."

Lois yanked out a tomato slice that had been slipping precariously from her sandwich. "Oh, stop it, Mal. Don't give me that noble martyr routine again." She pointed a finger at Mal. "Look, you'll probably get mad at me, but here's what I think: First, you definitely underestimate Brad. He has more strength of character than you give him credit for. And he's crazy about you. Let's not forget that. Secondly, I think you're trying to con yourself as well as your parents and everyone else, including me."

Mal raised her brows in mock indignation. "Really? And how am I doing that, Dr. Phil?"

Lois ignored her playful sarcasm and continued. "I think deep down you're crazy in love with him but you put on this façade. You probably have your parents convinced that he's been nothing more than a good friend who happens to be of the opposite sex."

"That's not true. They know our relationship ran deeper than that."

Lois drew a breath and paused for patience. "Listen Mal, all I'm trying to say is, if you love Brad, go get him, damn it!

Just because he moved to Atlanta doesn't mean the situation is irreversible. There are plenty of jobs in New York."

Mal gave up on the rest of her club sandwich, pushed her plate aside and sipped on her Coke. "Lois, you're a good friend. I know you're trying to help me, but I'm confused myself about my feelings for Brad. I can't figure out whether I'm miserable because I love him so much or whether the emptiness I feel is because I got used to depending on him all these years. I feel like I lost one of my limbs. Anyway, what I *do* know is I'm not going to call him. When he called to see how my mother's CAT scan turned out, he made sure he called when I was working. He never left his number. What does that tell you?"

"It tells me he's given up the fight, I'm afraid. And so will I, for now." She went back to her hardly-touched food and changed the subject. "Tell me how your novel is going. That always puts you in a good mood."

Mal smiled, glad to get off the subject of Brad. "Well, it's my story, so naturally I'm partial. But the teacher and the class cheer me on, give me the confidence I need to keep up with it."

"How's that actor you were telling me about? He sounded like an interesting character."

"Yeah, that's Quentin. He's a strange dude. I like him and I don't like him."

"Has he made any moves on you?"

"Would you believe me if I told you I'm not sure? Sometimes I think he does, and sometimes I chalk it up to my vivid imagination. We have our conversations over coffee—in and out of class—but just friendly stuff, mostly about our writing. Other than that, he doesn't say much; subtle little flirtatious hints here and there."

"Whoa! Sounds interesting," Lois said.

Chapter Thirty-five

He was off again on another one of his "business" trips. How convenient it was for the bastard to be gay, Georgia realized. There was no need to hide the fact that Jeffrey Townsend would be traveling with him. Why not? They were both partners in Templeton Associates; both successful, aggressive businessmen, both interested in securing accounts all over the country for the betterment of the firm. Their reservations were made in the same hotels. Who would know they used only one room? Yes, how very convenient.

Every time Georgia visualized Harry and Jeff Townsend locked in a passionate homosexual embrace, bile would rise in her throat. Yet she hadn't been able to confront him. The revelation had been so emotionally overwhelming, she wasn't ready to deal with it. She was afraid she'd lash out at him and never stop screaming for deceiving her all these years. Besides, she was still trying to hang on to that tiny sliver of hope. She didn't want strong suspicion to become fact. She was still searching, reevaluating what she had overheard, hoping to draw a different conclusion.

Classic case of wishful thinking. No matter how she tossed it around, there was no way to get around those words that would stay with her forever. "I miss you too," he had said in a sugary voice that sounded foreign to her.

More importantly, she had to think of the children before she made any moves. When that confrontational bomb explodes, what does she tell them? Daddy is in love with another man? A man Daddy had the nerve to invite for dinner a few weeks ago. *I actually had him at my table and shared my pot roast with him!* She cringed at the memory.

Could she and Harry simply claim irreconcilable differences with no explanations and expect her children to say, okay, fine? Could she shield their father's sexuality from them for a lifetime? If so, they'd probably blame her, Georgia concluded, for throwing their precious, faultless daddy out of their house. Not great choices.

She had called Althea and Jennifer to switch plans. Instead of meeting at Althea's house, she preferred that they come to her. She didn't want to drive alone at night while her blood was boiling.

Ordinarily, she would have enjoyed concocting a new and fancy dish for them. Georgia loved to cook and fuss with her table setting. But tonight, cooking was not a consideration. She had opted to order Chinese food, which they all loved anyway.

*   *   *

"I say confront him the moment he comes through that door," Jennifer said. The three women had been discussing Harry and his secret life from the cocktails through the last pot of tea.

Althea was at the counter struggling with the rock-hard ice cream and decided to sit and let it melt awhile. "I'm not sure that's a good idea, Jennifer. Think about it. Without a doubt, the scene is bound to get explosive. In a few weeks her kids will be home from college. Maybe she should wait until after the holidays, before they go back."

"I could blow up by then," Georgia threw in.

Althea responded only to Jennifer, as though it was their responsibility to come up with the right answers for their friend. "I hate to recommend divorce to anyone, especially a couple who have three happy, normal kids. It's bound to screw them up somehow," Althea said. "But how can she go on living that kind of lie? Being married to a womanizer is bad enough, but this—"

Jennifer interrupted. "She has no other choice. Divorce is her only option. How much is a woman supposed to sacrifice for her children? Now that she knows, she can never live with him and pretend everything's fine and dandy. Half the children today live with divorced parents. Georgia's children will adjust. It's not as if they'll feel like misfits."

Georgia faked a laugh. "Excuse me. Do you ladies mind if I join this conversation? I thought it out and made my decision. You're right, Althea. I don't want to ruin the holidays for my children. I'll keep my mouth shut and stew for a while, but as soon as they go back, I'll insist on a divorce. The children won't have to know why."

"What if he gives you a hard time?" Jennifer asked.

Georgia shrugged. "He wouldn't dare."

Chapter Thirty-six

Nearly breathless, Jill approached Brad's desk looking like she had just won the lottery. Her smile was contagious; he couldn't help but smile back, curious to hear what she had to say.

"Brad, tell me, *please* tell me you have no serious plans for tomorrow night."

He gave her a cautious glance, but the smile lingered at the corners of his mouth. "I think I should ask why before I answer that."

"You can wipe that suspicious look off your face. You're gonna love this. My brother had two tickets for the Knicks game and now his company stuck him with an unscheduled trip to San Diego. He's livid."

"So you're saying he gave them to you and you're asking me to join you?"

"You got it."

Brad was thrilled, but surprised at the invitation. "Geez, Jill, you don't have to ask me twice. You know what a Knicks fan I am, but what did I do to win this coveted prize? Don't you have a friend you want to ask first?"

Jill crossed her arms and peered at him. "Excuse me? I thought I *was* asking a friend."

Brad laughed. "Sorry. That was stupid of me, I guess. And hey, I'll be happy to pay for the tickets."

She shot him a look that required no verbal response.

Brad's hands went up in defeat. "Okay, okay. I wouldn't feel right if I hadn't offered. But dinner's definitely on me."

"I don't think we'll have time, Brad. We can grab a couple of candy bars to hold us and eat a light dinner after the game. How does that sound?"

"Sounds great. I'm looking forward to it, Jill."

"Me too," she said. "I've got to get back to work. Talk to you later."

Jill turned away from him and tried to keep the cat-that-killed-the-canary smirk off her face as she walked down the aisle back to her department. She licked her lips and had to bite down hard to suppress a fit of giggles. When she got back to the privacy of her workstation, she had to cover her mouth to keep her emotions in check.

*   *   *

Brad was pleasantly surprised Tuesday morning to find himself in an up mood. He had been dragging his ass back and forth to work and not much else since he walked out on Mal. Lou had all but given up trying to fix him up with a date. His girl had several friends who weren't bad to look at, he had said. Was that dubious description supposed to convince him to say yes? Thanks, but no thanks, was basically what he had told Lou. When I'm ready, you'll be the first to know.

Should he consider this night out with Jill Eaton tonight a date? Not really. Who could pass up a free ticket to a Knicks game? Besides, he liked Jill. She had a perpetually pleasant personality. You couldn't sulk in your depression too long once she got a hold on you. If the company gave a Miss Congeniality award, Jill would come out on top. And, unlike the date candidates Lou had to offer, Jill was a step above "not bad to look at." Make that a few steps above. Her body curved in all the right places, and she made sure she wore the right clothes to flaunt those curves. A little too much makeup for his taste, but he couldn't deny that her overdone gray eyes and full, mocha-brown lips grabbed his attention. She had a wide Julia Roberts smile and dark, ramrod straight, shiny hair that bounced when she walked. Her legs were not to be ignored either.

Jill had one imperfection, though, that clothes or makeup couldn't help. She wasn't Mal.

He flipped the razor on as if the buzzing sound would drill thoughts of Mal from his head. When that didn't work, he turned up the volume on his CD player, and concentrated on Jill and the Knicks.

*   *   *

Jill chose her new black Jones New York pants suit with a lemon yellow turtleneck sweater underneath. She selected the diamond stud earrings her parents had given her last Christmas over all the larger, more ostentatious gold earrings in her collection. On her neck, hanging just under the collar of her sweater, she wore her gold and diamond nameplate necklace, which was delicate and tasteful.

When she was completely dressed, she checked herself once more in her full-length mirror. Yes, perfect, classy. More Brad's type, she suspected. A little much for a Knicks game, but after all, she did have to spend the day at work first, right? And then there was that late dinner afterwards. Her stomach tumbled in anticipation.

Stay cool, Jill, she warned herself. Take it slow. This fish is the grand prize. You don't want him swimming away.

Chapter Thirty-seven

Jordan arrived at the Blue Ridge Diner at ten-thirty, the prearranged time, and sat in his car to wait for Anne Bishop. Less than five minutes later, she pulled into the parking lot.

"I guess a midmorning breakfast was a good choice," Jordan said after they were seated in a booth and the waiter left with their orders. "It's not crowded now. These diners are usually packed and noisy."

Anne fumbled out of her down jacket. Jordan immediately jumped up to hang it on the coat rack attached to their booth, but left his bunched up on his seat. When they had their first cups of coffee before them, Anne wrapped her cold hands around the steaming mug and met his gaze. "Frankly, Mr. Hammer—"

"I think we can use first names, Anne, considering the severity of what brings us together. Do you mind?"

"Not at all, Jordan," she said, placing emphasis on his name. "I'm uncomfortable with formalities too. Anyway, what I was about to say is I had second thoughts about meeting you. I'd hate to bump into someone I know and give them the wrong impression. But I decided that's stupid. I'm not doing anything wrong, and I don't have to answer to anyone but myself." She lifted her chin and threw her shoulders back to underscore her statement.

Jordan smiled. "Good for you. It's funny that you should say that because that same feeling crossed my mind, although I never entertained it for more than a second or two."

Anne's face grew serious. "Okay, now that that's out of the way, where do we start? How do we find the answers we're looking for? I've been racking my brain since that horrible night trying to make sense of it, but I still can't believe it of Wayne. You had to know him as I did to understand. He was the most loving, considerate and affectionate husband. I never doubted his love for one minute. To believe he was involved in an affair is mind-boggling to me. And I'm sick of all those patronizing faces. Everyone gives me that pitiful, condescending the-wife-is-the-last-to-know look."

Jordan rolled his eyes up. "Boy, do I know that look!" he said, shaking his head, but deep down he couldn't emphatically vouch for Gloria's faithfulness. He had looked back on their marriage and examined his conscience ad nauseam since she died and couldn't rule out the possibility. But with this Wayne Bishop? Where did he come from? Where did they meet and how did they die together? Neither he nor Anne would ever know the whole truth behind their alleged relationship, but maybe they could put some pieces together.

"Tell me about your husband, Anne. What was he like? What was his daily routine? Did he come home for dinner with his family at night? Where did he work? Was he involved in any outside activities that would have given him the opportunity to have an affair with my wife?"

She shrugged, then gave him a bittersweet smile. "I'm looking for answers to those same questions about your wife too, Jordan."

"I have no problem with that, Anne. It's the only way we can ever find out for sure. Let's face it, we're the only ones who care."

"That's for darn sure. Okay, I'll go first. Where do I start?" Her eyes went up as though searching her mind for pertinent details.

For over an hour after their breakfast dishes had been cleared away, they continued to probe. They picked at each other's brain looking for some commonality in the lives of their spouses that would have brought them together. But the more they talked, the more unbelievable it was to swallow that these two people, who were as dissimilar as any two people could get, were in fact lovers. Ludicrous, they both concluded. There had to be more to the story, and they both would never have peace or closure until they uncover the truth behind their deaths.

They parted that day with a warm handshake and promises to stay in touch. They should each feel free to contact the other with any questions or troubling thoughts he or she wanted to share. As he drove away from the diner, Jordan's mind was swimming with more nebulous thoughts than he had when he left his apartment that morning. All they accomplished, really, was to be more convinced than ever that Gloria and Wayne had not been lovers. There had to be another explanation. Yet, he felt their time together was not a total loss. There was some comfort in knowing he had made a good friend. Anne Bishop was a decent person who would gladly join in his quest for answers.

Chapter Thirty-eight

Quentin had only been driving five minutes when he realized he left his reading glasses at the theater. He muttered a few obscenities and swung his car around.

Snow flurries swirled in a whipping wind. Illuminated by the streetlights, they created a picture-perfect winter scene in the quaint suburban village of Brockford, but a biting ten-degree temperature left its streets virtually abandoned.

Up ahead, huddled in a long black coat with a fur-trimmed hood, was a woman struggling against the force of the wind, obviously headed for her car. He watched her turn, trying to walk backward to keep the blinding wind and snow off her face. Bertie. All alone.

Keeping his head down to fight the wind himself, he ran towards her and shouted her name, but Mother Nature's angry roar drowned out his voice. When he caught up to her, she let out one short, horrified shriek. The whites of her frightened eyes were like searchlights peering through the arch of her black hood. Then she recognized him and the fear drained from her face. Through his narrowed eyes, he saw the flash of her white teeth. Quentin assumed she was smiling, relieved that the strange man running towards her was not an assailant, but a friend.

"Where are you parked?" he shouted. "I'll walk you to your car."

Bertie pointed, then gasped when she saw the two faint funnels of light shining into the trees in front of her car.

"You left your lights on, Bertie. How the hell did you do that? Doesn't it buzz to remind you when you open the door to get out?"

Bertie's gloved hands turned outward. Her rueful expression told him she either couldn't hear him or couldn't imagine how she could have forgotten the lights.

"Give me the keys," he said, taking them from her hand. He pressed the button to unlock the doors, and with one twirl of his finger, motioned for her to go around to the passenger seat.

Inside the cold car, but at least safe from the gripping wind, Quentin tried to start the engine, knowing it was a futile attempt. "Battery's too low, of course," he said, turning to her. "I always have jumper cables in my car, but now, of all times—"

Bertie stopped him with a hand wave. "Doesn't matter, Quentin. Even if you had them, I wouldn't let you go through that trouble in this weather. I'll have to leave it here and deal with it in the morning. Can I impose on you to take me home?"

He gave her an incredulous look. "Of course I'll take you home. What do you expect me to do, leave you here stranded?"

"Well, ordinarily, I'd call Alan, but he's staying in the city overnight because of this snowstorm."

"Forget it, Bertie. There's no need to explain. It's no trouble for me at all. What kind of a heartless monster do you think I am? You stay here. I'll run and get my car and pull up here for you, okay?"

She gave him a humble smile. "Thanks, Quentin. You're a lifesaver."

When the heat of Quentin's car started to defrost their chilled bones, Quentin decided he couldn't let this opportunity pass. He had her alone and needed to know what exactly she knew about his relationship with Gloria.

"Are you in a hurry to get home, Bertie? Or can we go for coffee and something light to eat? I'm a little hungry. How about you?"

She shrugged. "I could always eat."

Quentin pulled into the parking lot of Charlie's Place, a steakhouse four miles north of Brockford on the way to Bertie's town. "This place has a reputation for great burgers and sweet potato fries, but I haven't eaten here yet. Want to try it?"

Bertie wrinkled her nose to nix the idea. "In this weather, we can't be choosy, I know, but it looks a little raunchy," she said. "I have a better idea, Quentin. As long as you're taking me home anyway, you might as well come in. I make a mean cheese omelet."

"How's your coffee?"

"Hot."

He gave her a half-smile. "Steamy hot?"

"Absolutely," she purred.

Quentin obliged her with a playful, devilish smile, but the thoughts in his head raced in a direction far different from the one portrayed on his face.

They rode in silence for a few minutes. The pounding of the windshield wipers fighting the blinding snow became a ticking clock. Quentin fought with his thoughts. One way or the other, he had to make a decision soon. Very soon. *Oh, what a tangled web we weave . . .* The words bounced in his head in rhythm with the wipers.

"They're predicting six to eight inches," Bertie said, planting her own seeds.

He threw her a look. "Maybe I can do better."

Bertie roared with laughter.

*   *   *

Quentin had driven at a snail's pace, and by the time they reached Bertie's house, everything in sight was blanketed in snow. Fresh-fallen snow is the epitome of purity, he mused, yet it couldn't erase his dark thoughts.

After shedding their outerwear in the entrance hall, Bertie gave Quentin a pair of Alan's fleece slippers and went straight for her well-stocked bar. She threw ice into two glasses and poured Drambuie into one. She licked her lips after the first sip. "Ah! This stuff sure warms your body up on a cold night. What'll you have, Quentin?"

Quentin was pleased to see how Bertie enjoyed her booze. Nothing more effective to loosen a tongue than a good, stiff drink, he thought.

"I shouldn't have any—"

She cut him off with a wave of her hand. "Don't even say it, Quentin. You're not going anywhere in this weather." She poured Drambuie in his glass without waiting to hear his choice. "Here, this'll warm you up and knock the tension out of your system. That was one scary drive."

The weather opened up their conversation while Quentin tried to think of how he could steer her in the right direction. Bertie made it easy for him. She wrapped both hands around her glass and leaned forward, elbows on the bar. "So tell me, Quentin, what's going on with you and Deirdre? Don't go close-mouthed on me because anyone can see something happened between you two. You're both so polite to each other. That's not natural behavior for friends and lovers." She shot him a don't-try-to-tell-me-otherwise glance.

He laughed at her forwardness. "What are you, the twenty-first century's Hedda Hopper?"

She grinned back at him, as though the title pleased her, and waited for his answer.

"We talk," he said defensively. "We've had dinners together . . ." Quentin wasn't sure how to broach the subject, but decided to go for a partial truth. "To be honest with you, Bertie, although it's really none of your business, the distance you notice between Deirdre and me is your fault."

Bertie's head jerked back. Her eyebrows furrowed. "My fault? What the hell did I do?"

Quentin took a handful of the peanuts she offered and chewed on them pensively, allowing him time to think before he spoke. The actor in him put on a face of mild sensitivity, without revealing the depth of his concern. He sipped his drink knowing he'd better nurse it. He had no intention of spending the night there, snow or no snow.

"Yes, Bertie, indirectly, it was your fault. That one little comment you made to me on opening night irritated me. It put me in a lousy mood, and poor Deirdre got the brunt of it. I hate to think that such a vicious rumor might be buzzing around the theater. If it were anyone else, I might not care, but Gloria Hammer?" He gave her a look that suggested the thought was ludicrous. "She was Jordan's wife, my *friend's* wife, for goodness sake. How the hell do you think that made me feel? That was a wild accusation, Bertie."

The grin never left her face. Quentin didn't like it. It told him she didn't believe a word he said. Halfway through her second drink, she just sat there with her arms folded and that dumb, alcohol-induced grin plastered across her face.

She took another pull from her glass, then looked him straight in the eye and spoke slowly, pointing a finger at him. "Quentin, did you ever hear the expression, 'Don't con a con artist'? If not, you're hearing it now. What I said was not a wild accusation. I knew what I was talking about."

Quentin retaliated with a condescending look. "Well, why don't you fill me in? I'm sure you want to."

"You know, Quentin, how sometimes we look, but don't see? We're oblivious when we shouldn't be. Which is what you did one night in July at a certain bar, but I checked the place out too, and didn't see either. I thought to myself, who the hell do I know who would come to a dive like this? But I never stopped to think. Another cheater, that's who."

Quentin remained silent, waited for more.

"I didn't notice you and Gloria, Quentin, until I got up to use the bathroom. Before that I was seated with my back to you."

Quentin let some of his anger seep out through his sarcasm. "And who, might I ask, were you cheating with that night?"

"Doesn't matter, and it wouldn't help for you to know anyway because my Alan knows all about my outside interests. He closes his eyes as long as I'm discreet. And he's not the perfect husband everybody thinks he is. Alan has his own stories to tell, I'm sure, but we understand each other."

"For your information, I hate to disappoint you, Bertie, but Gloria and I met that night to discuss a business venture of Jordan's which Gloria was vehemently against. She wanted to blow off steam and get my opinion. I hate to deflate your vivid imagination, Bertie, but that's all you saw."

"Forget it, Quentin. No sense denying it. Once I spotted the two of you, it was easy to keep a watchful eye. Maybe you don't remember the place too well, but from where I sat, I faced a mirror. I had a bird's-eye view. No one had to draw me any pictures. That was no business discussion."

Bertie was clearly enjoying watching him squirm, which grated on Quentin's nerves. She grabbed a handful of peanuts from the dish and munched away.

Quentin was determined not to let Bertie think he felt at all threatened by her disclosure. He put on a warm smile, like someone who good-naturedly accepts defeat. "So, okay. You caught me. What does that mean, Bertie? We never meant for it to happen, but it did. We both felt guilty. Every time we met was supposed to be our last. Neither Gloria nor I wanted to hurt Jordan. Do I have to worry about what you witnessed getting back to him? Have you spread that around to any of your friends? I can well imagine what a juicy piece of gossip that would be to share on girls' night out."

"Quentin, shame on you! What kind of degenerate do you think I am? Besides, even if I were tempted, I would never want to hurt Jordan either. Especially now that his wife is dead. Nor would I want to hurt you. You know how much I care for you, don't you, Quentin?" She had stopped chewing only long enough to put emphasis on her last words.

"Yes, I think I do." At this point, the crux of their conversation was being said more through their eyes than their lips, but Quentin found himself repulsed by her attempt to ooze sexuality.

From the other side of the bar, she squeezed his hand and winked. "Good. That's why, if you're the smart and sexy man I think you are, I'll never breathe a word about the last time I heard Gloria's voice."

Quentin sensed she was about to throw her ace on the table. "I'm listening," he said.

"It was back in September, the night she died. Alan was at a meeting in the office of the theater with several other backers of an upcoming production. I had been out shopping and stopped in only to pick him up, but there were six or seven people in there involved in a heated discussion. He told me not to bother waiting; he'd get home on his own."

"And? I think you'd better put this story on fast forward, Bertie. I don't think I like where it's going, and you did promise me a cheese omelet."

She laughed amiably. "Oh, I'm sorry, Quentin. You'll get your omelet. I did promise to feed you." She glanced out the window, made another comment about the intensity of the snowstorm, then ignored it and continued her story. "So where was I? Oh yes. Well, anyway, I left, but sidetracked into the ladies' room. It was empty, but I didn't use the first set of stalls. I like to go around the back where there are more stalls that don't get as much use. I figure they're cleaner and more private, you know?"

Quentin rolled his eyes.

Bertie laughed. "Oh, I'm sorry. You're right. Alan complains that I go on and on too. Well, while I was over in a corner stall on the other side, she came in. I didn't see her, of course, but I certainly know her voice. She was on her cell phone, calling you."

He drew a breath, starting to object to her assumption.

"No, Quentin, don't bother. She called you by name. The last thing I heard was 'Okay, ten-fifteen. See you then. Love you, Quentin.'"

Quentin stared at her. His insides were on fire.

"Was she good, Quentin? Or is Deirdre better?"

His continued silence was his reply.

"Quentin, I'll be better than both of them put together. I suggest you dump Deirdre for good. I promise you won't be disappointed. You'll have the best lover ever and, more importantly, the most loyal friend." She came around to his side of the bar, took his hand and pulled him off the stool. "C'mon. Forget your omelet. You'll eat it for breakfast."

Chapter Thirty-nine

Anne Bishop was sharing too much space with Gloria in Jordan's thoughts lately. Now, more than ever, their lives and problems became enmeshed. Roberta Bookman's murderer had seen to that.

An early riser, Anne had read the newspaper article and learned of Bertie's death while Jordan was still in a deep sleep, thanks to the two Tylenol PM he had taken at three o'clock in the morning. Her phone call had seemed like a dream. His head was heavy with the need for more sleep and his eyelids hung like two wet mops. When her message finally registered, it was as though he had been injected with a month's supply of adrenaline. He shot out of bed, told her to hold on, and raced to the front door for his newspaper.

Too stunned to talk, he picked up the receiver while he stared at Bertie's photograph on the first page. "Anne, can I call you back in a few minutes?"

"Sure."

He read through the article twice to let it sink in and make sense of it, but the shock ran through him like an electrical charge. Bertie Bookman? Someone strangled Bertie with her own scarf and literally put her on ice? Left her in that wooded area adjacent to the golf course? Unbelievable! Was this a mugging/robbery gone bad or an intentional hit? His mind began to spin with wild ideas, but he couldn't clear his head yet to sort them out. He had to pee, and he needed coffee. Until he took care of both, he wouldn't be able to think straight.

After he relieved himself, he put up his coffeemaker and watched it drip, letting the aroma fill his nostrils while he stood at his kitchen counter, still trying to absorb Bertie's death. Once he had steadied himself and downed half a mug of coffee, he called Anne back.

"Are you okay?" she asked. "I don't even know the woman, but it shook me up terribly too, Jordan. I'm *very* suspicious. What are the odds of two people, both active in the same theater, dying unnaturally six weeks apart?"

"My thoughts exactly. There has to be a connection."

"The paper doesn't mention anything suggestive of a connection. They're looking at a mugging gone bad."

Jordan refilled his mug and didn't bother with the milk. He gulped a mouthful and scalded his throat. "Yeah, well," he said finally, "you know what they say. Don't believe everything you read in the newspapers."

"I'm scared in one way, Jordan, but glad in another. Maybe the police will dig a little deeper and find the answers we're looking for. You know, I've thought and rethought this whole horror about Wayne's death and come to terms with it. If I never find out the whole truth, that element of doubt will give me something to cling to. But for my sons . . . that's different. For them, I want Wayne to come up totally innocent so they can love and respect him in death as they loved and respected him in life. Am I making sense?"

"Absolutely. Every single word. Try not to make yourself sick over it, Anne. Somehow we'll find out what we need to know. Let's have faith and think positively."

"With you in my corner, that's been getting easier. Power in numbers, right?"

He imagined her smile and wished he could see it and draw comfort from it again. "What are you doing today? You have such a calming effect on me, I'd love to see you."

"On a Sunday? Could never happen," she said with a laugh. "My mother's been coming every Sunday since Wayne died with her trunk full of my sons' favorite dishes. The more they fuss over her cooking, the more she cooks for them."

"I guess that's good for all concerned."

"Oh, sure. Even me."

"So how about tomorrow? Is that good?"

"Same time, same place? Ten-thirty at the Blue Ridge Diner?"

"That okay with you?"

"Fine. See you then."

*　　*　　*

Jordan woke up Monday morning in a much better frame of mind than the day before. After spending most of Sunday on the phone, making and receiving calls discussing Bertie's horrific death, the shock was wearing off and reality was slowly setting in. Even Quentin took the time to call before his matinee performance to ask how he was handling this second shock.

Nice of them all to call, but Jordan had no desire to spend time with any of them. Anne Bishop was the only person he felt comfortable talking to lately. She was probably the only other person who couldn't believe that Gloria and Wayne were sexually involved. But, if not, what in heaven's name brought them together that ill-fated night? Once the police summed it up, found them guilty partners of an illicit affair, they slammed the book shut and closed the investigation.

Apparently, everyone else followed suit. That left only Jordan and Anne to probe for the truth. Up until now. Bertie's murder should prompt the police to move their behinds a little and delve further. Aren't they the first ones to say they don't believe in coincidences? If any good could come out of Bertie's death, he hoped it would generate enough interest to reopen the investigation of Gloria's and Wayne's supposedly accidental deaths.

*   *   *

Their smiles connected like steel to a magnet when they met at the diner. Partners in misery and amateur sleuths who couldn't find misplaced car keys, much less solve a crime or investigate an accident. She was there first this time, already drinking coffee.

Jordan's pleasant greeting came naturally. "Good morning, Anne. How are you?"

Her lips tightened, erasing her smile. "Okay, I guess." The words rolled out on a sigh.

He gave her face a quick study. "You sound tired or depressed. Probably both, right?"

She gave him a full laugh this time. "Right. I went through another stir-crazy evening last night. I try to read or watch television, but I can't seem to concentrate on anything. My attention span is shot to hell lately."

"Understandably."

"Then, when I go to bed, I can't sleep. I'm all wired up trying to play Nancy Drew and end up feeling edgy and frustrated because I come up empty."

Jordan patted her hand. "Don't make yourself crazy, Anne. I think the police will link the three deaths eventually."

"I hope so. They'd be pretty stupid not to look for a connection."

"I haven't had a full night's sleep either since it happened. If it weren't for my work in the theater, I'd really

135

crack up. That keeps me somewhat stimulated, but when I come home, between the loneliness, the memories . . ." He stopped short, then said, "I walked into the bathroom last night and broke down because it doesn't smell like peaches anymore. I opened her bottle of shower gel, sniffed the fragrance and lost it. Guess I needed a good cry."

Anne's eyes filled, as did his. She swallowed hard, cupped her hand over his. "Oh, Jordan. I'm sorry. I don't know what to say."

He waved it off. "No, words are unnecessary. I'm sure you're going through the same agony."

She cocked her head as though not agreeing totally. "To be honest, being a mother, the worst part is seeing how Wayne's death has affected my sons. That's the way it is with parents. When they're in pain, you're in pain. They're holding in a lot of rage because of the way he died . . .you know, with your wife."

Jordan winced at the image. "Oh, geez. That's got to be rough. What exactly do they know?"

Her brows and shoulders rose simultaneously in a defeatist shrug. "Everything *we* know, actually. Hey, they're thirteen and fifteen; old enough to read newspapers. I certainly can't feed them lies. They adored their father, but now it's like they're trying to hate him for his infidelity—"

"— *alleged* infidelity, Anne. We don't know that for sure."

"Okay, *alleged* infidelity. Anyway, it's almost as if they welcome the hatred; like it can help them bury the love. But I can't get them to open up to me."

Listening to her sent guilt pangs through Jordan. Her problems were multiplied by three. "How are they with each other, Anne?"

She drew a breath and took a pensive moment. "Actually, their relationship seems stronger. Closer. I guess tragedy often does that."

"Give them space, Anne. Just let them know you're there to listen whenever they're ready to talk. They do need to release the rage, the shock, but you can't push them. Let them move at their own pace."

"I do. It's just that with the holidays coming up, it's getting harder to deal with. For them and for me."

"I know. I dread Christmas coming too. Let's be sure to stay in touch these coming weeks. We'll need to lean on each other."

She forced a weak smile. "Definitely. We have our own private support group. We dump all our feelings on each other and try our best to defuse them. What's wrong with that?"

"Not a thing," he said as he signaled for the waitress.

Chapter Forty

The second Monday in December would have been their last class until late January, but Georgia had called everyone over the weekend and unexpectedly cancelled. All she said was she had family problems, without offering any details and, of course, no one questioned her.

Quentin called Mal soon after she got home from work to ask if she would have dinner with him. During the run of the play, Mondays were his only nights off, and he was disappointed to find himself with no plans, especially now, he told her.

"Gee, Quentin, you sound like death warmed over," Mal said, sincerely concerned. "Is anything wrong?"

She heard his forced laugh. One short grunt that she interpreted to mean "that's putting it mildly."

"I guess you haven't read yesterday's papers."

"Yes, I did. Not cover to cover, but most of it. Why?" There was a note of alarm in her voice now.

"Did you read the article about the woman they found frozen in the snow? Roberta Bookman?"

"I do remember seeing the caption but I never read it through. I didn't want to know the gruesome details." Mal's hand went to her mouth. "Oh, no, don't tell me she was a relative of yours."

Quentin blew out a sigh. "No, not a relative, but someone I've known for years. She and her husband are very active in the theater. Or she *was* active . . ."

Mal heard the catch in his voice and she filled with sympathy. "Oh, that's awful, Quentin. I'm so sorry. When I saw the article, I never dreamed the victim would be connected to anyone I know. I can't believe it. Two horrifying deaths, both victims involved in that same theater group. It's scary."

"I know, but at least we know that Gloria Hammer's death was an accident. Shocking yes, but explainable. But Bertie—I can't stop thinking about her. She was such a nice woman. The thought of anyone wanting to kill her is incomprehensible. For what possible reason would someone want her dead?"

Mal had no answer for him. She was dealing with the shock herself. The thought that someone even remotely connected to her had been heinously murdered was chilling. From what she recalled of the article, the breath had been crushed out of her by the overpowering hands of a ruthless killer who then left her to be buried in the snow. Why? And so soon after Gloria Hammer's death. Sounds fishy.

"Anyway, I could use some company tonight. Maybe if I talk it out, I can work the shock out of my system, so to speak. What do you say, Mal? Can you help me out? We'll go someplace close by."

Mal glanced over at her parents. Russ was chopping chicken and vegetables for a Chinese recipe he wanted to try and Liz was trying her best to help. It warmed her to watch them. Although Liz's strength and appetite hadn't improved much yet, Dr. Vargas assured us she'd start feeling better soon. How long could cancer stay in remission? she wondered. Forever, she hoped.

"I guess it's workable tonight, Quentin," she said. "Where and when?"

"I can pick you up. Can I come in? I'd like to meet your parents and tell them what a great daughter they raised."

"Sure you can come in. Why not? My parents are already impressed that I have a friend who's a real, live professional actor. They'd love to meet you too." She gave him the address and told him to come about 7:30 so her parents wouldn't have to rush through their dinner. By that time, they'd be settled in comfortably to watch the annual tree lighting ceremony at Rockefeller Center, an event they both enjoyed each year. She wouldn't be missed and could enjoy dinner out with a clear head.

*   *   *

Quentin couldn't keep the smile off his face. He had a feeling of déjà vu. When he had asked Deirdre out for the first time, after Gloria's death, he had used similar words. Now, after Bertie, the same sympathy technique had worked with Mal. A guy had to see the dark humor in that.

*   *   *

Attracted by its spectacular Christmas decorations, Mal chose Casa Justina, a small Italian restaurant ten minutes from her house. Quentin sliced the warm, round loaf of bread, which they ate with their steaming cups of lentil soup.

"Your parents are good people, Mal. They made me feel very comfortable. It's a shame what life dumped on them."

"It's not so bad, really. My dad had a lot of anger and self-pity to deal with for a while, but eventually it burned itself out. He accepts his disability now because he knows it's irreversible. Actually, once my mom was diagnosed with cancer, his whole attitude changed."

"Sure, I can imagine. He probably figured her disease is life-threatening, his disability is not. Sometimes it takes a tragedy to wake you up. It motivates you to put your

140

priorities in order and learn to appreciate all the good stuff we take for granted."

"Absolutely." Mal paused to butter another slice of the doughy bread. She sipped her wine and stared at the tall tree in the center of the room. It had hundreds of twinkling lights and a set of electric trains chugging around its base through little snow-covered villages. Charming winter scenes of tiny houses and tiny people with painted smiles were scattered around the tree creating images of small-time life decades ago. Americana long gone.

Quentin's eyes followed hers. "You were right," he said, looking around. "They do a real bang-up job with holiday decorations here."

"Yes, that's why I suggested it." She crossed her arms on the table and leaned forward. "But Quentin, you gave me the impression on the phone that you wanted to vent your feelings about that poor woman's murder."

Quentin winced as though he couldn't tolerate the thought. "I did, but since I arrived at your house tonight, I've been able to blot it out of my head a bit. It's so hard to believe that actually happened. I hate to get into it." He shook his head. "Her poor husband. What a shock this must be for him. He must be half out of his mind."

"After I spoke to you, I found the article and read it. The paper said the medical examiner concluded that she was already dead when she was left in the snow. Strangled." Mal shuddered at the image. "Did you hear anything that wasn't in the paper? Where she was that night; if she was seen with anyone?"

"She was at the theater, her usual cheerful self. I saw her and waved goodnight as I was leaving. She was busy talking to some people I didn't know."

"How did you find out she died? Don't tell me you saw it in the paper."

"No, but an early morning phone call is just as shocking. Jordan Hammer called me. That poor guy. Sometimes I think he's having a harder time dealing with his wife's infidelity than her death. He was in bad shape himself trying to tie Gloria's death with Bertie's somehow."

"I can't blame him. Doesn't it make you wonder too? It gives me a creepy feeling, like the theater is haunted. And we're all coming to see the play tomorrow night. Even Georgia decided to join us. But what lousy timing. It's a little spooky knowing a killer is on the loose."

He gave her a big brother smile. "Don't put those thoughts in your head. You can make yourself crazy suspecting everyone around you is a potential threat."

"These days those thoughts are not easy to dismiss. Remember those sniper killings in the D.C. area last October? There was practically an army hunting them down, but they still couldn't prevent those deaths." She hugged herself to shake the chill out. "You just never know where these sickos are hiding. With your play, there are so many people involved in the production, I would imagine any one of them might have reason."

"True, but it could also be someone she knew privately, or some guy she had on the side, like Gloria. On the other hand, there's still a strong possibility that Bertie was the victim of a mugging or a rapist."

"She was raped? The article didn't say that."

"No, but maybe that was the guy's intent. He might have unintentionally killed her in his struggle to subdue her. That would have scared him off."

"Sounds like a reasonable theory, but I still suspect there's some connection."

Quentin pulled his arm off the table when the waiter approached.

"I'll never be able to finish this," Mal said, wide-eyed, when the huge dish of veal marsala was placed before her.

"So you'll take a doggy bag," Quentin said digging into his linguine with clam sauce. "Why don't we enjoy our dinner and try to talk about something else? Let's leave the crime-solving to the police."

"Fine with me. It doesn't seem right to discuss a murder in the midst of all these holiday decorations, anyway. This is the season for love and peace, right? So let's switch our conversation to writing. That's a happy medium for both of us."

He gave her a long, hard look. "True, but I'd rather talk about you. You and me."

Quentin's suggestive remarks always caught her off guard. Mal never had the right answers ready. She squirmed involuntarily and hoped he didn't notice. Again pretending that his words passed unheeded, she let her gaze fall onto her plate and dug in. After a few bites, when even the Christmas music and other diners' conversations couldn't drown out the sound of her chewing, she threw out a few questions about writing, all of which she had already researched, but they filled the silent moments and Quentin got the message.

*   *   *

He dropped her off at home an hour later. With her fingers gripped on the car door handle, she thanked him politely, gave him a broad smile and said, "See you tomorrow night at the theater."

*   *   *

Later—much later—although curled up comfortably in bed with her down comforter, Mal was still too keyed up to fall asleep. Thinking back of her evening with Quentin, she felt that rush of embarrassment again. No matter how she pretended to be oblivious to his flirtatious comments, she knew neither of them was being fooled. Quentin had some definite pluses; he was a good conversationalist, had an amusing, dry sense of humor, and of course that sexy smile beneath his beard. But there was something about those eyes she just couldn't trust. Insincerity, lack of integrity? She couldn't identify what exactly it was that rubbed her the wrong way, but it made her squeamish. A perfect example was how he conned her into seeing him tonight, under the guise of a person needing the comfort of a friend, when in reality he had other motives.

In the middle of the night, after it had taken her so long to fall asleep, she woke up in tears and let herself dwell on memories of Brad. Although she regularly worked at locking him out of her conscious thoughts, she couldn't keep him out of her dreams. She hated him for leaving her and hated herself for pushing him to that point.

Chapter Forty-one

Georgia was having a rough time suppressing her rage. She had sat through dinner with Harry avoiding eye contact, and thought she was handling it well under the circumstances. Until the phone rang. If she hadn't been looking for it she might not have noticed, but once she knew it was Jeff Townsend on the line, Harry's smile was unmistakable. It was clearly that certain smile that lights up a person's eyes when speaking to or about that someone special.

The scallops, potatoes and broccoli she had eaten minutes before had gone down uneventfully, but they were back with a vengeance. She made a dive for the bathroom. When she felt her eyeballs were back in their sockets and the last of her dinner was flushed down the bowl, she opened the bathroom door with the intent of going anywhere in the house where she couldn't see or hear him. But Harry was right outside the bathroom door. He feigned concern, but the phone was still in his hand. "Are you all right?" he asked.

"I'm fine. Something went down the wrong way; got stuck, I guess."

He nodded in agreement while he listened to his lover without interruption and went into the den to continue their conversation.

Georgia's pots and dishes banged and rattled as she cleaned up her kitchen. They became her escape vehicle for all the screams that were burning inside. She didn't know how long she could keep up this pretense. With her two hands behind her braced on the sink, she drew a few breaths, exhaling slowly. Her mind stayed focused on her children. Soon all three would be home for the holiday break. She only had weeks to tough it out, but once they were gone again she could explode. In the meantime, she had Althea and Jennifer as sounding boards and she'd have to settle for that.

She was on the floor with paper towels and a sponge cleaning up some food scrapings that missed the garbage disposal when she looked up and there he was, in her face. "What the hell's wrong with you lately, Georgia? You've been in one bitch of a mood."

Georgia flashed him a Suzy Homemaker-from-hell look, then bit down on her lip, pulling a breath through clenched teeth. She stood up, arched her brows as high as she could stretch them, then averted his gaze. Grabbing a fresh paper towel, she targeted the counters for another spraying spree with her Windex. "I'm surprised you noticed," she said, making no attempt to veil her sarcasm.

Harry pulled out a kitchen chair, sat down and crossed his arms. "Okay. Apparently, you have something to say. Why don't you just spit out what's bugging you and get it over with." He gave her a smirk, as though nothing she could say would have any substantive value; just some bitchy, feminine complaint, but he would humor her and listen.

If she sat across from him and looked in his face, she'd never be able to hold it all in. Instead, she continued with her spray bottle, attacking the already gleaming chrome and glass in her spacious kitchen.

She decided to feed him just what he had assumed and save it all for the kill that was sure to come in a few weeks. "It's nothing that would concern or interest you, Harry. Just some of the usual dissention at school that's been getting on my nerves."

His head tilted, he gave her a dubious glance. "So bad that it made you vomit?"

"I told you, I vomited because I choked on something, not because I was upset." She brushed it away. "Harry, I can't get into a conversation with you now. I'm going out soon and need to freshen up and get dressed."

"Where to? And with whom?"

Her eyebrows shot up again. "What's the difference? Do I interrogate you when you go out?"

Harry's eyes rolled impatiently. "I'm not interrogating. I'm just asking."

"I'm going out with my boyfriend, okay?" She imagined his mind saying *me too*.

His hands gripped the back of the chair. "Georgia, your attitude is uncalled for. What the hell's wrong with you?"

"Nothing. I'm fine," she said, removing all traces of hostility or sarcasm from her voice. "One of my students has a lead part in the play at the Emily Forrester Theater. I'm going with some of the others to watch him perform."

"Good for you. Enjoy yourself. Maybe you'll be in a better mood when you come home. I'll be going out soon too."

She couldn't resist. Her hands went on her hips. "Can I ask where and with whom too?"

"Sure. Jeff and I are meeting with some potential clients. The usual stuff."

"Yes, strictly business, but pleasant business, I'm sure."

"Oh, definitely."

I'll never get through these weeks, Georgia thought, as she climbed the stairs to her bedroom. Sometimes the sacrifices a mother makes for her children are beyond the call of duty.

Chapter Forty-two

The arrangement was that Georgia would pick up Mal, Marybeth and Evelyn, and Martin Roth would pick up Philomena, Amanda and Carolyn. Only Wally would be missing from the group. He had already seen the play with his wife and told the class they found it more entertaining than he expected. While Wally had praised Quentin's performance, Quentin had tried his best to feign humility, but that trace of arrogance seemed to fight for its rightful place in his smile, Mal remembered.

The seven writers and their teacher, who had become their friend and their crutch, met in the theater's lobby. Their conversation soon fell into speculative discussion of how this poor woman, Roberta Bookman, was murdered, and by whom. None of them knew her but she was a local; an active and influential member of this theater. Understandably, everyone was chilled by the story of her murder. Since they were out for a night of entertainment, they were only too happy to drop the subject when they were escorted to their third-row-center seats. They'd have plenty of time to talk later at the diner, where they had agreed to meet after the show.

Tonight Georgia's exaggerated cheerfulness caught Mal's perceptive eye. There was something unnatural tugging the corners of her mouth when she spoke. Like the weight of her false smile was too heavy a burden to carry. Those eyes that usually danced with enthusiasm during class had a lackluster emptiness that gave them a slightly droopy look. Mal guessed she hadn't had much sleep lately.

She didn't want to pry, but between the classes and the private phone conversations they had shared these past weeks, Mal considered Georgia a good friend, despite the difference in their ages. And Mal suspected Georgia needed a friend to talk to. God knows she'd been there herself many times over. She'd call her tomorrow, she decided, but when Georgia excused herself and took off for the ladies' room, Mal followed.

"Georgia, are you okay?"

That did it. She made the mistake of using those key words that unplug the dam releasing an explosion of tears. Those words had the same effect on her at her office recently, and now her big mouth had caused Georgia embarrassment. Mal squeezed her shoulder while Georgia sucked back the tears.

Mal regretted her well-meaning action, but when Georgia emerged from the bathroom stall, she was composed.

"I'm sorry, Georgia. I should mind my own business, I guess."

Georgia gave her an assuring pat on the cheek. "No, Mal, don't feel that way. I didn't realize my troubles are that transparent. It's just that this is not the place . . ."

"Well, I just wanted you to know if you need to talk to someone, just pick up the phone."

"Thanks. I might take you up on that."

To add to his charm, the little devil had talent. His singing voice was strong and smooth. He danced with graceful masculinity. His co-star, Dierdre Grange, was not to be believed. With a touch of the blended immortal styles of Fred Astaire and Ginger Rogers, they complemented each other's performance to perfection. And his character was lovable. Every time he flashed those pearly whites at his audience, the place was a sea of smiling faces. None of the group had ever heard of Deirdre before, but they all agreed that this part, particularly if and when the play opened on Broadway, would skyrocket her theatrical career.

At the end, when they joined hands and bowed, the audience went wild.

Quentin had invited his classmates backstage after the show. Like star-struck teenagers, they waited to meet the show's stars, particularly the beautiful and multi-talented Deirdre Grange. Anxious to shower her with praise, Carolyn Graham asked Quentin to introduce them to Deirdre first before she slipped away, which he did. Initially, Mal thought perhaps her exceptionally striking looks were attributable to stage makeup, but she soon discovered that was an erroneous assumption. The girl was even more gorgeous close up. A flawless face.

And then she knew. For one fleeting moment, she caught an exchange of looks between them and knew. What Mal read into that exchange was a fiery relationship gone bad. No, not bad, cooled maybe. There were no traces of anger she could discern, only that polite chill.

*   *   *

Mal wasn't the only one who noticed. Quentin and his co-star were the topic of discussion at the diner.

"I don't care what you say," Carolyn teased. "Maybe he had something going with her, but I think it's pretty obvious he has eyes for Mal."

Mal felt the blush of heat rise in her cheeks. "Oh, no, you're wrong," she said waving it off. "Quentin's a flirt. He flirts with everybody. Haven't you all noticed?"

"Yes, we noticed," Amanda threw into the conversation. "But he flirts primarily with you." She said it playfully, teasingly, but her words were laced with just a breath of envy. Mal felt a sudden surge of sympathy for her.

When everyone agreed with Amanda, Mal laughed it off and threw her hands up in defeat. "Okay, I give up. So maybe he does flirt mostly with me, but let's face it, I'm the only single woman in the class. Hasn't anyone taken that into consideration?"

"Sure, we did," Amanda said. "But since when does that matter?"

That drew a round of laughs and Mal was off the hot seat when someone put the spotlight on Amanda. The hour among friends flew by and ended with an exchange of affectionate goodnight kisses.

Just as she was about to pull out of her parking spot, Mal jerked back. Startled by the tapping on her window, she pressed the button to open it when she saw Georgia standing there, looking like a bundle of nerves.

"When's a good time to call you? When we can talk privately, that is?"

Mal thought about it a few seconds. "What's wrong with right now? Get in," she said, hitting the button to unlock the car doors.

Georgia ran around to the passenger side, opened the door and slid in. "You're an angel, Mal," she said, slightly breathless. "I do have two close friends I can talk to, but the distance between us leaves only the telephone. It helps, but I need warm, friendly eyes to look at, a sympathetic shoulder and someone to share a drink or a cup of coffee with. Someone I can trust. Sorry, Mal, but you fit all those qualifications."

Incredulous, Mal yanked her hands away from the steering wheel and faced the person she had assumed was totally in control at all times. A self-confident all-together person. This new image of the friend and teacher she wished

to emulate was strange. It brought to mind the scene from
The Wizard of Oz, where the once-powerful wicked witch
melts away to nothing.

"Georgia, talk to me. Is it *that* bad?"

"No," she said. "It's worse."

Chapter Forty-three

It was a rotten thing to do but he did it anyway. Brad bought two tickets to see *Crush* with the intention of taking Jill. She seemed thrilled when he invited her, but he felt lousy; low enough to crawl under a worm. His only motivation when he bought the tickets was to check the guy out; this Quentin Kingsley, and to see if Mal might be hanging around the theater, waiting for him. If so, he wanted the satisfaction of having her see Jill clinging to his arm. She'd be shocked speechless, not only to see Jill but to discover he hadn't gone to Atlanta after all.

Yes, a childish, totally immature plan, but he couldn't help himself. Seeing her get into Kingsley's car that night had turned his stomach. His imagination had worked overtime and had defeated his otherwise passive temperament. Images of her in his arms, or worse, kept popping up. He'd shake his head and squeeze his eyes closed, but the ugly picture had taken up permanent residence in his memory bank. Maybe if Mal *was* involved with this guy, he could learn to hate her and get her out of his system. Sure. As though he could turn her off like a light switch after loving her for years.

"To thine own self be true," he mumbled aloud as he grabbed his car keys and left to pick up Jill. This was their second formal date. He couldn't stall too long; he knew that. Without definitive words, the invitation to step beyond the "just friends" stage was blatantly clear. There was no denying his body was ready to respond, but his heart and mind weren't ready to let go of Mal. Yet, every time he thought of her with that Quentin Kingsley, the temptation grew stronger.

*   *   *

The Emily Forrester Theater was exceptionally crowded for a weeknight. "This was a great idea, Brad," Jill said. "I'm glad you thought of it. I haven't been to a play since *Cats,* and that was two years ago." She hooked her arm into his as though she didn't want to lose him, but that arm remained locked with his long after they were seated.

When the lights went up for intermission, Brad's eyes scanned the crowd. He hoped to God he wouldn't see her, and he didn't, but then what does that prove? Even if she were dating this creep, it's unlikely she'd be here for all his performances. Highly unlikely.

They left their seats to stretch their legs and headed for the refreshment stand in the lobby. "Looking for someone?" Jill asked.

This one never misses a trick, Brad thought. He shrugged. "No one in particular. I always seem to run into people I know at these places, so I'm just looking around for a familiar face."

"Aren't you enjoying the play?" she continued. "You never cracked a smile during the first act."

He twisted his lips as though her observation was way off base. "Where'd you get that idea? It's a musical. An upbeat, happy musical. What's not to like? And I smiled plenty. You just didn't notice. You were wrapped up in it yourself."

"Oh, okay. No big deal. I guess I got the wrong impression. It's just that you looked stone-faced sometimes. Angry almost. Especially when that guy who plays Joey St. John was on. Do you know him?"

Brad tried to look amused, but couldn't filter out the edge in his voice. "What is this, twenty questions? No, I never met the guy in my life."

Jill's smile faded. "I'm sorry, Brad. I didn't mean to get you in an uptight mood. I'm just trying to be sociable."

Seeing how he had unintentionally hurt her feelings, Brad eased off. He cupped her chin with his hand. "I'm sorry too. If I sounded like an irritable S.O.B., I apologize, okay?"

Relieved, Jill nodded and met his gaze, her eyes questioning his. "Okay. Apology accepted."

Sipping their Cokes in the lobby, their conversation shifted to shop talk, but Brad's hand went up suddenly to cut her off. He put a finger to his lips to stop her from talking, and darted his eyes to the left. Two women standing next to him were talking about something that grabbed his attention. They were discussing the recent murder of that woman who was strangled and left in the snow. She had been active in this theater. From what he could glean, no progress had been made in apprehending the killer. Other than that, he hadn't learned anything more than what he had read in the paper.

When they took their seats for the second act, Jill looked at him curiously. "What was that about? Why did you shut me up?"

"I'll tell you later," he whispered in response. He rolled his eyes from side to side to make her understand that this was no place for a private conversation.

Brad did enjoy the play despite his hostility, although he hated to admit it to himself. The guy had talent but that didn't mean he had to like him personally. He wondered if Mal had seen the play yet, then assumed she had. He hoped she didn't confuse the real Quentin Kingsley with Joey St. John, the character his audiences fell in love with.

*   *   *

In the privacy of the car Jill asked again, her tone light, playful. "So, I'm dying to know, Brad, what was so interesting about that conversation you were listening to? You don't strike me as the type to eavesdrop."

"I'm not, but I thought I might pick up some inside information." He told her what they had been discussing, but she had no recollection of the story at all and seemed disinterested.

"No, I don't follow stories like that. Too depressing," she said, and waved it off.

From the corner of his eye, Brad noticed how she dismissed the distasteful subject by crossing her arms and looking out the window. For all her pleasantries, that simple gesture revealed another side of her. Any person with half a heart would show some sympathetic reaction for the victim of such a heinous crime. But Jill merely fell silent for a few minutes until she felt the moment had passed. Then she flashed her Miss Congeniality smile again and cocked her head toward him. "Where to now?" she asked. "It's still early."

"I don't know. I'm not too hungry after that dinner, but if you're in the mood for a snack, name the place. I'm game."

"No, I'm not hungry either. Maybe just a beer or a glass of wine." She placed her hand over his on the steering wheel. "Let's go to my place."

Brad searched his mind for the right words to politely refuse her invitation. His heart wasn't quite ready to block out all memories of Mal. But involuntarily another part of him took the lead, and Brad drove in silence towards Jill's apartment.

What the hell, he thought. It's time to move on. It's over. He wasn't about to face a few more years of Mal playing the martyr even if she did want him back. If she loved me, *really* loved me, he concluded, *she'd* be sitting next to me in this car, not Jill Eaton.

Chapter Forty-four

Brad had made a complete ass of himself with Jill, but now that it was over he felt as though a thousand-pound weight had been lifted off his shoulders. He should have made his decision earlier though, instead of embarrassing the hell out of both of them. Sitting on the edge of her bed, half-undressed, with this gorgeous, desirable girl in his arms, he had pulled away from her as if he were stepping off hot coals. All the desire he had felt moments before drained out of him in one fleeting moment. His stomach seemed to take a nosedive to his feet, and he had felt sick and dirty with guilt. He mumbled a bunch of incoherent apologies while Jill had stood frozen with the shock and humiliation of his rejection. But one minute later, he was dressed and out of there.

His eyes glazed over with tears as he drove, partly for his near-betrayal to Mal, and for hurting Jill. How the hell he was going to handle facing her at work was unimaginable.

*   *   *

When he got home, he heaved a sigh of relief to find the apartment empty. Lou was a good friend and had a heart as big as a house, but Brad wasn't in the mood for company or another soul-searching conversation. He was consumed with self-hatred. First, for what he had done to Jill. He had led her on when in his heart he had always known he was using her to help him forget Mal. As though sex from a casual acquaintance could substitute for the love he felt for Mal. He was an idiot to think it could but he had his head on straight now. He knew exactly what he had to do and first on his agenda was to call in sick tomorrow morning.

*   *   *

Surprised that he managed to get six hours of uninterrupted sleep after battling restlessness for hours, he jolted out of bed. The pot of coffee Lou routinely made every morning before he left for work sat on its warming tray. Brad filled his mug with the steaming brew, but first gulped down a full glass of orange juice. His thoughts unscrambled now, he picked up the phone. Although the clock said only 8:10, he decided to make his sick call. Better to leave it on voice mail and avoid the need to lie to someone who'd know he was lying but would pretend not to, or worse, someone naïve enough to believe his sudden illness and pour on all that unwarranted sympathy.

That done, he showered, dressed, smoothed out his bed, washed the coffeepot and threw a load of laundry in the washing machine. By 9:30 he felt he had stalled long enough. He could make his second call now.

Anxious about how he would be received, his heart pounded while the phone rang. A familiar and welcome voice answered. "Russ, it's me, Brad. Before I say anything, first tell me . . ." He paused, almost afraid to hear the answer. ". . . how's Liz doing?"

"Brad! It's so nice of you to call, but wait. In answer to your question, I'm gonna let Liz tell you herself."

Relief washed over Brad's apprehensive feeling. He didn't need to hear it from Liz. From Russ's tone, he had already surmised good news, but he talked to her a few minutes, asking questions with sincere interest and enjoyed hearing the optimism in her voice.

"So how are things going for you down in Atlanta, Brad? Do you like your job there? Have you made any friends?"

Liz's questions flashed a childhood memory before his eyes. He felt that same queasiness in his stomach that a diet of guilt, anxiety and fear are sure to cause. That sick stomach was a given every time he stepped into the confessional box. How he had feared the reprimand, but it never came. Not to the degree he had anticipated. He had always come out feeling scrupulously clean, unburdened and full of promises to avoid those same sins.

Confession time again. "Liz, I never took that job in Atlanta," he said. "I'm calling you from my apartment here. I'm not working today and would really like to see you and Russ. We can talk then and I'll explain. Would it be okay if I came over?"

"Well, when would you like to come?"

"Now? Within an hour?"

Liz laughed, then cut away to tell her husband. "Now's fine, Brad. We're both looking forward to seeing you."

"Me too," he said, his foot tapping away, ready to run out. "I miss you guys."

*   *   *

Brad's reunion with these two special people who had been part of his daily life was charged with emotion. More than he or they had anticipated. Liz and Russ Triana had become like second parents to him during the past few years. Like a son, he grieved for every sorrow they suffered and delighted in any occasion that brought them joy.

Liz tightened her lips and shook her head. Brushing away the tears that welled in her eyes and threatened to fall any second, she forced a laugh. "Gee, Brad, I had no idea I missed you this much." Her arms opened wide. "C'mon. Give me a hug."

When he finally broke away from the silent embrace he shared with Liz, he leaned over and gave Russ a shorter, more masculine hug, but full of the same affection.

Liz pulled out a large Christmas box from the kitchen cabinet, which was lined with lace doilies and filled with cookies. "Look Brad, we have those cream cheese cookies you always loved. The little green wreaths and the tiny trees with colored sugar, remember?"

"Of course I remember. I still love them," he said. How could he forget baking them with Mal every year? He got the job of mixing the dough every time.

"Sit down. We made a fresh pot of coffee to have with the cookies," she said. "And we have cinnamon crumb cake too."

After ten minutes of dancing around the subject they all were avoiding, Brad zeroed in. He brought his gaze first to Liz, then to Russ. "How is she? Tell me. You both know I've been dying to ask."

Liz took a deep breath, exhaled slowly, and clasped her hands in her lap. "Physically, Mal is fine, Brad," she began. "Emotionally—how she's doing since the two of you broke up, that I can't say. Mal doesn't open up much to me or her father. I think I know why."

"Me too," Brad said.

"She has to keep up this constant pretense, doesn't she?" Russ offered to the conversation when no one else spoke. "Like she doesn't have a care in the world and there's no problem she can't handle. Like she's Superwoman. And all because of me and Liz. Mal figures how can she possibly complain about any of her problems when she's perfectly healthy and we're not. That's it in a nutshell, right, Brad?"

Brad kept his gaze on his teaspoon, twirling it playfully. "That's about the size of it, I think."

"And I have a strong suspicion that's what broke you two up, isn't it?" Russ asked, although he knew the answer.

Brad couldn't admit to that. Confirming their suspicion would only hurt them. "I wouldn't go that far," he said instead, then steered away in another direction. "I need to know something important. Is Mal seeing someone else— that you know of?"

Russ's and Liz's eyes connected like a laser beam hitting its target. A telltale sign for Brad. "I guess that means yes," he said, defeated.

"No, Brad. Not really," Russ said.

Not really. What the hell does that mean? Brad wondered. That she's not really seeing the guy steadily? That she's not really serious? Not really what? An angry jealousy filled him, but he masked it, kept his voice even and calm, all signs of anger safely tucked away.

"What exactly does 'not really' mean?" he asked, then picked up two cookies and ate them as though they were more important than any answer they might offer.

Liz looked totally confused, but Brad couldn't discern whether it was because she truly didn't know, or whether she knew and didn't want to hurt him. He turned to Russ and raised his brows in question.

"Brad, 'not really' means it's not really our place to answer that. Maybe you and Mal should talk this out. If she'll talk to you, especially when she finds out you lied to her. You never went to Atlanta."

Brad jumped to his own defense. "Oh, no. I never lied. I did intend to take that position, but changed my mind later."

"Okay, but still," Russ said. "You need to talk to Mal, not us."

Brad stood up and apologized. "You're right. I want you both to know I did come here to see both of you too. I thought about you a lot and wanted to know how you were doing. But, of course, yes, I wanted to find out about Mal."

Liz got up, brought the coffeepot to the table and refilled their cups. "Brad, we can see you're hurting. And all we can tell you is Mal is hurting too. Call her. Maybe you can both have a Merry Christmas after all."

Chapter Forty-five

Lois couldn't make up her mind whether or not to tell Mal. For sure the news would hurt her, but maybe she needed to know. Maybe she'd pick up the pieces of her shattered heart and move on. Sounds dramatic, but Lois couldn't deny the line held elements of truth and sound advice.

She and Mal had plans to Christmas shop after work tonight, then have a quick bite before going home. That's when she'd tell her, Lois decided.

*   *   *

The Golden Dragon had been the agreed upon Chinese restaurant of choice, having won first place in their deliberations because of its fat, crunchy noodles. They went to work on the bowl of noodles as soon as it was served, dipping them in the duck sauce while they sipped through their first pot of hot tea and waited for their meals.

Lois lifted her teacup and examined it as if it could reveal some long-held secret. "Why is it I can never enjoy a cup of tea at home like I do in a Chinese restaurant? Even if I get take-out and use their teabags, it never tastes the same."

Mal laughed. "I could never figure that one out either. Maybe it's the cups. I even went as far as buying a set in a Chinese gift shop, but that didn't do the trick either. Just to make use of them, I would pull them out every time Brad and I brought Chinese food home to eat with my parents."

Brad. Sooner or later, he always slips into the conversation. She saw the waiter coming with their wonton soup and waited until he served them, then said, "Mal, remember when I went to see *Crush* last week after you raved about it?"

"Yeah . . ."

Lois watched Mal as she ate, obviously enjoying her soup. She hated to ruin her appetite but forged on. "Mal, I didn't want to tell you this, but I think I should."

That got Mal's attention. She gave her friend a guarded look. "What?"

"I saw Brad there. He didn't see me but I saw him."

Nonplussed, Mal paused to make sense of what she heard. "But how is that possible, Lois? Brad's in Atlanta. You probably saw someone who looked like him." Dismissing it, Mal went back to her soup.

"Mal, it was Brad. He wasn't more than fifteen, twenty feet away from me."

"Are you sure?"

"If I weren't sure, Mal, I wouldn't be telling you. And there's more . . .he wasn't alone. He had a very attractive girl clinging to his arm. Of course, I have no idea who she was, but sexy-looking."

Now Lois turned her attention to her soup rather than see the hurt in her friend's eyes. Without raising her own, she could see how Mal was trying to absorb this shock.

In a short span of seconds, Mal shrugged. "Well, Brad's a normal, healthy male. I wouldn't expect him to shoot for sainthood. After all, we did break up."

Lois gave her a long, hard look. "Are you all right, Mal?"

Mal feigned indifference. "Of course, I'm all right. I'm a little ticked off that he lied to me about Atlanta, but I'll shake it off. It doesn't matter anymore anyway."

Lois dropped the subject, but recognized the sharp change in Mal's attitude and appetite. She continued to eat but at a much slower pace and with minimal enthusiasm. How do you start another casual conversation after that? The silence was killing them. Lois searched her mind for something meaningful to say.

She threw her shoulders back and put on a false smile so wide her cheeks hurt. "So, have you decided what you're wearing for your New Year's Eve date with Quentin?"

"I have two or three things in my closet I was considering."

"Forget all of them. We'll go shopping right after Christmas. You should get something hot, something knock-'em-dead fabulous."

Mal cocked her head and rejected the idea with a sour expression. "Why?"

"Because you should. That's why. It's time."

Chapter Forty-six

Mal's body felt like a volcano about to erupt. When she pulled into her driveway, it was 9:45. Considering the state she was in, she hoped to find her parents deeply engrossed in a TV program because she was in no mood for conversation. She had filled with anger when Lois told her about Brad and that "sexy-looking" girl. But, of course, her pride had kicked in and provided her with what passed as a normal reaction from a person whose heart had healed and was now content with the status quo.

And did she think Lois had fallen for her act? Not a chance. Lois knew Mal too well, but was smart enough to know when not to push her.

Mal heard the sound of the television the moment she turned the key in the door. She knew immediately what they were watching by the familiar background music. Her mother was a lifetime Cary Grant fan and the melody she heard was from his movie, *An Affair to Remember*. Her plan was to say a quick hello and good-night, then complain about total exhaustion and escape to the privacy of her room.

That plan fell flat when she saw them both waiting for her. She couldn't read their expressions too well. What she saw were two half-smiles with a message attached.

"What?" Mal asked.

Liz stepped forward. "No, don't get scared. It's nothing bad, but we do have something to tell you. Put your packages away and get yourself settled." She grabbed Mal's coat to hang it.

Mal dumped her shopping bags on her bed, then made a quick trip to the bathroom. Hours of shopping followed by two pots of tea had necessitated that priority action. The nip of cold winter air when she left the Golden Dragon had upgraded it to an emergency.

They were both in the kitchen waiting for her when she came out of the bathroom. Russ took the lead. "Mal, we're not sure if this will be good news or bad news, but we had an unexpected visitor today. Brad." He paused for her reaction, but she returned none, and he continued. "He never did take that Atlanta job, Mal. He's been here in New York all the while. And he misses you. He's going to call."

Mal's hands went on her hips. The anger and jealousy Lois's tale had stirred were percolating inside her and about to boil over. She started slowly. "Oh, is he? Well, isn't that nice of him?" Her words were icy and dripping with sarcasm. "What's even nicer is the fact that we have an answering machine. When he calls, he can leave his damn messages and I can have the pleasure of erasing him!"

Liz and Russ exchanged perplexed glances. In a few short sentences, their daughter's temper had escalated from calm to furious. Slowly, Liz followed Mal into her room. Her energy level wasn't ready for this yet. "Mal, aren't you overreacting a bit? I had no idea you were this angry with him. Can't you at least talk to him?"

Mal lashed back at her mother, something she had rarely done in her life and never since her illness. "No, Mom, I'm not overreacting and I wasn't angry with him, but I sure as hell am now, and no, I can't at least talk to him!"

Her words shot out like bullets and as soon as her wave of blind rage passed, Mal recognized the shock and hurt on her mother's face. She pulled her close and kissed her cheek, wetting it with tears she never felt coming. "I'm sorry, Mom.

I didn't mean to take it out on you. It's just that I'm very upset about Brad, and I don't want to talk about it. If he calls and you talk to him, you can just tell him not to bother to call again. I have no intention of talking to him."

Without words, Liz gave her daughter a pleading, confused look.

"Please, Mom, no questions. That's the way I want it. Period. Done." She turned away, went into the bedroom and closed the door.

Russ and Liz went back into the living room where they could talk without Mal overhearing. Liz was still shaking her head in disbelief as she stared ahead at the television screen. Even Cary Grant, on his knees professing his love to Deborah Kerr, could not cushion her pain. Her daughter's love for Brad was deeper, stronger than she had ever imagined. The fact that she probably gave him up because of her hammered away on her conscience.

Russ maneuvered himself from his wheelchair to the sofa to soothe his wife's hurt. Liz put her head on her husband's shoulder and stayed that way, quietly watching the fire die out in the fireplace.

Russ kissed her forehead. "She'll be okay. That was the shock of hearing he called; of finding out he never left New York. I think she'll calm down and talk to him eventually."

"I'm not so sure about that, Hon. I think there's more to this story than we'll ever know."

Later, in the comfort of her room, Mal calmed down. She felt awful for subjecting her parents to her bitchy mood. She assumed her writing position; propped up in bed, knees raised, pillows stuffed behind her back. But her thoughts were elsewhere. One end of her pen was positioned and ready between her index and middle fingers, but her thumb merely tapped away at the other end, raising it repeatedly like an out-of-control seesaw.

Why didn't I just tell them the truth? she asked herself. Why protect him? He doesn't deserve all the respect my parents shower on him. Why let them think I'm the bad guy here? No, tomorrow when I get home from work, they'll hear about their precious angelic Brad. How he barely waited till the body cooled.

With that decision centered in her head eradicating all others, Mal grabbed her steno pad. Her angry mood had its rewards. She wrote continuously for an hour, transferring her fire to Emma, her protagonist in *On This Rich Earth.* Words flooded the page, seemingly on their own, fed from an unknown source. Her eyes sparkled with excitement. Stimulated by what she was seeing, she continued to scribble at a rapid pace across the blue lines. When she reached the end, she reread it entirely and grinned with pride. Pride for what her meek, young Emma had accomplished in this high-tension scene, and pride in herself for managing to concentrate on her story, rather than fuming about Brad.

She slipped her writing materials back in her nightstand, and crossed her arms behind her head. Lois is right, she concluded. It's time to move on. Brad would be swept from her mind and her life.

She focused on her New Year's Eve date with Quentin. I *will* buy myself a new dress, and I *will* enjoy myself.

Chapter Forty-seven

Georgia had mixed emotions about the arrival of her children from college. She wanted them and she didn't want them. Dorothy and Elaine would be home this afternoon; they'd spend a respectable amount of time with their parents, then they'd be on the phone making arrangements to meet with friends. Alex would come storming through her door sometime tomorrow, undoubtedly loaded with dirty laundry and ravenously hungry. Normalcies that would soon change.

Although they had all been home for Thanksgiving, so much had happened since then, she needed to hug them. It had been hell these past weeks trying to put up a front for her children. At least she hadn't had to face them. While they were at school, they couldn't see the tension in her face. She wanted this holiday break to be special for them, but no matter what pleasures she planned, ultimately she knew how it would end. The thought of confronting Harry with the knowledge of his homosexuality was almost insignificant compared to the impact that revelation would have on their children. She shivered just thinking about it.

Jennifer and Althea had been calling almost every day, trying to help Georgia build courage for the inevitable. Never in her life had she felt so emotionally unstable. It would be a different ballgame if she and Harry were the only players. There would be a clean break, she'd let her lawyer handle the details, and try to get on with her life. But with three children in the picture, a simple dissolution of the marriage was not possible. Should she shield them from their father's homosexuality or be honest with them? Shielding them from the truth would shift the blame to her. What possible reason for divorce could she give her children that would carry enough strength to gain their support and acceptance? Nothing she could think of. And I'll be damned if I'd alienate my children in order to protect his deceitful lifestyle, she told herself. *No way.*

The phone interrupted her ruminations. She thought for sure it was Jennifer or Althea again. They wouldn't be seeing each other until late January, after the children went back to their colleges, and both these friends worried about Georgia like mother hens.

Comforted by their concern and the warmth of their friendship, she picked up the phone with a smile. Another voice took her by surprise.

"Georgia? It's me, Mal."

Georgia's smile widened at the sound of her newfound friend and confidant. "Mal, it's so good to hear from you. I miss the class already and we just started our holiday break." Her voice lowered, grew serious. "Mal, I'm sorry I dumped on you after the play. You caught me at a bad time. Or I should say I caught *you* at a bad time."

"Georgia, don't be ridiculous! That's why I'm calling, to see how you are. Are you alone now? Can you talk?"

"Yes, the girls are due this afternoon and Alex tomorrow."

"How about Harry? Where's he?"

"He left a few minutes ago to gas up and get his car washed, he claimed. Then he was going to the bakery to pick up some desserts for the kids. Such a good daddy he is." Her last line came out sounding like she was sucking on a sour lemon.

"Have you made your decision yet? Are you going to tell them before they leave? The more I think about it,

Georgia, the more convinced I am that you should do it while they're home. You can't lay a bomb like that on the phone."

"I know that. I just want to drag it on until after New Year's. They have celebration plans, parties. I don't want to spoil it for them. And then there's that little matter of my imminent confrontation with Harry. Needless to say, that has to come first."

"Gee, Georgia, I feel awful for you. I wish there were some way I could help. Since you told me I've been thinking about you constantly. It certainly took my mind off my own troubles."

"You have plenty on your plate too, Mal. I guess it's stupid to ask, but have you heard from Brad at all? A Christmas card, maybe?"

"Oh no, and I don't expect to hear from him. It's over. Period."

Georgia wanted to tell her again to try contacting him, like her friend Lois had also suggested, but Mal had been dead set against it then, and she was sure she'd get the same reaction now. Instead, she asked about her parents because she knew Mal would give her a positive response. They had also discussed her parents at length that night after seeing *Crush*. In that short period, both women shared stories, the highs and lows of their lives. Two lifetimes condensed to ninety minutes. An unlikely, but binding friendship was born that night, and Georgia hoped it would be nurtured for years to come.

"And what about the other Mr. Wonderful, Quentin? Have you heard from him again?"

Mal drew a deep breath. "Yes, as a matter of fact I did. He called to ask me again if I enjoyed the play, and would I go out with him after his performance tonight or tomorrow. All in the same breath, I might add."

Georgia's voice picked up a slight sparkle. "See, I told you. We *all* told you. Watch it, girl. That guy's looking to get in your pants. What did you tell him?" The sudden turn of their conversation swept Georgia back decades to her teenage years.

"I told him I was too busy until after Christmas, so he jumped ahead to New Year's Eve since he doesn't have an evening performance that night. He invited me to go with him to one of his theater friend's house party. Before I had a chance to think, I heard myself saying yes."

"So? What's wrong with that? You're a young woman, Mal. As long as your parents are doing okay, you should take advantage. I'm not saying you should marry the guy or sleep with him, but get out a little, have a few laughs."

Mal's delayed response created an image for Georgia. She didn't need to see her face to know the expression it carried. The silence was indicative of her understandable hesitancy.

"I don't think I can laugh with Quentin the way I used to with Brad, Georgia. It's not that I don't like him, but—"

"But what?"

"—but there's something about him I don't trust. And I don't say that with any sexual connotations. There's just something different about him. I can't put my finger on what it is, but it throws up this imaginary caution sign in my head."

"Oh, geez," Georgia said with a laugh. "Maybe he's gay like Harry and he's only after your brilliant mind."

Mal didn't return the laugh. "Georgia, it's good to hear you laugh, but you don't have to pretend with me. I know what's going on inside you. I have to go now, but will you promise to call me when you need to vent? I know you'll be busy with all your children around the next few weeks, but try to squeeze in a call to me anyway. I'll be worried about you."

"Yeah. I'm worried about me too. And Dorothy and Alex and Elaine. The only one I'm not worried about is that bastard I'm married to. And don't get me wrong, Mal, it's not the gay issue. People can't help what they feel. My anger is because he deceived me all these years, making me feel there was something wrong with *me*."

Mal couldn't think of any consoling words to offer. She hung up the phone and had a good cry. She hadn't allowed herself to cry in weeks. For Georgia, for her mom, for her dad, for the coming Christmas and, of course, for Brad's betrayal. She cried for them all until she was spent. Then she picked up her steno pad and started a new chapter of *On This Rich Earth*. All else was temporarily forgotten.

Chapter Forty-eight

Quentin had several balls to juggle but it had become a challenge that he found strangely amusing. He hadn't dropped a ball yet, so to speak, and smiled smugly at his ability to weave this web of deceit.

Tonight, the moment he spotted Deirdre enter the theater, he couldn't keep his eyes off her. Holding her in his arms on stage, watching her perform, were teasing temptations he had to deal with night after night. He was growing impatient with this cat-and-mouse game they were playing. The passion he felt for her was reaching explosive proportions. And putting aside the dynamic sex, the memory of her exquisite body wrapped in satin sheets, the smell of her captivating fragrance, he missed her. He missed talking to her, listening to her, watching her laugh, the sound of that laugh. But not enough to crawl at her feet. He was tired of apologizing. There's a limit to what lengths a man will go to satisfy his sexual urges.

His thoughts turned to Mal Triana. He was losing patience with that one, playing the perfect gentleman part. It's time for more aggressive action, he decided. Maybe a hungry male is what the young lady needs. And hasn't Quentin Kingsley always been one to accommodate the ladies? Of course.

But Mal had put him off to New Year's Eve. Okay, so he made it to first base with her. She accepted a formal date, not just an after-class cup of coffee. He intended to give her the rush treatment, to charm her right out of her pants. It had worked on all the others before her, and he saw no reason not to expect the same from Mal. It might take slightly longer, but he sensed a deep sensuality behind that innocent façade. Once he brought it out and worked on it, she'd succumb like the rest of them.

In the meantime, New Year's Eve was two weeks away. How the hell was he supposed to entertain himself till then? He could think of no woman from his list of past lovers that he cared to resurrect. Except Deirdre.

Stubborn pride can be a pain in the ass sometimes. It gets you nowhere. And once it curtails your sex life, what the hell good is it? Bearing that in mind, he decided to reverse his thinking, and give Deirdre one more try. But he had no intention of being reduced to begging.

He caught her backstage just as she was going in to dress for her first number. With as much humility as he could muster, he stopped her. "Deirdre, how long can this go on?" he asked softly. "I miss you something fierce. Is there anything I can do to make you forget that one stupid day?" With soulful eyes and child-like pouted lips, he waited. At least she didn't turn away and rush off this time like his previous attempts at reconciliation. *Progress,* he thought.

Deirdre crossed her arms, drew a breath and blew it out slowly. She kept her eyes fixed on the floor as if Quentin were laid out there rather than standing beside her. "I don't know, Quentin. You really hurt me that day. That mood came from out of nowhere. It scared me. It was as if you had a dual personality or some weird behavioral problem."

"Deirdre, *please.* Give me a chance to make it up to you. If I behave that way again, you can dump me and never look back. How's that?"

Arms still folded, she pursed her lips and gave him a long, sideways glance. "I nccd time to think about it. Right now I have to change and get into makeup. Call me at home tonight. We'll talk."

"Can't we just go somewhere after the show?"

"I don't think so. We need to talk first," she said.

Quentin smiled like an alley cat eyeing a plump little mouse as he watched her walk away. *In the bag,* he said to himself. Satisfied for now, he headed for his dressing room where he would once again assume the role of Joe St. John, Mr. Nice Guy.

After the show, Quentin's spirits were high as he changed into his street clothes. Things were looking up. First, and more importantly, his fears about being somehow connected to the three deaths were dissipating. He had been extremely cautious to cover his tracks each time. He hadn't panicked and allowed himself to trip up. Every move he made was carefully and succinctly planned.

Secondly, tonight he had made a breakthrough with Deirdre. Third, he had an upcoming date with Mal, and fourth, he had met and talked with two people during intermission who could further his career if Jordan's efforts failed. Everyone needs a Plan B, right? Jordan had offered to buy him dinner tonight, but Quentin had wormed out of it. He was in no mood to pamper him with sympathy again. Jordan's grief was a waste. Certainly, Gloria was an unworthy recipient.

Besides, he had his own demons to fight. He wasn't completely heartless and without feeling, after all. When you cause the death of three people, whether accidentally or impulsively, it doesn't just slip from your mind like a boring book or a bad movie. He felt bad about all of them and, ironically, the one he hadn't known at all, Wayne Bishop, had hit him the hardest. That poor jerk was the most innocent among the three. Gloria was getting too bitchy for her own good. He never wished her dead, but now that she was, well, so be it.

Bertie played with high stakes and she lost. Simple as that. She wanted an exclusive on him and his body in exchange for her silence. If she hadn't enjoyed herself taunting him, she'd still be alive. Jackass.

*   *   *

The streets were alive with people when he left the theater. Stores and restaurants were still open to accommodate the late shoppers, their windows and store fronts all lit up and decorated with seasonal displays to help people cheerfully part with their money.

Quentin filled his lungs with the crisp December air and walked through the parking lot to his car. Tonight he had no desire for any pleasures other than the comfort of his home. His plan was to fire up a few logs in the fireplace, have a couple of beers in his leather recliner, and call Deirdre. The thought had him grinning from ear to ear.

Less than an hour later, that image became a reality. After a quick shower, he slipped on a T-shirt and flannel lounge pants. Yellow tongues of flame snapped in the fireplace. As a matter of habit, he put the TV on, tuned it to CNN, and hit the mute button. If anything catastrophic had happened, he could tune in with the flick of his finger. Meanwhile, he dialed Deirdre and felt that familiar rising heat in his loins. His voice found its way out, but came up deep and raspy. "Hi," he said.

"Hi yourself," she responded and waited.

The intimacy of her two simple words triggered vivid memories and stirred up dormant passions that turned rising heat to burning desire. But again, he exercised caution. It hadn't been easy to get this far again, and he wasn't about to let her slip away.

He kept his words down to a whisper. "I miss you like you could never imagine, Deirdre. How long are you going to punish me?" Then, playfully, in his child-like voice that

Deirdre used to find irresistible, "Please, Mommy, I promise I'll be good. Pretty please, Mommy? Can we hug?"

He hadn't lost his touch. Deirdre's resolve went out the window. She laughed heartily into the phone. "Stop it, Quentin. That's not fair! You know that baby voice routine of yours always cracks me up. I'm not ready to forgive you yet. Not totally. There's a certain satisfaction I'm enjoying watching you suffer."

"Deirdre, wouldn't you prefer to watch me suffer in person? I can suffer like a bastard in your bed or mine." He added a touch of humility to his tone and said, "Really Deirdre, we *need* to be together. Considering how it was for us, I can't believe you don't miss me too."

"I *do* miss you, Quentin."

"Then what are we doing here? Why aren't we together?"

A long pause. Quentin could only hear the rhythm of her breathing.

"Okay," she said finally. Her tone sounded like a peace offering laced with a concession of defeat. "Tomorrow morning, I'll strip the bed. I know how you love my satin sheets."

Quentin stretched way out in his recliner, put his hands behind his head, and wore a smile broader than a Halloween pumpkin. Talk about satisfaction! he thought. *One down, one to go.*

Chapter Forty-nine

Anne's eyes rolled upward, then bounced side to side like a Mexican jumping bean. As if the shocking, unexpected loss of her husband hadn't sliced her in half and given her enough to cope with, she had to listen to these sermons. Who knows, maybe her friendship with Jordan Hammer wouldn't have the same comforting effect if she weren't being hounded about it. A couple of innocent breakfasts, and they were giving her the Mary Magdalen treatment.

This time her sister was dishing out the lecture. It was easy to funnel through the cacophony of her admonitions and pinpoint their origin. The crux of her words echoed the sentiments of their mother, whose turn to blast her warning had come up only hours earlier.

Finally, after an exhaustive effort to contain her temper and feed her sister false promises, she hung up the phone with a deep sigh and reached for her wallet to pull out that little piece of paper. Jordan's home phone number. He had told her to call whenever she felt the need.

She felt the need now.

Her act of defiance caused her fingers to tremble as she punched out the numbers, but the welcome blush of a weightless smile warmed her face like a spray of sunshine. Her smile soon faded into that dark well of disappointment at the sound of his answering machine. She should have known. It was still early, only 10:20. Surely a man of his stature could find something more entertaining to do than sit home alone with only dark thoughts and regrets for company.

Anne stumbled through her message while trying to ignore the fluttering feeling in her stomach. A feeling so deeply buried in a past life of youth and innocence, she fought the curious urge to surface it for reexamination. Twenty years later, as the newly widowed mother of two young boys, that feeling could be fraught with peril.

Is that what Elizabeth Taylor felt when Eddie Fisher opened his sympathetic arms to the grieving widow? A shudder ran through her at the comparison. *Don't even think it,* she admonished herself. Jordan and I simply lean on each other toward a common goal. Tragedy brought us together and perhaps our perseverance will shed light on the mysterious deaths. Wayne was a loving husband and an adoring father. If he had to die such a horrible death at such a young age, he certainly had earned the right to die with dignity and respect. If this is the road to travel to realize that goal, I've got to take it. And at thirty-eight years old, I owe no one an explanation.

With a firm nod of her head, she punctuated her resolve, tucked the flyaway strands of hair behind her ears and occupied herself with mundane household chores, none of which demanded immediate attention.

She peeked in the doorway of the bedroom her boys reluctantly shared. The advent of computers had commanded that families designate an entire room for the efficient functioning of computer equipment and its related paraphernalia. Like countless others, Keith and Adam fell victim to such technology.

Anne tiptoed into the room, smiled over them, and ran gentle fingers through their hair. She brushed her lips against their cheeks. Slumber had smoothed the adolescent roughness back into warm, baby-soft satin, though tinged with the unpleasant aroma of sweat and dirt. She smiled away a silent reprimand and made a mental note to discipline them in the morning for going to bed with dirty faces.

She darted out like a frightened mouse at the shrill sound of the phone pealing in the late night quiet. It had to be Jordan returning her call. Who else would call her at this hour, barring emergencies?

Slightly breathless, she answered it before the third ring.

"Anne, I can't tell you how pleased I was to find a message from you."

That voice had become her tranquilizer. She let the tension drain out of her and took the phone into the living room. She curled up on the sofa, threw a fleece lap blanket over her bare feet and settled comfortably for her forbidden fruit conversation.

"I had a day fraught with problems—business problems," he continued. "Hearing your voice was like a breath of spring."

Oh geez, here comes that Liz Taylor feeling again.

"Jordan, you've told me several times to call you if I need anything you can help me with—"

"Absolutely. I meant that."

"Well, there's something I need to do. And you're the only person who would understand."

"Name it, Anne."

"Can you take me to where it happened? At first I thought I'd never want to see it, but now I feel differently. I don't know why. Like I'm being drawn there. But I'm afraid to go alone. I might crack."

"Anne, don't say another word. You don't have to explain. Not to me. Just tell me when."

If his words were floating on a cloud, they couldn't have sounded softer, more soothing. Those haunting warnings to abort this friendship were like a sledgehammer beating her over the head, but her voice took command and chose to ignore them.

"Anytime within the next few days, before the boys are off from school for the holidays."

"Is Friday okay?"

"Friday is perfect."

They agreed to meet at the diner for breakfast first. She could leave her car there and ride with him.

What did she expect to accomplish by going there? She had no idea, but some compelling force was driving her.

Guilty tears welled in her eyes at the silent admission that the compelling force might be Jordan Hammer.

Chapter Fifty

Quentin wiped off his stage makeup, which clung stubbornly to his coarse beard. His image in the mirror returned an anticipatory smile, recalling his recent reunion with Deirdre. Thanks to his unrelenting efforts, she had melted like ice cream at a summer picnic. He intended to duplicate that incomparable pleasure tonight.

This game of deception had become exciting; an entertaining challenge. True, balancing his love life was small potatoes compared to dancing his way out of the dark circle of suspicion surrounding Bertie's death, but he so loved the flirtation with danger. He wished he could come forward and take credit for his two cover-ups.

Now take the demise of Roberta Bookman. There was a class act he could boast, albeit only to himself. Considering the fact that his decision had been instantaneous, allowing no time to think it out, he had done an exemplary job. With a deep breath, he threw his chest out and grinned, proud as a victorious general after a grueling battle.

Recently, the newspapers had been silent on the investigation of Bertie's murder, but buzz around the theater was electrifying. The cloud of suspicion on her husband was darkening. Speculation being tossed around was that Alan might have hired a professional to cut short the life of his gregarious and wealthy wife. However, acts of "The Snowman," as the killer had been nicknamed by the newspapers, bore no resemblance to classic methods used by hired hit men. Any spouse who contracted with such a person would no doubt collaborate with him to effectuate results suggesting an intruder; someone who had abducted his poor wife while he was away on a business trip.

Such were the flying rumors.

Quentin was not without sympathy for the poor guy, but a sneer of satisfaction crept up to form an involuntary smile on his lips. To get away with murder in this age of such advanced technology is quite an accomplishment, worthy of this surge of dubious pride.

The Snowman. Quentin laughed to himself at the tag they had given him, their unknown subject. He liked the title, he decided, along with its suggestion of power. He had to admit, though, that some credit should be given to Mother Nature. In the first incident, had it not been for the downpour of torrential rain, and the heavy blanket of snow in the second, obliteration of his presence at each scene would have been far more burdensome, particularly since not one of the deaths was premeditated. Quentin was somewhat humbled for the unsolicited but welcomed assistance from the heavens.

*   *   *

Deirdre had given him the spare key to her apartment should he arrive before her, which he did. He stripped out of his clothes and stepped into her shower, sucking in her lingering fragrance. His stomach growled ravenously, reminding him he hadn't eaten since late morning. He made it a practice not to eat a full meal before a performance, but had forgotten to have a light bite before leaving the theater. His mind had been preoccupied with visions of Deirdre and the pleasure that awaited him. And now, at 11:20, his body was starved for both the food and the woman.

Clad only in a towel wrapped around his waist, he walked from the bathroom, through the large, rectangular room that combined both living room and dining room, into the galley kitchen. He made himself at home, first studying the contents of the refrigerator, then swinging open cabinet doors in search of something interesting to snack on.

He settled on nachos and salsa and dumped generous portions of both onto a royal blue glass platter he found. His face lit up at the discovery of a half-used jar of processed cheese spread on the refrigerator door. He popped it in the microwave and watched till it bubbled, then drizzled the creamy topping over the chips, licking his fingers clean of its oozings.

On the counter behind him stood a large bottle of his favorite brand of merlot with two long-stemmed barrel-shaped wineglasses. Deirdre's thoughtfulness warmed him. She even remembered to leave the corkscrew. He was about to reach for it, but reconsidered. Where were his manners? He popped open a Diet Coke instead, opting to wait to enjoy the wine with his hostess. In bed.

When he heard the sound of the door opening, followed by boots being kicked off, Quentin was showered and comfortably propped in bed. The half-devoured snack platter rested on his thighs, his Coke and remote on the night table. Cheese streaked his black beard.

Deirdre laughed a hearty laugh when she saw him. "You look like a hungry leopard!"

"Don't get cute," he said with a playful smirk. He pushed the platter aside and got up to greet her. His mouth was already on her neck.

"Quentin, stop! I'm still in my coat. Give me a chance to get undressed and warm up."

"My thoughts exactly."

She smacked a fast G-rated kiss on his lips and shoved him away. "You know what I mean, wise guy. I need a hot shower and a soothing glass of wine to get my motor going. Did you open the bottle I left?"

"Not yet, but I will now. I wouldn't dream of letting your battery go dead," he teased.

She called out to him from the shower. He was back in bed, working the second half of his platter and sipping wine.

"Hey, what did you think about Alan? I just can't swallow that. Does he seem capable of murder to you? It's mind-boggling."

Quentin pretended disinterest. "Oh, you know how it is. They always go after the husband first. Unfortunately because he's usually the guilty one," he yelled back.

She entered the bedroom, her hair dripping, but gleaming in the lamplight. Her shortie robe only reached the top of her thighs. Lust burned his body as her arms went up to towel-dry her hair. He watched the robe rise and fall precariously. She continued to chatter, but her words bounced off him unheeded while he watched an everyday female task turn into a seductive performance to the eyes of a hungry male.

"I'm sorry. I didn't hear what you said," he said.

"That's because you weren't listening," she shot back amicably, but with a pointed, disciplinary finger.

He folded his arms, smiled and gave her his full attention. "Okay. Let's start again. What did you say?"

"I was talking about the slippers. Did you hear about them?"

His heart began to thump like war drums. *That* he hadn't heard. "What slippers?"

She sat on the edge of the bed, her excited eyes a prelude to what she was about to say. "Oh, see? I *thought* you didn't have a clue. They found Alan's slippers not far from where Bertie's body was found. I guess once those piles of snow melted, there they were in plain view. They're saying if Alan didn't do it himself, he might have hired someone to do the job."

His threw her a look of disbelief. *"Give me a break.* How the hell can that make sense? Alan was away on business, right? Do they think he came home from wherever he was, put on his slippers to kill his wife and bury her in the snow? Or maybe this guy he supposedly hired to kill her asked if he could borrow her husband's slippers?" He waved it away dismissively, as though the information was ludicrous.

"Don't give me that look! It sounds crazy to me too, but I'm just telling you what I heard."

"Okay, forget it. That's for the police to figure out, not us," he said, but his mind raced back to that night and the issue of the slippers. When he choked her with her own scarf and watched her eyes bulge and her tongue hang out, he experienced a fear that probably paralleled hers—well, maybe not quite.

He had thrown his own shoes in the car, just in case they could identify him in some way, and completed his deed wearing Alan's slippers. He thought he had disposed of them far enough away from where he had left Bertie's body, but then decided it didn't matter whether the police found them or not. As long as they couldn't be connected to him. And he was certain they couldn't be. Especially after being buried for weeks in all that snow.

None of those consoling thoughts had yet calmed his thumping heart.

When Deirdre slipped in bed beside him, that thumping heart seemed to be his only operating organ. For a while.

Chapter Fifty-one

Under hooded brows, Martha, the waitress who had served Jordan and Anne twice before, gave them a quick, knowing glance. Just one silent, slanty-eyed gaze before she walked away revealed her thoughts. An air of self-confident superiority enveloped her gait and raised her heavily penciled brows. Another two married people, not married to each other, her condescending look said. If they think those polite words and innocent faces can fool me, they can guess again. When you work in a diner, after a while you can spot the cheaters a mile away.

Anne and Jordan easily discerned this keen observation of the woman's thoughts. They exchanged a knowing glance of their own and both tried to suppress a smile. Then, suddenly, they broke into simultaneous laughter.

"Maybe we should pour it on when she gets back," Jordan suggested.

"Like how?" Anne asked, ready to play along.

Jordan stared with absolute pleasure at her sudden burst of enthusiasm. Since they met, although their friendship had strengthened, they had never shared a laugh before. It felt damn good.

"I'll think of something," he said. "You just follow my lead."

"Oh? You direct as well as produce?" she teased.

"Among other things," he answered, thinking of all the titles used for financial backers. Jordan not only had sufficient funds to fool around with, but the courage to take a chance on the dream of an unknown with potential. But then, he could afford to buy that courage. Not like the poor slob who throws his every dollar into it, plus every dollar he can borrow. Now *he's* the courageous one, not me.

When she smiled, Anne's cocoa-brown eyes were radiant under sandy-colored eyebrows that arched upward like angel wings. Now, succumbed to a quiet moment, the sparkle faded, shadowed by a veil of sadness. Sipping his coffee, Jordan gazed at her flawless complexion crowned by lovely high cheekbones. Her cheeks had a natural peachy glow, her nose a bit too short, but barely noticeable over the swell of full, sensual lips accentuated with frosty taupe lipstick. When she spoke, and particularly when she smiled, dazzling white teeth illuminated her face like sunshine.

"Why the serious face?" he asked. "I liked it better before when you laughed. I realized I'd never seen you laugh before."

"Well, Jordan, let's face it. We haven't had much to laugh about lately. If we did, we wouldn't have met in the first place." Her face went from serious to somber. She kept her gaze on her place mat and toyed with the silverware. "Don't you wish we could turn back the clock?"

Jordan saw the sadness ruling her face again and was about to sink down with her when he saw Martha coming with their orders. He made a grab for Anne's hand and winked.

"Sweetheart, how long can we go on like this? We have to tell them."

She bit her lip to stop the giggle she felt coming, then played along with his little soap opera. She leaned forward and spoke softly through pouted lips while Martha pretended to have better things to think about. She took her sweet time in serving their breakfast, though.

"I haven't been able to work up the courage," she said, meeting his gaze with exaggerated adoring eyes. "I'm afraid of what he might do to you." From the corner of her eye, Anne caught that quick spark in Martha's eyes. For an unguarded moment, she dropped her shield of indifference and stalled, hoping to hear more.

With their hands clasped together on the table, Martha became unnerved. She rubbed her dry, red hands on her apron and left. After her clumsy departure from their table, Anne and Jordan burst out laughing, but were soon silenced when they both gazed down at their hands, still comfortably joined.

Anne was grateful for the plate of food in front of her. It gave her good reason to pull away. Their hands separated for the simple business of eating and the food excused their silence.

Jordan sensed her discomfort and spoke first, seemingly amused. "Poor thing. We probably went too far. She was embarrassed."

"Yes, she was, but I can't say I'm sorry. That was fun. I almost forgot what it's like to have a good laugh."

"Feels great, doesn't it?"

*   *   *

Anne never felt it coming, but she sobbed like a baby when they arrived at the accident site. One look down the steep, jagged embankment where Wayne had met his death was enough to trigger an avalanche of pent-up tears.

Jordan wrapped his arms around her and his own eyes filled as she trembled in grief. "I shouldn't have brought you here," he said ruefully. "This was a bad idea."

191

The realization that she was in another man's arms at the very place where her husband died shocked Anne like a bolt of lightning. She pulled away abruptly, as if she were committing a sacrilegious act. "No, it's not your fault, Jordan. Don't you dare blame yourself. This was my idea, remember? I called you." She sniffed away her tears. "I'll be okay. This was just a little tough to take and I'm still not sure why I needed to be here. Maybe because this is where he spent his last moments on earth, and where I felt I needed to pray and say good-bye. I'm a little crazy, probably, but—"

He pressed a finger over her lips. "No, Anne. You're not at all crazy. I'll leave you alone and wait in the car. Take as long as you like."

She patted his arm with gratitude for his gentle nature and unwavering kindness, then turned away to face the bleak sunless sky. She clasped her hands, bowed her head and prayed. She prayed for Wayne, for her sons, for herself and for Jordan, who understood her pain.

Jordan sat in his car, deep in troubled thought. He wished he could let go and accept the facts as the police had presented them, but what did they really know? No one was there to see except the victims themselves.

He tried not to stare out at Anne while she communicated silently with God and her husband. He turned his head away, not wanting to impose, but after almost ten minutes, he called out to her. "Anne, I don't mean to rush you, but it's bitter cold out there. You'll catch cold—or maybe worse."

She pulled tissues out of her coat pocket, dabbed at her eyes, then blew her nose. "It doesn't matter. A good bout with the flu might be the perfect excuse to sleep through the holidays."

Jordan got out of the car and opened the passenger door for her. He raised the heat and looked at her with concern. "Geez, Anne, you're trembling. I should have dragged you back in the car sooner."

Her lips quivered as she spoke. "I'll be fine. And my trembling is not just from the cold."

He could hear another flood of tears rising in her throat and decided to leave it alone. He had an urge to hold her until her chills and her tears subsided, but steadied his hands on the wheel and pulled away instead.

They rode in silence for a while, each alone with their thoughts, and each wondering what the other was thinking.

"Feel better yet?" Jordan asked finally.

"Physically better, yes. But I can't get that scene out of my head. I keep seeing him falling down that embankment hitting all those rocks. I can go mad imagining what went through his mind while—" Her hand covered her mouth and she squeezed her eyes closed. "That image will forever haunt me."

"Stop, Anne, please. You've got to try to chase those thoughts away. Fight them or they *will* drive you crazy."

"Is that working for you?"

"Well, not completely," he admitted, "but I think I'm handling it a little better than you."

She cracked a bittersweet smile. "Misery is a woman's prerogative."

He looked at her, amused, and they both found themselves laughing again.

*　　*　　*

They indulged in small talk on the way back to the diner, but when they arrived, before she got into her own car, she brought the subject back. "Another thing that bothers me, Jordan, is the rainstorm that night. If Wayne had car trouble, and it was pouring rain . . . okay, so maybe he was under the hood trying to find the problem with the car, but why the heck was your wife . . . God! I still can't believe she was

193

with him . . . Anyway, why the heck would she be out of the car getting soaking wet for no reason? Wouldn't you think the average woman would sit in the car and wait?"

He thought about it a moment, then shook his head. "It's funny you should ask that, Anne, because the question crossed my mind too, but I didn't allow myself to dwell on it. I'm trying to accept the fact that we'll never have the answers. But yes, that's stranger than you think, if you knew Gloria. She was a very vain person. She'd complain even with a slight mist in the air because it would make her hair limp. I can't believe she'd stand in pouring rain and let herself look like a drowned rat.

"Secondly, Gloria was terrified of electrical storms, so much so that she gave up golf, which she loved. One day we got caught in a bad storm out on the fairway. She was petrified of being hit by lightning and couldn't run for cover under the trees because she knew trees attract lightning."

"Sounds like a phobia to me," Anne said. "Especially if her fear was so intense it made her give up the sport entirely."

"That's my point. Her fear would have kept her in that car, where she'd be safe."

Anne wrinkled her brows pensively. "That does sound weird, Jordan. Do you think we should mention it to that sergeant what's-his-name, Kennelly?"

Jordan dismissed her suggestion with a cynical frown. "Nah. Do you think they'd reopen the investigation on that? No way. They see us as two poor souls who can't deal with our spouses' infidelity. You know that, Anne. You've seen their attitudes."

Anne sighed. "Yes, I know," she said, a defeatist tone in her voice. "I'm just reaching, hoping." He held her car door open and she got in, looked up at him.

Without thinking, he bent down and brushed a kiss on her cheek. "Take care, Anne." A brief numbness gripped him. He didn't know if it was caused by regret from his unconscious act or his reaction to a forbidden pleasure. He wondered what Anne was thinking. He looked into her mesmerizing sad eyes for an answer, but they were vacant. She merely thanked him, offered a weak smile, and pulled her car away.

As Anne drove away from the diner, her conscience went to work, aided and abetted by the ominous warnings of her mother and sister. Break off this friendship with Jordan Hammer. It's dangerous, and it looks terrible! To whom? she asked her conscience. To them, not to me.

Chapter Fifty-two

There had been nothing merry about Georgia's Christmas, though she had made her best effort to mask her misery. Harry had given her a knockout diamond and sapphire necklace and she could barely look at him to acknowledge it. Even for the sake of the children she could not bear the thought of brushing lips to thank him, knowing where his lips had been. The repulsive image sent shock waves through her.

Celebrating New Year's Eve with him was out of the question. She had decided not to wait until after that holiday too. Sooner or later, the children had to be told. They'd be devastated to hear her intention to divorce their father, but not to be compared to what they'd feel if they learned why. She was still up in the air on that one.

Tonight looked like the opportune time to confront Harry, but she still wasn't certain she was ready. All three children were out for the evening. As bitter as she felt towards him, his dinner was still sitting on a warming tray, like the good little wife, straight out of a fairy tale. Everything had to look normal until she was ready to blow.

She lit the logs in the fireplace, poured herself a glass of wine, and sat in her club chair. Over and over again, since she was shocked out of her mind by that phone call that was never meant to reach her ears, she had practiced what she would say to him. The wine was supposed to relax her so she wouldn't become hysterical and drown all her words in tears, but so far it hadn't done its job. She sat up stiff and straight, her fingertips drumming on the arm of the chair, and waited.

He came in quietly through the kitchen door, as always, wearing that same expression of boredom and arrogance. That would soon change. She remained seated and watched him hang his coat and put his briefcase in the hall closet. He mumbled an icy hello when he saw her. Still she watched as he routinely lifted the lid on the casserole dish to examine its contents. She had made chili and rice, a favorite dish her children had requested, but apparently to him it was as appetizing as dog food. That disagreeable face was just what she needed to launch her out of her chair.

She stood in the archway that separated her kitchen and living room, arms folded across her chest. Her tone began calm and slow, like a simmering pot. "Don't fret, Harry, you won't have to tolerate my meals any longer. I've just about had it with that look of repulsion anyway. I see it too often."

"That's not true, and you know it. I just don't happen to be in the mood for chili. That's no reason to fly off the handle."

"Oh, really? Well, maybe I'll give you another reason." She felt the heat rising in her face and her balance unsteady, but there was no stopping her now. The lid was about to blow. "How's this one? I'll give you two words: Jeffrey Townsend!" She spit out the name as if it were poison.

Harry stood frozen, speechless.

"How dare you sleep in my bed after you've been *with a man?* How dare you give my children a gay father? You're disgusting!" Georgia screamed every word, then rage sent tears streaming down her face. "I hate you. I hate the sight of you and want you out of this house and out of my life. *Tonight!*" She screamed until her words were too garbled to be coherent and her voice too hoarse to be audible.

And all that time, Harry stood there; numb, dazed, defeated.

And when his wife ran from the kitchen, he remained there, stooped over, staring at his feet. Then he wept and wept until he was spent. When his sobs subsided, he could hear his wife's agonizing cries muffled into her pillow, and he wept again.

Sometime later, he climbed the stairs to pack a bag and beg his wife's forgiveness for ruining her life.

Chapter Fifty-three

With half a heart, Mal dressed for her date with Quentin. She hadn't been out with anyone other than Brad for years, and simply wasn't ready yet. All week she had struggled with regrets and considered breaking this date, but canceling out at the last minute was a rotten thing to do. None of the excuses she came up with sounded too convincing either, so she abandoned the whole idea. Who knows? She might have the time of her life. Isn't that what usually happens when you least expect it?

Quentin had called her twice this past week, once to ask if Santa treated her well, and again last night to tell her how he was looking forward to spending New Year's Eve with her. He spoke amiably about the people she'd meet at the party; which ones he liked or disliked and why.

During one phone conversation she had never bothered to leave the living room where she had been watching *Jeopardy* with her parents. They pretended to be disinterested in her conversation, but she caught her father's cautious gaze. Not that he had exhibited any particular displeasure after meeting Quentin, but clearly the presence of a new man in his daughter's life did not sit well with him. Brad had long ago become the son her parents could never have, and they were still hoping he and Mal would reconcile. In their eyes, Quentin posed a threat to that hope.

Mal took a last look to check over the fit of her black crepe dress. If it had been custom-made for her size eight figure, it couldn't have fit her better. The feel of it clinging to her skin gave her a million dollar feeling, worth every painful dollar she had paid for it at Lord & Taylor's. But her hair was driving her crazy. It was 8:40 already and Quentin was due at 9:00. When Russ wheeled himself to the doorway of her room, he caught the annoyance on her face as she continued to struggle with her hair. He started to back away, but she saw his reflection in her dresser mirror. "Want something, Dad?"

"No, Princess, nothing important. Just thought if you were finished fussing, we could talk a little."

Mal rubbed one more shot of mousse in her hair, then fingered the flyaway strands until they stayed put. She sealed them down with a thin coat of hairspray, then turned away from the mirror, accepting her less-than-perfect appearance.

"I'm done, Dad," she said, then threw a few articles of makeup, tissues, keys, breath mints and a few dollars into her evening bag. She sat at the foot of the bed, ready to give her father her full attention. "And I have twenty minutes to spare, if Quentin is punctual. Did you need to talk to me about anything specific?"

"Not really. Just to tell you how pretty you look in that dress and to say that I hope you enjoy yourself tonight. Do I have to worry about my Princess out with this Quentin guy?"

Mal's laugh was tinged with affection. She kissed his forehead. "I knew you had something like that on your mind, Dad. It's no use. No matter how old I get, you never stop worrying."

"Guilty as charged. When you're a parent you'll under-stand."

"But I'm not a love-struck teenager anymore, Dad. Give me credit for knowing how to pick them. Quentin's an okay guy." She stopped for a brief moment to give it more serious consideration. "I think his only fault is that he's slightly conceited; a little too self-confident. But that's only my impression. I could be wrong. Besides, conceit doesn't make him a bad person."

Russ cocked his head in agreement. "True," he said, "but you can't go by my impression either. I've only had one other person to compare him to."

Brad's name hadn't been mentioned since the night she had come home livid after her dinner with Lois. Now his presence hung between them again, intangible but formidable. To dismiss any discussion of Brad before it began, Mal stood up, gripped the handles on her father's wheelchair, and moved it from the doorway so she could leave the room.

"Well, don't compare him to 'that other person,' Dad, because sometimes you think you know a person, but find out you never did. And that's all I'm going to say on the subject. It's New Year's Eve and I don't want to work myself into a bad mood. I intend to have a wonderful time tonight and never give 'that other person' a single thought. Okay, Dad? End of discussion." She stormed away in a huff, impervious to the hurt and bewildered look on her father's face.

Her mother stood up from the living room sofa and blocked Mal's approach with disapproving eyes, but she said nothing.

Mal heaved a sigh, allowing the surge of anger to drain. *Here I go again. Look who I'm taking it out on,* she thought to herself with disdain. The sting of her mother's eyes hung over her like a black cloak. She kept her own eyes downcast and sat down on the rocker, hating herself for the biting words she had lashed out at her innocent father. Then, impulsively, she sprang from the chair and reached out to hug them both, first her father, who was beside his wife now. Russ welcomed her embrace with a forgiving smile, dismissing her apology before she got it out. "Don't start crying now, Mal," he said, wagging a finger at her. "You'll mess up that pretty face. It was my fault. I upset you. I didn't think before I opened my big mouth."

Mal returned his loving smile, blinked away the tears before they could begin and smacked a noisy kiss on his cheek. Then her arms went out to her mother, but her mother's eyes still held a message that Mal easily interpreted as a warning. No matter how she was hurting inside over her breakup with Brad, these immature emotional outbursts would not be tolerated. There could be no justification for lashing out on her father whose love for his daughter was immeasurable.

Mother and daughter exchanged a long, silent glance, acknowledged each other's thoughts, kissed each other's cheeks, and pulled apart at the sound of the bell. Quentin. Another look was shared by mother and daughter. A questioning look. A look of uncertainty. Both wondered what was to develop between Mal and the bearded actor/writer.

Mal went to the door to let him in. He looked dazzling in a black tuxedo, crisp white shirt, black tie and cummerbund, complemented by that killer smile.

He stood there a moment and just stared. "Mal, you look absolutely breathtaking. Fabulous! I'm gonna be proud as a peacock walking in there with you."

"You look pretty cute yourself," she said.

Chapter Fifty-four

When Quentin drove into the circular cobblestone driveway of his friends' mansion overlooking the Hudson, it took Mal by surprise. He had warned her this would be a formal affair, but as she watched the women stepping out of their fancy cars like movie stars at an awards ceremony, her dress with the million dollar feeling suddenly plummeted in value. Is this how Cinderella felt when her coach turned into a pumpkin and her dress to rags?

Quentin caught her staring at the exquisitely dressed women walking up the brick walk and read her mind. He laughed to put her at ease. "Mal, the only thing they possess that you don't is money. And lots of it. Trust me, when they get a good look at your face and luscious figure, they'll be green with envy and every man will have his eyes on you. What you have money can't buy."

Mal's face turned crimson, but his complimentary words, albeit laced with sexual connotations, did wonders for her ego. With renewed confidence, she linked her arm with his and walked through the huge entrance hall, an impressive mix of sand-colored marble and rich brown oak, into the Grand Room, where the festivities would begin. Massive crystal chandeliers hung from the dome-shaped ceiling that had been hand-painted to recreate an azure blue sky with puffs of drifting white clouds, all framed in gold. Reflections of soft-colored lights danced on the ceiling, conjuring up romantic images of an enchanted time long past, the Gilded Age of the early twentieth century.

On an elevated floor, an orchestra comprised of more than twenty musicians took up one wall. Four bar stations were set up for the cocktail hour and the duration of the evening. All musicians, bartenders and wait staff were handsomely dressed in tuxedos and royal blue bow ties, male and female alike. At least a dozen servers circled the oval-shaped room carrying trays of hot hors d'oeuvres for more than two hundred guests gathered for the celebration.

Some mingled at small round tables, talking and drinking. Others stood on the burgundy-carpeted steps of a winding staircase that led to bedrooms and other private corners not to be explored.

Mal took it all in, trying not to let her mouth hang open in awe. Quentin hadn't given her the slightest clue that the party would be held in a place like this! She dragged him a short distance away where she could scold him without being overheard. "Why were you so secretive about this party? You told me a 'house party.' I never dreamed it would be anything like this. I don't even know how to talk to these people. They're way out of my league."

"That's exactly what I thought you'd say. And that's exactly why I chose not to tell you. I was afraid it might scare you away. And see? I was right, wasn't I?"

Mal grinned up at him and nodded, conceding the point.

"Lewis and Joan Gilbert, the host and hostess," he continued, "had skipped their annual party last year. September 11 was still too raw in everyone's heart, particularly New Yorkers'. This year their attitude reversed. Glad to be alive and proud to be American, they said, they decided to go all out for a gala celebration. Ergo, the request for formal attire."

Mal hadn't even met the Gilberts yet, but liked them already.

"According to their invitation, they're even providing drivers for any guests who want or need a ride later, so if you don't mind, walk with me back to the bar. I'm ready for a refill."

As the clock moved closer to midnight, memories of past New Year's Eves with Brad brought tears to Mal's eyes, but this was no place to lose control of her emotions. She steeled herself to blink those memories away.

By the time 2003 was only ten minutes away, to her surprise, she was actually enjoying a conversation with a group of down-to-earth interesting people. Not until she saw him coming towards her, did Mal realize that she hadn't noticed how many trips he had made to the bar. He had obviously decided to take full advantage of the Gilberts' offer. One long look and she was sorry she hadn't kept a watchful eye on him. He approached her with rubbery legs, an idiotic grin induced by alcohol consumption, and a mock salute. She had thought he looked gorgeous when he picked her up hours earlier. Now he looked repulsive.

"I came to get my twelve o'clock kiss, Princess Mal." He feigned the customary bow reserved for royalty and nearly fell over.

Mal made no attempt to hide her displeasure for the sake of onlookers. "The princess title belongs exclusively to my father, Quentin, so please don't call me that again. And as far as your twelve o'clock kiss is concerned . . ." She shook her head. "I don't think so."

He wrapped both arms around her in a bear hug. She looked into glazed, droopy eyes and involuntarily inhaled his ninety-proof breath. "Quentin, don't make a scene, *please,*" she whispered, trying to peel his arms off her waist.

The orchestra leader saved the moment. He called for everyone's attention to count down the end of 2002 and welcome in 2003. A drum roll started to bring the already partying crowd to this ultimate height of celebration. Quentin released her without incident and joined in with the cheering and hand clapping.

While his attention was diverted, Mal backed away and lost herself in the crowd. This was a special moment to share hugs, kisses and happy tears with people you loved or cared for. All week she had psyched herself to believe that Quentin was a possible candidate for that circle.

She was wrong.

Chapter Fifty-five

Quentin's New Year's Eve inebriation had turned out to be a blessing, Mal realized. The Gilberts were quick to offer one of their drivers to send the couple home safely. By 2:00 a.m. he was in no condition to resist the offer.

At 4:00 a.m., Mal was home in bed, but still awake, thinking about what Quentin had said in the car on the way home. He had talked nonstop the entire trip, like your usual, run-of-the-mill drunk. Just a lot of nonsensical, unintelligible chatter. But one line had piqued her attention. She tried to recall exactly what he had said and what he had been mumbling before she heard those key words.

Something about him being a prince. *The* prince. She thought he was mouthing off some mumbo-jumbo about Cinderella's prince. Had she said something earlier about feeling like Cinderella? That would explain it, but she had no recollection of being verbal about it. Well, maybe I did, and don't remember, she thought. If so, that may be what steered his head in that direction. He had even called her *Princess.*

Mal closed her eyes and tried to remember that scene. Quentin had plopped his Happy New Year foil hat on his head to crown himself, then raised his glass and babbled, "I am prince of the magic slippers." What the hell did that mean, if anything?

She'd ignored it at first. Who pays attention to a drunk? But then again, alcohol often triggers soul baring. The word *slippers* is what put the imaginary light bulb over her head.

He'd said it more than once and she was certain he had said *slippers,* plural.

She turned off her TV. Two *Three's Company* reruns had failed to take her mind off Quentin, or Brad, who seemed to take up permanent residence there. She punched a hole in her pillow the size of her head and slipped a sleep mask over her eyes. Tomorrow's a holiday, she reminded herself. Another long day with family that she planned to enjoy. She and her parents had accepted her aunt and uncle's invitation to spend New Year's Day at their house if Liz was up to it.

The next day she'd call the one person who might help her separate fact from fiction. Together she and Georgia could determine whether Mal had valid reason to suspect Quentin Kingsley of murder.

*   *   *

Mal, at work, took a break for a cup of coffee and a quick phone call.

"Hi! Happy New Year," she said when Georgia answered the phone. I didn't wake anyone, did I?"

"At eleven o'clock? Are you kidding? Everyone's up and out already, going about their business. It's just me and Lulu, our cat."

"Ah, too bad. I guess you're free to talk, but I'm not and I do want to discuss something with you."

"Why? Is something wrong, Mal? You sound so serious."

From the corner of her eye, Mal saw one of the young attorneys pacing at her doorway, waiting for her to get off the phone. Damn! Why is it they can be on their phones all day, unavailable when you need them, but as soon as you pick up your phone, they stand there stiff as a cactus plant until you give up? She pretended not to notice and continued her conversation with Georgia.

"I'm not sure anything's wrong, Georgia. It's probably just my writer's imagination gone wild, but I would like to talk to you, privately if I could."

Georgia fell silent for one long moment, then said, "It's funny you should say that because I'd like to talk to you too. I have a few troubles of my own."

Mal immediately picked up on the tension in Georgia's voice. "Oh, no. Don't tell me you had your showdown with Harry already."

"You got it."

"But I thought you planned to wait until just before the kids go back to school."

Georgia blew a sigh into the phone. "I did too, but you know how it is. Sometimes your emotions get in the way of your plans."

The waiting attorney made himself more visible and Mal shot him a give-me-a-minute look of annoyance, then spoke back to Georgia. "Geez, Georgia, now I'm more concerned about you. Can I call you when I get home from work? Will you be able to talk then?"

"Probably not. But maybe we can meet someplace for coffee later, say around eight o'clock?"

"No problem. Just tell me where, Georgia."

They settled on the diner near the library.

When she hung up, Mal had the distinct feeling Georgia had some heavy-duty troubles to unload. Knowing the gist of the problem, she could well imagine. Her bizarre thoughts about Quentin seemed incredulous now. Maybe I should chuck the whole subject for tonight, she considered, but decided to wait and see if Georgia could handle it.

With a pleasant smile, she waved the impatient attorney in and swallowed her annoyance. But all day Quentin dominated her thoughts. The sober Quentin and the drunk Quentin and his flighty remark about slippers. *Prince of the Magic Slippers,* he had called himself. As far-fetched as it sounded, she couldn't dismiss a nagging suspicion. The more it haunted her, the more she hoped she'd get the opportunity to delve into it with Georgia tonight.

Chapter Fifty-six

Jill Eaton wasn't about to give up on Brad despite how he had humiliated her. But the guy was hurting for his precious Mal. His wounds were still raw and she had every intention of helping them heal. This time she'd play it differently, though. Slow and easy. So slow he'd never see it coming.

Carefully, she bided her time and waited for the right moment to make her move. She found it one evening, when most of the staff was gone for the day. As was the norm, several project managers were working late researching their clients' leases, checking their voice mail and returning only the calls they deemed necessary. Two associates also remained, Jill being one of them.

No one occupied the immediate area near Brad's office; at least no one within hearing distance. Jill couldn't let the opportunity pass. She waited until he concluded his phone call, then walked over to his office and knocked lightly on his open door.

"Mind if I come in?" she asked. She kept her voice soft, adding just a touch of shyness.

Brad heaved a sigh, remembering what had passed between them, but said, "Sure, why not?" He nodded to the chair in front of his desk, leaving a safe and formal distance between them. Before she had a chance to speak, he began to reiterate his apologies. "Jill, this has been rough on me . . . on us, after—"

Her hand went up to stop him. She shook her head with a gentle smile, as though what he was about to say was unnecessary. All was forgiven. "Brad, that's what I wanted to talk to you about, sort of. I've always considered you one of my good friends in this office, and still do. Sure, I was hurt and angry that night, but I got over it. Later, when I cooled off and gave it enough thought, I rationalized. What you did was not an insult to me or my femininity—"

"Absolutely not, Jill—"

"No, let me finish, Brad. Then you can speak your piece. Anyway, as I was saying, I realized that night should not have happened. It was too much, too soon. Neither of us was ready, particularly you, coming out of a long-term relationship. I want you to know I understand all that, and I'm not angry. Not at all."

Again Brad opened his mouth to speak, the apologies waiting to pour out, and again Jill stopped him and continued, "I've noticed how you haven't been able to even make eye contact with me since that night. I could see how uncomfortable our relationship—or lack thereof—has made you. It's totally unwarranted. We're both adults and we have to work together. There's no reason why we can't continue being friends, right?" Jill extended a hand across the desk.

Brad quickly sandwiched it between his. "Right, Jill," he said. "It *has* been uncomfortable and we *should* continue our friendship. And never, ever think that what happened that night was your fault in any shape or form. I think you're a very decent person and a very desirable woman. Believe me, I was the one who lost out that night."

She stood up. "It's nice of you to say that. My wounded pride appreciates it and I feel much better now." She sucked in a long breath and gave him one of those special smiles she was famous for.

"Me too, Jill," he said. "And again, thanks."

She scrunched her face and waved him off. "Brad, wipe that humble look off your face. There's no need for thanks. Thanks for what?"

"For being a good, understanding friend and a great date."

She kissed her fingertip and blew it towards him as a thank-you gesture, then left his office. *Step one completed.*

Chapter Fifty-seven

Life in the Pappas household had blown apart. Five lives shattered into fragments of what they once had been. Yes, even Harry, although the eye of the storm, was to be pitied. He had shriveled into the shadow of the man he was, or pretended to be. But then again, in the end, Georgia realized she had helped him. If she hadn't overheard that one conversation and confronted him, chances are Harry would never have had the courage to tell her or his children about his homosexuality. She still couldn't believe how he had sobbed, expecting her to understand his love for this man, this Jeffrey Townsend. Was he the first? How many others had there been? And even if she could understand, which was not remotely possible, she couldn't forgive him for the life he had forced her to lead.

In social and family circles, they were husband and wife, and both played their parts to perfection. In the privacy of their home, they were polite and civil to each other, but never lovers, never friends. Not for the past fifteen years.

Again, as she had done countless times, Georgia relived that scene, those few hours that ripped her family apart . . .

At first, while she screamed, he cried. Harry just sat on their bed with his head in his hands and cried. When Georgia had no screams left inside her, she looked at him with contempt, but her anger had dissipated. Pity for this stranger she had called her husband for twenty-six years replaced the rage.

With her arms folded, Georgia watched him, her jaws clenched. Harry pulled a large suitcase out of the closet and threw it on the bed. He appeared disoriented and confused, probably wondering how to put a lifetime into one suitcase. Georgia made no effort to help him.

"I don't know where to begin, Georgia, what to take. And I'm upset . . . we have so much to discuss, but you're angry now . . ."

"I'll be angry for a long time to come, Harry. You stole a whole lifetime from me."

"I gave you a good home and three beautiful children. It wasn't a total loss."

"Yes, you did," she said, her anger escalating again. "How did you manage that?"

"I wasn't being honest with myself then."

"Oh, let me guess," she said, her tone mocking. "I'd venture to say you've been honest with yourself for the past fifteen years, isn't that correct?"

He shot her a look of disgust and continued stuffing shirts, underwear and socks in the suitcase. "If you say so," he mumbled.

"But not with your wife and family, huh? With them you could be dishonest and live your sick double life, couldn't you?" She was pacing the floor now, waving a finger at him.

He flung a garment bag with two suits packed inside onto the bed and lashed back at her. "What the hell did you expect me to do? I was putting you and the kids first then. I didn't want to upset your lives, and I knew I had a responsibility to my family, so I stayed."

Her arms flew up. "How noble! The children and I should be grateful for the sacrifices you've made all these years. How selfish of us to keep you from your lovers. Tell me, Harry, how many men have there been in your life? Five? Ten? When did Jeffrey Townsend take the number one spot? Why don't you call him? He'll be elated to know you're free now."

For the first time in all their years together, Harry grabbed her throat. "That's enough!" he screamed, his face red, his eyes glazed with anger.

The bedroom door banged open, hitting the wall. Alex stood there in the doorway, enraged and stunned by what he had heard.

Father and son locked eyes and the shock of the moment rendered both silent. Then Alex walked right up to his father, hate burning in his eyes. "You're a disgrace to all of us. I can't even look at you anymore. And I hate you for what you did to my mother. For that I'll never forgive you. Just get out of our house. Go to your friggin' lover and leave us in peace."

"Don't you talk to me like that, young man. This is *my* house. I pay the bills here."

"Yes, and you'll continue to do so, I'm sure." Alex's words held a warning tone. He put his arms around his mother, who cried silently. "Let's go downstairs, Mom. Let him finish his packing and get the hell out of here."

Harry was gone before the girls came home. Alex held his mom until she was too numb to shed any more tears. Georgia stared into space, deep in her own thoughts and memories. Now, in retrospect, she realized that she should have known. There were signs, but she had always suspected other women, given their nonexistent sex life, but never once did she consider homosexuality. It was a double blow she couldn't fathom.

Alex heard the car pulling into the driveway and went to meet his sisters at the door. Thankfully, Dorothy had picked up Elaine from her friend's house, so he and their mom wouldn't have to get through this scene twice.

Death. Accident. Heart attack. All these fearful images crossed both girls' minds simultaneously when they saw their brother at the door, his face solemn.

Dorothy covered her mouth with her hands. Terror filled her eyes. "Oh, my God. Something happened . . . Mom? Dad? Who is it, Alex?" Then she saw her mother's tear-stained face and swollen eyes. Elaine ran to her and held on tight, afraid to hear the inevitable bad news. Dorothy remained frozen in fear.

"It's Daddy, I know," Dorothy said to her brother. "Just tell me, is he dead?"

"No, he's not dead," Alex assured her. "He's alive and well, but he's gone. As far as I'm concerned, he might as well be dead."

He brought his sisters into the living room and broke the news. Their immediate reaction was to scream at him in disbelief. He had to be wrong. How dare he say such ugly things about their father? But when they looked to their mother for support, she offered none. Her eyes were blank, her shoulders slumped.

The shock triggered anger, denial. Alex tried to calm them, but it had to run its course. When their anger subsided into mournful tears, Georgia and her children sat for hours trying to comfort each other from this shock that rocked their family. How could they possibly shield themselves from the disgrace Harry had brought upon them?

Georgia would never forget his face when he left the house that night. He was relieved and happy. Happy to be free. And she had done it for him. Without meeting her gaze, his last words were, "Get yourself a lawyer. I won't give you a hard time. And again, I'm sorry, Georgia."

"No, you're not!" she screamed back.

She had told the story of that memorable night twice already, separately to her friends, Althea and Jennifer. Now she had found Mal, another friend who conveniently lived in her neighborhood. Someone she could talk to face to face. Mal would listen to her story tonight. She could pour it all out again, and temporarily feel better, but the poison would stay inside her forever.

Chapter Fifty-eight

More than three months had passed, yet Anne found dealing with the grief worse rather than better. Today, like every other day, she walked around in a daze. Nothing she could do in or out of her house seemed important enough to motivate her. Depression's ugly head hovered over her, its massive arms held her captive. Wayne's face, his smile, his scent, were fading from her memory. She couldn't visualize him as vividly as she used to, nor could she hear his voice in her mind.

One o'clock in the afternoon, she was still in her pajamas, curled up on the sofa, her hair disheveled. Since her boys left for school, she had tortured herself watching old video tapes. She had laughed and cried at the same time, watching her family enjoy simple pleasures; water fights in their backyard, Fourth of July picnics with the neighbors, fun vacations and Christmas mornings with everyone in red pajamas and messy hair, sitting in a sea of crumpled wrapping paper. She watched until the pain overshadowed the pleasure. Knowing how innocent they all were to the impending tragedy, the tapes had become unbearable. Foolishly, she had turned off the VCR and switched to the noontime news. Constant reminders of imminent war and threatened terrorist attacks only added to her dark mood. Nothing could obliterate that gripping fear.

The shrill sound of the phone jolted Anne to her feet. A surge of inexplicable pleasure flashed through her, thinking it might be Jordan. A sigh of disappointment escaped her at the sound of her mother's voice.

"What are you doing?" she asked. "Still moping around?"

Anne took a long look down her pajama-clad body and ran fingers through her tangled hair. A sour taste in her mouth reminded her she still hadn't brushed her teeth.

"No, Mom. I've been busy. I know I promised to call."

"Busy doing what?"

Here we go again. "Just the usual stuff around the house, Mom. Nothing earth-shattering."

"You haven't taken care of Wayne's clothes yet, have you?"

It was more a reprimand than a question.

"No."

"I can come over today and help you with that. You shouldn't do it alone."

Anne thought of how she loved to fondle his clothes that still hung in their closet. When her boys weren't around, she'd wear one of his flannel shirts and slip her feet into his slippers, which she still kept under her bed.

She squared her shoulders and responded to her mother's offer. "No, Mom, I'm not ready. And when I am, that's something I have to do alone." Anne heard the edge in her own voice, but offered no apology. This wasn't the first time her mother had mentioned the clothes.

"Okay, okay. You don't have to bite my head off. Let's change the subject. How about if I take you and the boys out for dinner tonight? It'll be good for you to get out of the house a little." Rose Drummond's voice lowered an octave. "Have you seen that Jordan Hammer again? Has he been calling you?"

Anger seeped through Anne. She had intended to accept her mother's invitation to dinner just to please her, but when she threw in Jordan's name, she felt her temperature rise. Especially when she referred to him as *that* Jordan Hammer, as if he were a bug or a social disease.

No, Mom. Actually, I called him last, she wanted to say, but said instead, "Mom, I wish you'd get off my back about Jordan Hammer. You're making something out of nothing. Jordan and I have only one thing in common and I've already told you several times what that is. If you bring his name up again, Mom . . . well, I'm sorry, but I'll have to hang up on you." Her own words made her cringe. She had never been that sharp with her mother before. Well, desperate situations require desperate action.

Her mother's silence hung between them for a second. Then softly, almost in a whisper, she said, "Oh, my God, Anne. Don't tell me you have feelings for this man?"

"Yes, Mom. I *feel* for this man. I feel right now he's the only friend I have. He doesn't patronize me because I believe in my husband's innocence. He doesn't think I'm a mental case, too distraught to think clearly and accept other people's preconceived thoughts."

"I never said that, Anne. Your sister never said that either, I'm sure."

"No, but you both think it. That comes through loud and clear."

"Okay, Anne. You're upset now. Why don't you hang up so you can calm yourself down? If you feel better later, my dinner invitation is still open."

Anne hit the off button without saying good-bye. She had let loose with more emotion than she had planned, but if it would keep her mother and sister off her back about Jordan, it was worth it.

Only she and Jordan still struggled to hold on to that element of doubt concerning their spouses' deaths. Funny about element of doubt, she thought. It swings both ways. As strongly as they believed in Wayne's and Gloria's innocence, until it could be proven, the faint shadow of guilt would never give them peace. Sometimes Anne thought perhaps that element of doubt had fueled her attraction to Jordan, like an act of revenge. But no matter how many times she bounced it around in her mind, Wayne always came up not guilty. Never in a million years could he have given her all that love, physically and emotionally, and have a woman on the side. Not even Denzel Washington could pull off an acting job like that.

The conversation with her mother had sparked her with nervous energy. She showered, dressed and was out an hour later despite the frigid fifteen-degree temperature. First, she made a necessary stop at the bank, then Staples for computer supplies the boys needed. A long overdue trip to the supermarket was last on her to-do list.

Back in the warmth and security of her home now, she made herself a cup of hot chocolate to warm her shivering bones. It reminded her of the night Jordan had sat in her kitchen, politely drinking hot chocolate while she spoke to her mother on the telephone. A devilish smile crossed her face as she imagined what her mother and sister would have said if they had witnessed that scene. She sipped the hot, sweet bubbles that crowned her mug. That line about forbidden fruit tasting sweeter certainly rang true today because she couldn't wait for her next chance to call Jordan. Her mother's not-so-subtle reprimand had triggered that.

Still energized by her resolve, she cut up chicken and veggies, which she would stir-fry later. A little rice on the side and her boys would be happy. Maybe she'd even throw some biscuits in the oven. They'd never miss Grandma's restaurant meal. Later when they were asleep, she'd make a pot of decaf, bring a cup to the privacy of her bedroom, and call Jordan. On second thought, maybe she'd have wine instead of decaf.

She smiled as she busied herself in her kitchen, aware of her mood reversal, and glad to have something to look forward to. And she had her mother to thank.

Chapter Fifty-nine

The twenty-three year age difference between Mal and Georgia had no bearing on their new friendship. Initially brought together by their common interest in writing, their relationship had strengthened the night they had shared confidences.

They were seated in a corner booth of the diner with two cups of steaming hot, fresh coffee and one generous serving of chocolate cake to share. Small talk took them halfway through their coffee and the cake was long gone.

"I'm almost afraid to ask," Mal began, "but do you want to tell me what happened now? If you changed your mind, that's okay too, but judging by all that tension in your face, I think you need to let it go."

"Yes, you're right. I do need to talk. Not that I can expunge the shock out of my system in one thrust of words, but it helps." Georgia twisted her napkin so many times, it began to shred. She reached for another.

Mal saw the watery glaze in her eyes and cut in. "Will you be all right? Would you rather sit in the car and talk?"

"No. I'll be fine." She drew a breath. "I've done so much crying since this happened, I should be dehydrated by now."

Mal returned a gentle smile and patted Georgia's hand.

For the third time, Georgia told her story. She had been through it twice before with Jennifer and Althea, but both by telephone. To look across at a sympathetic face that understood your agony and listened to your babbling offered far more comfort. For a while anyway. Until all that poison starts to simmer again inside and eventually boils over.

When Georgia appeared sated, Mal groped for what she hoped were the right words. "Georgia, in most marital crises, I guess the logical thing to say is try to work it out, go for counseling, but in your case, I doubt that would help. Not with that problem. Divorce seems to be your only option. Dealing with the knowledge of another woman is bad enough," she said. That image of Brad and the "sexy-looking girl," as Lois had described her, shot through her like a tongue of fire. She chased it away and continued. "But another man, well, that's something else. I'm no expert, but as far as I know, that's irreversible. Fifteen years is a long time to live with a man who gives you no physical affection at all. Get your divorce. I know that's what you plan to do anyway, but if you're looking for support, lady, you've got it. No one in the world would blame you.

"And by the way," Mal added with a bright smile, "you should be proud of yourself. You got through that whole story without crying. That wasn't easy."

Georgia forced a smile and nodded. "Sometimes when you have no choice, you can control yourself. Probably if we were in some private place, I'd be crying like a baby. Anyway, thanks for listening, Mal. I do feel better now, after spilling my guts." She sucked in a deep breath, blew it out slowly, and excused herself for a bathroom break.

She returned with an apologetic face. The waitress trailed behind her with a fresh pot of decaf and refilled their cups. "Mal, when I got my head together again a minute ago, I remembered you wanted to discuss something with me when you called. I was so drowned in my own troubles, I totally forgot. I'm so sorry. What was it you wanted to say?"

Mal waved it off. "Forget it. You're upset and you'd probably think I'm nuts anyway."

"No, I can't forget it. What I need to forget is my own messed up life. C'mon, distract me. And then I want to hear about your date with Quentin; what you think about him."

Mal began to pleat her napkin, then stopped abruptly, remembering that Quentin had that habit. She clasped her hands and preceded her words with a nervous laugh. "What I think of him is what's bothering me. You're the only one I can confide in about this, really."

Georgia read the expression on Mal's face and sensed trouble. "About this what?" she asked.

"No. I *know* you'll think I'm crazy. It's probably just my bizarre imagination again."

"Maybe, maybe not. Talk to me, Mal. I can see whatever is on your mind is serious. Talk to me."

"Okay, but don't say I didn't warn you. Here goes. I think there's an outside chance that Quentin is a murderer."

The shock hit Georgia like a charging bull. Her hand went to her mouth, but "Oh, my God," still came out a little too loud. "Quentin a murderer?" Her look was incredulous; a cross between a question of Mal's sanity and macabre amusement. "The guy may be a little over-confident, in love with himself, but murder? Mal, c'mon!" Georgia searched Mal's face, waiting to hear this was some sort of joke. All she saw was firm determination, so she spent the next few minutes listening, then tried to peel off Mal's layers of suspicion with reason and logic.

But Mal held fast. Exasperated by the haunting feeling, her hands went up with a shrug. "I know it sounds crazy, Georgia," she said. "Maybe I'm losing my marbles, or maybe I have some sort of psychic power stirring to life inside me. I haven't the faintest idea what's behind it, but all of a sudden I see him as that woman's murderer."

"Roberta Bookman."

"Yes. Bertie they called her. She was very active in that theater. I'm sure he knew her well."

Georgia sat up straight, folded her arms across her chest. Deep in thought, she pursed her lips. "And in your mind that makes Quentin a suspect?"

"That and what he said about the slippers. When people are drunk a lot of stuff slips out that they would never reveal sober. Then there's this tiny trace of insincerity that comes across sometimes. Tiny, tiny," she said with squinted eyes. She held her thumb and index finger a half-inch apart to illustrate. "I picked up on it when he first talked about Bertie Bookman's murder. Suddenly, I was looking at Quentin, the actor, not Quentin, that gregarious, self-confident, in-love-with-himself guy you described." Her hands went up in defeat again. "So maybe I *am* crazy. So shoot me. I have nothing concrete to support the feeling, but it's there and I can't shake it."

Georgia cocked her head and nodded. "Yes, maybe you are a little crazy. And maybe not. Let's try to analyze. Come up with hypothetical situations. First we need motive. Let's use our writers' minds and *think.*"

And they did. Before the night was over, Georgia was hooked. She wasn't as convinced as Mal, but Mal had created enough smoke to generate Georgia's interest in looking for the fire.

Chapter Sixty

Quentin screwed up royally with Mal and Deirdre was getting on his nerves like a bad case of shingles. Jordan had asked him to join him for a quick dinner at the pub across from the theater. Half business, half pleasure, he said. Maybe he had something good to report. His spirits could use a little lift. Maybe he connected with the right people and they'd springboard *Crush* to New York.

The pub was three deep with its usual Friday night crowd and the noise level so high you couldn't hear yourself think. They hung out with a beer until a table opened up in the back. Once seated, they ordered a second round of beers and hot pastrami sandwiches that came out so high only the mouth of a hippo could tackle them.

"So, what's happening, Jordan? Any progress?" Quentin asked, his mouth stuffed.

"Things are looking good. I need to connect with a few more of the right people to put the whole package together, but I don't anticipate a problem. Once I smooth out all the kinks, we're looking at a late summer or early fall opening."

Quentin slapped the table, clearly elated. "Yes!" he said and reached to pump Jordan's hand. "I've gotta hand it to you, Jordie Boy. You are one hell of a salesman."

Jordan brushed off the praise with a modest shrug. He pulled a bunch of pastrami slices out of his sandwich and put them aside in his dish. "How the hell did you bite yours?"

Quentin laughed. "If you're hungry enough, you manage." He looked Jordan square in the face and felt no remorse at all for screwing his wife, then causing her death. The only thing he felt guilty about was not feeling guilty.

"Oh, before I forget, Alan Bookman called me about an hour ago. Boy, is that guy down in the dumps. I thought I was bad. Looks like the police don't have enough evidence to arrest him yet, but they're breathing down his neck and he's scared to death."

"Can you blame him? If I were in his shoes, I'd be scared shit too." *Well, I sort of was, wasn't I?* Quentin thought, not allowing the smile he felt coming to take shape.

"Anyway, I told him I was coming here with you and said he could join us if he wanted. That's okay with you, isn't it, Quentin?"

"Of course. The guy can use all the friends he can get right now." He couldn't help but laugh inwardly. *What are the odds of a guy breaking bread with the husbands of two women he killed? Well, only one was intentional.*

Quentin steered the conversation back to *Crush* and its New York opening.

Jordan pushed his plate aside, still half-full. "Listen, Quentin, don't mention to Deirdre yet what I said tonight about the New York opening."

"No problem. I understand. She's been flying high just hoping you work it out. No sense getting her all excited in case it falls through."

Jordan cocked his head. "It's not that. Nothing is ever for sure, but I'd say it's practically a given. But as you know, all these deals come with stipulations, compromises."

Quentin stopped chewing; shot him a long look.

Jordan shook his head. "No, no, it doesn't affect you," he said, "Not directly, anyway."

"I hear a 'but' coming . . ."

Jordan nodded. "You've got that right, I'm afraid. Truth is the backer with the deepest pockets wants Deirdre replaced."

Quentin stared at him with sincere incredulity. Deirdre's performance on stage could be matched only by her performance in bed. "Why?" he asked, though he could easily guess the answer.

"The usual. The guy's been drooling over this knockout dancer he's been seeing. Spent a few years in Vegas, now she's using him to break into Broadway. Everybody sees it, including him, but he doesn't care. Whatever it takes to keep her in his bed is okay with him."

"Geez. I don't want to be around when Deirdre gets that news." Although sympathy was his initial reaction, he felt a wave of relief. Deirdre had become a little too possessive lately. Shades of Gloria Hammer. He was still holding the reins, and he wasn't about to allow her to take control. If she were dumped from *Crush*, their daily contact would cease, leaving their relationship to cool and fade away.

"I'm sorry, Quentin. There's no question the two of you make magic together on that stage, but you know how it is. Money talks."

Quentin took a long pull on his beer, watched the foam settle. "Yeah, unfortunately, we all know that's the name of the game." He looked Jordan straight in the eye, then added, "But I was under the impression you were controlling the purse strings on this."

That drew a quick laugh from Jordan. "Well, as a producer I am, but you've been around long enough to know it takes a concerted effort to fill that purse."

Quentin never got to respond. Alan's appearance at the dining room entrance cut their conversation short. Besides,

230

he was far more interested in what Alan had to say than in Deirdre's career opportunities, or lack thereof.

He shook Alan's hand with both of his and let the actor in him fill his face with profound concern. Alan took the seat next to Jordan and slipped his jacket over the back of his chair.

Jordan gave him a hang-in-there pat on the shoulder.

"What's going on, Alan?" Quentin asked, back to his sandwich now. "What the hell are those bastards doing to you?"

Alan shook his head and waved the question away. His lips tightened in disgust, then sucked in enough air to ramble out a response. "They're killing me. That's what the bastards are doing. Boxing me in until they get me where they want me. There's one sonofabitch ADA, a woman, who's after my blood. She doesn't give a shit that I lost my wife, that just maybe I'm innocent. All that bitch is after is an indictment so she can score points for her political career. I'm a convenient target, easy to nail—to set up, I should say."

"That's bullshit, Alan," Jordan said with sincere concern. "What does your lawyer say?"

"He says they're trying to hammer the nails in my coffin, but I shouldn't worry. He's working on it. Like that's supposed to comfort me." He paused to give the waiter his order of Johnnie Walker Black.

Quentin used that opening to feign sympathy once again. "It's a tough break, Alan. I can well imagine how this is tearing you apart. Bertie was a good woman, everybody's friend. Yours especially, I'm sure."

Alan's arm rested on the table. His hand went to his forehead to support his overburdened mind. "Absolutely," he said, his eyes downcast.

Sweet poison oozed from Quentin's lips. "Then to be accused and harassed because they have nowhere else to point a finger—" He shook his head for emphasis. "Geez!"

Alan digested the proffered support and drowned himself in a moment of silent self-pity. The arrival of his drink broke his reverie. He refused the menu the waiter handed him, but ordered two more beers for his friends. Both Jordan and Quentin declined the offer, their mugs still half-full. Alan lifted the glass to the waiter and said, "Give me ten minutes and bring me another." He then turned to Jordan. "Hey, I'm sorry, Jordie. I've got a hell of a nerve dumping my troubles on you after the shock you've been through."

Hidden somewhere in there were those unsaid words again. Jordan sensed them every time. He wished he could reach out and squeeze them to death. The image of Anne's empathetic face and sweet smile surfaced and soothed him. His rising anger cooled. *It's you and me, kid, against the whole damned world,* his mind conveyed to her.

"No apologies necessary, Alan. Yes, I'm still going through that shock," he said, putting emphasis on *shock*, "but at least no fingers were ever pointed at me. Man, that's got to be hell on wheels."

Alan let out a laugh laced with bitterness. "Tell me about it," he said, then turned to Quentin with hopeful eyes. "Quentin, you were at the theater that night. Are you sure you didn't talk to Bertie at all? Maybe you forgot at first, and maybe she mentioned something casually about what she planned to do later or someone she had to meet?"

"Alan, I'm *so* sorry. I wish I had some little piece of information that could help, but the police already questioned me. There was nothing much to tell. You know how friendly Bertie was. She talked to everyone. Yes, I did see her, but she was involved in conversation with people I didn't know, so we just exchanged hellos with hand waves.

After that, I went backstage to change and go home. She wasn't around when I left. At least I didn't see her."

Alan heaved a sigh and reached for his second scotch before the approaching waiter had a chance to put it on the table. "Yeah, I know. I've been through everybody's story over and over again, hoping to hear something that might give them a little clue that could open new doors. I'm getting the feeling that ain't gonna happen. You guys can't imagine what it's like to have all the walls closing in on you."

Both men gave silent sympathetic nods while their minds raced along different paths.

No, I can't imagine, Jordan thought, *but I can relate to the need for clues to open new doors.*

Yes, I can imagine, pal, Quentin thought. *That's exactly why I have no intention of boxing myself inside those walls. Too bad Alan, but as the saying goes, better you than me.*

Chapter Sixty-one

Two nights after Mal met with Georgia, Quentin called to attempt another apology for his New Year's Eve behavior. Mal stiffened at the sound of his voice. If the guy turned out to be innocent, she'd be humbly sorry, but right now she was slightly afraid of him. Well, maybe slightly more than slightly.

He pleaded his case with the usual confident charm. "Mal, I'm no drunk," he said. "Not really. I guess I just got carried away when I heard they were providing rides home. I can count on one hand the times in my life when I got drunk. Well, maybe on two hands," he offered with a laugh.

Mal fell silent, searching for the right response. Their writing classes would resume Monday night. She wanted to keep their relationship amicable yet distant.

"Are you there, Mal?"

"I'm here."

"C'mon, Mal. Don't tell me you're gonna punish me forever for one stupid mistake. Geez! Presidents have pardoned hardened criminals for a lot worse than that."

A chill ran through her. Why did he choose that line for an analogy? *Stop it. Don't get paranoid now*, she admonished herself.

"Did I do or say something that offended you? If so, I apologize."

She had to find a way to cut him off permanently without provoking anger or disdain. With Brad gone, Georgia's writing classes were all she looked forward to. She wasn't about to let an insignificant fact like he might be a murderer jeopardize the pleasure and learning power of those classes.

All by themselves, her lips found the words. "No, Quentin, I can't say I wasn't disappointed that night, but offended? No. A little embarrassed, yes. But not much. You weren't the only one riding high that night, but—"

"Great. That's a relief. So . . . when can we get together?"

"Quentin, I was about to say that it can't work for us. It wouldn't be fair. I can't get Brad out of my head or my heart. That's going to be a long struggle, I suspect."

"Friends can be very comforting when you're down, Mal."

"Yes, I agree. But friends don't date. I'm sorry, Quentin. You're a nice guy. I enjoy your company, but I'm just not ready to see someone else."

He blew a sigh into the phone. "I guess I'll have to respect that for a while and hope you change your mind somewhere down the road. You'll continue with Georgia's classes, won't you?"

She found a laugh for her killer friend with the killer smile. "Are you kidding? Without Georgia and everyone else's critiques, *On This Rich Earth* would never have a chance."

"You're really enjoying writing that novel, aren't you?"

"Oh, yeah. Once I got into the research it became more and more fascinating. It's an exciting project. And it's doing wonders for my dad too."

"That's great. I'm happy for you, Mal. I can see and hear that adrenaline flowing when you talk about it. Makes me want to pick up my novel and throw myself into it again."

"You'd better. You got us all interested in that plot. Don't you dare abandon it," she said congenially.

"Oh, no way. I've just been exceptionally busy these last weeks," he said.

Yeah, murder can really tie you up, Mal thought.

"Okay, I'll say goodnight, then. I'll see you Monday night. Still friends?"

"Definitely, Quentin. Still friends."

He sounded so convincingly innocent, she thought when she hung up, that her weird thoughts became clouded with doubts. Why would he kill Bertie Bookman? What possible motive would he have?

Mal fell asleep that night content with her new resolve. Just because she couldn't put her finger on the motive didn't mean she hadn't put her finger on the killer. Call it instinct, call it intuition, call it psychic phenomenon, call it anything you want. All she knew was Quentin Kingsley had killed Bertie Bookman. If Georgia would help her, maybe their two heads could come up with the answers long before the police.

Chapter Sixty-two

Brad had fallen into the routine of hanging around the office after five o'clock, regardless of whether it was necessary or not. Despite his best effort, he was having a hell of a time trying to erase all those years with Mal and get on with his life. He had always been in love with her, but hadn't realized the depth of that love until he lost her. Without her, his life had changed drastically. For years, he had seen her four or five times a week. Now he didn't know how to fill that void. And he had no one to blame but himself.

A bittersweet smile formed on his lips as he reminisced. He thought of how often she mentioned how sorry she was for him that he should be burdened by her problems. Then she'd stumble to rephrase her feelings. Guilt would rush through her for referring to her parents as "problems."

Yes, certainly seeing her dad in a wheelchair, still struggling with therapy that can never undo the damage his legs had sustained. Still, compared to that first year, he'd come a long way, emotionally and physically.

Her mother's illness—well, that was another story. In Liz's case, "problem" was an understated word. No one would disagree that cancer is the ultimate "problem" that could snake its way into any healthy body, at any age. It might curl in a dark corner and lie dormant for a while, then rears its ugly head again to spit out its life-threatening poison. Still, although not often enough, we hear those cancer survival stories, some even suggestive of miracles.

And we grasp, we cling to that hope. Which is where Liz, Russ and Mal are at now. Clinging.

But Brad loved them all. Differently, of course. A deep, intense, consuming love for Mal, and sincere, warm affection for her parents. He clenched his teeth and shook his head thinking how stupidly, in one impulsive moment of self-pity, he swept them all away.

With a little too much force, he flung the pen he had been chewing down on his desk. It rolled off and sailed along the floor. When he bent to retrieve it, he saw Jill's long legs swinging into motion from around the hall that led to her department. He stood up and smiled.

"Hi. I didn't know you were working late too," she said.

"Well, when you work in different departments and never come up for air, you don't know who's still around."

"I've had enough, though. After a while you get bleary-eyed. I just want to put these files away, and I'm out of here."

"Yeah, me too," he said, although he hadn't accomplished enough work to earn bleary-eyes.

Jill smiled, said nothing, and replaced the files in a nearby file cabinet.

Brad slipped his hands in his pockets and stood quietly watching her.

"Listen," he heard himself say, "I was planning to pick up a meatball hero and eat it at home, "but if you have nothing better to do and would like to join me, we can sit and be served. I could use your good company." He hoped his tone implied just that.

She gave him a long look. "Still hurting, huh?"

He shrugged, making an ineffective attempt at indifference. "It's better. Just a matter of getting into a new routine. Making new friends. Whatever."

Unconvinced, Jill cocked a brow, but she quickly wiped the doubt off her face. "Oh, yeah, you're still hurting," she said, with a dismissive hand wave. She flashed him one of her luminous smiles, suggesting that his situation was merely temporary. "But we won't talk about it if you don't feel like. And yes, I'd love to join you. I used my lunch hour to shop, and my usual Hershey bar didn't quite cut it. My empty stomach is sending up messages."

"Italian okay?"

"Fine. I could go for a huge dish of pasta. That and a fat glass of wine to flush away the tensions of the day would be perfect."

"Great. Grab your coat," he said as he grabbed his, "and we'll be sipping that wine in twenty minutes."

"If we get a table that fast," she said, her step perkier as she rushed down the hall for her coat.

"Think positively," he called back and found himself feeling suddenly energized for the first time that day. With her coat flung over her arm, he watched every step she took as she walked towards him. He couldn't figure out why he shouldn't be thrilled to have her attention and her friendship. She was one hell of a substitute. But he had leveled with her the last time they had spoken. He certainly didn't want to rehash that uncomfortable situation and certainly didn't want a repeat scene of their last date.

But no one likes to eat alone, right?

*   *   *

They went to Mia Cuccina, a well-established Italian restaurant two blocks from their office. Both chose melon wrapped in prosciutto as their appetizers. For entrees, Jill ordered the veal picata and Brad decided on the gnocchi bolognese that they would each share. And the wine, of course, was a must. She chose white, he red.

Two hours passed without a lull in their conversation. Brad began to feel intoxicated not only by the two glasses of wine he had drunk, but the warmth of a budding friendship, the feminine fragrance of Jill's perfume blended somewhat incongruously with the rich, hearty flavors of the delectable dishes they had shared.

He took her home in a cab, and by then he had steeled himself to act with his head, not that part of him that ached for attention. With a split-second kiss on the cheek, Jill thanked him for the superb meal and the pleasure of his company. She did not invite him in, for which Brad was grateful. Maybe she was content to have a good male friend in her life right now until someone better showed up? He couldn't tell for sure, but knew that if he continued this *friendship*, he'd be treading on dangerous ground. If things went sour, working in the same office would be hell.

Chapter Sixty-three

Anne knew she'd have to deal with it eventually, but kept putting it off. One night, in early January, Jordan called her a few minutes past eleven. For the first time, the sound of the phone had awakened thirteen-year-old Keith, her younger son. She heard him go into the bathroom and hoped he'd plop right back in his bed. But no, there he was standing in the archway in his athletic shorts and T-shirt, rubbing the sleep out of his eyes. His rumpled hair formed peaks, making him look as though he had caught his finger in an electrical socket. Yet, even if he were wearing a tuxedo, that hairstyle would be perfectly acceptable, and probably preferred these days.

"Who's that, Mom? Anything wrong?" he asked. No one ever called them at that hour, even when their dad was alive.

"No, sweetheart," she said, her hand cupped lightly over the mouthpiece. "Go back to sleep. It's a friend of mine. I had left a message for her to call me when she got home." She hated lying to him, but some lies are unavoidable.

"Who?"

She shooed his concern away with a hand wave, then wrinkled her nose and shook her head to indicate a no-one-you-know response.

She blew a sigh of relief when he bought it and stumbled back to his bedroom. When she heard the door close, she whispered into the phone. "Jordan, you still there?"

"Yes, I'm here. I'm sorry. I guess no time is a good time to call. If I try to reach you earlier, your boys are around and you can't talk. If I call this late, I disturb them and invite their curious questions. Do you think they could handle our friendship if you told them? They might, you know, if they understood what we're trying to do."

"First of all, Jordan, don't worry about disturbing them. When they sleep, an earthquake couldn't wake them. I think Keith never got around to going to the bathroom before he fell asleep tonight. That's what woke him up, not you. And in answer to your question, yes, they might understand if I spoke to them, but I can't be sure, so I'd rather not get into it. Especially since I can't trust them not to casually say something to my mother or sister. *That*, I'd rather avoid."

Jordan took a pensive moment before responding. "I feel awful that my presence in your life causes you such trouble. You have enough on your plate. If you want me to stop—to go away quietly—"

Anne cut him off faster than she intended. "The only problem I have in my life is all the people who try to tell me how I should live it. To be honest, Jordan, your friendship is a comfort to me. Tragedy gave us this common problem with common feelings. The things we've shared could never be said in conversation with others. They all think we're crazy for believing in our spouses."

Some things Jordan still couldn't share. Like the fact that deep down he didn't have the same faith in Gloria that she had in Wayne. He felt awful every time that doubt invaded his thoughts, but he could never say with absolute certainty that his wife would never have cheated on him. And yet, he had no concrete evidence to think otherwise. The only thing he felt sure of was that she was not involved in any way with Wayne Bishop.

He put a smile on his face and brushed away his negative thoughts. "Okay, then. I'm glad you feel that way.

Actually, I called you to discuss something entirely different. Something potentially pleasant for you."

Anne welcomed the change of pace. "Well, that sounds promising. Shoot."

Well, you've heard me mention Quentin Kingsley—"

"Yes, the actor in your play. I remember."

"Right. Quentin has mentioned to me a couple of times about these writing classes he attends. He loves the teacher and enjoys the exchange with the other students. Well, I remembered you saying one day that you had always wanted to be a journalist, but never got around to pursuing it. Since you like to write—"

"You figured I would be interested in this class?"

"Yes, I did. It might be just the kind of boost you need. And it would only be a half-hour ride for you."

"But if the classes are already ongoing, it's probably too late to think about it, right?"

"Maybe, but maybe not. This woman routinely starts new ones anyway with a short break in between, he says. I think you should give her a call. Can't hurt."

Anne liked the idea, but hesitated. "Would I be going in over my head? How do I know what level of writing they're on? I wouldn't want to embarrass myself."

"Anne, don't put yourself down. I get the feeling from all the conversations we've had that you'd fit in just fine. Why don't I give you her number and you can question her?"

She reached for a pen and felt a surge of enthusiasm that she hadn't felt since before Wayne's death. "If I don't lose my nerve by tomorrow, Jordan, I will. Give me her number. And what's her name, by the way?"

"Georgia Pappas. Quentin says she's an absolute doll and a great teacher."

"Okay, Jordan. If you trust Quentin's judgment, I'll trust him too."

"That's the spirit," he said. "Call me after you speak to her and let me know how it goes."

"Definitely. And thanks for thinking of me, Jordan."

"I'm always thinking of you."

Chapter Sixty-four

Georgia had dreaded going back to work so soon after the traumatic breakup of her marriage. She considered not mentioning the split at all, but what would be the point? Why prolong the agony? And so, she addressed the problem head-on; stirred up the fire and stomped it out in one short sentence.

When Lydia Talbert, one of the teachers she was fairly friendly with, asked her how her holidays were, she simply replied, "Fine, actually. With all my kids home, I had a wonderful Christmas, but before New Year's, Harry and I agreed to separate."

Lydia's brows shot up like a rocket. The whites of her eyes formed wide circles. Words escaped her, but sympathy replaced her look of surprise.

Georgia yielded a sour laugh. "Yeah, it shocked me too, but it was a long time coming, I guess. And truthfully, Lydia, I'd appreciate it if you'd spare me the questions. I'd rather not discuss it."

"Oh, of course. But hey, if ever you want to talk . . ."

"Sure. Thanks, Lydia." *Slim chance of that happening,* Georgia thought to herself. Anything she said to Lydia would be broadcast throughout the school faster than a tornado. Now, by throwing out those few words, Georgia had put a lid on all other supposedly well-meaning inquiries.

*   *   *

That was a week ago. Over and done with. Now tonight she had her writing class to face. Not that she owed them any explanations about her private life, but if and when any reference to her husband came up, she'd make a short, simple statement that they would soon be divorced, and get on with the business of writing. None of them would probe further, she was sure. Except for Mal, of course, whose input she had solicited and welcomed. But never in the presence of the other students.

When she had their attention, Georgia gave them all a warm greeting. Quentin took a seat next to Mal, and Georgia shuddered to herself at the remote possibility that Mal's instincts could be correct.

"Okay, class, now that you've all had a chance to welcome each other back, I want to make a quick announcement."

Mal made a noticeable, spontaneous jolt in her seat.

Georgia threw her a quick no-not-that look of assurance. "I'm sure none of you will mind, but I took it upon myself to invite someone new to sit in tonight, just as a silent observer. A young widow who's thinking of joining our class. She's a little afraid it might be over her head." Her eyes went straight to her friend. "Sound familiar, Mal?"

Mal responded with a nod and a grin. Contagious smiles and chuckles of laughter circled the table.

"She should be here soon. I'm sure you'll all make her feel welcome. This gal really needs some breaks. She's been to hell and back."

Piquing their interest, she explained. "You're all familiar with the story, I'm sure. We've discussed it briefly here." Then, to Quentin, "Quentin, you particularly should be interested in this. Remember that horrible accident that killed your producer's wife and the man they claim she was having an affair with?"

Quentin barely nodded.

"Well, this woman, Anne Bishop, is the wife of that man."

Despite the dark, heavy beard, Georgia's keen, observant eye watched the color drain from his face.

Chapter Sixty-five

With a little discipline, Quentin had learned to chase away those little guilt pangs about Wayne Bishop's death. After all, he kept reminding himself, it was an accident. If anything, he should have felt guiltier about Gloria. He had known her well and intimately but, where she was concerned, he couldn't feel anything but relief.

Wayne Bishop had been a faceless and unintentional victim. That also made it easier to dismiss him from Quentin's thoughts. Until tonight, at Georgia's class, when Wayne's widow sat inches away from him. It unnerved him at first, but he pulled himself together and joined in the welcoming remarks voiced by the others.

"Welcome, Anne—Bishop, is it?"

"Yes."

"Glad to have you with us. Hope you decide to join our class. We're all good people around this table," he said, putting his killer smile to work as he acknowledged everyone seated. "And Georgia—" He formed a circle with his thumb and index finger. "—she's the best. How did you hear about our class?"

Anne had prepared herself for that question. Jordan would not be part of her answer. "A friend of mine had seen Georgia's flyer months ago, but only mentioned it to me just the other day. He knows I love to write, but also knew I was in no position to handle it months ago. Now I think it might do me good to get involved. Anyway, I called the library, and they put me in touch with Georgia." She shrugged and smiled pleasantly. "And here I am."

"Okay, class, I think we'd better get started," Georgia said, cutting off further conversation. "We have to leave the socializing to break time or we won't finish our lesson and readings."

Quentin's mind wandered. His intent before this surprise visitor was to use the refreshment break to work on Mal. He wasn't ready to accept defeat with that one yet. His ego wouldn't allow it.

While Georgia's voice went on and on about the uses and misuses of introspection, Quentin studied with quick glances the faces of the two most attractive women in the room. Well, maybe Georgia could tie for second. Mal bore a striking resemblance to Jaclyn Smith; a magnetic mix of wholesome beauty and sensuality. Lots of dark corners there to be awakened and explored.

Anne Bishop, if one had to compare her to a screen star, would come closest to a dark-haired Meg Ryan. Warm cocoa-brown eyes, although shadowed by grief and probably sleepless nights, and an adorable smile that could melt the most hardened heart. Probably pushing forty, but she could easily pass for late twenties if she tried. Beyond those sad eyes and forced smile Quentin guessed was a woman longing for the comforts and joys that had once been part of her life. Like sex. He smiled to himself at the image. Wouldn't that be a gas? Better than playing friend and confidant to Gloria's and Bertie's husbands at the bar the other night.

Clasping his hands on the table, he blinked away his thoughts and concentrated on listening to Georgia. None of the past months' incidents had quashed his desire to become a proficient writer.

Later, with an empty coffee cup in his hand, he stood in line behind Mal while she helped herself to coffee and a croissant. "Still mad at me?" he whispered in her ear.

"Quentin! Gee, you made me jump. Don't ever do that when someone's holding a cup of hot coffee."

"Sorry, that was stupid of me, I guess. You're right. I'll never, never do it again. Promise." He put his hands together in mock prayer for forgiveness.

She shot him a look. "You're not being sarcastic, are you, Quentin?"

"No way," he said with a defensive laugh. "I'm trying to get you to be my friend again."

"We talked about that. I told you how it is. And why."

"And I respect that. No dates. Friends don't date, you said. But what's wrong with two friends having a cup of coffee or a meal together?" He folded his arms defiantly, but held his killer smile.

Mal sensed the eyes and ears around them. "Quentin, please. This is not the time or place."

"Okay. Then you tell me where and when."

"Nowhere. Not ever."

Annoyed by her adamant rejection, he snarled his response. "Fine. The hell with you too."

He wormed his way across the room and invited himself into the conversation in progress between Georgia and Anne Bishop. "I don't mean to interrupt," he said, "but I wanted to say if you'd like some help in catching up on what we've covered so far in this class, I have all my notes. I'd be happy to help."

"Well, isn't that nice of you. I might just take you up on that." Anne wished she could tell him they had a common friend, but saw no need to advertise her relationship with Jordan. But she could tell Jordan how impressed she was with his friend.

Chapter Sixty-six

Mal's smile spread like a slice of moonlight. She wished she had a loaded camera on hand to capture the memorable moment. Her mother baking cookies! A sight she feared she'd never see again. Liz was trying to fudge through her grandmother's recipe for S cookies, but that generation rarely bothered to follow rigid recipes. A little of this, a little of that and good judgment was supposed to produce successful results.

Liz looked as though she had showered in flour. She scratched the tickle off her nose with the clean part of her arm and clutched another handful of flour. No matter how she rubbed, she couldn't free her fingers from all the pasty dough mixture.

Mal burst out laughing. "Ma, you look like the Pillsbury Dough Boy! Whatever possessed you to try making Grandma's S cookies?"

Frustrated, Liz threw her sticky hands upward. "God only knows. I should have had my head examined instead. It was your father's fault. He mentioned Grandma's cookies the other day and I remembered how we used to love dunking them in milk. I was feeling pretty good this morning so I decided to try baking a batch." Accepting defeat, she ran her messy hands under the warm water.

Russ wheeled himself into the domestic scene and snickered at the slimy cookies that looked more like fat worms than the prelude to Grandma's delicious, plump cookies. He tried not to laugh. "Honey," he said, "these are a sorry sight. I think the only place those things will get dunked is the garbage."

In response, Liz stuck out her tongue. "It was too dry to form a workable dough, so I kept adding eggs and milk. Then it got too mushy, so I added more flour." She drew a breath and blew out her frustration. "Nothing works. Guess I'll dump the whole mess."

Mal looked over the sorry-looking specimens on the cookie sheet, then at the huge ball of dough in the bowl. Its texture reminded her of elephant skin. "No, Mom. Don't dump it. As long as you made this mess, why don't we separate them into two trays? If we bake them we can taste which are bad and which are awful," she said, enjoying the opportunity to tease her mother. "Then maybe next time you'll come up with a happy medium."

"There won't be a next time." Liz continued to rub her hands under the faucet until her fingers were visible once again, then pointed one in her husband's face. "Next time you get a desire for S cookies, we'll take a ride to Capizzo's Bakery."

The three of them laughed and Mal prodded her mother away from the sink. "Go get cleaned up, Mom. Dad and I will finish up." She concentrated on working the elephant skin dough into S-shaped cookies. Their resemblance to Grandma's was dubious.

Liz pulled the scarf off her head as she walked towards the bathroom. Mal got a better look at the curly clusters of hair that were cropping up on her scalp. Still sparse and by no means attractive, but a welcome sight. Signs of life returning, she thought. Her dad, who had the identical thought, squeezed his daughter's hand and smiled. *She's gonna make it,* his expression conveyed. Mal held her smile and nodded.

While the disastrous cookies baked and Mal and her dad cleaned up, he tried to ease into the subject of Mal's love life. Of course, that was her own business, but he hated to think of her missing Brad and wondered why there was no second date with Quentin. He broached the subject gently, sort of like entering a house through the back door. "So, what's happening in class, Mal? Anything new?"

She gave him an incredulous look. "Are you kidding, Dad? I told you Monday night what a shock we all got when Anne Bishop showed up. What could be newsier than that? That poor woman. I feel so sorry for her and her sons. Bad enough they had to lose their husband and father, but the way he died . . ."

"Does Quentin ever mention how his friend is doing? The husband of the woman in that accident?"

Mal took a peek at the cookies in the oven. The ele-phant-skinned ones looked like they would die from dehydration and the eggy ones looked like they were melting under a hot sun.

"No, never," she answered her father. "We don't get much time for side conversations. We're all thirsting on the need to hone our writing skills. All talk is geared in that direction."

"How about your teacher? How is she doing?"

Mal shrugged. "As well as can be expected, I guess. Georgia and I have become friends and yes, I have talked to her privately. You'd never know it to see her in class, but she's pretty shaken up. Divorce has got to be the pits." Although Mal had told her parents about the breakup of Georgia's marriage, she had omitted the reason. If Georgia had trusted her enough to confide something so personal, she could never betray that trust.

"Whose divorce? What did I miss?" Liz was back, wearing fresh, clean flour-free jeans and a red turtleneck. Her wig remained on her dresser, framed around a styrofoam head.

"Your hair is coming in fast and furious, Mom. And so curly!" she said with forced enthusiasm. Her mom was so happy to see a growth of hair again, she seemed oblivious to the fact that most of her scalp was still barren.

Liz beamed. "Yes, I know. I think I'm going to like the new curly look." She reached to touch one of the new clusters, happy to feel its presence. "So, what were you guys saying about divorce? Were you talking about Georgia, your teacher?"

"Yeah, she's having a rough time. It came as a complete shock to her. Apparently, he doesn't love her anymore and wants out. Plain and simple, after twenty-six years." It wasn't a total lie. Just an omission of truth.

"Such a shame. The whole family suffers in a divorce. But if he doesn't love her . . ." she paused with her musings, then said, "Sometimes couples who *do* love each other break up for stupid reasons. Like pride. And pride doesn't keep your feet warm at night."

"True, Mom. But pride had nothing to do with the collapse of Georgia's marriage."

"I wasn't thinking of Georgia," Liz said.

Mal rolled her eyes and fell silent.

Liz slipped between her husband and daughter to fill the Farberware pot with water. "I want to make some coffee for when those fabulous cookies come out of the oven."

Again, they all laughed in unison, which pleased Mal. Her mother had obviously been trying to put the subject of Brad on the table again, and she was in no mood to beat that dead horse.

No words were exchanged while Mal and her dad cleaned up the last traces of gummy flour from the countertop. The aroma of perking hazelnut coffee filled the air.

"Okay," Liz said, trying again. "So you don't want to talk about Brad. Then let's talk about Quentin. What happened with him? Can you tell us?"

"He seemed pretty nice, friendly enough," Russ said. "Once you get past all that hair."

Liz's lips thinned, her eyes narrowed. "I'm not sure I agree with that. Don't ask me why. Sometimes a person is too nice. It's almost phony." She twisted her mouth and frowned, unable to define her skepticism.

There you go, Mal thought. *Guess I am my mother's daughter.*

"Quentin's okay, I guess," she said. "But all we really have in common is our writing. And *because* of our writing, I thought it best not to get involved with him. If the relationship didn't work out, sitting through the classes with him would be uncomfortable. We're friends—acquaintances, really, and I'd like to leave it at that." *Another lie.* Mal would never categorize as a friend anyone who used "the hell with you too" as his parting words.

The guy had a nasty, almost evil, underlying streak in him. The more she got to know him, the more she saw him as Roberta Bookman's murderer. No one could convince her otherwise. Now all she had to do was prove it.

Chapter Sixty-seven

Misery loves company, they say. Is that why I'm on my way to Jill's house again? Brad asked himself. But this time, on a weeknight, it was just a casual, impromptu date. Al Pacino's latest film had come up for discussion at the office, both wanted to see it, and neither one wanted to go alone. Then maybe a stop at The Muffin Man's for coffee and conversation. After that, he'd drop her off, watch her walk safely into her building, and drive off. That's how he had it planned out in his mind. Now if only he could get his mind and body to agree.

She was waiting in the lobby of her building when he drove up, watching for him through the glass doors. That fantastic Julia Roberts smile lit up her face when she spotted him. Like Brad, Jill was casually dressed in jeans, sneakers and a hooded down jacket.

"You look good in those jeans," he said when she buckled up. "Do you realize we've worked together for what . . . three years? And we've never seen each other in these everyday clothes."

"Yeah, well, casual Friday can't get this casual in our office. 'Casual, but in good taste,' Mooney says. 'No jeans, no sneakers.' I pay big bucks for my designer jeans. They *are* in good taste."

Brad laughed with her. He enjoyed her extroverted personality. If he let her, she could entertain him for hours if she didn't drive him crazy first. She could bounce from story to story without missing a beat, but she managed to hold his interest with her humorous delivery. She was also well read, as exhibited at work, and could jump into any discussion on world events with knowledgeable, intelligent facts. Her face and body scored just as high.

I should have been a salesman, Brad thought. Any guy who could actually sell himself with his own snow job has to be doing something right.

He shot her a sideways smile and let his eyes lock with hers for one brief moment. His look was meant to convey *I enjoy your company and yes, I'd love to, but I won't*. At least that's what had been floating through his mind, but Jill could easily have interpreted it differently.

Unsaid words and memories of their last date, its intimacy and ultimate humiliation, hung between them like a smoky curtain. Although they had cut through it somewhat soon after, it wasn't easy to pretend it never happened. But here they were, still trying.

A whipping wind took their breath away as they left the theater. Brad laced his fingers with hers to cross the busy street to the parking lot. They ran to the car and laughed with relief when they slammed the doors shut. Brad rubbed his hands and blew into them while they waited for the car to heat up and defrost. "That Pacino is one hell of an actor," Brad said when he found his voice. "He never disappoints me."

Jill kept gloved hands over her icy cold face. "I don't always like the roles he plays, but whatever it is, he does damn well."

"That's for sure. No one would disagree with that, but even if he weren't such a great actor, I'd still love just looking at him. He has the most piercing, sexy eyes. They sort of drill right through you."

"Through you, not through me," he said with a laugh.

She punched his arm playfully. "You know what I mean, wise guy."

"Are we still going for coffee?" Jill asked, her tone hesitant, almost timid.

"The Muffin Man. That was your suggestion originally, and that's fine with me if it's still okay with you." He gave her a questioning glance. "Did you change your mind?"

Jill kept her eyes focused straight ahead, as though more interested in the surrounding sights than their conversation. "No, that'll be fine, I guess. It's just that it's so darn bitter cold, I hate getting in and out of the car again."

"Oh, so are you saying you'd rather skip it and go straight home?"

She parted her lips to answer, but pulled the words back.

"What?" he said, his gaze curious.

"No, nothing. I was just thinking about the leftover lemon meringue pie going to waste in my refrigerator. I ate at my parents' last night, and my mother made one, knowing it's my favorite. The two of them are always watching their diets and insisted that I take the rest home. Like I want to get fat."

"I doubt you'll let that happen," Brad said, remembering the tight, perfectly proportioned body buried under the down parka.

"Well, if you like lemon meringue pie and you'd like to come up, you're welcome. We can make it quick."

Make what quick? Brad thought. The throbbing in his groin sent words to his mouth. "I *love* lemon meringue pie," he said.

* * *

Brad poured the coffee into two large mugs that Jill had set on the coffee table in her den. She came in seconds later with two slices of the loaded-with-calories-but lick-your-lips delicious pie. A huge piece for Brad and a sliver for herself.

"Geez!" His eyes widened when she put it in front of him. "I'll have to run an extra mile in the morning, but I can't pass it up."

They fell into easy, light conversation with him seated on the sofa, and she on the club chair. "Do you mind if I put the news on, Brad? I want to see what's happening with the Iraq situation. Actually, I don't *want* to see it, but it's compelling, to say the least."

Brad was surprised by her friendly, yet aloof behavior. He felt like a guest she was politely entertaining for the first time. "No, definitely. I'd like to see it too. I wouldn't want to be in the shoes of our president now. He's literally carrying the weight of the world on his shoulders."

They watched and discussed the news together and sat through Jay Leno's monologue to shade from their minds thoughts of the looming war. When the commercial break came, Jill released an exaggerated yawn. "Well, it's almost midnight, Brad. Cinderella needs her beauty sleep. Do you mind?"

Brad jumped to his feet. "No, of course not. It *is* late." He grabbed his jacket from the wrought-iron railing where he had thrown it and slipped it on." Well, thanks for a very pleasant evening," he said with an edge of formality. "Guess I'll see you in the morning."

He couldn't quite identify his feelings when he left her. Relief for avoiding what could have been another uncomfortable scene was strangely mixed with disappointment. But at least his throbbing groin had calmed down.

If he could have seen the complacent grin on Jill's face as she watched him walk to his car, he would have known she had definite plans to fire that storm up again. This time she'd play her cards differently and pull her ace in the hole when the pot is sweetest.

Chapter Sixty-eight

Anne waited until her sons stormed out of the house, late as usual, making a mad dash for the bus. She laughed and shook her head as they ran across the street. No matter how often she tried to rush them through their routine, they were hopelessly slow in the mornings, then had to move their behinds at fast forward speed in order to catch their bus.

She dumped the sticky remains of their waffles into the garbage and hurried through her kitchen cleanup. Today she intended to complete the depressing task of boxing and delivering all of Wayne's clothes to the church's thrift shop. She had already showered and dressed so she could leave the house as soon as the job was done, rather than reminisce through painful memories and hang around in her pajamas all day, drowned in depression. No more. Enough. She braced herself to accomplish the task without allowing her emotions to sweep in and swallow her up again.

And next week, she'd begin her search for part-time work. If she could find something that would allow her to be home before the boys, that would be perfect. Of course, when summertime rolled around, working would be a problem. Well, I'll deal with that problem when the time comes, she told herself.

Anne actually smiled at her image in the bedroom mirror when she got through every article of clothing in the closet without shedding a single tear. In some pockets, she had found insignificant items of everyday life; theater ticket stubs, gas receipts and even half of a Hershey bar long forgotten.

The dresser drawers were next. She yanked a fresh garbage bag off the roll for this job. Underwear and socks would have to go out with the trash. When she scooped out the contents of the first drawer, a yellow piece of paper fell on the floor. A receipt from a jewelry store across town, near his office. Her heart began to hammer in her chest.

The ink on the receipt copy was faint, but legible. On September 15th, two weeks before Wayne died, he had left a fifty-dollar deposit on a four hundred dollar gold locket. Anne's mouth went dry. She and Wayne were never that extravagant on their gifts to each other. They both much preferred to throw any extra money into their vacation fund. Besides, her birthday was in April and their anniversary in June. It couldn't possibly have been bought for her. Her insides numbed at the revelation. Had it been intended for Gloria Hammer? Had she really been an idiotic naïve fool all these years? Fury consumed her at the thought. She wished she could reach Jordan now to ask him Gloria's date of birth, but knew that would have to wait until tonight. And even if Gloria's birthday had been upcoming, that wouldn't prove anything conclusively. Men involved in illicit affairs don't necessarily wait for a special occasion to shower gifts on a woman. That's a pattern customarily reserved for their wives.

The top of the receipt had a barely visible scribbled notation, part of which had been ripped off where it missed the perforation. She smoothed out the paper and tried to decipher the illegible writing. *Inscription to be called in* is what she finally figured out. So clear and simple once you knew it.

Her shaky fingers reached for the phone to punch out the number of Jewels by Frederick, but she hit the off button instead. With her stomach in knots and her hand still trembling, she put on her jacket, grabbed her bag and car keys and headed out. The morning rush was over. At this time of day, she thought, it shouldn't take more than twenty minutes to get there.

*   *   *

It was still too early when she pulled into one of the spaces in the strip mall. A sign on the door displayed the store's hours, indicating a 10:00 a.m. opening. Fifteen minutes more. She turned, intending to wait in her car until the proprietor showed up, but paused when she saw a well-dressed man in a Burberry raincoat walking in her direction. When he noticed her waiting and flashed an apologetic smile, she knew he had to be the owner, Mr. Frederick Stone.

She agreed to allow him ten minutes. In the bagel shop next door, she sipped her third cup of coffee for the day until the jeweler was ready for business. At 10:05 he welcomed her with a broad smile, anticipating his first sale of the day. Anne cleared her throat and gave serious thought to turning around and forgetting the whole idea. Better to live your life with doubt than to uncover proof positive that your made-in-heaven marriage was one big lie.

But Mr. Frederick Stone stood there, hands clasped on his display case, still smiling. "Well now, I'm sorry you had to wait. How can I help you?"

"My name is Anne Bishop," she began, then paused. When no name recognition appeared on his face, she continued. "I found this receipt for a locket my husband had ordered. He's deceased several months now, but I wanted to know if he ever picked it up. The receipt doesn't indicate a final transaction, but knowing my husband, he might have forgotten to bring his receipt."

Now recognition crossed his face, wiping away his cheerful, businesslike smile. "Oh, Mrs. Bishop, I'm so sorry. I didn't recognize the name at first, but now I remember your husband. Such a nice young man. I was shocked when I read about his death in the newspaper."

Anne saw a look of discomfort taking shape and wanted to spare him and herself further embarrassment by avoiding any discussion of Wayne's fatal accident. "Did my husband ever pick up this locket?" she asked again. "And was it ever inscribed?"

Mr. Stone's lips tightened. He drew a breath, excused himself and came back a few moments later with a small jewelry box. "Mrs. Bishop, maybe I should have called you about this. I did a lot of soul-searching, but after reading about the nature of his accident—"

"—you decided to let sleeping dogs lie, assuming the locket might have been bought for the woman he died with and not his wife, correct?"

Grim-lipped, he nodded.

"May I see it?"

Wordless, he opened the box and handed her the locket.

Her stomach turned over and sent a wave of numbing weakness through her. She was afraid to look, but knew she must. *10-5 Love you, Buttercup,* the inscription said. A flood of tears surfaced, but she fought them away. Anne pulled out her checkbook, wrote out a check for the balance due, and beamed when she looked up. "Mr. Stone, I'm sure you've been curious about this. Let me put the mystery to rest. This locket was definitely purchased for me. My husband did not die with that woman the way the newspapers told it. And I'm not going to stop probing until I get to the truth." She walked out the door feeling immeasurable relief.

10-5 Love you, Buttercup. She couldn't believe it. This had to be the sweetest, most romantic thing Wayne had ever done. The first time he had called her *Buttercup* was the night he proposed, on October 5th, and had used it often after then, during their most intimate moments.

Before she turned the key in the ignition, she raised her eyes to heaven and whispered aloud, "Thank you, God." This time she didn't fight the tears that filled her eyes. Happy tears were always welcome.

Chapter Sixty-nine

Mal sat in the late night quiet of her living room with a mug of honey-lemon tea. She bit into her peanut butter rice cake, which was no match for the chocolate-covered donut she craved. The crunching sound between her teeth overpowered the smooth and easy sound of Kenny G's CD and broke her concentration, but she chewed on.

A fresh page on her steno pad stared back at her, thirsting for words. Initially, she had been pleased with her ability to create conflict, but now that it was wind-down time and she needed solutions to the problems she created, her mind was a total blank. Besides, she couldn't shake the more troublesome thoughts that kept snaking through her head. Right there in the forefront was Quentin Kingsley, an arrogant, promising actor, wannabe writer and womanizer with an inflated ego. But murderer? Heaven only knows. Sometimes she felt certain her instincts were correct, and during other more passive moods, she chalked it up to paranoia or, at the very least, a vivid imagination.

The Saturday class would have to go, she decided. Georgia's Monday night class was larger, and with Georgia at the helm, much more informative. Although the open exchange of ideas at the Saturday class had some positive impact as well, with Quentin leading it, she couldn't avoid eye contact.

She had become obsessive about Quentin's guilt in Bertie Bookman's murder. It's amazing, she thought, how much is revealed about a person in one brief moment. A few spoken words, one snarled expression, can expose a person's true personality like a neon sign. Even Quentin's smile, which Mal first thought to be loaded with sex appeal, could no longer mask who he really was. But none of those character flaws necessarily spelled out murderer. No matter how she tried to sort it out, she had no answers.

She toyed with the idea of confronting him with what he had said New Year's Eve night. Just ask him point blank what he meant when he babbled on about the slippers. But that would be flirting with danger, maybe even death. Suppose, just suppose, her suspicions were correct? No, she wasn't like those death-defying women you read about in mystery novels, the ones who perform superhuman feats that raise the reader's brow in disbelief.

But Georgia was right. If she went to the police they would cast her aside like yesterday's newspapers. And with Quentin, she had slammed the door shut on their friendly relationship the last time they spoke, so how the heck was she supposed to pursue her amateur investigation and push this insanity out of her head?

God must have heard her because her cell phone rang. The clock on the mantle said 10:20, a little late for social calls. She ran back to her room to answer it, a bit apprehensive.

"Mal, it's me, Georgia. I'm sorry for calling so late. That's why I used your cell. I didn't want to disturb your parents. Are they sleeping?"

"No, I wanted to write in the living room tonight so I could listen to a few CDs. Thought I could stimulate my dormant mind with mood music. Not that it worked. But my parents went in their bedroom anyway to watch a movie. What's up? Is something wrong?"

She heaved a sigh. "Well, I don't even want to get into the subject of what's been going on in my family. It's been hell. The kids try to avoid talking about him, and I do the same, like he never existed. They're trying to protect me, and I try to protect them. But we're not helping each other by clamming up and sweeping it under the rug."

"That's for sure, Georgia. Maybe you should take the upper hand, round them up, or take one at a time and have a good heart to heart. Let them cry, let them scream, but everyone has to pour it out, no matter how many sessions it takes. What about professional help?"

"I skirted that subject, but they're not buying yet."

"And you?"

"I'm thinking about it. But in some ways, Mal, I'm better off now than before. I was trapped in a dead marriage, blaming myself for losing my husband's interest. Now that it's out in the open, I feel relieved. I know now I wasn't at fault, so I have a more positive attitude about myself and my future. You know what I mean?"

"Absolutely. Now's the time to say: *This is the first day of the rest of my life.*"

"Exactly. That's exactly how I feel. Like I was reborn. Anyway, how did we get into this again? That's not why I called you." She paused, then laughed. "You have me just as crazy as you are, Mal. I can't stop thinking about Quentin. And to tell you the truth, I'm beginning to see him through your eyes too."

"I thought we already agreed on that," Mal said with the same touch of humor.

"We did. But something else has been bugging me. I won't be able to sleep tonight unless we toss it around."

"Shoot. I'm all ears."

Georgia cleared her throat. "Okay, here goes. Ever since Anne Bishop joined our class, I can't stop thinking about that tragic accident and the disgrace she had to deal with on top of losing her husband."

Only someone as unselfish as Georgia would worry about someone else's problems when she had monumental problems of her own, Mal thought. Maybe that's what helps her deal with it. Whatever the motivation, she knew her friend would be okay. That confidence put a smile on her face.

"I don't mean to sound insensitive, Georgia, but we drained that story dry when it first happened. Anne took a step in the right direction by joining our class. Once a person starts making moves to pull out of depression, half the battle is won. But Georgia, get back to what you were saying. What keeps bugging you?"

"I'm beginning to feel like Jessica Fletcher in *Murder, She Wrote,* but doesn't it seem too coincidental that Bertie Bookman's death occurred so soon after that accident? And both she and Gloria Hammer knew each other?"

"The police have already alluded to that, according to the newspapers. It's crossed my mind too, but where the heck would Wayne Bishop fit in?"

"That's where I get stuck in neutral. Other than what I've heard myself in our class discussions, has Quentin ever discussed anything else about that accident?"

Mal paused to search her memory once again. "Nothing, really. Just the usual sympathetic remarks about what a horrible tragedy it was, et cetera, et cetera."

"Okay. Let's forget Wayne Bishop for now," Georgia said. "We'll concentrate on the two women. What or *who* did they have in common?"

"Well, that's obvious enough. The theater's the *what,* anyone involved in that theater could be the *who.*"

"And you say Quentin is on top of that list." Georgia presented it as an accepted fact, not a question.

"Yes. Maybe because he's the only one I know, but what I *do* know, I don't like."

268

"Me too. Particularly since the slipper remark. We need to get him talking about it again. Maybe we can trip him up."

"That won't be easy. He's a little mad at me for giving him the brush-off. To get rid of him once and for all, I told him I'm still hurting for Brad."

Georgia fell silent a moment, then said, "And you are, aren't you?"

"Sort of. But I'm getting better."

"Okay. We won't go into it now, unless you want to. Let's try to figure out how we can get our loquacious, gregarious Quentin to open up again about those three deaths."

"There's only one solution," Mal said with a sigh. "I'm going to eat humble pie and put myself in his good graces again."

Georgia's voice came through cloaked with alarm and caution. "Mal, that's a bad idea. If we're barking up the right tree, Quentin Kingsley doesn't have good graces."

Chapter Seventy

The news came two weeks before *Crush* was due to close at the Emily Forrester Theater. For the past month, the entire cast had been apprehensive awaiting word about the fate of the play. Almost all the reviews during its run in Brockford had been favorable, but small town success did not automatically skyrocket a production to the Broadway stage.

Now, after a Friday night performance, Jordan had them all gathered on stage, ready to make his announcement. He scanned the sea of anxious faces and when Deirdre's hopeful gaze met his, he realized he should have handled this differently. He should have told her the bad news first, privately. Now he was about to give her the most exciting, thrilling moment of her life, send her spirits soaring to unparalleled heights, only to shoot her down soon after. He hated himself for the oversight. If he hadn't been so wrapped in myriad problems, business and personal, he could have spared her. All eyes were on him, waiting for him to speak.

Jordan allowed his face to break into a slow smile, then simply said, "We open at the Lionel Reiss Theater September 19th."

The cheers were deafening. Everyone came to him with hugs and handshakes, then embraced each other. A lump shot up in his throat when Deirdre put her arms around him and kissed him on the cheek. "I *knew* you could do it," she said.

"Deirdre, I'd like to talk to you before you go home tonight, okay?"

"Sure. No problem," she said, still euphoric. "Quentin too?" she asked, assuming it had something to do with changes or cuts in their dance routines.

"No, just you," he said, unable to meet her gaze.

A troubled look invaded her beautiful face. "Why? Is something wrong?"

Jordan raised a finger to his lip, silencing further discussion. "It's personal," he said.

*   *   *

He sat on a wooden swivel chair in the theater's Green Room, which served as a lounge for cast and crew. He had a pile of paperwork he could have gone through while he waited, but never bothered to open his attaché case. Tonight he didn't have the patience. Especially not now, while he waited for Deirdre. He dreaded this scene. Deirdre didn't deserve this bad break. She was talented, reliable and cooperative. A pleasure to work with and a pleasure to look at. But those attributes were not enough to save her. He wished he could have told Douglas Banion, the backer who wanted her out, where he could shove his money, but the pleasure of that satisfaction would have caused the ax to fall on the entire company.

"Close the door behind you, Deirdre, please," was all Jordan said when she walked in, but no further words were necessary. Once their eyes met, she knew. Jordan took one look at that fright—that shock reflected in her eyes—and knew his message had already sunk in. He steepled his fingers over his nose and avoided her gaze.

She hovered over him, refusing the chair he offered, her eyes on fire. "Tell me this is not what I'm thinking. Tell me, Jordan!"

He stood up and reached for her hands. "I'm sorry, Deirdre. You have no idea how I fought for you."

"Why?" A steady stream of tears fell on her cheeks. "The reviews were great, the audiences loved me. What did I do wrong?"

He wanted to level with her, say something like, *you didn't sleep with the right person,* but why pour salt on her wound. Instead, he squared her shoulders and lifted her chin with one finger. "Deirdre, you did nothing wrong. Absolutely nothing. Someone else just stuck a foot in the door and threw in a stronger hook."

She plopped herself down in the leather chair and sobbed, but with barely a sound. She just sat staring through him, as though in shock. "Who's the bastard that gave me the boot? And who's replacing me?"

Jordan's arms were folded across his chest. He looked down at her, overwhelmed with sympathy, but powerless to help. "Would it really make a difference if I told you? You're so upset now. You'll find out soon enough."

Her anger escalated again. "Yes, it would make a difference. I need to know who to hate."

Jordan sighed, then said, "Okay. It's Douglas Banion and he's bringing in Melissa Lamont."

Deirdre shot out of the chair. "That bastard is replacing me with that fat-assed slob? She has no talent whatsoever!"

"Apparently, Mr. Banion thinks she's good at something." He pulled a business card out of his jacket pocket and handed it to her. "Look, do yourself a favor. Call this guy. He's a new agent who's building a nice clientele. He's not on overload yet and he might be able to handle you. I already spoke to him."

Deirdre fingered the card and gave him a piercing look fraught with skepticism. "Throwing me a crumb, Jordan?"

He shrugged. "Just trying to help."

The sincerity in his voice melted her anger. She forced a smile, brushed a faint kiss on his cheek. "I know you are, Jordan. I'm sure if you could have avoided this, you would have."

He only nodded.

She held the card between two fingers and snapped at it with her thumb. "Who knows? Maybe with this little thing, I'll make Douglas Banion live to regret giving me the ax. I'm sure as hell gonna try."

Chapter Seventy-one

Anne sat at her kitchen table, lost in thought. The sun hadn't even come up yet on this Saturday morning, but she hadn't been able to stay in bed. Before, all she ever wanted to do was sleep, now anxiety kept her awake. But she wasn't about to complain. She hadn't felt this charged up and energetic since before Wayne died. First it was her decision to join Georgia's writing class, then the discovery of her treasured locket. Together, those happenings became the catalyst to unleash her from depression's cold and heavy chains.

She stood up with her coffee mug and stared out at the early morning winter scene. Streaks of golden-hued orange fanned upward, staining the blue sky. Like God's introduction to his magnificent morning sun, Anne thought. And suddenly, there it was, peeking on the horizon, about to rise in all its glory.

Just as suddenly, the words began to take shape. She sat back down at the table, picked up her pen. Monday night would be her first class as a full-fledged paying member. Georgia had told her to write a few pages on anything she wished, preferably something positive. There it was, all along, staring her in the face, but she hadn't seen it. With fingers that couldn't move fast enough to catch all her tumbling thoughts and words, she began her first assignment.

Depression is a dark, heavy blanket that can bury you alive. Recently, two incidents in my life enabled

me to lift that ugly blanket. This morn-
ing I watched the sun rise and realized
that's how I feel now, uplifted...

A rush of adrenaline pushed Anne to complete writing her piece in less than an hour. With a fresh cup of coffee, she moved to the computer to polish it up for presentation at class. When she reread it, she realized she had emptied her heart.

Later, while the boys were still asleep and would most likely stay asleep for most of the morning, she showered, dressed in a brand-new outfit, then blow-dried her hair. Satisfied with the results of the new stylish cut she had treated herself to this past week, she picked at it with her fingertips, pleased with her new image.

She wished she were meeting Jordan today. A touch of sadness clouded her good mood. How long could they pretend they were nothing more than friends with a common goal? Neither one was fooling the other, but neither one whispered the words they each held in their heart. Once those words were spoken, they would have to deal with them. Jordan was his own person; no children, no parents or siblings to cling to his conscience. Perhaps he'd be ready for an intimate relationship, but Anne shivered at the thought. How could she admit to such feelings for another man, a stranger to her family, only four months after the death of a husband who gave her nothing but love?

So friends they'd be for as long as they could keep their feelings at bay, and as long as they keep meeting in public places that offered no opportunity to succumb to moments of weakness. She wouldn't see him until Tuesday, but their late night phone conversations would sustain her until then.

*   *   *

By dinnertime Monday, Anne was so energetic, she moved around her kitchen as though her legs were motorized. Tonight she had her class and tomorrow morning she'd see Jordan again. They were trying a new coffee shop that opened up not far from the Blue Ridge Diner, where they had been meeting twice a week. For a few moments, she allowed herself to fantasize. She dreamed of the warmth of his arms around her, the feel of his breath on her face, his lips on her cheek, on her mouth . . .

She shook her head vigorously, as though it were being attacked by unknown demons. *"No. Stop. Don't!"* she cried aloud. Her hands crossed her chest as if to lock in the emotions that filled her body with physical desire and her mind with the heart-wrenching, stinging pain of guilt.

A few deep breaths and slow exhalations brought her back in control again, but she knew, no matter how she tried to suppress the thoughts, in her heart she knew she was already in love with Jordan. Those proverbial floodgates could hold back the tide only so long before they burst.

*　　*　　*

At class, when Anne's turn finally came up, she prefaced her reading with a short comment. "When I arrived here tonight, I had asked Georgia if I could read last. Now I realize that was a dumb mistake. I see I have some tough acts to follow." In unison, the class waved away her discomfort and threw out a medley of encouraging words.

When she finished, a hush fell over the class. Anne felt as if her heart had plunged down to her stomach. Then came showers of praise. Her face relaxed and burst into a radiant smile.

At the break, Mal was quick to approach her. "Anne, you brought tears to our eyes with that piece. It was really something special."

"Thanks, Mal. Actually, I hadn't intended to dig down that deeply when I started writing, but once I did, I felt such a sense of relief."

"Unburdened. Yes, I know the feeling." Mal darted her eyes to be sure no one was close enough to eavesdrop, then whispered, "Listen, Anne, would you mind if I called you at home? Georgia and I would like to talk to you about something we can't get into here."

Anne responded with a quizzical look, but noting Mal's troubled expression, she simply said, "Sure. Georgia has my number."

*   *   *

The next morning, Anne greeted Jordan with her sunniest smile. "What a great job they did with this place," she said looking it over. "They gave it a real cozy charm with these Early American touches."

Jordan pulled out a captain's chair for her at their window table. Clean, calico ruffled curtains framed the windows, tied back with bows. "Well, don't you look happy this morning," he said. "It's a pleasure to see you like this— not that seeing you isn't always a pleasure."

"Oh, Jordan, I have so much to tell you. I couldn't wait to get here. Last night, of all nights, my son Adam was still awake at the computer when I got home, so I never got the chance to call you."

He gave an understanding nod and a slight sigh of relief. "I *was* disappointed when I didn't hear from you, but I figured—or I *hoped,* I should say—that you didn't have the privacy to call. And I know you don't want me to call you anymore when the boys are home."

The smile left her face for a moment. "I'm sorry, Jordan, but that's too risky."

His hand went up. "No apology necessary. I understand perfectly. So tell me what you're bursting to tell me. I assume you liked your writing class?"

"Oh, Jordan, I could kiss you for recommending that class!"

He dipped his head and smiled. She blushed.

"Oh, stop," she said playfully. "You know what I mean. In all these months, last night was the best medicine for depression—except for our friendship, of course . . ." Her voice ran off like a racing train, filling him in on every detail from the moment she walked in until the moment she left. She only reluctantly paused for air when the waiter came for their food orders. Even though it was near noon, she stuck to her usual scrambled eggs, with ham and toast.

During the whole time, Jordan looked at her, laughed at her bubbly enthusiasm. He loved everything about her and wished he could tell her. Instead, he reached for her hand, but she was so animated, she needed it to emphasize and punctuate her story.

"So, what did you think of my friend, Quentin?" he asked when he could get a word in.

"Oh, yes. I almost forgot about him. He seemed very friendly. Even offered to help me. Wants to be a playwright someday." She made a face that told him how impressed she was.

"Yes, I know. Quentin's an ambitious guy with a good head on his shoulders. He might just make it—" Jordan stopped short. Anne's happy face took a sudden switch to pure shock. Her eyes were fixed in the direction of the entrance.

"I knew this would happen to us sooner or later," she said.

Jordan didn't want to turn to look, but it was obvious she had seen someone she knew. "Who is it, Anne?"

"Georgia Pappas, my teacher, with another woman."

"Oh, God," he said, knowing how this would embarrass her and make her feel threatened.

Anne, to Jordan's surprise, threw her shoulders back and handled it differently. She stood up and greeted her teacher since the waiter was leading them to a table near them anyway. "Georgia, what are you doing here? What a coincidence!" Without the slightest hesitation, she introduced Jordan as her "good friend," and Georgia introduced her companion as Lisa Roman, a fellow teacher.

"We're on a short lunch break and decided to check this place out. Looks great, doesn't it? Hope the food is good."

"Me too, because I love the atmosphere. I was just chewing Jordan's ears off about how much I enjoyed your class last night."

"Good for you, Anne. We're all glad to have you. Don't mean to be rude, but we're real tight on time."

Anne chased them off with a hand wave. "Go. Enjoy."

Jordan arched a brow. "I'm proud of you. You handled that very well. I thought you'd be devastated to have someone you know see us together."

"I was at first, but I get so damned tired of living my life for other people. I want to be selfish. I don't care anymore."

He reached across and sneaked a pinch at her cheek. "That's the spirit I like to hear. Now I'm *real* proud of you."

A troublesome frown creased her face. "Georgia's appearance interrupted my story. I didn't get to the end. I want to see what you make of this." She leaned closer, her elbows on the table. "This woman, Mal Triana—she's the youngest of the women there—she approached me during the coffee break. She asked if she could call me; said she and Georgia wanted to speak to me about something that was directly connected to what I had written. Jordan, I wrote about Wayne's death, about the smear in the newspapers that I never believed, and about how I found the locket. What do you think they could possibly want?"

Jordan matched her perplexed look. "Can't figure that one at all, but I'm just as anxious to find out. When did she say she'd call?"

"She didn't, but I'm considering calling her first. I can always say the curiosity was killing me. Which it is."

"Good idea. And call me first chance you get."

"Naturally."

Chapter Seventy-two

Mal and Georgia convinced Anne to meet with them at Georgia's house despite the fact that they hadn't offered even a hint of the reason for the meeting. But Anne, although afraid of what might be disclosed, felt compelled to go, knowing that it had some connection to Wayne's death.

After the initial amenities, all three women sat in the comfort of Georgia's living room, where she poured each of them a glass of white wine. Anne sat in one of the club chairs, Georgia and Mal shared the sofa. Flames crackled and glowed in the fireplace, but neither the wine nor the fire alleviated the strained moments that passed among them.

Georgia broke the silence. "Look, Anne, I'm sorry we had to keep you in the dark about this, but once we explain, you'll understand. Monday night, after you poured your heart out about the facts surrounding your husband's death, we felt we had to try to help you somehow since the police have apparently concluded their investigation."

Anne arched a skeptical brow and forced a polite smile. "Forgive me, but how do the two of you intend to help? Do you know something the police or I don't know?"

Mal threw out her hands and sighed. "We don't have anything more than a hunch to go on, but that little hunch has been snowballing. We don't mean to get your hopes up. This may all be a huge misconception on my part." She shot Georgia an apologetic look, then said, "I'm afraid I dragged Georgia into this by convincing her to look at the facts through my eyes."

"Stop beating up on yourself, Mal," Georgia said. "If I didn't think your suspicions had merit, you couldn't convince me if you stood on your head."

Anne stood up. "I wish you'd both tell me what this is all about. I don't know whether to be frightened or optimistic."

"You're absolutely right, Anne." Georgia took a slow sip of her wine, smoothed out the imaginary wrinkles on her slacks, then continued. "First, we should tell you that we're waiting for two other visitors who should be here momentarily. I'm sorry to spring this on you without warning, but our decision to contact these two gentlemen was a last-minute thing."

Anne sat up straight, tensed by the thought of Jordan's possible appearance. "Who?" she asked.

"Initially we had intended to speak only with you, but to be honest, after seeing you Tuesday morning with Jordan Hammer, we felt comfortable enough to contact him too."

"And the other gentleman?"

"Alan Bookman."

It took a second for the name to register, but Anne's hand went to her mouth. "Oh, my God! What's going on?"

Georgia threw Mal a look that silently conveyed *I hope we know what we're doing,* then said, "Ball's in your court, Mal."

Similar to Georgia's nervous gesture, Mal chose picking at nonexistent lint on the sleeve of her sweater. Finally, she opened her mouth to speak the explanatory words she had practiced, but was literally saved by the bell.

Alan Bookman wore the face of a man angered by this ludicrous invitation which he too felt compelled to accept. Although she had given her name, this woman was a total stranger who only alluded to the fact that she could possibly shed light on the identity of his wife's murderer. For all he knew, she could have been the killer herself. But the urgency in her voice and his obsessive desire for digging out the truth sent him out of his house, cursing and mumbling to himself during the entire car ride. A sense of foreboding overcame him, not knowing what he would be walking into.

Anne, still stunned to hear that Jordan would show up unexpectedly, and shocked to find herself looking up at the man whose wife had been brutally *murdered,* was rendered silent. The hostile look Alan Bookman wore when he entered the room quickly dissipated when he was introduced to her. An empathetic nod was their only exchange when Georgia went through the formality of introductions.

For Georgia, he resumed the attitude he came in with. "I have to tell you, your phone call had me very upset. I almost didn't come."

Heeding the this-better-be-important warning in his tone, Mal jumped in. "Mr. Bookman, believe me, neither of us wants to upset you, Anne Bishop or Jordan Hammer. I hope and pray something positive comes of this, but if we can all be patient until—" She was about to say until Jordan Hammer gets here when she saw headlights turn into the driveway. All heads turned in that direction.

Jordan and Anne locked eyes when he came in. "Why didn't you tell me you got this call too?" she asked, then waved her question away. Of course, he couldn't tell her. Since the night her son Keith got too inquisitive about her late night incoming call, they had agreed that she would make nightly calls, and only if the opportunity presented itself.

Alan pumped Jordan's hand, somewhat relieved to see a familiar and friendly face. "You know what the hell's going on here, Jordie?"

Jordan shrugged. All eyes were then riveted on Mal, who was now standing, pacing slowly, arms folded across her chest. "Mr. Hammer, you and Mr. Bookman might be in the best position to help us out of this maze."

"Please, I'm sure we can all dispense with the formalities, considering the nature of what brings us together. *Jordan* will be fine."

Alan merely nodded his acquiescence.

Mal felt like a nervous, straight-out-of-law-school attorney stumbling through her first summation. "Please don't jump out of your seats to tell me I'm a complete lunatic when I say this, but I've had a strong, nagging suspicion that someone known to both you gentlemen was responsible for the tragic deaths of your wives, and probably your husband too," she said, turning to Anne.

All eyes widened, but no one spoke. Georgia took this opportunity to busy herself with pouring wine for both men. She handed each a glass, then sat quietly to watch the drama unfold.

Mal scanned the three anxious faces, then blurted it out. "Okay. It's Quentin Kingsley." She paused to let the shock and disbelief sink in and come to rest. "I know it sounds insane," she continued, "but please bear with me. Let me explain why I suspect him and why I decided to turn to all of you rather than the police."

No one raised any objection, which fueled Mal's courage. With rapt attention they waited to hear her theory.

"My first impression of Quentin was that he was an extroverted kind of guy. Sociable, confident, enthusiastic about his goals in life and willing to work hard to realize all his dreams."

"Can't fault him for that," Jordan said, still unable to swallow this absurd accusation.

Mal fanned her fingers in a let-me-go-on gesture. "Right. And I don't," she said. "But through our writing, we became friends with a common goal; to be successful writers, of course. Quentin, however, expressed the same burning desires to succeed in his acting career." Anticipating a defensive remark from Jordan, she turned to him. "And yes, I agree drive and ambition is a commendable attribute, but sometimes it can obsess a person and blind his ability to distinguish right from wrong."

Now a cynical-faced Alan cut in. "Excuse me, I don't mean to sound condescending, but aren't you being too analytical for someone with no background in that field?"

Mal rolled her eyes upward. She drew a breath. "Maybe so, Mr. Bookman—"

"*Alan*'s okay."

"Yes, Alan," she acknowledged and went on, "but I'm only trying to lay a foundation here so that my theory may sound more credible. However amateurish it may sound, please keep in mind that our motives are good. We brought you all together to hear us out and maybe pick your brains for anything that might help." She raised her hands as if to concede defeat. "Listen, I'd be just as pleased to find Quentin innocent. There's a part of him I like. But I'll never rest until I find out, one way or the other."

Georgia, noticing Mal's discomfort, thought she might need a break. "Do you want me to continue, Mal?"

Mal waved her off, forced a laugh. "No, it's okay. I'm on a roll. Besides, I'm the one who started this, so I should finish it." Her gaze fell on Alan again. "Alan, let me jump ahead to the crux of what's been troubling me. I accepted a date with Quentin for New Year's Eve. He brought me to a house party. When he heard the hosts had prearranged car service for anyone who might want to over-indulge, he took full advantage. Although I was repulsed by his inebriated state and paid little attention to his nonsensical ramblings, a couple of his comments shot through me and stuck here." She tapped her temple, then paused and sat down on the sofa again.

The two men were seated opposite her next to Anne, Jordan in the second club chair and Alan in a rocker. She glanced at the anticipation in their faces, then focused on Alan once again. "Alan, I can't quote him verbatim, but what I *think* he said was, *'I'm the prince of the magic slippers.'*

"Then he mumbled something that sounded like *'friggin toes'* or *'frozen toes.'* That part I can't remember exactly."

"No one spoke for a minute. Mal watched their expressions change. Then, "Oh, my God," from Anne. "Are you sure?" from Jordan.

Alan Bookman shot out of his chair. "And you didn't tell this to the police?"

"I agonized over that one. But then I decided not to. What if I were wrong? What if those words had nothing whatsoever to do with your wife's murder? How could I do that to someone who might be totally innocent? It could ruin Quentin."

Georgia cut in. "Mal thought maybe we could make a concerted effort to sort through the facts and hopefully come up with something concrete to present to the police."

"And I'm here because I know Quentin well, I guess," Jordan said. "Why Anne, though?"

"No, Jordan, that's only part of the reason you're here. The real reason you're here—and Anne too—is because like Anne, I don't believe the investigation of the accident that claimed the lives of your spouses should have been closed. I have this feeling I can't shake that Quentin is responsible for that too."

Incredulous, unable to digest these insinuations about his friend, the star of his show, Jordan rejected the accusation with a dismissive hand wave. "Oh, c'mon, Mal. This is insane. Even after what you told us, I can't see Quentin involved in anything malicious or downright evil, like murder. He's too self-centered, too ambitious about his career goals, as you said. That's where all his passions are centered."

"My point exactly," Mal answered.

Anne, with an eerie calm, sat quietly through the discussion. She barely knew Quentin, and therefore could evaluate him more objectively by merely listening to what was being said. Her mind was not clouded with preconceived images of Quentin's underlying personality traits.

"What exactly put that feeling in your head, Mal?" she asked.

"Again, this is mere speculation," she reminded her audience, "but Monday night, at our writing class, something Anne said when she read sent bells off in my head. I asked her to bring a copy so I could read it aloud tonight."

Anne pulled the folded single sheet of paper from her bag and handed it to Mal.

"Okay, guys, here's the part," she said, and began to read. *'The last time I spoke to Wayne, when he called me that afternoon, who ever dreamed it would be the last conversation we'd ever have? We talked about such trivialities, like what odds and ends we had to buy the next night to begin the renovation on our basement. But first on the agenda would be to bring the car in to the mechanic. It had been acting up lately and he didn't want to get stuck in the middle of nowhere.'* I'll stop there." A quick observation told her no one was making the connection.

Her gaze went to Jordan. "Jordan, another of Quentin's casual remarks surfaced a couple of days ago. Somehow we got on the subject of relationships. He admitted how he sometimes gets bored, especially if the woman gets too demanding. I answered, sort of jokingly, that maybe that's why some men prefer married women. They're safer, they say. I could see I hit a nerve, because he vehemently disagreed. He gestured with a vigorous hand wave and said, *'Don't you believe it! They're the worst to get rid of!'* She let her voice drop to almost a whisper, then asked, "Jordan, is it at all possible that Quentin and your wife were together that night?" She didn't give him a chance to respond."And isn't it also possible that Wayne Bishop might have pulled into that clearing in the road because of car trouble?"

Anne, wanting Mal to be correct, albeit painful for Jordan, tried to disprove her theory. "But he would have called AAA. They would have had a record of his call and his location. To their credit, the police already covered that possibility."

"Not necessarily. Let's check out this scenario. Suppose he was under the hood? Maybe he was checking it out himself first—"

Jordan finished her sentence. "—and maybe Quentin came around the dark bend in the road and hit him, throwing him down the embankment."

"With your wife in the car," Mal added with a rueful edge of finality.

Jordan nodded, soaking it all in. "And you're saying he killed Gloria to keep her quiet?"

Mal shrugged. "That's what I'm guessing. Not that it will bring your wife back, but if I'm right, at least you can have peace through justice."

"It's also possible he killed her accidentally too," Georgia said.

"But how?" Jordan asked. "If what Mal says is true, she would have been in Quentin's car."

"Yes, but think about it, Jordan," Georgia continued. "If you had just witnessed the driver of your car hit someone, would you just sit calmly in your car and wait for him to investigate?"

Jordan felt stupid for not instantly realizing that himself. "No, of course not," he said. "And with Gloria's temperament, she would have been hysterical."

Still dumbfounded, Alan asked, "So what do we do now?"

Mal threw her hands out again and shrugged. "I'm mentally drained from all this heavy-duty thinking. I was hoping you guys could tell me."

Chapter Seventy-three

After four months, memories of Mal still haunted Brad; the sweet, the bittersweet. The 5" x 7" framed photo of them together at a Fourth of July picnic was no longer a permanent fixture on his night table, but every now and then he'd pull it out of the drawer to look at that face he had loved for years. And still did, maybe more than ever. The pain seemed to deepen with the passage of time. He'd close his eyes to remember, but couldn't visualize her face as sharply as he used to. He reached for that photo more and more these days.

The sound of the phone startled him. No one ever called at 10:45 at night. He reached for it with concern.

"Brad, it's me, Jill."

He eased into a smile. "Hey, what's up? Anything wrong?"

"No, I'm sorry to call you this late. Were you sleeping already?"

"No, just relaxing, watching Law & Order." *And aching for Mal.*

"Well, I wanted to catch you before work tomorrow. My friend Jenny's latest boyfriend is appearing at a comedy club downtown. She and four other couples are going to see him and she asked me to go, but I won't feel comfortable hanging out with all couples. And it sounds like fun, something different."

"Say no more. Sounds great. So what's the plan? Dinner first with these couples and your friend, or what?"

"Oh no, we'll do something on our own first, then meet them at the club. The guy doesn't go on till ten."

Brad thought for a minute. "From five to ten is a long stretch. Too long to sit in a restaurant."

"I agree," she said, "so here's my thought. I have four lobster tails in my freezer. We can pick up a few grocery items and go back to my place. We'll throw the lobsters in a marinara sauce, and that with linguine, a salad and a fresh, warm loaf of Italian bread, will be perfect. What do you think?"

"My taste buds are watering already," Brad said with a laugh. "Who could pass up an invitation for lobster?"

"Great. Then I'll see you in the morning."

"Sure. And thanks, Jill. Looks like you're becoming my social director."

She hesitated, thinking that's not exactly the targeted position, but she answered pleasantly. "No problem. It's my pleasure."

*   *   *

The weather cooperated for a change. After weeks of windy, bitter cold weather, a balmy mist with an unseasonal fifty-five degree temperature filled the city streets with more than the usual number of pedestrians. And no one seemed to be as rushed to get where they were going. They walked leisurely along the avenue in Jill's neighborhood until they reached Dominick's Italian Village, the deli where they picked up far more Italian delicacies than they could ever eat in one evening.

Soon after, in the comfort of Jill's apartment, she put on a Dean Martin CD of Italian love songs. "An Italian meal should have soft, Italian background music. Don't you agree?"

"Absolutely," Brad answered. Mocking the style of a waiter in a fancy restaurant, he folded a dishtowel over his arm, bowed, then reached for the wrapped-up bottle. "And what's an Italian meal without a good, rich red wine?"

She played along. "Oh, that's like tomato sauce without pasta." She pulled out two wineglasses and a corkscrew. He poured them each a glass and they busied themselves with their respective tasks. Jill set the table and fussed with the lobster sauce while Brad created an antipasto so impressive he hated to disturb it. But appetites ruled, and they both ate hearty portions while the sauce simmered and the pot of water was put on to boil for the linguine. The smooth chianti was indeed the perfect complement to wash it all down.

"I must admit you did a better job with that antipasto than I could have done. Even all those fancy ingredients you picked up—I wouldn't have thought of half of them. And you arranged it so beautifully on the platter." She raised her glass. "My compliments to the chef."

Pleased by her praise, he gave her a wide grin. "Presentation is everything," he said. How could he explain that he developed and honed that skill from the countless meals he and Mal had put together with her parents? After a while, it had become a competitive game they looked forward to. Each of them would try one specialty dish from a cookbook and try to outdo the others. They worked in teams, two at a time, in the modest-sized kitchen. It often got chaotic, but always fun. Lots of laughter and lots of good food.

He chased the memories away and plastered a wide, clown-like smile on his face. He liked Jill, and she didn't deserve to be dragged down by his aching heart. This too shall pass, he told himself. *But when?*

When their stomachs had more than they could handle, Brad insisted on cleaning up the kitchen while Jill went to freshen up. He brewed a small pot of espresso, sliced slivers of lemon peel and placed them in the tiny cups. As a final touch, he placed miniature chocolate-covered biscottis in the little saucers.

Jill came out looking fresh and energetic. And desirable. "What? No gelato?" she teased.

"You wouldn't let me buy it!" he answered in defense.

She laughed. "Just kidding. Don't get excited."

He poured the espresso for both of them and took a pensive moment to stare at her. He watched her full, creamy lips blow short, gentle breaths in the coffee to cool it. Jill's a beautiful, sexy-looking woman with a sparkling personality, he mused. If I had met Jill and Mal at a party before I knew either, the male part of me would probably have been drawn to Jill. But it hadn't happened that way. Mal had come into his life first, wrapped herself around his heart, and he still couldn't shake her free.

Jill's eyes shot sideways to her kitchen clock above the refrigerator. "We rushed like crazy, but we still have an hour to kill."

He couldn't read into her this time. Was that just a filler for a quiet moment or a subtle invitation?

"Let's take our espresso into the living room," she suggested. "It's more comfortable than these hard chairs."

She put their cups on the coffee table, then went to retire Dean Martin for the night. She replaced the CD with Celine Dion and joined Brad on the sofa.

While they were preparing dinner, they talked, they laughed, they enjoyed themselves. Now, with only the little cups to occupy their hands, an awkward silence fell between them. Coincidentally, they both leaned forward simultaneously to place their empty cups on the table. Their eyes held and a wave of desire consumed them, taking full control of the moment. Within seconds, Brad found himself leaning over Jill. The creamy, pink lipstick that had made her full, sensuous lips irresistibly inviting, was now gone, devoured by their passion.

Jill's arms wrapped around his neck, her fingers pulled at his hair. Hunger blinded them as they groped at each other, anxious to satisfy the urges that washed away all other thoughts.

With an unexpected thrust, Jill pushed his face away, then his chest. She shot to her feet, grabbed his jacket off the railing, threw it at him, and pointed to the door. "Go, Brad. Do me a favor and just get the hell out of here and out of my life. I'll be damned if I'm gonna let you use my body to make love to your precious Mal."

If she hadn't screamed those words, it probably would never have dawned on him that in the height of his passion, he had called out to Mal. Without looking back, he left the apartment, feeling like shit. Again, he had unintentionally hurt Jill. Only God knows how much he wanted to feel for her what he felt for Mal, but you can't will your heart to love. It's either there or it isn't.

On his cab ride home, he sorted out troublesome thoughts of Mal and Jill. He had a long, lonely weekend to get through first, but after this second round of rejection, seeing Jill at work would be miserably uncomfortable for both of them. He gave a fleeting thought as to whether that Atlanta job might still be available, but immediately rejected the idea. He wasn't going that far away from Mal. Even though he never saw her, there was some small comfort in knowing she was nearby.

By the time the cab pulled up to his apartment building, his mind was made up. He was going after Mal full force this time; not like a wimp with his tail between his legs. He loved her, wanted her back, and until she told him face-to-face that she had lost all feeling for him, that all their years together meant nothing, he wasn't giving up. At first he'd decided to show up unexpectedly at the house tomorrow, but he didn't want to cause Liz and Russ any embarrassment. Besides, he needed to catch Mal where he could talk to her privately.

Monday, he finally decided. He'd skip out of his office early and wait for her outside her building. She'd never make a scene in public, and maybe, just maybe, he'd get to first base.

Chapter Seventy-four

It took a hell of a lot of convincing, but she finally got everyone to agree. Long before the meeting at Georgia's house, Mal's mind was already made up. She didn't have all the details in place yet, but with careful planning, she felt she could pull it off.

The first order of business was to get him talking about the so-called accident. That investigation was a dead issue as far as the police were concerned. They had already concluded that it was an accident and Mal suspected they would do everything in their power to keep it that way to maintain their reputations as polished professionals. If Mal and the others could make a concerted effort to present strong enough evidence against Quentin, they would have no choice but to reopen the investigation. If the police still refused, well, they could talk to the press. The newspapers would have a field day with the story. An accident turned crime scene and a bungled police investigation would make great copy.

Then if they could nail Quentin and charge him with manslaughter or whatever for the accident, it would just be a matter of time before they connected him to Bertie's murder. But for now, at least that investigation was still open. They had to concentrate on probing the accident first. She promised the group that she would proceed with extreme caution, as long as they all maintained their cool and treated Quentin normally, like the friend they had all assumed he was. Any behavior to the contrary would compromise Mal's safety and their common goal. No one was at ease with Mal's plan, but when she told them she'd do it with or without their consent, they all reluctantly agreed.

All weekend, the anxiety was killing her, but she couldn't call Quentin. Too suspicious, unnatural, she thought. At Monday night's class, she'd start step one of Plan A. Not that she had a Plan B in place yet, or a step two for that matter.

She hadn't been able to write a single paragraph on her story with this on her mind. Her parents noticed her jitteriness and both questioned her separately. She made one or two lame excuses related to her job, but the looks they returned told Mal they were unconvinced.

*   *   *

Finally, at the break Monday night, Mal made it her business to beat Quentin to the coffee urn. With much trepidation and a racing heart, she put step one into action. He hadn't greeted her with more than an icy nod when she walked into Georgia's house earlier that night. She hoped her previous attitude hadn't turned him off completely.

He was making small talk with Evelyn Shapiro as he walked toward the refreshment table. With the friendliest grin she could manage, she handed him a cup of coffee and a slice of chocolate layer cake. "Here, Quentin. Peace offering?" With pouted lips, she posed it as a question.

He gave her a puzzled, but pleased look and accepted her offerings. "Well, this is a pleasant surprise," he said. "What caused the sudden change?"

"I feel I owe you an apology. Sometimes I act on emotions, then later regret it. After I cool off, I think about it with a clear head and see things differently." She lowered her voice and shot him a humble smile. "In other words, I was a jerk. To be honest, I had no right to be so critical of you just because you got a little drunk."

"A little more than a little, I admit."

"Anyway, my conscience came back to haunt me. Many years ago, Quentin, when I was a stupid teenager, I got drunk at a friend's sleepover party. Her parents were away for the weekend. I'm ashamed to say it, but that night I was so far gone that I threw my guts up in her bathtub."

Quentin winced, then laughed. "Yuk. Not a good memory."

"No, but in a way it was. I was so sick for the next twenty-four hours that I never, ever had more than two weak drinks in one evening. I swore that would never happen to me again."

He sipped his coffee, took a man-sized bite of the cake. "Good lesson learned."

"Definitely. But that's why I felt guilty for pulling that righteous attitude on you. I'm no paragon. Who am I to pass judgment? What's that biblical line? *Let he who is without sin cast the first stone.*"

"So does this mean I get another chance? You'll go out with me?"

She gave him a tilt of her head that said, I'm considering it if you still want to.

"What about your Brad? I thought you had eyes only for him?"

From across the room, Mal caught Georgia's dagger look. Her eyes sent a caution warning so strong that Mal gave thought to abandoning the whole idea, but there was no turning back now.

"I did, I *do*," she answered. "But that's over, totally over, and it's time I accepted that and enjoyed the company of others."

"Now you're talking, Mal. That's the positive attitude you should have. And I have no qualms about stepping in the number two spot," he said. Then, with a sideways glance and that smile that could melt ice, he added, "Until you're ready to push me to number one."

Partly for realism, and partly because it appeared involuntarily, she gave him a we'll-see-but-don't-push-your-luck smile.

"Okay. We'll take it slow and easy. But do I have to wait for the weekend? Can I see you before that?"

She thought about it a moment, then said, "But this is the last week of your play in Brockford, isn't it? You have performances every night through Friday, right?"

"Right. But I was thinking tonight, after class."

Her heartbeat went back on double time, but she forced a smile. "Okay, but only for an hour or so. Tomorrow's work."

"You never did give me more than an hour after class. I hope to change that," Quentin said with a grin.

Chapter Seventy-five

Georgia was worried sick. She had no choice but to watch Mal implement her plan to get on the good side of Quentin again. Distracted by conversational interruptions from other students, she hadn't been able to keep a protective eye on Mal, not that there was much she could do to stop her. She did, however, manage to whisper a quick message to Anne to hang around after the others left. Mal and Quentin had already left together. Assumptions were made by all, but none verbally.

Everyone seemed to linger at the door longer than usual, throwing questions at her that she had no patience to answer, but couldn't escape from without being blatantly rude. Anne picked up the problem and came to her rescue. "Well, I could stand here and listen to this discussion all night, Georgia, but we've already held you up an extra twenty minutes. I don't want to wear out the welcome mat, so I'll say goodnight." She squeezed Georgia's hand tightly, hoping she'd get the message, but, more importantly, the others did and floated out, as did Anne.

Georgia's phone rang as she waved goodnight to the last of them. She closed and locked her front door and ran to answer it.

"Georgia, it's me, Anne. I'm calling you from my car. I had to leave to help you get rid of the others, but I'll just ride around the block and come back."

Georgia blew a sigh of relief. "Oh, good. I need to vent some of my fears. Hurry back."

Minutes later, when they were finally alone, they each fixed another cup of decaf coffee and sat with them at the table.

"I'm scared to death about Mal, Anne. I could kick myself for letting her talk me into this. Do you realize if Quentin really is guilty, that we're putting her in grave danger?"

"We all realize that. But what choice did she give us? You heard her. She's determined to go after him. Jordan thinks she's crazy too. He can't believe his friend is a murderer. Still, he did try to talk her out of it—you heard him—but he had just met her that night. He certainly has no control over her."

Georgia nodded her agreement, then sat pensively for a moment. She was tempted to ask what kind of relationship she had with Jordan, but it was none of her business, and that wasn't priority discussion anyway. A slight smile tugged at the corners of her mouth. "You know, Anne, Mal's confident, tenacious attitude is so unlike the Mal I first met. I like to think my class and her desire to be a proficient writer were instrumental in effectuating that change. Now she sets her goals and goes after them."

"And proving Quentin's guilt is one of them," Anne said.

"First and foremost. She had negative vibes about him from day one, but never in my wildest dreams did I imagine we'd be thinking *murder.*"

Anne raked her fingers through her hair and shook her head. "Sounds far-fetched to me too, Georgia, but after listening to her present her case, she made me a strong believer. I had a hell of a time sitting at the same table with him tonight. I wanted to get up and strangle him with my bare hands."

Georgia gave her a sour laugh. "Get in line. I don't trust Alan Bookman to keep a lid on. He was *livid.* You saw him."

"Jordan was just as angry, but then, of course, there's that part of him that's in denial. Besides, he would never be as demonstrative as Alan. That's not his style. Forever the gentleman, that's Jordan."

Their eyes met, the obvious question hung between them. Georgia, embarrassed by her own silence, fixed her gaze on her coffee cup.

Anne first broke into a smile, then laughed, but her laugh held no trace of embarrassment. "It's okay, Georgia. I'd be just as curious if I were in your shoes. The answer is yes, Jordan and I are friends—*good* friends, but no, we are not having an affair."

Georgia's huge brown eyes darted sideways to meet her gaze again. "Not yet," she said. Her expression relaxed into a knowing, approving grin.

"Right. Not yet," Anne conceded. "But that's another story."

Georgia saw the immediate change in Anne's demeanor and understood. Moisture built in her eyes; her lips thinned and quivered slightly. She had experienced that emotional reaction herself countless times and still did. She went to sit next to her on the sofa and held Anne's hand. "Are you all right? If you need to talk about it, I'll listen. If not, I won't bring it up again."

Anne blotted up the runaway tears, but quickly composed herself. "No, it's okay, Georgia. Believe me, I'm desperate for someone to confide in. I need someone to tell me it's okay to have these feelings. When my mother and sister got wind of it, they made me feel like the scum of the earth." She waved her hand. "I'm sorry. Let's forget it for now. If I start pouring that story out, I'll be here all night. And I told my boys I'd be home by ten."

Georgia handed Anne the phone. "Call them if you'd like. Make it eleven."

Anne just stared at the phone for a second. "But we were supposed to talk about Mal. I'm afraid for her too. Is there anything we can do to help her?"

"Pray that she's wrong about Quentin."

"And if she isn't?"

"Pray harder."

Anne gave Georgia a look of despair and tapped out her phone number.

Chapter Seventy-six

Even allowing for traffic, Brad never figured more than twenty minutes, tops, to get from his office to Mal's. He hadn't anticipated, but should have, the possibility of a fender-bender accident that would stall traffic for who knows how far back. Tempers flared, horns honked, and motorists desperate to reach their destination screamed out their frustrations. Simmering road rage.

Brad sat on the edge of his seat in the back of the cab. He looked at the tangled mess of cars around him, as if it were possible to find a way out of the quagmire. He wasn't angry, only disappointed. He had psyched himself all weekend for this chance with Mal. He had planned what he would say, and let himself daydream about a romantic reconciliation with Mal's arms wrapped around his neck, smothering his face with kisses.

It seemed to take forever to get past the accident scene, but finally, when they did, it was long past five o'clock. He wished he could try again the next night, but leaving at 4:30 again would most definitely be frowned upon.

Then he remembered. Idiot, he told himself, it's Monday. Barring catastrophic illness, Mal would never miss her writing class. The bitter memory of the last time he had waited for her outside her teacher's house made him think twice about a second attempt. But maybe jealousy blinded my sense of reason that night. Maybe her going off with the bearded actor had an explanation he could live with. Not for one minute had he considered anything sexual. He couldn't believe that of Mal. She barely knew the guy. But this Quentin Kingsley could have more in mind than to discuss their writing.

He let his thoughts drift away from that unpleasantry, but they settled on something worse. He wondered how Liz was doing; hoped she was still okay. He had wanted to call, but kept procrastinating. And he missed Russ. He had become half-friend, half-father over the years, and Brad suffered the void of that friendship as well.

While the driver weaved in and out of the city streets with a vengeance, Brad frowned and shook his head. Every time he thought about Mal's completely erroneous evaluation of the part he played in her family relationship, it made him crazy. He loved all three of them and never considered anything he did for them a sacrifice. Why couldn't she get that through her stubborn head?

The cab fare was outrageous but Brad didn't mind. He liked being alone with his thoughts and what the hell else could he spend his money on?

*   *   *

When he walked into his apartment, Lou and his girl, Barbara, were sharing a pizza in the kitchen.

"Hey! Did you eat?" Lou asked with his mouth full. "Come finish this up. It'll only get thrown out."

The smell of sauce and cheese whet Brad's appetite. He realized that his stomach had been sending him messages all afternoon after he had skipped lunch. He popped a Coke can open and joined them. "Are you sure you guys are done?" he asked. "I can down these two slices in two minutes flat."

Barbara pushed the box his way. "No, we're stuffed. Enjoy."

"So what are you up to tonight?" Lou asked. "Gonna sit home and make mad love to your computer again?"

Brad could only shake his head and flashed a don't-start-again grin. His mouth was occupied trying to catch the dripping sauce and cheese.

"We were gonna check the newspaper to see if there's a halfway decent movie we could catch. You're welcome to join us, buddy. It's better than sitting home alone." He glanced at Barbara who, without hesitation, echoed the invitation.

"No, thanks, but actually I *do* have plans tonight," Brad said.

Lou threw him a curious look. "Female plans, I hope?"

Brad merely tilted his head and returned a sly smile. "You could say that, I guess."

Lou's face brightened. He wanted to ask if things were developing with Jill, or whether someone new had entered the picture. Either way, his friend needed to work at letting go memories of Mal. Brad had been so down in the dumps these past months and Lou hadn't been able to pull him out. "I guess you'll tell me when you're ready?"

"Right."

"Fine. As long as you get the hell out of the house. Computers are a great pastime, but they can't provide the kind of entertainment you need."

Barbara gave him a playful shove. "Lou, mind your business! I'm sure Brad is old enough to decide what he needs and when."

"He *is* my business. He's my friend and I want to see him happy again."

"Thanks, Lou. But I'm working on it, so don't worry so much about me, my love life or my sex life. You guys go to your movie and I'll clean up. I've got time to kill before I leave."

"Smells like a real date to me. I hope so."

Brad gave him another grin, but said nothing further. He folded the remaining slice of pizza and gave it all his attention, closing off his friend's inquisitive remarks. Lou's heart was in the right place, but Brad didn't want to tell him of his plan to make one last try with Mal. If it worked, fine. If not, well, Lou's a good friend, but his friendly talks about "moving on" were beginning to sound like sermons. Brad didn't need anyone to tell him what was good for him. He knew exactly what he wanted and tonight he was going after it, after *her*.

*   *   *

Hours later, he sat in his car, parked discreetly down the street from Georgia's house. The classes, he remembered, ran from 7:00 to 9:00. The talkative good-nights stretched them to 9:30. But here he was, at 9:45, still waiting for Mal to come out. All the others came out more or less together, but no Mal. Had she missed the class tonight? Maybe something was wrong at home? His eyes narrowed with concern. Maybe she was still in there, involved in conversation with Georgia. But when the porch light went out, he knew Georgia's class was officially over and all her students gone.

Missing Mal for the second time in one night sunk his spirits. He pulled away with the decision that tomorrow he'd call the house, just to be sure everything was still okay with Liz.

He tried not to dwell on it, but another troublesome thought nagged him. Apparently, Mal had missed class tonight for some reason. But someone else was noticeably absent. Quentin Kingsley also hadn't come out that door. Either Mal was with him again or maybe she was home and his absence was completely unrelated. In which case, that would leave the trouble at home theory.

Either way, he didn't like the possibilities.

Chapter Seventy-seven

The next morning Mal made a fast call to Georgia while she dressed for work.

"Why didn't you call me last night?" Georgia scolded while Mal listened with a smile smeared across her face. "I was sitting on pins and needles worried about you."

"It was close to eleven when I got home. I thought you'd be sleeping."

"Oh, sure. You go out with a killer and I'm supposed to conk out and have sweet dreams. Sure!"

"Well, didn't you?" Mal teased.

"Yes, eventually. But it wasn't easy. I think I'm chickening out of this plan of yours. And you should too. Why don't you just talk to the police and take your chances?"

Mal was having a hard time doing her makeup with only one free hand. "We've been through that, Georgia," she said. "You're becoming like my second mother. Stop worrying so much. I know what I'm doing. As long as Quentin doesn't know what I'm up to, I'm in no danger. And who's gonna tell him?"

Georgia blew a sigh. "You're impossible. Thick-headed. What happened to that timid little girl who joined my class last September?"

"Oh, you mean the old Mal," she said playfully. "She died. Thanks to you and the class, she was given a strong dose of confidence and the new Mal was born."

She didn't want to prolong the conversation, but her mother's remission played a major part of her turnaround. Before, the smell of death filled her with fears and negative thoughts. Brad had always been there to lean on. Without him now, she had to force herself to be a take-charge person for her parents' sakes, as well as her own.

"Seriously, Georgia, I really have to go. I need two hands to put myself together. Just keep in mind that Quentin has absolutely no reason to harm me."

"Quentin's a clever young man with a razor-sharp mind. He has an innate ability to see through people. You'd be surprised how much people reveal about themselves in our class discussions and their writings. It's like they lift a dark shade, open a window and let us all in."

Mal made a disagreeable face that Georgia would have challenged if she could have seen it. "I haven't got time for an argumentative discussion, Georgia, but that's not entirely true. Didn't you just say you had a completely different impression of me at first?"

"Yes," she argued, "because you *were* different."

"Okay, then what about Quentin? Would you ever in a million years have pegged him as a killer?"

"No, but—"

"No buts, Mrs. Pappas," she said, mimicking the theatrical sound of a trial lawyer. "No further questions of this witness, Your Honor." She had thrown her voice to the side as though a judge were really there.

Georgia didn't need to see or hear her to know Mal was laughing. "You think this is a big joke, don't you?"

Mal's voice fell serious. "No, I don't, but I don't want to scare myself out of this. If you and the others strip me of my confidence and start throwing doubts in my path, I might trip up for sure. Then I'll really be in trouble. Trust me, I know what I'm doing."

Georgia blew a sigh. "Okay, I give up. But you never told me what happened last night."

"Nothing happened. Quentin was exceptionally talkative. He went on and on about the class, his writing, my writing, and then the good news about his play. I had hoped to shift the conversation to Anne so that I could ease into the accident, but the opening never came. My questions have to flow naturally into the conversation, spaced far apart. I don't want him to realize he's being interrogated."

Georgia's voice calmed. "I'm glad to hear you haven't lost all your senses. So now what?"

"So now I try again. I'm seeing him again Saturday night. He's taking me out to celebrate the success of his play."

"Oh, dear God . . ." were Georgia's mumbled words.

Mal returned with a tone strong on reprimand. "What happened to you, Georgia? Talk about personality changes! I thought you were with me all the way on this."

"I was. I am, really. But it was different when we were in the talking stages. Now that it's happening, I'm scared to death for you. *Please* be careful."

"Careful's my new middle name," she answered. Then, when Liz suddenly appeared at her doorway wearing a quizzical what's-going-on look, she ended the conversation. "Georgia, I'm gonna be late for work if I don't get off this phone. I'll try to call you tonight."

"What was that all about?" her mother asked.

Mal brushed the inquiry off with a clipped laugh. "Plot twists, believe it or not. Georgia is good that way. If she knows we're stuck on something and she comes up with a helpful suggestion, she calls us."

Liz's eyebrows arched. "Nice to hear there are still some dedicated teachers. I'm impressed."

"Georgia's not only an excellent teacher, but she's become a very special friend. She has plenty of her own personal problems to battle, but she's always there for us."

Liz gave her daughter a warm smile. "Sounds like the young lady your dad and I live with."

A lump rose in Mal's throat. She reached for her mom, hugged her thin body, and kissed her cheek. "I love you too, Mom," she said.

When Liz turned away and faced the kitchen once again, her husband's unexpected presence startled her. "Oh, I didn't hear you get up," she said.

He returned her good morning peck on the lips, then followed it with a long, hard look. "Are you all right?"

"Sure. What makes you think I'm not?"

He shrugged. His forehead creased with lines of concern. "I don't know. I thought I saw you make a face when Mal hugged you. Like it hurt."

Liz laughed and waved it off. "Oh, no," she said. "I haven't been able to put weight back on since my treatments stopped. Without all that padding I used to have . . ."

She left the sentence to hang unfinished.

Russ didn't say a word. Every day was a day closer to Liz's next CAT scan. And every day his fears intensified.

Chapter Seventy-eight

All day Saturday Mal was a nervous wreck. Despite her cool, confident façade, her stomach was so queasy she had no idea how she could fake her way through a meal with Quentin. He had told her they had reservations at The Boathouse, a pricey seafood restaurant up near West Point known for its fabulous view of the Hudson River. Even though she'd be tagged the fool of the century, she hoped to God all her suspicions were wrong. Wouldn't it be refreshing to discover all Quentin wanted was to get in her pants? Fat chance.

She pretended not to notice the glaring questions in her parents' eyes as she bounced around the house getting ready for her dreaded date. It was what they didn't say or hadn't asked that bugged her.

Liz looked her daughter over as she picked at her hair. "Don't bother fussing with it, Mal," she said. "It's so windy out tonight, it'll blow around the minute you step outside."

Mal put the hair pick back in her makeup case and zipped it closed. "I know. Force of habit." She struggled to keep her voice light and even, but her emotions were fighting to let loose. Throwing herself in harm's way to play amateur superstar detective was pure insanity. She had put her foot into this almost fearlessly while it was in the talking stage, and had nixed all Georgia's last-minute warnings, but now that her insane plan would momentarily become a reality, her courage was melting faster than a snowball in July. With nothing to do now but wait, she folded her arms across her chest to tuck her trembling fingers under them, out of sight.

"That color looks great on you, Mal."

She had chosen an angora raspberry sweater with a cowl collar over a long black skirt. High-heeled boots complemented her G-rated outfit. She hadn't changed her jewelry, though. Her everyday tiny gold cross and small, unpretentious gold earrings remained on her neck and ears.

"How come you didn't wear the necklace and earrings Dad and I bought you for Christmas?" Liz asked. "The gold and pearl setting would be perfect with this neckline. Don't you like them?"

Mal wasn't about to explain to her mother that there was no way she was shedding her cross tonight. If *He* didn't protect her, who would? "That's for special occasions, Mom," she said instead, then steered in another direction. "So do you guys need anything before I leave?"

"No, we're fine," Liz answered. "There's nothing good on TV tonight, as usual, so your father agreed to watch *Indiscreet* with me if I keep him company through one of his John Wayne movies."

"Sounds romantic," she teased. "Shall I get out the wine glasses?"

Russ, who had been watching a sports news program in the living room, chimed in. "If your mother and I want to be romantic, we don't need wine for stimulation."

"Whoa!" she shot back. Mal loved the playful banter she often shared with her parents. "You have big ears in there. Besides, I didn't say you *need* wine. It's just conducive, sort of, right?"

"Right."

Although she had said it only in jest, she pulled out two glasses anyway and set them on the counter. "There. Just in case you want them," she said with a smile. For the few moments, she had escaped the fear. Then the bell rang and sent her stomach tumbling.

Showtime.

When Mal opened the door, she almost didn't recognize him. "Wow! What a difference!" His face was clean-shaven, his hair cut enough to conform with acceptable style. He wore a black turtleneck over black pants. A gray cashmere sport jacket broke it up handsomely. And that smile, no longer shadowed by all that hair, was more captivating than ever. She could be fooled by it herself if she didn't know better.

He flashed it on Russ and Liz and greeted them warmly. Once they congratulated him about the play, he poured on his charm and provided them with a brief synopsis of his success story, although neither Russ nor Liz had encouraged him to do so.

"I think we'd better get going, Quentin," Mal said to rescue her parents from his nonstop, self-centered stories.

Liz stopped them just as they were about to leave. "Oh, Mal, what's the name of that restaurant you're going to?"

"The Boathouse."

"Oh, that's it, okay," Liz said, nodding. "Just in case of an emergency. You never know."

Mal gave her mother a probing look. "Why, Mom? Are you anticipating an emergency? Are you not telling me something?"

Liz waved them towards the door. "I'm fine. Go out and enjoy yourselves. I know you're a grown woman, but a mother never stops worrying about her child."

"Don't worry, Mrs. Triana. Your daughter will be in good hands."

Mal imagined those good hands around her throat and shivered.

"I'll leave my cell phone on, Mom. Call me if you need me."

"Sure, sure," Liz said. Again she waved them off and this time closed the door in their faces.

Alone with his wife now, Russ wheeled under the kitchen's bright light and looked her over with narrowed eyes. "Are you sure you're okay?"

Her arms flew up. "Yes, I'm fine," she insisted. "You guys watch me like a hawk. That's enough to make me feel sick even if I'm not. Don't nag, *please.*" She lowered her voice and changed the subject. "Tell me, Hon, what do you think of that guy?"

Russ shrugged. "He's sociable, good-looking—not that that matters—and it sounds like he's headed for a successful theatrical career . . ."

"But?"

"But I don't like him; don't trust him. He's egotistical and comes on too strong."

"I'm not crazy about him either. Don't ask me why. No one will ever measure up to Brad, I guess."

"That's for damned sure."

Chapter Seventy-nine

As promised, The Boathouse had a spectacular panoramic river view. Mal and Quentin sat at a window table on the enclosed deck sipping their cocktails. She had ordered one of their tropical drinks served in a pineapple. The sweet taste of fruit juices mixed with rum relaxed her somewhat, but she was well aware of how these harmless-looking concoctions can hit you later without warning. With that in mind, she nibbled on breadsticks.

Quentin looked like a new person with his clean-shaven face and short haircut. His smile illuminated his face and his eyes sparkled like the restaurant's lights that danced on the rippling river. To look at him now, it was hard to think of him as a killer. Yet, smile or no smile, when his eyes peered down at her, it was hard *not* to believe it.

She slid the maraschino cherry and pineapple chunk off the stirrer and ate them. Quentin was never at a loss for words, but at the moment his flirtatious eyes were doing the talking and it unnerved her. She couldn't keep eating just to keep her mouth and hands busy. Instead, she plucked the paper umbrella out of her pineapple and twirled it between her two fingers. The action kept her hands busy and gave her eyes somewhere else to focus.

"You were right about this place, Quentin," she said. "The ambiance is elegant and the view from up here is magnificent."

"The food is excellent too. Their lobsters are the best I've ever eaten. You should have tried one."

"No, I'll just watch you struggle with yours. Lobsters are too challenging for me, too messy. My stuffed sole will be fine, I'm sure."

He reached for her hand, which took Mal by surprise. Instinctively, her body jerked, then stiffened.

Quentin looked at her quizzically, then laughed. "What are you so uptight about? I wasn't going to bite you. I was just going to say how happy I am that we're out together. I like being with you."

To free her hand, she reached for her water glass since she wasn't about to lift and cling to a pineapple. The gesture did not go unnoticed by Quentin. He gave her a sly smile. "Relax," he said. "It's not as if I'm a total stranger. We've been friends for a while now." He creased his brows, then said, "I hope this has nothing to do with your Brad. Is it still uncomfortable for you to be with someone else?"

No, just you, she thought, but said, "The awkwardness you notice has nothing to do with preferences, Quentin. I'm past that. It's been months since I've seen Brad." She struggled to keep her voice light and not to be afraid to meet his gaze. "To be honest, I had been with only Brad for years. My dating skills are rusty."

He reached across the table and lifted her face with one finger. "Don't you worry, sweet princess. We'll take it slow. Leave it to me," he said with a confident grin. "If you let me take care of you, you'll be fine."

Obviously, he had no recollection of their last date, when she told him not to call her "princess," a nickname strictly reserved for her father's use.

"That's sweet of you, Quentin. I'm sure I'll be fine too, eventually. I just need a little practice." He had unknowingly provided her with the perfect cover to mask her tense demeanor and she'd use it to her advantage. Her problem now was how could she get him on a different track? How do you introduce death and tragedy into this romantic setting?

She had time to ponder it because when their entrees arrived, eating their food would keep them too busy for any deep conversation.

Later, while they drank their coffee and shared a huge slice of chocolate cheesecake drizzled with strawberry sauce and topped with slivered almonds, Quentin again came to her aid. He talked about *Crush's* success, what it would mean to his career, and how everyone credited Jordan. "Without his perseverance, we wouldn't have made it this far. I've got him to thank," he said.

Was that actually a touch of humility I heard? Mal wondered. She slid smoothly into the opening he provided. "Speaking of Jordan, Quentin, how is he doing? And how about that other man—I forget his name—the one whose wife was killed."

"Alan Bookman," he said, his face draped with pathos.

She shook her head in disbelief. "What tragedies those two suffered. Jordan not only lost his wife, but had to learn she had been unfaithful, and this guy, Alan," she said with extreme caution not to disclose any hint of having met him, "it's got to be sheer agony for him to know how brutally she was murdered. And with no justice to ease the pain. I hope for his sake they at least find her killer."

Quentin, unaware of the complacent grin that first crossed his face, sent her a look replete with pessimism. "Don't hold your breath. They can't even find a motive."

Mal leaned forward, not bothering to shield her curious interest. How often does murder come that close? Sadly enough, it made for interesting conversation. It would be perfectly natural for her, or anyone else, to be caught up in the mysterious details surrounding Bertie Bookman's murder. With that resolve, she pressed on.

318

"Did they ever find out how she got home that night? Her car was still in the theater parking lot as I recall, right?"

"Yes, it was. With a dead battery. And if they knew how she got home that night, they'd probably have her killer. So obviously they don't."

She wanted to ask where he was that night after he left the theater, but that would be pushing it. She circled her thoughts and came in from a different angle. "Had you seen her earlier that night or talked to her?"

"No, I was backstage. How could I have seen her?"

She shrugged. "I don't know. I thought maybe she was backstage too, or maybe sometime after the show you ran into her."

"No, I didn't. Why do you ask?"

His body language was offering her some involuntary answers. His face took on a hostile look and he threw his shoulders back. She made an outward gesture of hopelessness with her hands. "No particular reason. It's just that sometimes long after a casual encounter passes, something clicks. You remember an incident that was insignificant then, but *is* significant later. Especially in a murder investigation."

"True," he said, then covered her hands with his. "But we don't want to talk about death and murder, do we? I don't mean to sound insensitive, but we're here to celebrate, right?" He flashed a bright smile, but the look in his eyes warned Mal that it was time to move on. Death in small doses was the plan.

Thank God for their writing. She opened up that subject and, for the rest of the evening, clung to it like a safety net.

Chapter Eighty

Anne was too upset to wait until the boys were home and asleep to call Jordan. They weren't due home for more than an hour. She didn't know where Jordan was or whether he would be able to talk with her. Still, she took the chance.

As soon as he answered his cell phone, her words tumbled out in tears and she hated herself for losing control so easily. The guy is putting on a Broadway production and he could do without her whiny interruption. "I'm sorry, Jordan," she said, sniffing, "these darn tears always take me by surprise. Where are you? Can you talk?"

"For a few minutes, maybe, but if we get interrupted, stay put and I'll call you back. I'm at the Lionel Reiss Theater. What's wrong, Anne?"

The concern in his voice calmed her. If he were there with her, she would not have been able to resist throwing herself in his arms. She inhaled a long breath and answered his question, her emotions in check now. "My mother and sister just left."

His voice fell. "Oh, no. Tell me."

"They know I've been meeting you and, of course, blew it all out of proportion. I admitted we did, but they actually got angry when I said we only meet for breakfast and talk on the phone."

Jordan couldn't help but laugh a little. "I can understand that."

"'Don't insult our intelligence,' my mother said with her nose in the air. My sister just rolled her eyes and groaned. That was enough. The two of them had me tried and convicted before they walked in, so why bother trying to convince them otherwise?"

Jordan shook his head. "That's so unfair. Were they always this overbearing with you?"

Anne's eyes went up as she gave his question serious thought. "Not really. Not like this. But then again, nothing like this ever came up. I guess my friendship with you put their trust to the test and they both failed. Miserably. All of a sudden, I see them so differently. It hurts."

The sadness in her voice touched Jordan. He wished he could reach for her hand or, better yet, hold her in his arms. "I feel awful about all this. If I hadn't come looking for you in the first place—"

"No, Jordan. Don't say that. Despite this fallout, you've been my crutch and I wouldn't want to lose what we have because of their narrow-mindedness."

Jordan wanted very much to discuss exactly what it was they had and where it was going, but this was not the time. She was too upset. "What about your dad? You don't say much about him. How does he feel?"

Her face softened at the mention of her father. A rueful smile appeared; affection mixed with hopelessness. "The subject never came up between us. If I know my mother, she's probably been giving him an earful, but . . ." She paused to find the right words, or rather, to *avoid* the right words, but coming up empty, she pressed on. "You have to know my dad to understand. He's sweet, easygoing, would never hurt a fly, physically or verbally, and has always been there for us." She stopped for a sigh. "But in plain words, he's henpecked." She followed with a quick laugh, but her tone was devoid of humor.

"So even if he disagreed with your mother, she'd come down hard and fight him until he gave up."

"Or allowed himself to agree with her, externally, at least. You have to understand, Jordan," she tried to explain, "my mother is not all bad, but she's very opinionated. Until you agree with her, she never quits. I'm sure over the years my father found it easier to agree than to subject himself to her laments."

"Well, I'm on the outside looking in, of course, but maybe you should try to have a good talk with him, alone. Maybe before the issues weren't important enough, but if you let him know how much you're hurting . . ." He left the thought suspended.

She considered his advice momentarily. "I can't say I haven't toyed with that idea. Not that I think he could influence my mother, but it would be nice to have him in my corner, if push came to shove. We'll see."

What she didn't say was she had planned to use that option if and when her relationship with Jordan went beyond this simmering stage. Love has to be nurtured to survive, they say, so she either had to resolve to break away from him completely or prepare herself for the repercussions. She cringed imagining herself trying to spring Jordan's existence on her sons, but giving him up was even more disheartening.

Jordan eyed the small group of people who were patiently waiting for him to rejoin their discussion, but still he waited while Anne ruminated. "Anne? Are you okay? What are you thinking?"

The words poured out before she could stop them. "I'm thinking that maybe I should have that talk with my father sooner, rather than later. But not before you and I have a serious talk of our own."

The short silence that followed brought Anne instant regret. Then Jordan finally said, "Do you think you can get away one night soon? Maybe we can find someplace quiet where we can talk without eyes and ears all around us."

"A shopping trip to the mall sounds credible. I do need some new spring clothes."

They agreed to talk again later that night when they could decide on a date and time that would work for both. When Anne hung up the phone, her heart raced with anticipation of her clandestine meeting with Jordan. She chased away memories of her mother's and sister's admonishing words, but Wayne's face held fast. She let herself imagine him smiling softly, telling her it's okay.

Chapter Eighty-one

Mal had an after-work bridal shower to attend for one of her co-workers. Liz chose that night to invite Brad for dinner. If he was nice enough to call, still concerned about her and Russ after all this time, why shouldn't they reciprocate his kindness?

That's how they justified the invitation that would have made their daughter furious. Externally furious.

"Don't give me any back talk," Brad said after they finished eating. He stopped their objections with an outstretched arm. "If you guys went to the trouble of cooking this awesome roast beef dinner for me, the least I can do is clean up. Now just relax, both of you."

Russ gave him a rueful smile. "Brad, all we do is relax. Besides, Liz and I like to cook; you know that."

Liz didn't get up, but she scraped and stacked the dirty dishes and passed them to Brad for the dishwasher. "Truth is, Brad, your name comes up often," she said without looking at him. "Between us, that is." She made a hand gesture to clarify that she meant only Russ and herself.

"That's nice to know. I miss you both too, but . . ." He cut off the rest with a tight-lipped shrug, then turned from the sink to face them. "Look, you know how close I've always been to you, how I respect your judgment. Tell me honestly, am I beating a dead horse with Mal? Is she seeing that actor guy from her writing class?"

He caught the look that crossed between Russ and Liz.

Liz heaved a sigh, then clenched her teeth when that knifelike pain stabbed at her again. Neither of them noticed, thankfully. It passed quickly and she sat pensively for a moment, then said, "I think we'd have to say yes and no to that question."

Brad gave a half laugh and waited. "What's that supposed to mean?"

"It means yes, she's been out with him; twice that we know of. But something is very fishy about that relationship." She shook her head as though she could offer nothing to substantiate her impression, then looked to her husband for help.

"Let me explain what's been going on, Brad. Then you can make your own conclusions.

"At first, when Mal talked about her class and everyone in it, including this Quentin, the actor, she was full of enthusiasm. It seemed she particularly liked to converse with him. From what she told us, he's friendly, helpful and a wealth of knowledge when it comes to the craft of writing. He's ambitious and tenacious about his goals for the future. That's their common ground. Mal is a darn good writer, Brad."

"She always was," Brad started to say.

"Yes, but this is her first attempt at a novel," Russ cut in. "Once she settled on a story line that was right for her, it set a fire in her gut. Anyway, the result is a whole lot of powerful, passionate writing." Papa-pride put a wide smile on his face.

Before the subject drifted away, Liz swung it back. "We're very proud of her accomplishment and her spirit, Brad, but let's get back to what we were trying to explain. The bottom line is although she said he's got a swelled head, she liked this Quentin because they shared the same interest. Apparently, most of the other students are excellent writers, but I get the impression Mal and Quentin are the most dedicated to their work." She caught Russ's hand wave to put her explanation on fast forward and stopped herself. "My mouth does have a habit of running far afield," she said. "Anyway, somewhere along the line, Mal's feelings about him changed sharply. She doesn't say much, but her attitude is very noticeable." She threw her hands up. "Yet, she goes out with him again. It's almost as though she's determined to. It doesn't make sense."

"Initially, Liz and I assumed that determination was because of her breakup with you. A 'moving on' sort of thing, but it's more than that. Mal has these whispered phone conversations with Georgia, her teacher. From what we pick up, Quentin is the subject matter, but their talks are much too serious. I think Georgia is concerned about something because Mal responds with words like 'don't worry, I'll be fine,' or 'I can handle it.' We tried to get her to tell us what's going on, but she pleasantly brushes us off."

Brad sat there, his hand cupping his chin, his forehead creased in thought. "I don't like the sound of this." His lips became a tight line across his face. "I'm not in a position now to call and question her. She'd be angry with you for telling me, and she'd probably tell me to mind my own business."

"Right on both counts," Russ said.

"I can't disagree," Liz said. "I keep repeating to myself that Mal is a twenty-five- year-old-woman, entitled to make her own choices, but to this mother's heart of mine, she'll always be my baby. And mothers never stop worrying about their babies. It starts from the moment you discover that a life is beginning inside you and it lasts an entire lifetime." She shrugged with a weak grin, suggestive of an apology.

Brad patted her hand and returned a loving smile. "Nothing wrong with that. Sounds like something my own mother would say."

A disconcerting silence fell among them.

"I'm sorry we dumped this on you, Brad," Liz continued. "It's not the reason we invited you. You were like a son to us and we missed you."

Russ kept his gaze on his wife, but spoke to Brad. "That's true, but Liz and I are glad to have you share our concerns. There's probably nothing we can do, but it's something of a relief to discuss it with . . ." His words stopped short.

Brad completed what Russ chose not to say. "With someone else who loves her. It's okay." His words carried a gentle tone tinged with sadness, then grew stronger as determination tightened his face. "Maybe there *is* something *I* can do. Mal's mad at me anyway, so what's the worst she can do, get madder?"

Russ and Liz gave him a long, hard look, waiting to hear what was on his mind.

"It might be easier if I paid a visit to Georgia. Supposedly she's a classy lady. She just might talk to me. What do you guys think?"

Liz smiled broadly and, after looking first to her husband, answered. "We think we're awfully glad you came to dinner, Brad."

Chapter Eighty-two

Secretly meeting Jordan in the mall's parking lot brought Anne's guilt to a soaring new high. She tried to flush the feelings out of her as she drove. You haven't done anything wrong, she told herself, and you won't be doing anything wrong tonight. A little talk in a mall parking lot is not exactly like a tryst in a motel room.

The image of being with Jordan in a motel room had been flashing in her mind too often lately. It made her stomach sink and turn over like a roller coaster ride. Tingling sensations rippled through her body.

They had planned to meet in the southwest corner of the parking lot, far from the entrance. She didn't spot his car when she pulled into a parking space which gave her an edgy feeling. This far back, there were no people walking to and from their cars. She felt like a sitting duck for some psycho who might be lurking in the shadows.

Blinding headlights coming towards her made her imagination run wild, but relief washed over her when she recognized the car. She popped the lock open when he approached her passenger door. Her thumping heart refused to calm down, but it was no longer fueled by fear. Anxiety replaced it now, along with an uncontrollable longing to be wrapped in his arms. They had never been alone together in this semi-darkness. Their eyes held for one long, silent moment when he sat in her car only inches away. Anne suddenly wished her car had a bench seat, but the gearshift panel stood stubbornly between them like a chastity belt.

Jordan had only said "hi" to her, but his eyes revealed that he shared the same thoughts.

He reached for her hand and brought it to his lips, then kissed her open palm. "I always wanted to do that," he said.

The gesture charged through Anne. She felt numb, weightless, as though she were floating. Abruptly, she turned her eyes away, afraid that her every thought and feeling would be exposed within them.

He cupped her face in his hands, forcing her to look at him. His voice was a gentle whisper. "Anne, it's not as if we're still married to other people."

Here come the tears, she thought. They were stuck in her throat and spilled out as soon as she spoke. "I know. I keep trying to tell myself the same thing, but it's so soon. If anyone ever told me I would feel this way about someone else, I'd say they were crazy. I loved Wayne . . ." She couldn't go on.

"You have nothing to feel guilty about, Anne. I loved Gloria too, but this is different, stronger, and I'm not ashamed to admit it."

Their eyes met once again and no more words were spoken. All those suppressed feelings exploded when finally their lips met. Through the thick layer of winter jackets, four hands groped to touch, to explore and to feel the warmth of each other's body.

"Can we go somewhere?" Jordan asked, his voice a raspy whisper.

Frustrated, she shook her head. "I'm supposed to be shopping, Jordan. I don't have much time. Besides, we were supposed to talk." She said it with a little laugh at the absurdity of her words. With all their pent-up emotions, they barely said hello to each other before they were tangled in each other's arms.

He smiled at her, ran his pinky playfully over her eyebrows. "We did talk in a way. Sometimes words are superfluous. What we shared in our first kisses said it all. I love you, Anne. You're in my thoughts day and night. Who ever said love has to come at a designated time, when everyone else says its okay? It hits you over the head whenever it wants to. You have no say in the matter."

"How true," she said with a tight smile. She rubbed his cheeks gently, then pulled his face closer, hungry for those lips again. "I love you too, Jordan, and I don't care anymore what anyone thinks about it. I'm ready to face the music."

He squeezed her tighter. "That's what I hoped to hear. And the sooner, the better."

With a determined look on her face, she said, "First, I'm going to have that talk with my father. If he can't set my mother and sister straight, I'll do it myself."

Jordan kissed her forehead. "Good for you," he said.

"And then I'll have to tell my boys."

Jordan's face grew serious. "How do you think they'll handle it?"

She shrugged. "I've always had a good, open relationship with them. We talk. But this is going to be a lot for them to swallow. They loved their father."

"But they love their mother too, right? I'm sure they'd want to see you happy again."

"I'd like to think that, Jordan, but we're going to ease into this. It'll take a while for you to win them over. And I'm not sure you ever will."

"Don't be pessimistic, sweetheart. I'm going to work at it real hard. I don't ever want to lose you."

"Ditto," she said, and reached for him again.

Chapter Eighty-three

Brad waited until after five o'clock to call Georgia, when most of his co-workers left for the day. He had tossed around the idea of just ringing her bell without warning. An advance phone call would give her time to think about whether to talk to him or not and what to say. She might decide not to get caught in the middle and tell him to speak directly to Mal about this Quentin guy.

On the other hand, he could go back and forth a half-dozen times and not find her home. He opted for the phone call. He pulled the little piece of paper from his wallet where Liz had written Georgia's number. He waited through four rings, expecting an answering machine to pick up. Instead, he heard a breathless "hello." She had obviously run to catch the call.

"Is this Georgia Pappas?" he began.

"Yes. Who's calling?"

"Mrs. Pappas, we never met, but I'm sure you know of me. I'm Brad Winslow. Mal and I used to—"

"Oh, of course," Georgia said, but her brows creased with curiosity, then concern. "Why are you calling? Did something happen to Mal?"

"No, no," he assured her. "But I paid a visit to her parents, and as a result, I'd like to speak to you. They're concerned about Mal, and frankly, so am I. Do you suppose we could talk somewhere? Or I'd be glad to come there if you'd prefer."

Georgia couldn't imagine what they could be concerned about. Certainly, Mal hadn't said a word to her parents about her suspicions. She wanted to question him right then, but responded instead, "Here would be fine. Is seven o'clock okay?"

"That's perfect. I'll see you then."

*　　*　　*

He arrived at seven sharp and was surprised when Georgia answered the door. Mal had described her several times, but the image he created in his mind didn't do her justice. The woman was strikingly attractive and her warm smile put him instantly at ease. Liz had mentioned that her husband had left her for someone else and they were involved in divorce proceedings. Brad couldn't help but wonder why. She struck him as the kind of wife any man would want to come home to, but acknowledged that good looks and a warm smile weren't always enough to hold a marriage together.

"Can I offer you coffee or something cold to drink?"

"No, thanks. I just had a full dinner," he said, not mentioning that his full dinner consisted of a can of Campbell's tomato soup and a grilled cheese sandwich, slightly burned.

Georgia offered the comfort of her living room to talk, but he refused that as well. "Your kitchen is beautiful," he said, looking it over. He pulled out a kitchen chair and sat down. "I'm fine here."

Georgia did the same and clasped her hands on the table. "Before we get into anything else, I want to say I'm sorry things didn't work out for you and Mal. She mentioned you often before you broke up. Always lovingly, I might add."

Brad cocked his head. "That's nice of you to say, but that's not doing me any good now and that's not why I'm here. Incidentally, I know you're in the middle of divorce proceedings, and I'm sorry about that too."

Georgia faked a laugh and made a sweeping hand gesture. "Oh, that was a long time coming. We won't get into that either. But thanks for caring."

Brad tried to make light of it. "Now, with our failed love lives aside, let's get back to Mal. First, please assure me that you won't tell her you spoke with me. Her mom and dad don't want her to know their concerns triggered it. They try to stay out of her business, but you know how it is."

"Tell me about it. I have three children myself. That's easier said than done."

"Georgia—may I call you Georgia?"

"Of course."

"Anyway, Georgia," he continued, "Mal's parents told me about this actor in your class."

"Quentin Kingsley."

"Yes. I've seen him myself briefly. I must confess I sat in my car outside your house one night, hoping to talk with Mal, but when I saw her get into his car, I took off. Do you know what's going on between them? I have to first tell you that Mal's parents overheard bits and pieces of your conversations with her. They got the distinct impression that you're worried about her for some reason, and naturally, so are they. And so am I." He folded his arms together and waited for her explanation, hoping she wouldn't give him a whitewashed version.

Georgia tilted her head back and rolled her eyes upward. "Oh, this is so hard to explain. And if she knew I told you, she'd kill me."

Brad leaned forward on the table. "Told me what?"

"Brad, what I'm about to tell you could all be nothing. Pure speculation concocted by the imaginative mind of a writer. But just on the outside chance that it's not, I feel compelled to spill it out. Maybe you can find a way to stop her. To be honest, you, of all people, would be the last person she'd want to know."

"Georgia, you're scaring me. *Tell* me."

Georgia took a deep breath and blew a long sigh. "Mal is convinced, and I can't say I disagree, that Quentin Kingsley murdered Roberta Bookman. Remember that story? The woman who was found frozen in the snow?"

Incredulous, Brad only stared at her while he digested what she had said. "You can't be serious! On the basis of what?"

She filled him in first with the broad picture of Mal's impression of Quentin, then narrowed it down to what he said New Year's Eve when he was drunk.

Brad shot out of his chair. "And she went out with him?"

Georgia's eyes rolled upward. She shook her head. "She won't listen to me, Brad. Mal thinks this is a murder mystery game. She laughs me off. Her plan is to gain his confidence, get him talking and maybe he'll say something strong enough to present to the police."

"This *is* strong enough."

"Maybe. Maybe not. Besides, she has another reason for stalling with the police." She paused.

"I'm listening."

"Mal has a theory that Quentin was also responsible for the two other deaths connected to that theater. The way she presented the scenario to us was very convincing. She has no proof, but it *could* have happened that way."

"What way? And who's '*us*'?"

She answered both questions in a five-minute narrative.

334

"God Almighty! If she's right, she's hanging around with a murderer! Is she crazy?"

"Yes, she definitely is crazy. I liked her better when she was shy."

"Well, I have to knock some sense into that thick head of hers. She has to take this to the police. First of all, she's interfering with a police investigation."

"That's just the point. The investigation of the accident is closed. She won't go to the police yet. She feels they might not give any credence to the ramblings of a drunk. It's not as if he actually confessed to murdering Bertie Bookman. If she can squeeze something out of him to connect him to the accident, her theory will have more strength. Mal says the police won't want to lose face by reopening that investigation. Not without strong evidence to warrant it."

"She's probably right about that. But it's still not up to her to play detective. It's too dangerous. The police can keep an eye on him until he trips up." He grabbed his jacket off the kitchen chair. "I'd better go, Georgia. I have to call her."

"What makes you think she'll take your call?"

"I'll have to find a way to stop her from hanging up on me. I can't go to her house because I won't discuss this with her parents around. They'll go ballistic."

"Would you call me and let me know how you make out?"

"Of course. And thanks again for confiding in me, Georgia. Before I go, though, did she happen to tell you why the hell she's so mad at me? We didn't end our relationship in anger. I could never understand that."

Georgia walked him to the door. "I think I can answer that one in only two words, Brad."

His eyebrows rose.

"Jill Eaton."

"Oh, shit," he said, then apologized.

335

Chapter Eighty-four

Anne's mother and sister enjoyed a weekly ritual. Every Thursday morning, they had their hair and nails done, then lunched together. Before Wayne died, Anne had joined them occasionally, but not since.

Earlier this Thursday morning, her mother had called, insisting that Anne meet them at the restaurant. Sure, Anne wanted to say, so you can squeeze me in like bookends and attack from both sides? She made an excuse about brutal menstrual cramps, but promised to join them the following week.

She waited until 10:30 when she knew for certain her mother would be at the hairdresser's, then called her dad. Never before had she and her father discussed anything as serious and sensitive as what she anticipated today. She had no idea how he would react. He might be as shocked and opposed to her relationship with Jordan as her mother and sister were. But he'd never be as irritatingly demonstrative. He's too gentle a man for that. Like Jordan. That's probably why she fell for him so hard, so soon. Anyone who can measure up to her dad is the epitome of male perfection. If only he didn't allow himself to be so henpecked, she mused.

Her heart started that familiar heavy pounding again. "Daddy?" she said when he picked up. Involuntarily, her voice carried a childlike, pleading tone.

"Oh, Anne. Are you looking for your mother? She's out already with your sister. It's Thursday."

She tried to brighten her tone. "No, Daddy. Actually, I want to talk with you. Are you busy this morning? Can I come over?"

"Of course you can come over. Since when do you have to ask? You sound troubled, Anne. Is anything wrong?"

"No, not really. At least not in my opinion. That's what I want to discuss with you. Put on a pot of coffee, Dad. I'll pick up a few donuts and be there in twenty minutes."

*   *   *

When he opened the door, the warmth in her father's smile was as calming as a security blanket is to a toddler. His smile was brief though; quickly replaced by hooded brows and narrowed eyes.

In the kitchen, he poured them each a mug of coffee while Anne put the six donuts she had bought on a platter. She handed one to her father. "You'd better eat all you want now, Dad, because I'm taking the leftovers. I don't want Mom to know I came sneaking over here."

His face relaxed somewhat. "Oh. Now I think I know why you're here. I was afraid at first that maybe one of the boys got into trouble or something."

Her hands wrapped around her coffee mug. She blew into it, sipped and shook her head to allay her father's fears. "No, thank God for that, at least." She kept her eyes focused on her coffee, as though it required all her attention at the moment. She felt her father's eyes studying her.

"Help me out, Anne. I'm guessing by your discomfort that this is about that producer fellow you've befriended. The one whose wife was also killed in the accident."

Her words poured out defensively. "Dad, our friendship bonded almost immediately. Look at what we have in common!" She threw her hands up. "And we both hate what the press has done to us. Can you imagine the impact all that ugly publicity has had on me and the boys? And Jordan too."

He covered her trembling hand with his. Jordan often used that same comforting, protective gesture.

"Of course, I can imagine. And I've seen. Believe me, Anne, every pain you, Keith and Adam have to endure gets me right here." He pounded his chest. "My heart aches for you and the boys every day."

She saw her father's eyes grow watery. He covered his mouth with his hand in an attempt to conceal its quivering. Impulsively, Anne went around the table and hugged him. Her tears stained his face.

"Don't worry, sweetheart," he said. "We'll work it out." With a gentle tug, he unwrapped her hands from around his neck. "Sit down and let's talk. Tell me what's going on."

She made a face. "I'm sure Mom and Paige gave you an earful," she said.

He handed her a donut covered with coconut. "Here. Something sweet will calm you," he said with a smile.

She shot him a look and couldn't help but laugh. "If I had to eat something sweet every time I needed calming lately, I'd be fat as a horse!" She bit into it anyway and washed it away with a long gulp of her coffee, then grew serious. "Daddy, first of all, let me preface this by saying that nothing has happened between me and Jordan."

He smiled down at her. "But it's going there, isn't it? And that's why you're here, right?"

She nodded slightly. Two fat tears escaped from her eyes and fell onto her cheeks.

"That's what I thought. Do you love him? Does he love you?"

The sob in her throat made her simple response almost incoherent. "Yes, I do. We do."

He leaned forward and lifted her chin. Determination tightened his jaw line. "Then, you know what I think, my dear daughter?"

She looked up at him.

"I think it's wonderful. The only people you have to concentrate on are your sons. They're both good, intelligent boys. They may surprise you. If you want, I'll be with you when you tell them."

"Oh, Dad. I always knew I loved you for good reason. Not just because you're my father."

They both laughed.

"But Mom and Paige made me feel like Mary Magdalen. They say—"

Her father pounded on the table with his fist. "Stop! I don't care what they say and you shouldn't either. After we talk to the boys, you and I together, then we'll handle your mother and sister. Okay?"

She smiled ear-to-ear and allowed her tears to flow freely. A long sigh of relief followed. "Oh, Daddy. I don't know why I was so nervous about talking to you. I should have known better."

"Now, I want you to do one thing for me."

"Anything. What?"

"Next time you arrange to meet your Jordan fellow, invite me."

She beamed. "Nothing would please me more, Daddy."

"Good. Now go home, call him, and tell him what I said."

"Are you kidding? I *can't wait* to tell him."

"And one more thing. Don't you dare take those donuts with you."

Again Anne went around the table, hugged him and smacked a long, wet kiss on his cheek. This time laughter caused their tears.

Chapter Eighty-five

Mal would never admit it to Georgia, but she was fresh out of ideas. She had put her hopes high on gathering information, no matter how trivial, from Jordan and Alan. Neither one could come up with anything that would connect Quentin to the death of their wives. And Alan was getting mighty antsy. She had begged him for three more days. If she found nothing to hang Quentin by then, she promised to go with him to the police station and give it a shot.

Anne Bishop, bless her, by one fleeting phrase in her class story about Wayne's car trouble, had unknowingly provided the opening Mal needed to piece together her theory. But how far would that get her with the police? She could hear them already. Supposition. Conjecture, they'd say. An unsubstantiated scenario created by a young woman who likes to play detective. A writer, no less. She easily visualized their condescending facial expressions.

All she needed was another date with Quentin. The only problem was that it had to be soon. Like in the next day or two since Alan had given her that ultimatum. Then the idea came to her. She called Quentin from work to ask him a question relating to her Civil War novel. She could have done the research herself online or at the library, but this gave her an excuse to call him.

Her plan had worked out perfectly. She complained that she had a list of facts to authenticate and a ton of other things to research and hadn't been able to put a dent in it. He offered to meet her in the library that night and help her out. If he only knew, she thought.

This time she told her parents she was going to the library, but not with whom. Neither one of them liked him, so why let them worry that she's getting romantically involved?

Her cell phone rang while she was driving. "Mal, I'm glad I caught you," Quentin said. "Where are you?"

"On my way. I should be there in ten minutes or less."

"Don't bother. Turn around, make a left on Vandeveer until you get to Rosemont. Are you familiar with that area?"

"Vaguely. It's by the golf course, right?"

"Yes. Take the road around the golf course until you reach the Clermont Library. We'll do much better there. They have everything you could possibly need."

"Okay. If you say so. You're the Civil War expert, not me."

"Don't underestimate yourself. It doesn't take factual knowledge to give you plenty of smarts. A sharp, inquisitive mind is all you need. And that you have."

Mal frowned. Why did that not come through as a compliment? His last words sounded like something she'd be better off without.

* * *

The seventy-five-year-old Clermont Library was an impressive structure, inside and out. But more importantly, its shelves were well-stocked with Civil War material. Too bad she didn't have the head to concentrate on her novel tonight. She'd have to force herself to get into it, though. The information she needed right now was locked securely in Quentin's mind. Tonight would probably be her last chance to pry it out. By tomorrow night Alan Bookman would drag her to the police station, ready or not.

To his credit, Quentin was a whiz at research. He found shortcuts to attaining much of the information she would have struggled to find. And he provided it enthusiastically. He seemed genuinely happy to help and obviously proud of his ability to do so.

Two hours later, she had all the data she needed to fill in the blanks on her last few chapters and enough to keep her writing a few more. But a library is not conducive to general conversation, and Mal therefore had no opportunity to plant her seeds for information. What now? she thought.

She went to replace books on their shelves while Quentin made photocopies for her. She had not planned her next words, they just spilled out. "Quentin, it was so nice of you to spend all this time helping me out. I'd like to show you my appreciation."

He gave her his sexiest sideways glance and flashed his winning smile. Only these days that smile with the perfect white teeth no longer made her think of the handsome young actor/writer; more like a killer shark.

"Don't give me that look," she said. "You know what I mean. Are you hungry? I'll treat."

His expression didn't change. "*Very* hungry."

Something in her stomach went haywire and made her momentarily woozy, but she didn't dare let it show. "Want to try the Four Corners Diner? That's not too far. Get your car and meet me there."

They were out the front door when he answered. "Actually, Mal, I don't have my car. It's being serviced. I got a ride here," he said, letting her assume a car ride, not a bus. "Do you mind taking me home later?"

It bothered her that he hadn't mentioned it before. "Sure. No problem, but you didn't have to meet me tonight if you didn't have your car. This could have waited."

"I *wanted* to meet you."

The queasiness came back in her stomach when they approached her Honda. The thought of being along with him in a locked car . . . Her mouth went dry at the thought, but she steeled herself to stay in control. The last thing she wanted was to tip him off with a show of fear.

Then, to make matters worse, he slipped the car keys out of her hand and said, "Go around, Mal. I'll drive." She was scared to death, but now that they were out of the library and a comfortable break had been made from their Civil War-related talk, she couldn't let this last opportunity pass.

"All talked out?" he asked, keeping his eyes on the road. "You look so pensive. You okay?"

"Sure. I'm fine," she said, straightening in her seat. *You're here now. Go for it.* "Anne Bishop came into my mind again. I feel so bad for that poor woman."

"She's young. She'll adjust. Her boys will keep her motivated. And she joined our class. That alone means she's trying."

"Maybe. But neither her boys nor our class can replace her husband."

He threw her a look. "That goes without saying."

"How's your friend, Alan Bookman? Anything new on the investigation of his wife's murder?"

He tapped his fingers on the steering wheel before answering, then said, "Mal, are we going to get on this same topic every time we're together?"

Heat rose in her face and she hoped to God it didn't show. "No, of course not. It's just that a murder has never come this close to me before. I feel for the family. Every time I look at Anne, I imagine her crying in her pillow every night."

"Then why bring up Anne? You were talking about murder. Get your stories straight, Mal. Alan's wife was murdered. Anne's husband's death was an accident."

Mal noticed the pronounced veins in his forehead. His voice had a biting tone. Her nerves had put her tongue far ahead of her brain. She struggled to keep the fear off her face and out of her voice. "Well, from the way Anne describes her husband, I find it hard to believe he was having an affair with your producer's wife."

He laughed at her. "Now that's a naïve attitude. When a guy is having an affair, he makes a concentrated effort to be attentive to his wife. Not too much; just enough to make him seem like a contented married man."

"You sound as though you speak from personal experience. Have you ever been married, Quentin? Never mind," she quickly added, "that's none of my business." *Get back on track, Mal,* she told herself. "But anyway, I think once a woman finds out about another woman, she looks back on his behavioral patterns differently and realizes that yes, it is possible. But Anne is adamant in her defense. Besides," she said, making a face and waving it off, "Wayne Bishop and Gloria Hammer were so wrong for each other. Apples and oranges."

He threw her a curious look. "Now how can you know that?" His voice lowered. "And I'm surprised that you remember her name. There's been nothing in the newspapers for months."

Oh, dear God. This is what Georgia warned me about. Maybe you'll trip up instead of him, she had said.

"I was following the story when it did appear. After all," she argued, "I was remotely connected through you. Her being your producer's wife brought it home, sort of, wouldn't you say?"

Good comeback, she thought. *But I'm glad he's driving and can't study my face.*

That thought was swept away in a second. "Why are you so tense, Mal? Your eyes are darting around like search-lights, anywhere but at me and you're noticeably jumpy."

"I'm not jumpy. I've told you before, I have to get used to being out with someone else. Brad and I were together for years."

"Yes, you did tell me that, but I'm not buying it any-more." He reached over and pinched her cheek, but his touch was devoid of affection. The gesture clearly conveyed I've-got-your-number-honey, or words to that effect. The thoughts in her mind and the words on her lips were suddenly frozen in fear. His last gesture and the tone of his voice was confession enough for Mal.

Chapter Eighty-six

Brad could have kicked himself for waiting too long to call Mal. Calling her at work was not even a consideration, so he had decided to wait till about 6:45, which was about when the Trianas usually finished eating dinner.

"Oh, Brad, you just missed her," Liz said. "She went to do research at the library. Maybe you could catch her there?" It was more of a plea than a suggestion.

He didn't want to stir Mal's anger at the library, but on second thought, he considered, that might be just the place to get her to listen. She'd never make a scene at the library.

"No problem," he answered her. "I'm on my way. And I'll call you tomorrow to let you know what happened."

"Good luck, Brad. I hope you get through to her because Russ and I haven't had much luck. We'd like to know what's going on. She's too mysterious lately. And stubborn."

He tried a little levity to ease her concern. "Sounds challenging. I hope she doesn't throw a book at me when she sees me."

"Oh, she's not that bad, Brad."

He faked a laugh and hung up.

*   *   *

She wasn't there. He checked every aisle upstairs and downstairs. He even waited a few minutes outside the ladies' room. The library was probably only a cover story for her parents. Brad wasted an hour there, waiting for her to show up, allowing that she might have made a stop somewhere first.

His emotions were a tangled mess of anger and fear. Anger because she took it upon herself to take up this idiotic, dangerous cause, and fearful because he trusted her instincts. Mal's perceptive skills had always been sharp. If she felt vibes that this guy was a killer, chances were great that he was.

He made a thorough check of the parking lot looking for her car. When that search proved fruitless, he got in his car and called Georgia. After he briefed her on his attempts to locate her so far, he said, "Georgia, before I go any further, I'd like you to do me a favor."

"Anything."

"Please call Kingsley. If he's home and she's out, I'll feel better. I'd do it myself, but he'd be more receptive to you, I'm sure."

Georgia couldn't rule out the possibility that maybe crazy Mal might be there with him, but if that hadn't occurred to Brad, she wasn't about to suggest it. "I'm sure he would be. Stay where you are, Brad. I'll try right now and get back to you. I have your cell number."

One long minute later, his phone rang. "No luck, Brad. His answering machine picked up. If he has caller ID, he might call me back, if he should come in soon. Maybe he *is* there and on another call."

"That's possible, I guess," Brad said, but didn't place much hope on it.

"Brad, you still there?"

"Yes, sorry, Georgia. I'm thinking. Do you know of any other places she might be?"

347

"I can think of plenty of places, but not one that would necessitate lying to her parents. I don't want to frighten you, Brad, but that's the part that scares me."

"Forget it. I'm already scared."

"Look, Brad, I can't sit home while you drive around. I'd be a nervous wreck. I can always check my messages just in case Quentin does call. Stay there and I'll meet you in five minutes. Maybe if we put our heads together . . ."

He didn't let her finish. "No, don't bother. I'll pick you up. Watch for my car."

They went to the two diners where some of Georgia's writer students hung out to talk shop. Georgia spoke to the wait staff. No one had seen Mal or anyone else from the writers' class that night.

Back in the car, Georgia had another idea. "Let me try Anne Bishop. Mal and I sort of bonded with Anne lately because of this. Maybe they spoke on the phone today. It's worth a try."

But Anne wasn't home. Her son Keith answered. He hesitated when Georgia asked him for his mother's cell phone number. "Mrs. Pappas, I'm sure it would be okay, but my mother doesn't like us to give out that number. How about if I call her and have her call you?"

"Fine. That's what you *should* do. You have no way of knowing I am who I claim to be." She gave him her number and they waited for the phone to ring.

Coincidentally, Anne was on her way to meet Jordan again in the mall parking lot. After her talk with her father, she was feeling so euphoric she had called Jordan right away, but refused to tell him how it went. She wanted to tell him face-to-face.

Anne refused to believe that Mal could be in danger. With all she herself had been through, her mind couldn't handle another impending tragedy. "How do you know she isn't out shopping or doing something perfectly innocent and normal?"

"Why would she have lied to her parents?" Georgia asked.

"Maybe she *intended* to go to the library and changed her mind."

"Possible, but not probable."

"Why?"

"Because I know Mal. Look at it realistically. Alan Bookman gave her a three-day ultimatum. She was determined to connect Quentin to the accident before going to the police so they would have good reason to reopen the investigation. I'll bet you dollars to donuts she made some arrangement with him. *That* she would not have told her parents. Make sense?"

Anne heaved a sigh. "That stupid, stupid girl. Is she crazy?"

"Brad and I already established that fact, yes." Georgia's voice was veiled with hopeless resignation.

"Let me call Jordan. Maybe we can help you look for her."

"Thanks Anne, but hold off for now. Brad and I can't think of where else to look yet, much less tell you where to go. But keep your cell phone on, just in case."

"Absolutely."

Chapter Eighty-seven

They had passed the park and were driving along the golf course. By daylight, it was a scenic sight. By night, and with Quentin sitting next to her, the dark, lonely stretch was ominous. Mal tried not to visualize it, but the image of Bertie Bookman's frozen body on the snow-covered green wouldn't disappear.

When they turned into a bend of the road, he veered to the right and drove onto a graveled road. She was slightly relieved when she realized they were approaching the golf course restaurant until she saw the sign which Quentin ignored. "We can't eat here. Didn't you see that Closed for Renovations sign?"

He didn't answer.

Petrified, Mal began to tremble. It's too late to feign innocence anymore, she thought. He knows.

He swung the car around to the side of the building where it wouldn't be visible from the road. With an angry slam on the brake, he brought it to an abrupt stop. "What kind of an idiot do you think I am, Mal? Do you think I don't have eyes and ears?"

Mal stared in shocked silence at the glazed eyes and huge white teeth. The look of a hungry animal.

"Do you think I was stupid enough not to catch those eye signals between you and Georgia? I only had to see it once to figure out what was happening. But twice? No way, baby. Two times left no doubt in my mind."

Terrified, Mal couldn't cry or speak. "Please . . ." passed through her dry lips, but nothing more.

With gloved hands, he grabbed her throat. You should have minded your damn business, baby doll. That's what got Bertie Bookman in trouble."

"Please, I promise . . ." she began.

He let go but gave her a sardonic smile. "Don't beg, Mal. It doesn't become you. But tell me what you figured out. I'm very curious." He folded his arms and smiled.

"What about the others? How did you kill them? And why?"

"I *didn't* kill them. It was an accident, just like the police said."

"But you were there, weren't you? You caused that accident." Her voice was stronger now, fueled by survivor instinct. Every minute she kept him talking was another minute of life.

"Sure I was there. Gloria Hammer was with *me*, not Anne's husband." He paused, shook his head and smiled. "It's almost funny when you think about it. Here this jerk is out in the dark, probably with car trouble . . ."

She listened to his every word, shocked that the accident happened almost exactly the way she had theorized. "What about Bertie Bookman? Why did you have to kill her? And how?"

"What are you writing a book, baby?" He laughed at his own line. "Actually, it could work itself into a good story plot. Too bad you'll never get the chance to write it."

"Quentin, wait. Don't be crazy. Listen to me. If I'm found dead, Georgia would know immediately that it was you. If you let me live, you have a better chance. You haven't been under suspicion for any of the deaths yet, and chances are great you never will be. And you can't believe

351

for one moment that I'd be insane enough to say anything. I'd be putting my own life in jeopardy until you're tried and convicted. If it ever happens. Sharp lawyers help criminals get away with murder on a regular basis."

He squeezed her face. "Don't compare me with criminals. It was an accident!"

"An accident you didn't report. And let's not forget Bertie."

"I never planned to kill Bertie. It was her own damn fault. She was ready to stick her claws in me and never let go. She would have had me like a puppet on a string for life. No way! And if you think I'm gonna give you that chance, think again, sweetheart."

"Quentin, *please.* Georgia will go right to the police. They'll pick you up in an hour."

"Not if I get to her first. I had that base covered this afternoon." He tapped his head. "It's all up here."

Like a drowning person whose life supposedly passes through in those last moments, Mal begged forgiveness for the hell she created with her stubbornness. It would cost her her life and probably Georgia's too. At least she never told him about the others. Jordan, Anne and Alan would still be alive to tell Mal's theory, which would then undoubtedly be believed.

Still trying to stall and cling to hope, she said, "I guess you really are a good actor, Quentin. Tonight, in the library, I never had the slightest inkling that you suspected me."

He grinned. "Yes, I am," he said complacently.

"Did you also figure out what you'll do with me?" She couldn't bring herself to say *with my body,* but those were the words that crossed her mind. "Or my car? Or how you'll get home once you get rid of it?"

He pinched her nose and laughed. "You're always thinking, aren't you? But I'm ahead of you. Of course, I thought that out. I figured I'd leave you here, somewhere in this golf course. Now, instead of "The Snowman," the press will probably dub me "The Golf Course Murderer." Sounds impressive, doesn't it? Maybe someone can write a book. Not you, naturally, but they can title it *Murder on the Green.* How's that sound?"

He's going mad, she realized. It's all finally getting to him. She had to keep shooting questions. "And my car?"

"I'll leave your car somewhere in your neighborhood, all wiped nice and clean. I'm good at this now. From there I'll walk to Benny's Place, a bar in my neighborhood. That place is always jammed. I'll mix and lose myself in the crowd. Trust me, no one will know for sure when I came in or left."

"And you think all those pieces are going to fit together without a hitch?"

He shrugged. "Hey, if they don't, I'll go down trying. Let's face it, I have no other options. Understand one thing before we call it a night—or a life, I should say." Again he smiled at himself. "Understand that I never intended to kill you or anyone else. Sometimes shit happens and you do what you gotta do to survive."

Her heart thundered like never before when his hand went for her throat again. This time she was prepared. She reached for the flash of gleaming white she had spotted moments ago protruding from under her seat. Mal gripped the white trowel, still caked with dirt from her grandparents' gravesite, and plunged it into Quentin's body.

Chapter Eighty-eight

Jordan was already parked and waiting when Anne arrived. In her car, he took one look at her face and saw trouble. "What's wrong, Anne?"

Worry lines wrinkled her forehead. "Nothing with me. I told you my news is good. My father was wonderful about us, but I can't even talk about that now. I'm so upset." She began to cry.

Jordan held her face in his hands, brushed a light kiss on her quivering lips. "Talk to me, Anne."

She grabbed a tissue from her bag and wiped her eyes, then took a deep breath. "I'm okay now. It might all be nothing, but I got a phone call from Georgia while I was driving to meet you." She told him the gist of it.

Jordan slapped his forehead. "Geez! This is insanity. That girl could be anywhere and Quentin could be miles away doing his thing. What makes them think Mal and Quentin are together?"

"Mostly because she lied to her parents and because Alan Bookman put the pressure on Mal to talk to the police. Georgia feels, knowing how determined Mal is to tie him to the accident and the murder, she would have made moves to see Quentin again."

He digested what she said, then shook his head. "I'm sorry, but this is crazy. I just can't see Quentin the way Mal presented him. She had me going for a while that night, but later when I was alone, I was convinced that what she heard him say, or what she *thought* she heard him say, was blown out of proportion. Quentin's really a nice guy, Anne. I've known him a lot longer than all of you have. Granted, he has a bit of a swelled head, but I can't hang him for that. And as far as lying to her parents is concerned—" He waved it away. "That's ludicrous. Children have been lying to their parents forever."

"Mal's not a child. She's a grown woman; she doesn't have to lie. But apparently, they don't like Quentin for reasons of their own, so yes, she'd probably lie to them about seeing him."

He pondered that skeptically for a moment. Then his face brightened. "Hey, wait a minute," he said, and reached for his wallet. "I have Quentin's cell phone number in here somewhere. I'll call him and put this all to rest."

Anne perked up. "Gee, why didn't you say so?"

"It just dawned on me. I've never had to use it. I just have it in case of an emergency."

"Well, this is an emergency. Here, dial." She handed him her cell phone, then pulled it back. "No, use yours. Just in case Georgia has to reach us."

"Wait. I have to think of a good reason to call him."

Anne pursed her lips thoughtfully, then smiled. "Why don't you tell him about us? Pretend you need a friend to talk to. Don't male friends share these things too?"

He gave her a guarded look. "Yes, but are you sure that's okay with you? That kind of news spreads like wildfire."

"How can we even think about that now? Mal's safety has to take precedence." Anne read his face. "Don't worry. Call. I have a feeling you won't get an answer anyway. If he's out with Mal, and if he's on to her, he won't want to be tracked down."

Jordan called and waited. "No answer," he said.

Chapter Eighty-nine

It wasn't good enough. The trowel penetrated enough to cause Quentin to scream out, but not enough to render him harmless. Mal saw the whites of his eyes widen in shocked disbelief. She froze, but only for a second. Hysterical, she ran from the car, and left him clutching his side.

She ran as fast as she could, without looking back. Her instincts had been right all along, but at the moment that revelation offered no satisfaction or comfort.

Quentin clenched his teeth, still shocked by her attack. That little bitch tried to kill me, he thought. He rubbed the spot where it still stung but he was relieved to discover no blood. If they ever found his blood in her car there would be no way out. But right now, there was no turning back. He had no choice but to quash forever the two people who were determined to destroy his dreams. One at a time, and both tonight, he must silence Mal and Georgia, two women he had genuinely liked and respected. But that would be the easy part. Planning an airtight alibi for his whereabouts the entire night would be the greatest challenge he would ever face. And he wouldn't bet the farm on his chances that no one had noticed them at the library. But maybe that wasn't the way to go . . .

Mal's legs were numb with fear, but seemed to be driven by a force of their own. If only she had a split second to think clearly, she would have grabbed her bag off the floor of the car. She could have easily called 9-1-1 from her cell phone. But the terror she felt when his hands tightened around her throat erased all rational thoughts. Her mind and body, in their quest to survive, acted completely on their own.

She ran towards the road, where surely she could flag down a car for help. She had no idea how badly she had injured Quentin. Maybe she had severed a major artery and he could bleed to death. And maybe he was close behind her, not bleeding at all.

Breathless, more from fear than running, she finally saw the steady stream of headlights and knew she was home free. She sucked in a long, deep breath and ran up the small hill towards the road. But when she stumbled on rocky ground, an excruciating pain shot through her right leg. Her body fell to the ground. Mal bit into her lip to suppress the scream lodged in her throat, but the pain took control and released them anyway. She didn't have to see it to know her leg was broken.

The pain was unbearable and the total helplessness filled her with unparalleled terror. Even if Quentin's wound had immobilized him, who could rescue her from this obscure location? Her cries for help would never be heard over the sound of speeding traffic.

Mal began to sink into unconsciousness. The pain in her leg swirled with it but, strangely, lost some of its intensity. Her entire being was about to succumb to it for escape when she felt herself being dragged by her arms. Her screams pealed into the night at the sight of Quentin hovering over her, moonlight illuminating his furious face. She didn't even try to beg for her life, knowing it was useless. Instead, she willed herself into oblivion and, in answer to her last fleeting prayer, fainted away.

The sounds were dreamlike. She couldn't identify them at first. Mournful, distant sounds. Like a trapped animal in pain. Her own cries, perhaps, but weakened by her diminishing strength.

Quentin's face took shape again through the dizzying whirlpool that enveloped Mal. But the image was not the face of Quentin, the friendly egotist, or Quentin, the desperate, ambitious actor/writer being driven to madness by his own involuntary acts. No, this was a foreign face; once handsome and confident, now veiled with defeat. Tears fell from his eyes, mucus from his nose, saliva from his mouth. Oblivious, he let them all flow while he released all the emotion his mind could no longer cope with.

"Why are you doing this to me?" he screamed at her, but not in anger. His tone sounded more like the plea of an innocent victim crying out to his tormentor. "I told you I never meant to kill any of them." He grabbed her hair to pull her face up closer, as though his words might better penetrate. "They were accidents, all of them. Accidents! Even Bertie. She wouldn't stop teasing me, taunting me. I knew she'd never keep her mouth shut. What choice did I have? What choice?"

She almost felt sorry for him. "Should have reported the accident. First mistake," she said between labored breaths.

He used his sleeve to wipe his runny nose. "I was *drunk,* Mal. Don't you understand I was drunk? They would have *crucified* me."

"Oh, God."

"Now again I have no choice. See what I mean? I have to kill you and Georgia too. I never wanted anything from you but your friendship and maybe a little sex. This is your own damn fault!"

Still crying, and still oblivious to his tears, his hands went around her throat for the last time. "I'm sorry, Mal. I'm *really* sorry."

Chapter Ninety

Ironically, it was Jordan who got the ball rolling. He and Anne discussed Quentin in depth sitting in her car, creating hypothetical situations and picking apart the skimpy, nebulous facts Mal had presented. Dark thoughts about his friend entered his mind. Would Quentin take such drastic steps to protect his future? Yes, he concluded. It is possible that anyone driven by blind ambition, as Quentin most certainly was, might be capable of murder.

The possibility, however remote, prompted him into action. "Get Georgia on the phone, Anne. I want to talk to them."

"Why? What are you thinking?"

"I'm thinking that chances are great that Mal is out somewhere, safe and sound, but we can't afford to take that for granted. Not when her life is at stake."

"Oh, God, Jordan, I try not to think that way, but I *am* frightened." She waited to hear the ring, then handed him the phone.

"Georgia, this is Jordan," he said when she answered. "Any luck yet?"

"No, nothing. I even called her house and spoke to her father. Of course, I had to pretend it was just a hello-how-are-you call, but I thought maybe she might have called to tell them of a change in plans. She worries about them, particularly her mother."

"Georgia, where are you and Brad right now?"

"We're on Rutherford Road, headed back for the Melville Library. Thought we'd try again. We talked about going to the police, but if we said we needed help looking for a woman who was supposed to be at the library, but isn't, they'd laugh in our faces."

"Okay," Jordan said. "Do that. But don't leave. Anne and I will meet you there. I have a crazy idea in my head that we need to check out. It's far-fetched, but I won't rest if we don't."

"What is it?"

"I have to drive now, Georgia. I'll explain when we get there."

*   *   *

Georgia and Brad were already out of his car, waiting for them at the entrance to the library parking lot. Jordan and Anne pulled up in his car. He popped the lock. "Get in," he said to both of them. "I can drop you off here later to pick up your car."

"Where are we going?" an anxious Brad asked.

"Oh, don't get your hopes up," Jordan answered. "It's just a hunch I have to check out." Through the rearview mirror, he glanced at their faces, waiting for some encouraging theory. "Mal doesn't answer her phone. It's obviously turned off. Why? I'm asking myself. As convinced as she is that Quentin is this madman killer, she'd never forget to leave her phone on and ready to use in an emergency."

"If she could get to it," Brad interjected.

"True, unless she really was in a library. There she'd have to turn it off. I had this flash memory of a sign in the Clermont Library. As soon as you enter, there's a sign in the vestibule requesting that cell phones be turned off. That's when it hit me."

"What?" again from Brad.

"That we might be barking up the wrong tree. Quentin is the one who steered me to that library. He mentioned that although it's a little out of the way, they're better staffed and better stocked. Maybe he brought her there unexpectedly."

"You mean unexpectedly to Mal?"

"Probably."

Anne wrinkled her nose and nixed the idea. "But if he had dark, devious plans for her, why would he take her somewhere where they would be seen together?"

"That bothers me too. But the Clermont Library is huge. A person can get lost in there. The Melville Library, conversely, is small, intimate. He's a regular there. They know him by name. If, for some reason, taking her to the library first was part of his plan, he definitely would have chosen the Clermont."

"But still," Brad argued, "why wouldn't she put her phone on again once they left?"

"Maybe she did, Brad," Georgia said. "Maybe when we called, she was still in the library."

He nodded, allowing the possibility.

"I hate to say this," Jordan said, "but there's one other factor that might have attracted Quentin to the Clermont Library." He hesitated, reluctant to put the image in their minds.

Brad prodded him. "Well?"

"The golf course."

Chapter Ninety-one

Quentin couldn't afford the luxury of yielding to his emotions. He had to get out of there fast, but carefully. One hasty move motivated by fear could be his downfall. He drove her car near the entrance/exit and kept it hidden behind the tall shrubs that lined the edge of the property. Traffic was light, but steady. Getting out of the golf course undetected was his first priority.

He realized now that he'd better deal himself a new hand. His story would work better if he admits right off that he had been with Mal at the library. To deny it would be too risky. Too easy to prove he was. One strand of his hair in her car was enough to target him. If he makes it sound innocent enough they can find all the hairs and clothing fibers they want.

Still waiting for his chance to drive out inconspicuously, he planned out his next crucial moves. Yes, sure I was with her, he'd say. She called me—you can check the phone records—she wanted some research help and I gladly accommodated her. Perfectly logical explanation. But why did you use her car? they'd ask.

She offered to pick me up and I accepted. After all, I was doing her a favor. Again, perfectly logical. What the hell happened after she dropped me off I couldn't possibly imagine. I'll be shocked, horrified by the news and full of regrets for not using my car so she'd arrive home safely.

Too bad. Too damn bad. Everything in Phase One of his plan had worked well. He hadn't anticipated a problem from

Mal since she had an agenda of her own which required that she be pleasant and cooperative. Yes, they had walked in together, but Quentin relied on blending in with preoccupied people in a library out of their neighborhood. And the time spent at the library had been necessary. Without waiting out those two hours, traffic at that time would have been heavy. His chances of exiting the golf course unnoticed, with all those glaring headlights shining on him, would have been slim. The course hadn't opened yet for the spring season and with the restaurant temporarily closed, a car coming out of there would look suspicious to any conscientious passing motorist or worse, a cruising police car. With all these cell phones available, someone might easily call it in.

He waited less than a minute, but it had seemed like an hour. A long break in the stream of cars gave him the smooth clearance he needed to exit onto the road.

"Phase Two completed," he said aloud. "On to Phase Three." With renewed confidence, he threw his shoulders back and concentrated on his next steps:

A – Dump the car in the SuperSave parking lot; from there catch the bus to Cypress and Germaine. That stop is a busy intersection where loads of people get off and on. Again he could blend into the crowd.

B – Take easy bus connections all the way to home sweet home.

C – Wait till eleven o'clock, then get to Georgia's house and take care of business.

Okay, he thought, almost satisfied. What am I forgetting?

Chapter Ninety-two

When they met at the Melville Library, all four agreed to bypass the Clermont Library where they had initially intended to show Brad's wallet photo of Mal to the staff. Even if someone could confirm that she had been there, what purpose would that serve? They needed to know where she is, and how she is *now*.

Instead, they took off for the golf course in silence. Brad prayed to God in his own words, pleading that none of the gruesome images in his mind would become a reality.

"Geez," he said when they turned onto the graveled driveway. "I forgot that restaurant is closed." His mouth was so dry his voice came out crackly. He cleared his throat. "They're expanding the place. Drive around the back, Jordan." Fear painted that gruesome image again.

No one spoke. Almost in unison, Georgia and Anne covered their mouths with their hands, as though they anticipated screams. As if holding back the screams could hold back the horror. But everyone heaved a long sigh of relief when they found nothing but construction debris.

Brad got out of the car to give the area a closer check. There was nothing on or around the structure large enough to hide a body, and no windows were broken. A nervous laugh broke through when he ran back to the car. "Whew! What a relief. I was almost out of my mind when we turned in here, afraid of what we might find."

"Maybe we *are* all going nuts," Jordan said. "Let's get out of here. It was a crazy idea to begin with, even if Quentin is who and what we fear. There's no way he could have brought her anywhere on this golf course but behind that building. Unlike the course where Bertie was found, this is the only drivable entrance. What would he do with the car? He couldn't very well drive it out on the fairway. People would spot it immediately from the road and alert the police."

"You hope," Georgia said skeptically. "It's amazing what people ignore."

Jordan's eyes narrowed. "Not so much anymore. Not since 9/11."

"True," she agreed.

Anne interrupted with her own theory. "He could have parked the car behind the restaurant and carried her, couldn't he?"

"Yes, but he'd never take that chance. Think about it," Jordan said. "If you were driving by, and you saw someone running across the course carrying someone, what would you do, drive by and ignore it?"

"No, of course not. I'd call 9-1-1."

"Exactly. And that's why no one in his right mind would take that chance."

Brad's mouth twisted in a sour grin. "But if we all thought this guy is in his right mind, we'd never be here to begin with."

Jordan nodded in agreement as he drove out onto the road. "All I know is I'm still hoping that someday Quentin and I get the chance to have a long laugh about this."

"And I hate to say this, Jordan," Georgia said, "but I doubt that's gonna happen."

Brad leaned forward from his back seat. "Jordan, drop me off for my car. I'll take Georgia home and keep trying to reach Mal on her cell phone. If I don't get her, I'm going straight to her house and speak to her parents. God forbid Mal is in danger, they have a right to know. I'm sure they'll want to go to the police and I'll take them."

"And of course you'll call us the moment she comes home or you learn something," Jordan said. It was a statement, not a request.

"Of course."

Georgia's concern for Mal hung heavily on her face. She nibbled at her fingernails. An old habit. "Oh, dear God. There's no way I can put my head on a pillow tonight and sleep. Not until this is over and she's home safe."

"It'll be the same for all of us, Georgia," Anne said.

Georgia kept her gaze fixed out the window. "I know. But this is one night I hate the thought of being all alone in that house."

They rode in silence the rest of the way to the Melville Library for Brad's car, each with their separate thoughts, while Mal lay hidden behind the shrubs, terrified and helpless.

Chapter Ninety-three

Brad pulled the car into Georgia's driveway. "I'll wait here a minute," he said. "Check your messages. She could have called since you last checked."

Georgia gave him a doubtful look.

There were two messages on her phone; one from Jennifer suggesting that she, Georgia and Althea try this new restaurant she found for their next get-together. The second was from her eye doctor's office to reschedule her next appointment. Such trivialities, Georgia thought.

She went to the window in her living room and looked out to Brad. She shook her head sadly and watched him drive off.

Too keyed-up to sleep, Georgia kicked off her shoes, poured herself a glass of wine and sat in the rocker in her den, staring into the soft beam of light from the foyer lamp. Thoughts of Mal consumed her; even more terrifying now that she was alone. She clung to the hope of hearing good news when Brad reached Mal's house. Wouldn't it be wonderful to hear that all was well and he had awakened them all from a sound sleep? She smiled at the thought, sipped her wine.

"Want some company?"

Quentin. *Dear God in heaven.*

Her body went rigid as though entombed in concrete. A gasp escaped from her throat, but the broken sounds that followed were unintelligible. He stood before her, silent and expressionless for a long moment, a thin leather belt gripped in his hands, hanging loosely. Its silver buckle threw off an incongruous shine in the darkness.

Her voice broke through. "How did you get in here?"

"I watch a lot of crime shows." He relaxed his stance and drew a breath. His eyes were somewhat remorseful, but determined. "I don't like this any more than you do, Georgia, but I'm faultless here. I'm not sure if it was you or Mal who started snooping around where your asses don't belong. It doesn't matter anyway. I'm just here to sweep up the mess." A sardonic grin crossed his face. "And throw out the garbage, you could say." He waved his hand like an eraser on a blackboard. "No, I shouldn't say that. I never considered you or Mal 'garbage.' Not before I found out you were on to me."

"Where's Mal?" she asked, dreading his answer.

Quentin gave the belt a playful swing, made a condescending face. "Now why do you care? In another minute it won't matter." He held the belt outward to underscore his meaning.

"Where is she?"

He shrugged. "Who knows? She's up there somewhere," he said, pointing skyward.

He watched calmly as Georgia's hands flew to her mouth and waited through her cries of grief. "She's up there somewhere with Gloria," he continued, "and Anne's husband, Mr. Holier-than-thou Bishop, according to *her*, and Bertie. We can't forget Bertie. Turned out that bitch really deserved to die."

Georgia's body trembled with fear. The shock of finding him in her home, hearing him admit to killing Mal as matter-of-factly as if she were merely an item on his list of things-to-do-today, and knowing he planned to squeeze the life out

368

of her with her own belt. She had nothing within reach to use as a weapon. All she could do to stay alive is talk, throw questions.

Harry's collection of steins was still standing on a shelf behind her. Maybe if she could inch her way there, she could grab one. But what a long shot! Even if she could get her hands on one, he'd overpower her in a second. How could she expect the chance to hit him with it, and hard enough to escape his murderous hands? Still, she intended to try.

She stood up, stepped back and tried to hold him off with words. "Quentin, please, you've got to think clearly about this." Her voice was thick, her tongue dry as cotton.

"I *have* been thinking clearly, Georgia. That's why I'm here. You have to understand that this is no pleasure mission for me. I'm not some weirdo who kills for sheer pleasure. Like they say in the Mafia movies, 'It's strictly business; nothing personal.'"

Georgia's gaze was fixed on that belt. The way he played with it belied his words. Whether he could possibly be unaware of it himself, she didn't know, but what she did know was he was getting some sick pleasure from this ultimate control over her life. He liked watching her beg, and beg she would for every last breath. The guy always loved an audience and the sound of his own voice. She hoped to use that as ammunition until she reached the steins.

"But so far they haven't touched you for the first three. Maybe they'll never connect you to Mal's death either. How did you kill her? Where did you leave her?"

He smiled with dubious pride. "First answer, with these." He lifted his gloved hands victoriously. "Second, I left her to rest in a beautiful spot, actually. Again, like Bertie."

She looked deep into the eyes of this person she had known and liked and saw a sick young man on the brink of insanity. "What do you mean like Bertie? You left her in that same golf course?" She backed up another step.

He waved her off casually, as though they were discussing the time of day. "Oh, no. That would have been a bit inconvenient. I had a lot of ground to cover tonight. First her, then you."

"But Quentin, you don't have to kill me. Don't you see I can help you? I'd never betray you because my life would depend on it. And together we could think up a cover story. I could be your alibi. Think about it," she pleaded. "I'm worth more to you alive than dead."

Every step she took backward brought him a step closer. She stayed put, to think of an out. She didn't want to corner herself.

"Nice try, Georgia. You sound like Mal. I wish for your sake that I could trust you because having an airtight alibi would help, I admit—"

The shrill sound of the phone made him jump. His eyes darted to the end table, where it sat, as did hers. "Who the hell is that? Don't answer it," he said, panic in his voice.

A surge of hope flooded through her entire being. A half-hour hadn't passed, but could it possibly be Brad? Who else would call at this hour? She considered some kind of emergency for one of her children, but chased the thought away. She had enough trouble now without inventing new fears.

The ringing stopped. Without a message.

Chapter Ninety-four

Brad pulled into a parking spot outside the Triana house. It was 11:15. They'd probably be in bed, asleep and unaware that Mal should have been home from the library hours ago. Their garage was in the back, and from this distance he couldn't tell whether Mal's car was in it. He walked back to check, knowing the automatic floodlights would go on and scare the Trianas out of their wits. His stomach flipped over when he found the garage empty.

The sound of their doorbell ringing at this hour would also scare them but he had no choice. The Trianas were fully dressed, their faces fraught with concern. Liz didn't give him a chance to speak. "Why are you here, Brad? Do you know where Mal is?"

Hope drained from him in a long sigh. "No, I don't. Can I come in?"

Liz stepped aside and the three of them gathered in the living room. Liz and Brad sat on the sofa, both on the edge of their seats, while Russ hunched over in his wheelchair. Liz was straining to hold back a panic attack, her fingers steepled over her mouth.

Russ patted her thigh in his futile attempt to comfort her. Clearly for his wife's sake, he tried to remain calm. "First, tell us why you're here, Brad. Do you have something bad to tell us? The library closes at nine. It's not as if Mal hasn't been out this late before on a weeknight, but she never mentioned any plans for afterwards."

"But we haven't been able to reach her," Liz said. "We couldn't get you at home or on your cell. We even called Georgia a few minutes ago, but there was no answer."

Liz's words had spilled out with one long babbling effect. Brad hadn't been able to get a word in edgewise yet. It was almost as if they were afraid to hear what he had to say; their words intended to build a wall of defense.

Brad put his hand up and shook his head. "Wait. I know you're both upset, but let me speak. And let me preface it with saying that Mal may be fine and can pull into your driveway momentarily with a perfectly reasonable explanation."

"But?" Russ asked.

"Yes, there's a 'but,'" Brad conceded. "First—this is important—did you say you got no answer at Georgia's house?"

"Right. We didn't leave a message, but we did leave one at your house," Russ said.

Brad looked confused. "And you couldn't get me on my cell? Why? I had it on."

"Beats me," Russ said. "This is your number, isn't it?" He opened up the piece of paper in his shirt pocket. "555-7230."

Brad grabbed the paper. "That's not a zero, that's a six."

"Oh, my God," Russ mumbled while Liz threw her head back and rolled her eyes at the discovery of their careless error.

"Get back to that 'but,' Brad," Liz said. Her hands were all over; her fingers couldn't stay still.

An imaginary warning sign had flashed in his head when they mentioned not being able to reach Georgia minutes ago. He allowed that she might have been in the bathroom, but considering the urgency of the call she expected from him, wouldn't she have taken the phone in with her? But he had to tell them first and there was no way to soften the blow. He leaned forward, looked at those two anxious faces, and began.

"Russ, Liz, I should first tell you what Mal *really* thinks of this Quentin. She could be all wrong—" He stopped himself. Why bother? Once he told them, nothing would hold back the terrifying fears. "Mal is obsessed with her suspicion that Quentin is responsible for all three deaths connected to that theater." He paused for their anticipated reactions of shock, then continued with the worst. "She's also been playing detective, I learned from Georgia, and it's very possible she's out with him tonight. And, if so, that's why you haven't been able to reach her and she hasn't called."

Liz shot up and screamed. "Oh, dear God, no!"

The shock stunned Russ at first. When it registered, he punched the arm of his chair. "Give me that phone," he said to his wife. "We've got to call the police."

Brad was not hopeful that the police would jump into action when they got a complaint of a twenty-five-year-old woman being considered missing and in danger because she'd been out a few hours with no contact. They'd probably laugh, assuming she's out enjoying herself, in bed with a lover, and had the phone turned off. Understandable assumption.

Neither Liz nor Russ was interested in hearing the backstory before calling the police, not that he blamed them. He used that slice of time to call Georgia on his cell.

No answer. His stomach plunged down to his toes. The picture was so sharp in his mind, he grabbed the phone away from Russ. "Look, this is an emergency . . ."

Chapter Ninety-five

Quentin had already wrapped the belt around Georgia's neck when the police broke in. Hysterical with fear, sobs rocked her body as she tried to tell them coherently where they could find Mal's body.

Brad was forced to remain outside the house while the police investigated. He had called Jordan on his way there, and the two of them stood leaning against Brad's car, too tense, too horrified to speak.

Finally one of the detectives approached them and introduced himself as Detective Sergeant Anthony Ruggio. "Brad Winslow?"

Brad stood erect. "That's me."

"You were right, I'm afraid. But she's alive. We got here just in time. Another minute . . ." He didn't finish, merely illustrated with a hand gesture slicing his throat. "The perp, that actor, he's a basket case. Worse than the victim. Crying like a baby."

Relief for Georgia's safety filled him, but Mal was all he could think of. "Where's Mal? Did he tell you?"

Detective Sergeant Ruggio's mouth formed a grin line. "No, *she* did." He stroked his chin absently. "Police are on the way."

"On the way where?"

"The golf course."

Brad clenched his teeth, let out a mournful cry.

The detective cast his eyes downward. He had watched another man cry tonight. The first had repulsed him. This one brought a lump to his throat. "Mrs. Pappas claims he killed her."

Brad wouldn't let go. With Jordan behind the wheel of his car, they headed back to the Clermont Golf Course. He prayed all the way, holding on to that thin thread of hope that Georgia could have misunderstood. But deep down he knew that if Quentin had come to kill Georgia, surely he wouldn't have left Mal alive. Still, until they find her, Brad's mind and heart would continue to keep her alive.

*   *   *

Brad and Jordan arrived at the scene to see Liz and Russ being helped out of a police car. Both were out of control with agonizing grief, Liz screaming her daughter's name. Once they had opened Russ's wheelchair and helped him into it, he pulled his wife onto his lap, held her as if he never wanted to let go, and wailed on her shoulder. Their sobs were contagious. A silent crowd had gathered, but they maintained a respectful distance. Anyone who hadn't been crying before was crying now.

*   *   *

Georgia, still traumatized by her near-death experience, watched as they cuffed Quentin, read him his rights and took him away. What a waste! she thought for a second, then immediately focused on Brad and Mal's parents. She had to be there, she told the young detective, and he reluctantly escorted her to the scene.

*   *   *

Brad saw Georgia coming towards him. He ran to meet her and hugged her like a brother returning from war. Jordan did the same when Brad finally let go.

"Did they find her yet?" she asked through tears.

Words stuck in Brad's throat. He just shook his head and bit down on his lip. "I wanted to see her parents to offer my sympathy," Georgia said. It wasn't difficult to find them in the crowd. Their cries pealed through the tense silence slicing through the hearts of every onlooker.

Then, out of nowhere, Anne appeared, on foot, with both her sons. Jordan threw her a perplexed look, but asked no questions.

"Nothing yet?" she asked.

"No, nothing. What are you doing here, Anne? Haven't you had enough? This is so upsetting."

She waved it away. "I'm sure it's just as upsetting to you and everyone else here who loves that poor girl. She was such a beautiful, warm person. I keep thinking if only we would have forced her to stop this crazy plan. Sure, she proved herself right, but it cost her her life."

Jordan wanted to put a comforting arm around her, but seeing her two boys in the corner of his eye held him back.

Keith gave his brother a nudge and they both stepped forward to stand before Jordan. "I know this is a bad time, Mr. Hammer, but Adam and I wanted to introduce ourselves and tell you it's okay with us. But you'd better be good to her."

Beyond the suggestion of a smile, Jordan noted the boy's reluctant acceptance and clear warning. He shook their hands and smiled. "Your mother didn't tell me she told you."

"She didn't," Adam said. "Our grandpa did. We knew something was going on, so we squeezed it out of him."

Jordan's eyes searched Anne's. "How come you never told me?"

She shrugged, forced a smile. "Because I just found out today, and tonight when we met, this took precedence," she said, sweeping her hand to the horror story unfolding across the street.

"Has anybody called Alan?" Georgia asked.

"No, *I* didn't," Jordan said. "But I'm sure he'll hear about it. There were news crews at your house and they're here already."

A rush of movement across the street grabbed everyone's attention. Detectives, uniformed police, emergency medical technicians and crime scene personnel scattered like bees from a hive.

A man's booming voice rang out the miraculous words. "Over here! She's alive."

Cheering voices and applause brought joyful tears to the eyes of every onlooker. Brad broke through the crowd and ran across the street to join Liz and Russ. He squeezed them both in a bear hug. "The three people who love her most should be together for this," he said, his voice choked with emotion.

"They won't let us in there. I'm nervous," Liz said. "They didn't say how they found her. How she is."

Brad kissed her forehead. "Liz, God already answered our prayers. She's alive, that's most important. Let's hope whatever is wrong with her can be fixed."

Finally, the EMTs carried her out to the waiting ambulance. The crowd burst into applause and cheers once again, but more subdued this time seeing her on a stretcher. By this time, Georgia had finagled her way over to Brad and the Trianas. All four approached the ambulance with apprehension, but their frightened faces relaxed when Mal gave them a weak smile.

"I'm okay," she said, her voice raspy from Quentin's attack. "Just my leg. It's broken."

Liz smothered her daughter's forehead and hands with kisses while Russ could only touch her hand. Both cried with relief.

Mal's smile grew when Brad leaned over her. "Where you been?" she said, and Brad lost it. He let go the rush of tears he had been storing inside, but quickly wiped them away. "I'm never letting you out of my sight again! I'm sticking to you like glue for life!"

"Is that a proposal?"

"You bet," he said and kissed her cheek.

Mal's gaze went to her parents. Russ took over. "She can't talk too well, so I'll answer for her. Those eyes said yes. We all say yes!" he said, giving Liz another squeeze.

"Hang in there, Mal. We love you," Georgia threw in before they closed the ambulance doors.

Mal answered something that Georgia couldn't hear. "What was that she said?" she asked Brad.

With a smile mixed with pride and disbelief, Brad shook his head and answered Georgia's question. "She said, 'See? I *told* you it was Quentin!'"

Epilogue

The future looked brighter for the Triana family. Most importantly, Liz's pains that she had tried to conceal had turned out to be totally unrelated to her cancer. One doctor's visit could have saved her from all that anxiety. But it wasn't until she was scheduled for another CAT scan that she finally mentioned it to Dr. Vargas who referred her to a gastroenterologist. Her cancer was still in remission and they all resolved to look to the future optimistically.

Mal and Brad were busy planning a wedding and, to everyone's delight, Mal had enrolled in fall classes at the local community college. After that, she'd tough it out and continue her education until she had a Master's Degree in her hand.

They were also busy house-hunting and had suggested to her parents the idea of a two-family house for the four of them. But Liz and Russ had graciously declined, admitting they'd like them living nearby, if possible. Mal and Brad had no intention of leaving the area and had put a binder on an adorable Cape Cod only ten minutes away.

Negative thoughts had no place in their lives now.

Mal's relationship with Georgia was stronger than ever. She was both valued mentor and treasured friend. Mal had met Georgia's friends, Jennifer and Althea, last Saturday afternoon when she joined them for lunch. Both were likeable women with effervescent personalities. Mal couldn't have been happier when, after much protestation and lots of laughs, the two women had convinced Georgia to accept a blind date with Jennifer's divorced brother. Jennifer had spoken of him often and this time even produced her brother's photograph.

Anne and Jordan's once-secret love was no longer a secret. The thought of those two people finding each other and falling in love brought a smile to Mal's face. A happy ending to a sad story. Or happy beginning, really. As they had planned, Anne and Jordan were taking it slow, allowing Anne's sons ample time to get acquainted with Jordan. According to Anne, so far, he was winning them over with minimal effort. Jordan was such an easygoing gentle man that even Anne's mother and sister had melted.

*   *   *

By mid-July, with the wedding only three months away, Mal had something else to celebrate. After all those revisions, *On This Rich Earth* was ready for liftoff. This Saturday morning, she and Brad took a leisurely walk to the post office. Bursting with pride and an overwhelming sense of accomplishment, she handed the postal clerk three brown envelopes, each containing her query letter, synopsis and sample chapters for the first publishers on her list.

"I feel like a mother letting her baby take those first steps on its own." Her eyes searched Brad's face. "I can read your thoughts," she said, giving him a playful poke in the temple.

"Oh, really? And just what am I thinking?"

"You're afraid that I won't be able to handle the rejections."

The smile left Brad's face. His eyes narrowed thoughtfully. "Something like that. As far as I'm concerned, Mal, the book is a winner, but it's a tough market. It could take forever to find someone willing to take that first chance on you. You've got tons of competition out there."

"Brad, trust me when I tell you I can handle it." She made the blackboard eraser hand gesture to wipe away his thoughts. "Look at it this way. Compare it to a person who buys a lottery ticket. That person knows what she's really buying is a dream; something pleasant and positive to think about and hope for. When the ticket loses, what does she do? She says 'oh, well,' heaves a sigh and goes right out to buy another ticket."

He nodded. The rippled worry lines in his forehead relaxed. "Good analogy, Mal. If you can keep that attitude, you can see it through." He brought her hand to his lips and smacked a kiss on it. "Are you still gonna love me when you're rich and famous?"

"Are you still gonna love me when I drive you crazy with research questions and force you to read and edit every page I write?"

He threw her a look. "I wish we weren't walking on this busy avenue, or I'd show you how much I'd still love you."

She giggled. "And you let an insignificant detail like that stop you?"

Brad stopped short, pulled her into his arms and kissed her, long and hard. Across the street, people at the bus stop watched. Once again, Mal heard the distant sounds of cheers and applause.